ONLY TRICK

ONLY TRICK

by Jewel E. Ann

Copyright © 2015 by Jewel E. Ann
ISBN: 978-0-9961564-2-4
Print Edition

Cover Designer: © Regina Wamba, Mae I Design
Formatting: BB eBooks

Dedication

To my best friend, Jyl

Acknowledgements

Thank you readers for giving my art meaning. It's a beautiful gift to have the opportunity to share my passion with you.

A special thank you to bloggers for reading and sharing my stories with your trusting followers. It is an honor to make it onto your long TBR lists.

A special mention and thank you to Lori Chomyk, the winner of my Name a Character Contest. Tamsen Cross is a beautiful name and I hope my character did your name justice.

To my patient and hardworking editor, Maxann with The Polished Pen, thank you for your continued encouragement and mentoring.

Thank you, Regina Wamba with Mae I Design, for another creative and *very* HOT cover! You are such a talented artist. And a special thank you to the very handsome, Gabriel Charles, for finding the essence of Trick.

Thank you, Paul at BB ebooks, for your outstanding formatting and the *best* service. It's always a pleasure to work with you.

My "girls" aka, my beta readers. Thank you for combing through hundreds of pages of gibberish text laden with crazy and sometimes laughable errors and still loving the story and being my most enthusiastic cheerleaders. Leslie, Kambra, Sherri, and Jyl—I love you!

Finally, to my husband and three inspiring boys, you are my whole world and to say I live a charmed life is an understatement. You own my heart and Every. Single. Beat.

The mind speaks with reason and logic. The heart ... it doesn't speak, it just feels. But here's the thing about feelings ... they are the unspoken truth.

~Darby Lucille Carmichael

CHAPTER ONE

Health *n:* absence of disease and lack of stupidity.

M Y MORNING STARTS with a frequent flyer who hasn't been able to find his pulse for over a week. His previous visit was for chest pain during masturbation after smoking crack, so I suggested he give up either the crack or masturbating. Next up, removal of a rotten tampon, followed by an examination for "chicken pox on a penis." Hello herpes! Finally, while everyone else is actually saving lives, I'm given the old guy complaining of a tick on his butt, which turns out to be a Brach's butterscotch stuck in his ass hair. The funny part ... I've seen this patient numerous times and he has the most timid personality—a real "candy ass."

I crack myself up!

The truth: I love my job. Puzzles for me over TV any day, but none have ever been as challenging and addictive as the mystical human body. My nana has an old cedar chest she calls the graveyard. It's filled with baby dolls and stuffed animals that look like they've been maimed by a pack of wolves. Limbs that were cut and torn off then sewn back on, eye patches, bandages, toilet paper casts, and red fingernail polish aka dried blood—I received my calling early on.

As the piercing sirens draw near with a gunshot wound victim, my senses heighten. I feel stronger and faster while my vision sharpens and my skin tingles, like a numbing that makes me feel invincible to pain. I'm nearly panting like a dog waiting for its dinner; it's possible I'm even drooling a little. Adrenaline: It's my favorite drug.

"I've got this." Dr. Ellis shoves two charts into my chest before strutting his authoritative, pompous ass toward the ER entrance like God has crowned him king for the day. "Abdominal pain in room one; sutures in three."

Even in the adult world, bullies pop balloons. If I were a guy, I'd be grabbing my crotch looking for my balls. *Yep, they're there, shoe marks and all.*

"He's just pissed you're with Ashby and not him. His shift ended ten minutes ago." My straight-talking nurse, Jade, hands me a pen to sign off on a chart.

I huff out a fiery breath of evil contempt for all men. "Cute hair." I glance up, forcing a small smile. She fluffs her short, bouncy, black curls.

"I decided to embrace my African-American heritage."

I laugh, walking past her to the sutures in three. "That *or* you decided to try a new look for Doctor ... What's his name? Oh yes, Dr. I Buy Coffee For All The Nurses In Exchange For Blow Jobs. Please tell me you're not falling for Creepy Creighton."

"You're just bitter because you don't drink coffee."

"Well even if I did, it would never be *that* flavor. Sutures?"

Jade clears her throat. "Yeah, about that ..."

I turn, a cliff's edge away from the door to room three. "What about it?" Flipping open the chart, I read the medical history of Patrick Roth, age twenty-eight.

"He cut his hand, working on his bike."

I glance up from the chart. "And?"

"He's ... intense."

"Are you sweating?"

Jade swipes her fingers across her brow then looks at them. "No. Well maybe." She steps closer, glancing around as if we're surrounded by spies. "He's a squirrel."

I pull my head back, reclaiming my personal space. "He brought in a squirrel?"

Jade shuts her eyes, shaking her head. "No. He *is* a squirrel. Seriously, Darby? You don't know that a hot-ass guy is called a squirrel?"

I close the chart. "What moron came up with that?"

"I'm getting you an Urban Dictionary for Christmas. How can you work in the heart of Chicago and not be well versed in street-wise lingo?"

Jade receives my best stink eye as I open the door.

Oh hell!

Jade walks on my heels like an unexpected speed bump, nudging me a step farther into the room than what my legs would voluntarily go on their own. She pinches my arm. "Told ya," she whispers.

"Good—"

Good what? Good morning? Good afternoon? Good evening? Good God!

"Day ... good day, Mr. Roth. I'm ..." This is that moment, the one when you're jogging down the sidewalk with a strong stride feeling fit, confident, and then it happens—trip. Maybe no more than a quarter inch crack that catches the toe of your shoe sending your legs into a flailing panic to keep your body vertical. That's all it takes. One second to go from dauntless to dazed.

This "crack" and its colorful collage of ink canvasing skin over lean muscled arms holds my gaze captive, stopping time for a few awkward seconds. He's just so ...

"Ahem!" An elbow rams into my arm, jerking me out of my reverie—okay, flat out gawking. "Patrick, this is Darby Carmichael. She's going to stitch you up and get you on your way."

Dark, that's the word. Dark hair strategically styled in at least a dozen conflicting directions. Dark brows and lashes, dark stubble, and hazel eyes pinning me with a piercing *dark* look.

"Uh ... huh."

The most kissable lips twitch, not a smile—more of an amused acknowledgment of me ... Yes, me staring and using sounds like "uh ... huh" instead of real words that an educated medical professional should use. Then I notice a pearly faded scar above his eye, one of those perfect imperfections that give character and story to a person.

"Darby?" Jade holds up a pair of blue nitrile gloves, ticktocking in front of my face.

Her voice muffles like an echo from underwater, the eerie world of submersion when you feel like you can hear blood running through your veins against the cadence of your heart. I suck in a breath, more like a gasp. Scrubbing my hands at the sink with thorough intensity, I try to find my stride again—my voice. If there is a God, I pray he will grant me a small shred of dignity to go with it. "Tell me what happened." I dry my hands.

He holds up his hand wrapped in a blood-soiled towel. "Cut my hand ... tightening a bolt." Yep, his voice is just as dark as the rest of his suffocating sexiness. It's deep with a slight raspy edge that allows me to actually feel it, not just hear it. He might as well have said, "I just dropped by to suck on your nipples." Either way, I'm Frosty on a warm day—a guaranteed puddle on the floor by the time he leaves.

Fuck the threat of measles ... I'll take spots over this nasty case of stammering poppycock. Give me a vaccine for that!

I unwrap his hand then glance up to see his reaction to the deep cut. He cannot pass out. I've already reserved that right and it has nothing to do with his hand, just self-preservation. But he's not looking at his hand; he's looking at me.

Shit! Breathe, Darby, breathe.

He smells good. Is it his soap or cologne? Or is it just sexy? I didn't think sexy had a smell—until now.

Shit! Don't breathe, Darby, don't breathe.

Patrick is not my first *squirrel*, but my professionalism has never wavered. Patients are puzzles waiting to be pieced back together, nothing more. But dear God, all I want to do is nuzzle my nose into his neck and inhale like I'm taking my first breath.

"I'm going to clean the wound then you'll need a few stitches."

"You're the doctor."

Jeez! That voice …

I look down and get to work putting him back together. "I'm not actually a doctor. I'm a PA—a physician assistant." Voilà! With those words, my hands takeover what my brain has struggled to remember. I'm a physician assistant. I'm a professional and this man is nothing more than my patient.

His hand becomes just that—a hand. It no longer matters that it's attached to a body that … that … God, there are no words, not even in my head. I convince myself it might as well be a cadaver hand. I'm not sure what my glitch was a few moments ago. Maybe Jade's ridiculous squirrel comment messed with my head. But I'm back.

Good mental pep talk, Darby!

"Change the bandage every twenty-four hours and try to keep the wound dry for forty-eight hours. You can set up an appointment to have the stitches removed in eight to ten days. I noticed on your chart that you can't remember the last time you had a tetanus shot; I recommend one before you leave. Jade can get that for you." I peel off my gloves and wash my hands. "Do you have any questions?"

He shakes his head, I hope in response to my question and not my cringe-worthy behavior. My dignity sure is shaking her head as she frees herself from my smothering libido. It took years to get my degree and only minutes for my brain to melt into a pile of mush. I restrict my gaze to the sink, the floor, then his chart—anything to keep from looking at him. "Okay then, it was nice to meet you, Mr. Roth."

I risk a glance with a nervous smile. Those eyes flick to mine then fade along my body like a sheet being snapped over a bed, floating through the air until landing in its place. I wipe my brow with the back of my hand. *Shit! Now I'm sweating.*

I leave the room in desperate search of my missing confidence and professionalism. It was with me before I entered room three, so it has to be around here somewhere. From the computer at the nurses' station, I take a quick look up as Mr. Roth saunters out, leaving a wake of self-combusting females along his path. Sure enough he's staring at me, no smile. Ducking my head, I swipe my tongue along my teeth. *Do I have something in my teeth? Why the look?*

"Is it wrong that I gave him his tetanus shot in the butt?"

My head whips up from the computer. "What? You gave him——"

Jade giggles and plops the chart down in front of me. "Kidding. But holy hell, did you see the tats on that guy? A body like that could leave you speechless. Oh that's right ... you *were* speechless."

Focusing back on the monitor, I shake my head. "I was just distracted by the GSW that Ellis stole from me, that's all."

"Mmm hmm," Jade hums with a smirk that matches my own.

THE FIVE MILE commute to my condo in Lincoln Park takes twenty minutes to navigate in the massive crush of people, cars, and busses. Keeping with my normal routine, I strip then pull on my shorts and sports bra while listening to phone messages.

> *Darby, Cal wanted me to remind you about the fund-raising dinner this weekend. I'll send over your dress, and I can also arrange to have your hair and makeup done. Will Steven be picking you up, or shall I send a car for you? Call me, darling.*

"Call me, *darling!*" Sarcastic contempt leaks from every cell in my body. *Darling?* Seriously, at forty-one, Rachel, my "stepmom," is closer to my age than my father's. I think that's why she refers to him as Cal instead of my dad or father. She's caught in the middle— not quite old enough to be my mother but young enough to be

Calvin Carmichael's daughter. What can I say? My father has Hugh Hefner Syndrome. He had it when he married my mom. She was twenty-two years his junior. He's my father and genetically I'm programmed to love him, but Calvin Carmichael doesn't have a monogamous bone in his body.

I hop on my bike and spin out my legs because I *love* exercising! Who doesn't? It's good for my heart and I love the neurogenesis, mood enhancement, and endorphin release. *Just kidding!* I do it because I love food as much as boots and skinny jeans.

To take my mind off the sweat and burn, I channel surf. *Dating Naked* is on; I roll my eyes at the stupidity of it. Speaking of stupid relationships, I remember to call Steven.

He answers on the first ring. "I've got thirty seconds, Darb, go."

Yeah, that's our sex life too—lucky me!

"Are you still planning on going this weekend?" I ask like I actually care … which I don't.

"Oh crap! The fundraiser. I'm on call so I might have to miss it or leave if there's an emergency. Is that a problem?"

I laugh. *Fifty-thousand-dollar-a-plate dinner that your parents are paying for … Nah, it's no problem for me.* "Hey, you're saving lives."

"You know it, babe. Gotta go."

Dr. Steven Ashby, sole heir to Ashby Communications, drives a yellow convertible Corvette and calls himself a metrosexual. That pretty much wraps up his personality. Our relationship is convenient and approved by both his parents and mine—well, my father and evil stepmother.

"Hey, Rachel, sorry I missed your call. Steven is planning on attending the dinner this weekend, so I'll ride with him. However, he's on call, but I have the know-how and resources to figure out my own transportation. I look forward to seeing the dress you picked out for me. Tell my father 'hi.' See you Saturday."

I press *End* on my phone and crank up the resistance until my legs feel the fire. *Skinny jeans, skinny jeans, skinny jeans.* I hate lying, but with my family it's necessary for survival. The truth? I'm not sorry I missed Rachel's call, and I'm not looking forward to seeing the dress she picked out for me.

Rachel Hart founded Hart Designs in her mid-twenties. She has the look and the money my father likes. He has the clout and connections she likes. I may be bitter, but I'm not blind. She has insane talent and celebrities around the world flock to have her design one-of-a-kind gowns.

I have a closet full of them, mostly in hues of green. Rachel says purple, blue, and red are other suitable colors for my ginger hair and fair skin, but green is "stunning on me so why mess with perfection?" The problem is it feels too perfect. I have a Saint Paddy's Day birthday, and I'm not sure if it's because or in spite of it … I don't like green.

After an intense, sweat-dripping workout and a shower, I inspect the reflection in the mirror with a scrutinizing eye, then I call Gemmie.

"Is this a 9-1-1 emergency?" she answers with her usual snarky attitude.

I laugh. "Yes, Gemmie, it is."

"It wouldn't have anything to do with the ritzy fundraiser this weekend, now would it?"

"You know me so well. I was going to do my—"

"Yeah, yeah, you were going to do your own hair until you took a break from saving the sin-filled city of Chicago one stab wound at a time and looked in a mirror. Then you realized there's only one person who can transform your flaming mane into a work of art. Enter, yours truly."

"I hope all that gibberish is your way of saying you'll do my hair on Saturday."

"Ask nicely."

I sigh. "Please."

"Please will get you on my schedule in two months."

"Pretty please."

"One month, twenty-nine days …"

Another sigh. "You're amazing."

"One month … keep going."

"I need some help here, Gemmie—"

"Gemmie, you're a goddess … an artist, and true creator of miracles. I need you like my next breath and—"

"You name the price and I'll pay it." She's going to break me.

"I'll see you at one o'clock. Who's doing your makeup?"

"Me."

She gasps. "Oh hell no!"

"Why not?" I lean closer to the mirror and look at my skin. It's porcelain … ish. There may be a few minor flaws but nothing like the rutted surface I feared when I was going through the most torturous puberty ever. A little rouge, lip gloss, and mascara to accent my blue eyes should be all that's needed. I'm not into the gaudy, caked-on look.

"If you have to ask, then that's your answer. I've got a guy. I'll call him tomorrow."

"Gem—"

"Goodnight, honey."

MY *EMERALD* DRESS was delivered yesterday. Thankfully it fits. I'm not the runway giraffe Rachel is used to sheathing in the world's finest textiles. With good posture I'm five-six, and my hip region, while somewhat slim and toned, suggests I come from a line of women built for child bearing. Some things you just can't change.

"Is Dr. Drab accompanying you tonight?"

I peek out from under the foil because apparently I need just a dash of highlight around my face. "He's not drab."

"He is. That's why he drives that hideous banana on wheels. He's overcompensating."

"Gemmie, you've seen him once, and it was just a quick introduction. How can you conclude from 'Hi, nice to meet you,' that he's drab?"

She raises her penciled brows at me. "I don't trust him."

I laugh. "My stylist with half her head buzzed and the other half dyed blue doesn't trust my date because he drives a yellow sports car. Please tell me you see the irony in this."

She leads me to the sink and leans me back to wash out my hair. "You refer to him as Steven or your *date,* but never your boyfriend. Yet you don't date anyone else, and he hasn't put a ring on your finger. Please tell me you see the irony in *that?*"

"Steven's nice and an excellent doctor." *He's self-absorbed and a mediocre doctor, if I'm completely honest.*

Gemmie massages my scalp with her nails; I release a shameless moan. I love having my hair done. What girl doesn't? It ranks up there with facials and pedicures. If Steven could work a nice scalp massage into foreplay, I think I could overlook his unusual habit of talking in the third person during sex.

"He's convenient, and you're too lazy to find a better guy."

"I'm *busy,* not lazy. I don't need a guy, and I sure as hell don't need a ring on my finger. You may not trust Steven, but I don't trust *any* guys."

She wraps a towel around my head. "I hear ya, sister. I'm the youngest of four girls. All my sisters have drained my parents' wedding fund and showered them with grandchildren. I can't make it past a third date let alone find a guy worthy of meeting my family."

"Maybe your standards are too high."

Pursing her lips, she rolls her head like letting a fine wine breath before tasting it. "Nah, men just aren't made the same as they used to be—too much inbreeding."

A snort hijacks my ladylike laugh, sending us both into a fit of giggles.

I sigh after the silliness settles into a simmering smile. "So where am I going for this unnecessary makeup application?"

Gemmie spins me around so I'm facing the mirror and jerks her head toward the front window. "Across the street. You can thank me later. The only place that's possibly more difficult to get into on short notice than the chair you're sitting in right now. They're not as easily persuaded by the name-your-price offer."

I glance out the window. "*Rogue Seduction?*"

"Yep. They're not exactly listed in the phone book. In fact, you need a prominent referral to get an appointment."

I look at Gemmie's reflection. "You're my referral?"

She laughs with a wide-eyed *duh* look. "Yes, and I only get to make a few a year, so you should feel special."

My shoulders bob up and down once, unable to muster anymore enthusiasm. "It's just makeup."

"It's 'just makeup' and the ceiling of the Sistine Chapel is 'just a painting.'"

I don't argue. As much as it disappoints my father and Rachel, fashion and glamour, money and influence, are not my things. My father is "politician rich" meaning he does okay, but he lives like the rich and famous because of Rachel.

"So does this makeup guy know I'm attending a political fundraiser? I don't want to look like a street-walking cake face."

"It doesn't matter," she yells over the dryer.

"What do you mean it doesn't matter?"

"It's not about what you want; it's all about what you need."

I squint at her, hoping the pointedness of my gaze boring into her eyes will accentuate my words. "Well, I *need* to not look like a cheap tramp."

She's immune to my non-existent superpower. "That's not your decision. Trick will decide what you need. Don't worry, I promise you'll get the high-class tramp look." Gemmie winks.

"Trick?"

"Yep. Trust me, you won't care what he does to you once you

see him."

My face holds an untrusting scowl.

Gemmie smiles. "No worries. He's a guilt-free pleasure."

"Why is that?"

"He's gay."

CHAPTER TWO

PERFECTLY-SCULPTED GINGER LOCKS withstand the brutal assault of the muggy July air as I pad across the street in my flip flops. After sitting in Gemmie's chair for over an hour, the humidity has my dark jean shorts clinging to my ass like a sticker while my white button-down blouse has an equally appealing adhesive feel to my back.

CHIPPED GREY BRICKS, peeling red-painted trim, and *Rogue Seduction* drawn on the window in white with the perfection of a five-year-old makes this joint look like a real hole-in-the-wall. Gemmie's a miracle worker with my hair, but I'm not feeling as confident about how my face will look when I leave this dive.

Opening the door, Peggy Lee's "Fever" fills the air with a surprise appeal for all of two seconds. Then I take in my surroundings with a few slow steps toward the heart of the room. The seductive classic plays from an actual turntable in the corner, which fits in with the rest of the swing and big band era theme. If my Grandma Carmichael's ghost comes for a visit, I'm certain this is where she hangs out. This place reminds me of her attic: a pinup of Betty Grable, an old trumpet, a photo of Harry James, a Casablanca movie poster. It's a clash of generations. There's a photo of Marilyn Monroe next to one of Kelly Ripa and ... I look closer ...

"You must be Gemmie's friend."

No. Fucking. Way!

How does this happen to me? I don't even have to turn around.

That deep resonating voice has lingered in my ears all week. Squinting, I lean closer to the picture of Kelly Ripa. She's perched with her signature grin on the same stool that's next to me with the same trumpet hanging on the wall, and standing behind her is a guy that looks like a slightly gothic version of Patrick Roth. I turn.

Un—believable!

"Patrick?" I'm not sure why I sound unsure—it's him.

"Darby … Carmichael." My name sounds like sex dripping off his tongue. I feel dirty, embarrassed, pissed off, turned on, and scared shitless all at the same time. This city's too damn big for me to see the same *squirrel* twice in one week.

"Patrick?" I need to find a new word; I sound like a parrot.

"Trick. Have a seat." He tilts his head to the side, gesturing to the stool next to me.

Patrick was a wounded *squirrel* of very few words. He was a little dark and mysterious mixed with a whole lot of sexy. Trick is dangerous and intimidating—the lion circling the sheep. His sex appeal isn't just distracting, it's unnerving; a fitted white T-shirt exposes his toned arms and yes … tattoos. *God, I love those tattoos!*

I swallow; actually I gulp.

My torso sways forward a smidgen to inspect his face or what appears to be dark shadows under his eyes, doubling their intensity, in fact—oh hell, I think he's wearing black eyeliner or guyliner. I went through a brief goth phase in my early college years, but the guys I was with back then looked like amateurs with Crayolas for makeup. Trick looks like he stepped off the cover of *Rolling Stone*.

I ease onto the stool, propping my feet up on the lower bar. He moves in front of me—staring. I look at his eyes; I look away. I wet my lips then bite them together. I fold my hands then drop them to my sides. Then I repeat this cycle of nervous gestures over again.

"Look at me."

O-kay …

I've had my makeup done before, but this is a visual interrogation. Gemmie's parting words ring in my head. *He's gay.* It's weird that doesn't calm my nerves, cease the slow leak between my legs, or soften my nipples. *Time's up!* I can't look at him anymore.

"I'm thinking something soft and sophisticated." I look down at his black boots and black jeans, his hand still bandaged, and black leather wristbands cuffing the end of his sleeve tattoo. Steven wears a medical I.D. bracelet for his nut allergies, but it's not as sexy as Trick's leather bands.

"It doesn't matter what you're thinking."

I cock my head to the side, and if I were a dog my ears would be pricked forward. "Excuse me?"

He steps closer and brushes my hair back over my shoulders. "I didn't tell you how to do your job."

Gemmie failed to mention I'd be dealing with Mr. All-Star Personality. He turns and messes with things on his counter. I exhale louder than I intend to, not realizing I've been holding my breath.

"What color is your dress?"

"Emerald."

He glances over his shoulder.

"That's green." I relinquish a tightlipped smile.

His eyes go wide; he turns back around. It's possible he already knew that emerald is a shade of green. I can only imagine what my next brilliant statement will be … my eye color is sky … *that's blue.* He moves close with the stealth of a slithering snake—tempting, teasing. I can smell him … taste him. *He's gay. He's gay. He's gay.* I cringe at the way my body stiffens as he touches my skin.

"Relax." That damn seductive voice wrecks me!

His face, mere inches from mine, suffocates me with an awkward … *intimacy.* My heart drums against my chest over and over, and I can't control it. Surly he hears it or feels it. Hell, I think it's vibrating the whole room. I lick my lips and swallow. My body will collapse on itself if I look at his eyes, but I can't *not* look at them. They're right here staring at me. Why does he have to be so close? Is he nearsighted? Jade was right; he's intense.

I squeak and it's an actual I'm-so-pathetically-losing-it sound when his hand rests on my leg.

"Re-lax."

I hadn't noticed my pent-up energy being channeled into my leg, bouncing out of control. What is wrong with me? *HE'S GAY!*

The problem is … I'm not. His sexual preference doesn't take away from his scorching sex appeal. I bet my ass is singed from his nearness burning my panties right off.

"Close your eyes."

If he doesn't remove his hand from my leg I'm going to lean in and attack his neck like a rabid animal. *Just one little taste.*

"H-how's your hand?" I grasp at anything that might be a distraction.

He doesn't respond, but thank God he removes his hand from my leg.

"So you like the big band era, huh?"

Nothing.

"Are you the owner?"

Still nothing.

What's his deal? I give up. I'm pitting out, nipping out, and striking out. He doesn't want to talk. Fine—neither do I! My focus turns to the music, the long list of assholes I plan on avoiding tonight, and the test results I need to check on at the hospital in the morning. Then, against my will, he manages to draw me under his hypnotic spell with those black-framed eyes.

Time drags on and on. I need a shower, but given my hair and makeup I'll have to settle for a sponge bath. He outlines my lips with a pencil then makes a slow, torturous production of applying lipstick. I have to keep my lips slightly parted, which means he can hear and even feel my quickening breath … I'm panting.

Pathetic.

Trick steps back, leaving me naked to his scrutinizing gaze.

"Beautiful."

I choke on my tongue in disbelief that he just said that, then I look past him at the mirror. Words are inadequate. I'm … holy hell, it's like I'm staring at the cover of a glamour magazine. I didn't get it before, but now I do. *Hello, Sistine Chapel.*

"Is there a problem?"

I blink a few times and shake my head like I'm lost, and I am … for words.

"You look disappointed. That's not a look I'm accustom to seeing."

Lucky you.

I continue to shake my head. Closing my eyes, I give myself a much needed mental bitch slap for being disappointed that the gay makeup artist is admiring his work and not me. "It's perfect. Thank you."

I pay for the most expensive and most erotic hour of my life. Glancing at my watch, I realize I need to make haste if I'm going to beat Steven to my place.

Trick's enigmatic personality makes even a simple goodbye feel like an awkward conversing between two people who don't speak the same language. "So … thanks."

He nods. Once again, I'm left guessing what his simple body language says. Maybe it's "you're welcome," or maybe he's just dismissing me.

I shuffle in my flip flops to the door and give him one last smile, one last chance to say *something!* He doesn't reciprocate. I'm not sure he actually has teeth. He's never given me more than a barely detectable smirk. A full-fledged smile with the straight white teeth I imagine are behind those yummy lips would make me climax. Maybe it's best if I never know.

THE MASSIVE WASTE of money for political fundraisers, or politics in general, makes me physically ill. It's greed and gluttony. If I really think about it, it's all of the seven deadly sins. Ironically, I think committing them is a prerequisite to running for any higher office in this country "One nation under God." God has to be shaking his head.

I'm showered with compliments on my dress, hair, and makeup. If the school-girl popularity contest were my thing, tonight would make up for the debacle that was my prom. Sadly, none of it matters ... anymore.

"Hospital called. I have to go, babe." Steven hands me his empty glass and slips on his black Armani jacket.

"Can you drop me off?" I scoot back in my chair, reaching for my wrap.

"Your place isn't on the way to the hospital. You know that. Besides, don't you want to stay?"

I look around, a little nauseous, a lot unimpressed. Dinner was over an hour ago, and my father and Rachel seem to have vanished. *Wishful thinking.* If only aliens were real. "No. I don't want to stay. I'll get a cab."

"No you won't." Steven holds up his finger, walking a few tables over to where his parents are seated. He whispers something in his dad's ear then smirks coming toward me. "Jack will drive you home."

"I'm not taking your parents' car and driver away from them, Steven."

He helps me with my wrap, pressing his lips to my shoulder. "They'll be here for several more hours yet. Jack's just waiting outside anyway."

I agree with a reluctant lingering of guilt as Steven escorts me out of the hotel.

He bundles me in the back of the town car and kisses me with eagerness. "Did I tell you how sexy you look tonight?" He brushes his lips along my exposed shoulder.

"More than once."

"Take her back to my place, Jack." He calls up front. "I'll hurry. Don't take off your dress before I get there."

"Steven, I have to be to work at seven. It's already eleven."

"My place," he growls while sucking my neck like a hormone-crazed teenager.

"You give me a hickey and I'll cut your dick off."

He stands, straightening his tie. "No hickeys, then. Steven has something he'd rather you do to his dick later. Bye, babe." He closes my door and I shiver, but not like goose bumps of anticipation, more like the skin-crawling heebie jeebies begging for a stay of execution from the promise or *threat* of his words. That annoying third person crap didn't help, either. *Seriously, just massage my scalp!*

Both Gemmie and Trick have messed with my head today. Steven's not an unleashed tiger in the bedroom, but he has adequate skills. Though, he could use more tongue and less fingers. Sometimes I'm not sure if he's trying to turn me on or prep me for a pap smear. Regardless, since my afternoon tease, I could really use a good release. But now Trick is in my head. I can't stop wondering where the rest of his tattoos lead and what they all mean. Do they cover something or expose something? He's gay so none of this should matter, but I just—Can't. Stop. Thinking. About. Him!

The car begins to shake with the subtleness of a small earth quake as Jack pulls to the far right just before the stop sign. A barely detectable grumble escapes his chest as he gets out and walks around back.

"What's happening?" I ask, rolling down my window.

"Flat tire, Miss Carmichael. I do apologize for the inconvenience. It shouldn't take long to fix it."

"That's fine. It's not your fault." I open my door and step out.

"Miss, please stay in the vehicle. It's not safe—"

I wave a dismissive hand. "It's not safe to change a flat tire with a passenger in the vehicle. I'm fine."

Jack concedes and continues to rummage through the trunk. Rubbing my hands along my arms while hugging myself, I contemplate grabbing my wrap, but instead lose focus as I gather my bearings of where we are. Gemmie's neon sign is off, but I still recognize a few stores down on the other side of the street. That means ... I continue walking until I'm standing in front of Rogue Seduction. I move closer to the window to see inside. The lights are off limiting my visibility to a few shadows from the filtered street light.

"We're closed."

I jump, smacking my hand against my chest as I turn. "Oh my God! You scared the shit out of me!"

"Well that sounds messy." Trick shoves one hand in his pocket while the other twists a toothpick that's hanging from the corner of his mouth. A mouth that still refuses to relinquish a smile. His hazel eyes look black tonight as he looks me over like I'm asking for his opinion of my dress ... but I'm not.

I shiver, despite my heat-flushed skin. "You live here?"

"You stalking me?"

My head jerks back. His comment laced with a hint of narcissism sucker punches me. "What? No. I—my—I mean the car has a flat." I point down the street. Trick looks and nods just as Jack walks toward us.

"I'm so sorry, Miss Carmichael. There's not a spare tire. I've called for assistance and they should be here soon."

"Don't worry about it, Jack. I'll get a cab."

"I could call—"

"It's fine, Jack, really."

His backbone turns to Jello while he hangs his head, moping like a child all the way back to the car.

Trick looks around, fiddling with his toothpick. "Good luck finding that cab." He sidesteps past me to an alleyway cut between the buildings.

I assess my dark surroundings—closed businesses, broken street lights, and a few homeless people drifting in and out of the alleys. Digging through my purse, I grab my phone—it's dead. *Just perfect!* I look over at Jack leaning against the car, smoking a cigarette. After taking two steps in his direction, I pivot, for some insane, unexplainable reason, and waddle in my tight dress down the alley, heels clacking against the concrete.

"No cabs?" Trick asks without looking up as he unlocks a large metal door.

"My phone is dead. Can I borrow yours or pay you for a ride?"

He grunts, opening the door. "I don't want your money."

I rub my hands over the tight, chilled skin on my arms. "You didn't have an issue with it earlier."

"That was business. In." He gestures with his head.

I step inside like I'm testing it for quicksand. It's completely dark. The heavy door slams shut leaving an eerie echo bouncing off walls that seem wider and higher than my eyes can see. Trick flips a switch to a single light bulb that looks like it's dangling from nowhere. Dark shadows drape everything but a freight elevator with the old scissor gate a few feet in front of us. He opens the gate and steps into the elevator. I don't.

We have a silent standoff. I'm not getting on that old thing and he … well I don't think he cares what I do.

"Suit yourself." He starts to shut the gate.

"Wait!" I scurry into the elevator and he shuts the gate behind me.

It starts its ascent with a jerk as the old wheel and pulleys moan in protest. I lean against the back wall with my hands flat against it to brace myself. The fright in my face is palpable; I can only imagine how ugly it must look from the outside. My fear is met with another toothless smirk.

Smug ass!

The elevator grinds to an equally jerky halt. Trick slides open the gate and steps off, turning on the lights. With less hesitation than before, I follow him like a horse he's breaking with fear, not trust. He lives in an old warehouse. It has monstrous open ceilings with exposed duct work and conduit and a panoramic grid of windows at the far end. The walls are all naked red brick and there's a spiral iron stairway in the distant corner, leading to an open loft area.

"I'll get you a jacket."

"I'm fine." I force myself to stop the nervous friction of my hands rubbing against my arms. It has to be eighty degrees on this upper level, but I still have chills.

Trick continues to the stairway, of course not acknowledging a word I've said.

This place is void of interior walls with the exception of two translucent glass brick walls about ten feet high near a cluster of bedroom furniture. Watching the stairway for his return, I ease my way over and peek around the corner of glass—it's a bathroom. Shuffling on my toes to silence my heels, I move toward the kitchen so he doesn't see me snooping near his bedroom area. With my hands clasped behind my back in innocence, I wait for Trick. Beyond the sitting area in the middle of the room are multiple figures near the far windows. The dim lighting makes it impossible to tell if it's more furniture or something else. It looks like different things draped with sheets.

"Here," Trick says coming down the stairs, holding out a black leather jacket.

"I like your place."

He raises a single disbelieving brow at me.

"I do. I like the industrial feel."

He gives me a slow yeah-sure-you-do nod, clearly not convinced. In my own home I surround myself with modern decor trimmed in clean lines and very little clutter. Step-mommy Rachel thinks it has a hideous "sterile" feel to it: stainless steel appliances, white and shades of gray paint, and all hard surface flooring.

"You're a man of very few words, Patrick Roth." I smile, hoping to capture the ultimate prize—a return smile.

"It's Trick, and maybe you're a woman of too many words. Put the jacket on. Let's go."

"You could offer me a drink." Internally, I grimace. Where did that come from? I have no idea what I'm doing or what's my angle—my motivation. It might be fifty percent stupidity and fifty percent curiosity. *Okay, more like seventy-thirty.*

He sighs. "I don't have anything to offer you."

What does that mean? Are we still talking beverages or something else, as in he's gay and I'm not?

"Wine?"

He shakes his head.

"Beer?"

Another shake.

"Tea?"

No shake, just a glare—a you-just-woke-the-beast glare.

Don't say it; don't say—

"Water?" I whisper, a squint of apprehension on my face.

Gah! I'm pathetic.

His jaw clenches as he turns. Retrieving a bottled water from his refrigerator, he tosses it to me. I catch it and stare at it for a few seconds.

"What?" he says with biting aggravation.

My nose wrinkles. "Well, my teeth are sensitive. I can't drink cold water." God's honest truth.

He rests his hands on his hips and looks up at the ceiling, the muscle in his jaw working overtime.

"I'm fine with tap water." I squeak the words out like I'm waiting for the ceiling to collapse.

He grabs the bottle from my hands, screws off the top, and gulps down the contents. Then he fills it with tap water, glancing back at me with an evil scowl. "Jacket. Go. Now!" He hands the bottle to me, brushing past to the elevator.

The clicking of my heels echoes with each step as I hurry to catch up. On the descent, I take a small sip of the water and give him a sheepish sidelong glance. He doesn't look at me, eyes firm ahead, hands fisted.

LEAVING ME AND my lukewarm water on the elevator as if I no longer exist, he flips on another single light that illuminates a door off to our right. There's a keypad by it and he enters a long code before the door buzzes and he pushes it open. I hustle to catch up before the heavy door slams in my face. It's pitch black again until a large service door opens. Trick yanks off a cover with a magician's confidence, revealing a motorcycle.

Sucking my wet lips into my mouth, I release them with a pop. "I'm not getting on that thing."

We both stare at the motorcycle in silence for a few moments.

"Suit yourself." He tosses the cover over it and backtracks toward the elevator.

"Wait!"

He turns.

I point to a larger *something* that's also covered. "What's that?"

"Not mine."

I sigh, a lack of trust pulling my eyes into a tight squint. I know there's more beyond whatever isn't his, but I can't see that well in this meager lighting. I could share with him motorcycle fatality statistics and the life-threatening injuries I see come into the ER, but something tells me my words would be nothing more than miming to a blind person.

"I can't get my leg over a motorcycle in this tight dress." I gesture to my fitted skirt that falls just above my knees. There's an inch slit up one side, but not enough give to allow me to swing a leg over. It takes him three meaningful strides before we're standing toe to toe. I shrug in the most innocent it's-not-my-fault-I-have-this-dress-on way while looking up at him, thinking he surely understands my predicament. Eyes that give away nothing inspect the full length of my body, then he bends down and rips the skirt of my dress to my hip, exposing the waistband of my thong.

"What the hell?" I screech, grasping for the torn pieces in a losing battle to cover my bared ass.

Trick pulls the cover off his bike and grabs a helmet. Now it's my jaw that grinds in rage. He wedges the helmet between his knees and gathers my hair, twisting it until it's piled on top of my head before he shoves the helmet on me and flips down the visor.

"Jacket," he grumbles, picking it up off the floor by my feet.

He slips it on me and zips it like I'm a child; then he gets on the bike and brings it to a roaring start.

"Get on." He looks back at me, eyes drifting to my naked leg.

"Jerk!" I huff while throwing a leg over the bike and my patience to the wind.

"Hold on," he grates, reaching back, *palming my ass,* to scoot me closer to him, which just makes me more pissed. *And turned on in a praying mantis sexual cannibalism way.*

I hug his body out of necessity with a scoop of detest and a drizzling of lust. How did my night turn into this fiasco?

"What's your address?" he asks as we pull up to a stoplight.

I don't say anything. I'm too livid to speak.

"Suit yourself."

I flip up the visor. "What the hell does that mean? Why do you keep saying that to me?"

The light turns green.

"Address, Darby … now!"

I spew out my address like venom as he speeds forward. If I didn't know better—and maybe I don't—I'd think his mission is to send me flying off the back of his bike. My fingers make a death-grip claim to his abs. If I had long nails he'd be bleeding by now.

I say an instant prayer of thanks when we pull to a safe stop in front of my place. Nearly tumbling to the ground to get away from him, I jerk off his helmet and heave it. He catches it with a look of shock on his face. Shrugging off his jacket, I whip it on the ground.

"Have a nice life, asshole!" Turning, I stomp to my door. The lock evades me as I make desperate stabs at it with my key. It slides through the teeth, but before I can turn it Trick pins me to the door, my cheek pressed to the cool metal. I swear my ribs could crack from my heart beating in such a thunderous rage; every labored breath seethes through my clenched teeth.

His lips are so close to my ear I can feel their warmth. "I'm not an asshole. I just don't like rich-bitch women who think they can strut their whore asses around and own me because they have a bigger bank account. I offered you a ride ... *period*. So stop trying to buddy up to me. You don't have anything I fucking want. Got it?"

I wriggle out of his grasp and turn.

Smack!

Fire rages through my hand, the effects of which I'm sure will last longer than on his face. "You *are* an asshole." I shove him, but his feet stay rooted firmly to the ground. He doesn't even sway. "You don't know me, and you sure as hell don't know the balance of my bank account. So get the fuck away from me, and make sure you never end up in my ER again, because I won't lift a goddamn finger to put you back together! Got. It?"

I whip around and stumble inside, closing and locking the door behind me before collapsing to the floor.

"Fuck!" he yells. "Darby!" He bangs on the door, but I don't move.

I'm so pissed. The nerve of that jerk! But damn if I'm not as equally turned on. For the love of God, he ripped my dress. That was so damn hot! And when he slammed me against the door and rambled all that inconsiderate shit to me with a completely unwarranted judgmental attitude, I was even more pissed *and* proportionally aroused. I'm sure after a good night's sleep and the return of my rational thinking, the only memory I'll have from tonight will be his asshole attitude. But for now, the thing I'm most miffed about is that he's gay!

CHAPTER THREE

FOUR HOURS OF sleep—*not* enough. However, as I drag my emotionally drained ass to work, lack of sleep is not my biggest concern. My clutch bag with my wallet and phone, aka my life, trumps everything else. I left it at Trick's place. *Note to self: Never burn bridges if your purse is on the other side.*

I still can't make sense of what happened. Everything seemed fine until I asked for a drink—one drink. It was as if I asked him for a kidney transplant. I blinked and he went from agreeing to give me a ride home to accusing me of trying to what? Buy him? Control him? Own him? All over *one* drink? *He's* the asshole that ripped my dress and tried to kill me with his reckless driving! *Welcome back, rational thinking.*

"Good morning, sunshine. Long night?" Jade hands me a Green Lantern, my favorite raw green drink from Peel that I stockpile in the break room refrigerator. She's the closest thing to a best friend that I have, and that's pathetic considering we never see each other outside of work. But she knows I let my Green Lantern sit out thirty minutes so it's not so cold when I drink it, and she's kind enough to not act all exasperated about it like *some* people.

"Thanks. Mmm ... perfect." I lick my lips. "And yes, it was a long night. Steven got called into work and my evening went to hell in a handbag after that." *And now I'm in hell because I in fact don't have my handbag!* That reminds me, *Steven*! He's probably blown up my phone with messages wondering where I was when he got home.

"What happened?"

"Cardiac arrest ten minutes out," Ellen announces.

"Long story, I'll tell you later. I need to make a quick call and get dressed." I change into my scrubs and call Gemmie.

"Hel—lo?"

"Gemmie, it's Darby. I'm sorry for waking you, but I need a favor."

"Shit balls, Darby! It's six-forty-five on a Sunday!"

"I know, hence the apology. I need you to get my purse from Trick. I need my phone back ASAP."

"They're not open on Sunday." I can hear the growly yawn in her voice.

"It's at his place. He lives—"

"I know where he lives. Wait … how do you?"

"Long story." That seems to be the answer of the day. "Please … I *need* my phone. I'll owe you big time."

"The *long story*, that's all I want. Soon!"

"Deal. Gotta go. Thank you. I love you. You're the best!"

THE NEXT FOUR hours fill with a steady flow of weekend crazies. A looming cloud of exhaustion chases me so I just keep going.

"Room two, possible fracture." Jade hands me the chart.

"X-ray?"

"Not yet."

"Get one. What's next?"

"Five-year-old stuck a bean up his nose, room four."

I roll my eyes. "Lovely."

"Darb." Steven catches me on my way to bean nose.

"Oh, Steven, about last night—"

"Yeah, I'm sorry, babe. I was in surgery longer than I expected. I'm just now leaving."

"Oh, well … I went…" *Yeah, he doesn't need to know.* "…I mean, no problem. I'll call you later."

I glance up, searching for a nod of acknowledgement or something, but his gaze fixes over my shoulder. I turn to *Trick* planted behind me as if he just appeared rather than arrived. A glacier, he gives away nothing with his indifferent almost steely expression while holding my clutch in his hand. An icy chill sloths up my spine.

"Is that your purse?"

I look back at Steven. "Yes. Long story, I'll call you later." There it is again—my *long story*.

Snatching my clutch, I brush past ice man without a word.

"You're welcome."

I whip around with vinegar in my veins. "Tell Gemmie thank you."

He holds up his hand. "While I'm here, how about you take these stitches out?"

I fish my phone out of my clutch and hand my purse to wide-eyed Jade behind the counter. "It's been seven days, I said eight to ten."

"Suit yourself, I'll rip them out on my own."

I look at Jade with a desperate plea in my eyes, a silent SOS.

"Room two went to X-ray." She smiles, throwing me in the lion's den and swallowing the key.

I squint my eyes in a piercing scowl. "Jade, after you get the X-ray in room two, Mr. Douglas, curtain six, soiled himself and needs your assistance." My scowl morphs into vengeful smirk as I turn on my heel. "Follow me, *Patrick*."

He hops up on the table while I wash my hands. I grab several paper towels, taking a long breath and releasing it slowly. I hate feeling angry. Some people would say I act like a doormat, but if I were to react like I did last night every time a man pissed me off, I'd already be dead of a heart attack or stroke. Certain personalities crave that reaction; they love crawling under other people's skin like a chronic disease. If that's Trick, then I gave him exactly what he was looking for last night.

My focus stays on his hand, yet just his proximity does unwelcome things to my body that hasn't got the I-despise-this-jerk message. Thank God my hands are immune to the rest of my jittery emotions as I remove his sutures.

"I'm really not an asshole."

I release a cynical laugh. "Um … yes, you really are."

"I may have misjudged you."

"*May*? That's an understatement. But it doesn't matter…" I remove the last stitch and glance at him "…after today you won't have to see this *controlling rich-bitch whore* again."

He grimaces like I ripped his wound back open. "I shouldn't have said that. It was a knee-jerk reaction."

I pull off my gloves and toss them in the garbage. "No, you shouldn't have thought it in the first place." I wash my hands. "Whatever, I don't need another critic, and you made it perfectly clear that you don't want or need anything from me so…" I hold open the door "…have a nice life." Fake smiling. Teeth grinding. Breath holding.

He bites his lips together, dropping his chin into a thoughtful nod as he scoots off the table.

I stare at my feet like they're the most deserving thing in the room of my attention as he walks toward me. There's a tightness in my chest and a sinking feeling in my stomach from a toxic mix of anger, pain, and disappointment. Then there's my irrational side that's been gagged and thrown in the proverbial closet, all hot and bothered.

"What time are you done working?"

I raise my head, a what-did-you-say frown stealing my face. "Three. Why?"

"I'll pick you up at seven. Dinner's on me." He gives me his signature smirk, that small lip twitch that deceives his best efforts to act unaffected around me.

"Why would I want to go to dinner with you?"

"Because even if you won't admit it, something inside you needs to know that I'm not the *asshole* that drove you home last night."

I'm not sure what irritates me more, that he acts like he knows me or that he's right. I squint, but he's unreadable. It's insane that I'm even considering his offer, a likely round two of throwing my bruised ego into the ring.

I sigh. "I'll be starving by five and you're still an asshole."

He purses his lips to the side. "Grab a snack, I'll get you at six, and … you're wrong." He doesn't give me a chance for rebuttal before he's out the door.

I need a what-the-hell just happened moment, but I don't have that luxury because there's a bean up some kid's nose just calling my name.

I MANAGE TO slip out of the hospital before Jade has a chance to play twenty questions. Part of me is dying to talk about this situation I've fallen into, but that would require an explanation of my fascination with a gay man whom I've just recently met. That's an answer I don't have yet.

Steven is another "answer" I don't have. I'm sure "pleased" would not be the word to describe how he'd feel about me going to dinner with Trick, but can a straight guy really be jealous of a gay guy?

I finger through my long red waves that have been pulled back into a ponytail all day. Trick has seen my naked face so there's no need to fuss over makeup. I'm sure I'd do it all wrong in his eyes anyway. Faded skinny jeans, black boots, and a white off-the-shoulder top say casual … *friendly.*

"Seriously?" I mumble to myself, seeing him pull up on his mo-torcycle. This is Chicago; he has to have something other than a motorcycle.

As I open the door, he pulls off his helmet and gets off his motorcycle. I squeeze my legs together and second guess dinner being such a great idea. How stupid am I to torture myself like this?

Fuck. Me. Now!

There it is and ... Oh. My. God! It's even better than I imagined. I'm drowning in my own saliva as I attempt to keep myself from drooling—dark chaotic hair, intense eyes, the always present thick, dark stubble, and now a million—actually gazillion—dollar smile with teeth. *He has teeth! Pretty. White. Teeth.*

"I'll drive." I motion back toward my door.

He shakes his head and crooks a finger at me. Trick is grand master of the sexy come-hither look. How do gay guys do it better than straight guys?

"Are you going to try to kill me again?"

"Again?" He cants his head to the side.

I slip my purse strap over my head as he shrugs off his black jacket and puts it on me. "Yes, *again*. And don't be coy; you're not that good at it."

He repeats the hair twist from last night and slips his helmet on my head.

"If we took my car we'd both be safe."

He hops on. "What fun would that be?"

The moment I get my leg over, he palms my ass, *again*, and scoots me forward. Trick is dangerous in every way imaginable. Yet, I ignore all reason and just hold on. As crazy as it may sound, I'd rather be holding Trick with layers of clothing between us knowing it will never be more, than naked in bed with Steven and a future of possibilities.

This is so messed up!

TRICK TAKES THE helmet and jacket then leads me into the restaurant with long strides that leave me jogging to catch up. *What's the big hurry?*

"Have you ever had Moroccan?" He looks down at me as we wait to be seated.

"Not in Chicago."

"Where have you had it?"

"Morocco."

He grabs my hand and pulls me toward the door. "Let's go."

"What?" I follow him back outside.

Releasing my hand, he keeps walking. "Maybe you should pick the restaurant." He calls back with exasperation weighting his words.

"Why? I don't understand."

"Just ... let's go."

I fist my hands on my hips, refusing to move until he turns to look at me. "If this is about you gauging my rich-bitch whore status by the stamps in my passport, then you have just confirmed my earlier assessment—you *are* an asshole."

Trick turns, eyes giving away nothing as they stare intently at me like I'm a code to be deciphered. Then his hardened features soften a fraction. "I'm paying."

"Damn right you are," I reply as he brushes past me. I'm not certain, but I think the corners of his lips curl up a millimeter or two.

He looks at me with his million-thoughts-zero-words, completely unreadable expression. "Table for two, something more private please," he says to the maître d'.

Trick pulls out my chair for me, maybe as a peace offering.

"Trying to be a gentleman?"

A smirk. "I can assure you, I'm no gentleman."

I knew this, but his confirmation has a biting chill to it.

"Welcome. Can I take your drink order?" our waiter asks.

Trick looks at me.

"I'll have a glass of Riesling, please."

"And for you, sir?"

"Water's fine."

The waiter nods then moves to the next table.

"I was an addict."

This feels like a test, so I choose subtlety. With a minute raise of my shoulders, my eyes shift from my menu to him. "I didn't ask."

"You wanted to." He taps the rim of his water glass.

I glance back at my menu. "Alcohol?"

"Everything."

I meet his gaze again, and he dares me to flinch with his unyielding look.

"How long have you been clean and sober?"

"Nine years."

The waiter sets down my glass and pours the Riesling. "Shall I give you a few more minutes?"

We both nod.

I take a sip of my wine. "I used to chew my fingernails. My nana tried everything to make me quit—gloves, nasty tasting polish. I think she even considered shock therapy."

Trick's whole body visibly relaxes. I grin, relishing in his reaction to my unexpected confession. I'd hate to be predictable.

"How long's it been since your last chewing?"

I laugh. "I'm not sure. I probably still take a little nibble when I'm watching a scary movie or something like that."

He reaches across the table and takes my hand, rubbing his thumb over my short, neatly-trimmed nails. I hold my breath that's so easily lost to his touch, then slip my hand from his when I need to breathe again.

"So how'd you become the 'it' man in the world of makeup artistry?"

"My partner dragged me into the business."

I clear my throat. "Is he a makeup artist too?"

"No, he owns several salons, but when he met me he saw 'untapped' talent and decided to open Rogue Seduction."

"You must be quite the couple. Your business looks like a hole-in-the-wall from the outside, but Gemmie said you cater to the rich and famous."

He nods. "It's not supposed to attract anyone, hence the 'hole-in-the-wall' appearance. We don't exactly take walk-ins. The business is all Grady Cross, my partner. He knew everyone who's anyone before I was old enough to vote. I can't explain the decor. It's just … Grady."

I inwardly smile, thinking of Etta James and my Grandma Carmichael. "An older man, huh?"

Trick raises a single brow and smirks. "Yes, he's older than I am. Forty-five to be exact."

"Are you ready to order?" the waiter interrupts.

I order a salmon dish; Trick orders lamb.

I can't believe Trick's boyfriend, partner … whatever, is seventeen years older than him. Taking another sip of wine I try to mask my shock.

"So you know I was a junkie and that I live with an *older* man … and that I'm not an asshole, so what's your story?"

Pursing my lips, I squint one eye. "The asshole part is still up for debate."

"It's not—"

"It is." I insist. "So you and Grady live together?"

"Yes."

"Where was he last night?"

"LA"

"Oh?"

"He only lives in Chicago a few months out of the year."

"And you're okay with that?"

Trick takes a sip of his water. "Sure, why wouldn't I be?"

"I don't know. Long distance relationships don't usually work."

He dips his chin into a slow nod. There's something in his eyes that tells me for every word he does say, there are a thousand caught inside that tell his real story.

I wait to see if he wants to add anything, but he seems mesmerized by the flickering flame of the votive in the middle of our table. "Okay, me ... let's see ... I love working in the ER, and I like riding in vehicles with at least four tires."

Trick laughs and it's such a beautiful sound. It's like this frigid wall that's been between us is beginning to melt one laugh, one smile at a time. "That's it? All I get are two things that I already knew about you?"

"You know I work in the ER, but you didn't know that I love it. *And* don't forget about the nail chewing."

He shakes his head as the waiter brings us our salads.

"Thank you," we both say to the waiter.

"What's your favorite part about working in the ER?"

"The smell."

He squints, stopping mid bite.

"Yeah, it's the refreshing mix of alcohol, saliva, and dried blood. Some rooms smell like fresh plastic tubing. The nurses' station smells like coffee grounds, and the rest is just ..."

Trick still hasn't brought his fork the rest of the way to his mouth. "Don't stop, now. You haven't completely ruined my dinner yet."

I laugh. "Well if you insist. There's nothing like the smell of a freshly incised abscess, 80-proof vomit—"

"I get it!" Trick's eyes bug out.

I giggle. He didn't let me get to the good stuff like the ammonia and fishy odor of lady parts in need of help, or the pungent stool smell from a GI bleed. I'll save that for dessert.

"So what are you dying to know if it's not about my disgusting fingernail habit, my favorite mode of transportation, or the aroma of the ER?"

He stabs his lettuce. "I'm dying to know what you would be doing tonight if you weren't with me."

I chew my bite then dab my mouth. "That's easy. I'd be on my back getting a subpar lay."

Trick chokes on his food to the point where I scoot out of my chair and wonder if I need to do the Heimlich maneuver.

"Are you okay?"

He nods with his hand fisted at his mouth.

I ease back into my chair with apprehension. "Are you sure?"

"Yes," he says with a hoarse voice before taking a sip of water. He clears his throat. "I can't believe you said that."

"Really? What else would my 'rich-bitch whore ass' be doing?"

He flinches. I know it's a low blow since he's trying to make amends, but I've been judged my whole life and I'm tired of the Darby the Doormat role. "I'm sorry. I have trust issues with women and I shouldn't have said it."

Keeping my eyes on him, I try to gauge his sincerity. Then my gaze slips to my wine glass and I nod. "I forgive you. I apologize for being so crass with my remark. *I* have trust issues with men, and I've never had a real friend so my casual conversation skills aren't very refined—"

"Wait." He holds up his finger. "You've never had friends?"

"Not really." I look down at my plate and push my food around.

"How is that possible?"

"My *stellar* personality…" I wink "…was disguised by braces, zits, split ends, glasses, hips that developed before my boobs, and a painfully shy, introverted personality … get the picture? Oh, and how could I forget, I vomited down the back of the most popular boy in school who was sitting in front of me at a pep rally my freshman year. That's the day my name was officially changed from Darby to Barfy."

Trick's face morphs into a mixture of pain and humor. "And you chewed your finger nails."

I laugh and nod. "And that."

"Wow … that's just … wow. Well now you're …" His eyes move from my face to my chest and back up.

"Yes, now I have boobs to balance out my hips. They may not

be what wet dreams are made of, but they're functional and give my bra something to do besides cover my nipples under white shirts. And my face survived puberty without scarring. I had Lasik on my eyes and Gemmie pampers my unruly hair."

Another blinding smile. "You're…" Trick slowly shakes his head "…not trying to impress me."

I cock my head. "Is that a backwards way of saying that I'm unimpressive?"

"To the contrary, I've never been so impressed."

I squint one eye. "It's was the Barfy part, wasn't it?"

He chuckles. "Yes, definitely that. And your introverted personality?"

I laugh. "In college I crawled out of my little introverted hole. I'm still not the life of the party."

Trick's jaw goes slack.

"I know. How could I not be, right? My profession requires adequate social skills, but I still have trouble feeling comfortable around women. I think it's from years of never fitting into a clique or group of them."

Trick raises a single brow.

"I'm not a lesbian or anything—" I try to reel in the words, but it's too late. I grimace. "I mean … I don't have a problem with them or gay men or really the homosexual community in general."

Double brows peaked.

Shit!

Closing my eyes, I pinch the bridge of my nose, pausing just long enough to think before I speak. "I desperately wanted to fit in and have friends, I just never knew how. Even today I feel awkward with my female coworkers if I sit by them in the cafeteria. Unless it's about work, they do all the talking and I just sit and nod with a polite smile."

"Why, what do they talk about?"

I grin. "Men."

Trick chuckles. "But you have nothing to add?"

"No, I do. I just have yet to muster the courage to add my two cents. It's like my mind regresses back to high school and the nightmares I used to have. I imagine an awkward silence after I say something and then the whole room erupts into laughter—fingers pointing, eyes rolling, and me sinking into my chair."

Trick's lips pull into a bemused smile. "You're paranoid."

"I'm shy."

"You're scared."

"Screw you. Men are jerks anyway. What's the point in talking about them?"

"Well if you're getting a 'subpar lay' then maybe you need to talk about it."

"Why did you start doing drugs?"

He chuckles, giving me a slight head shake. "Yeah, I think we're done here." Standing, he tosses a wad of cash on the table. "Come."

I guess we're both done.

He goes through his routine of getting me ready to ride without saying a word. I let him, because I need the physical touch, even if it's just his hands twisting my hair or grazing my neck as he fastens the jacket on me. Then there's the really twisted part of me that hopes—*prays*—his hand finds its way to my ass when I get on the back.

It does!

I feel like such a fool … a desperate misfit. I'm not that girl anymore. The need to fit in has faded over time and been replaced with a healthy dose of confidence. But Trick has a way of drawing that repressed vulnerability to the surface. I'm not sure how I feel about that.

CHAPTER FOUR

*T*HIS IS ONE *fucking huge mistake, but this woman came out of nowhere. I'm fascinated by her. A distraction? Hell yes. A bad decision? Absolutely. Will I do the right thing? Unlikely.*

CHAPTER FIVE

I EXPECT TRICK to fast track to my place and bid me a permanent farewell. He proved he's not a total asshole and cleared his conscience while I proved I'm a total freak. I had the upper hand going into the evening, but somewhere along the way I lost it. Most guys would look past the freak part in exchange for a quick lay. So I'm surprised when he pulls into his mammoth garage. I have nothing to offer *him* ... at least that he wants.

He parks the motorcycle and removes my helmet.

I shake out my hair like one of those women in a Garnier hair-care commercial. Sadly ... I don't think I hit the sexy mark. It's tangled and knotted in my face. "Why are we here?" I paw at the hair stuck to my face like a dog with fleas.

He brushes a few stray strands that I miss then smiles. "I thought we could hang out awhile."

I squint my eyes like he's talking Chinese.

He grabs my hand and pulls me toward the elevator. "Maybe I'll be your first."

My grip tightens as the elevator ascends. "My first?"

"Yes, your first friend."

We step off the elevator and Trick turns on the lights.

"Why?"

He twists his mouth like he's chewing on the inside of his cheek. "I don't know. Maybe I need a friend too."

Just my luck. My first official friend is a guy, but not just a guy ... a *squirrel*, a gay squirrel. I'm not sure if he is a gift or a curse.

"So what are you thinking? Battleship or Scrabble?"

Trick gives me the you-just-grew-two-more-heads look. "You're serious?"

"No?" I cringe at my own awkwardness. *Okay, I'm a little serious.*

He chuckles. "You cannot be that socially inept."

Yes, I can and I am. I have proper social skills when it comes to dinner parties and medical conferences. I've dated several men since I graduated college, but the relationships have only been about sex. We didn't "hang out" much aside from the bedroom and restaurants. Number of slumber parties I've attended: 0. Number of girls' weekends I've been on: 0. If Trick doesn't want a blowjob or a quick roll in the hay, then I'm in foreign territory.

"So what were *you* thinking?"

Trick sits down on the couch and rests his ankle on his knee. "Well, I only have to beat a subpar lay so ..."

"Not this again! Steven is a surgeon and his mind is always on his work. It's not that he doesn't have *skills.*" I plop down on the couch next to him, leaving just enough room that I don't get a whiff of his pheromones that seem to make me a bit rabid. If this friendship is going to work, I need to get past my physical craving for him.

"He just has ADD in bed?"

I snicker. "I hadn't thought of it that way, but maybe."

Trick's smile could melt the north pole; I don't know why he's so reserved with it. "So how'd you meet Subpar Steve?"

I pull off my boots and tuck my feet underneath me. "Our fathers introduced us at a political fundraiser last year. My father is running for his second term in the senate, and Steven's dad is a wealthy son of a bitch that wants a shitload of favors. So they're a match made in campaign corruption heaven."

He chuckles. "Your dad must be proud of your glowing endorsement."

"My father has never been proud of me for anything." *Oh God!*

Those are cringe-worthy words, the ones I've never let myself say aloud.

"Daddy issues? Might that explain why you settle for relationships that are *subpar*?"

"My daddy issues extend way beyond my love life. But yes, guys love that I have no expectations of them. We can mutually benefit from meaningless sex without fear that I'll go all *Fatal Attraction* on them. And truthfully, I couldn't care less. Men are cheating, lying pigs." Trick frowns. "Present company excluded." I try to smile past the foot in my mouth. "My first two years of college I went through a black, sort of goth phase."

Trick rubs the back of his fingers across his bristly chin and raises his eyebrows.

"I don't know why you wear guyliner when you work, but I like the way it reminds me of the two best and worst years of my life. Finding yourself in college is such a cliché, but that's what I did … Unfortunately, I had to lose myself for two years first. I died my hair black, wore all black makeup and clothing, and experimented with sex, alcohol, and a few *recreational* drugs." I laugh. "God, my father was so pissed. But what did he expect? I hadn't had the best role models in my life, except for my nana, she's amazing."

"Where does your nana live?"

"Lincoln Park. Not too far from me. She's the only blood relative I have left on my mom's side, and she moved in with us after I was born." My voice fades to just barely above a whisper. "My mom died giving birth to me, so Nana basically raised me."

Trick gives me a sad smile that I return with a such-is-life shrug. The heavy air suffocates the moment leaving an awkward silence. "Mom died" is the biggest conversation killer.

"So … if you hadn't taken pity on me and offered dinner and 'hanging out,' what would you be doing tonight?"

He wets his lips then rubs them together. "Drawing."

"Drawing? Drawing what?"

"Whatever my current project happens to be."

I purse my lips to the side. "Are we talking crayons, markers, chalk?"

"Pencil."

"Really? Can I see?"

He looks at me with an unexpected frown on his face before diverting his eyes to his lap "No."

I laugh then try to choke it back when I see his lips pull into a firm line. "Are you serious? You're not going to let me see them?"

Trick shakes his head with absolution.

"But I thought we were friends."

"We are, but let's be honest, if this were a date would you have sex with me tonight?"

If you weren't gay? Yes! Yeah, that's so wrong of me.

"No. What's your point?"

"My point is that some things are personal and require a certain amount of trust."

I fidget with the frayed hem of my jeans. "So you don't trust me?"

"I don't trust women."

Rubbing my hands over my face, I sigh. "I guess I had that one coming. Do you want to talk about it?"

He looks up with tight brows. "Talk about why I don't trust women?"

I nod.

"No, I don't."

My phone rings. We both look at my handbag. "Excuse me." I dig through everything and find it buried at the bottom. Trick watches with unnerving intensity as I say a few okays and "be right there."

"Emergency?" he asks as I drop my phone in my purse.

"Yes, a shooting with multiple victims. Sorry, I have to go. Besides, you won't show me your artwork so we might as well call it a night." I love the way he tips his chin to hide his grin. He stands and I wave him off. "I can grab a cab."

"No, I'll get you there faster."

I raise an untrusting brow. "I think safer is better than faster."

"Come," he yells over his shoulder as I do the one-legged hop, trying to catch up while tugging on my boots.

HAIR TWIST. HELMET. Jacket. Ass grab. *Yes!*

Thankfully no one can see the Cheshire cat grin on my face as Trick weaves through traffic to the hospital. The past forty-eight hours have been surreal. After witnessing so many motorcycle injuries and fatalities, I swore I'd never get on the back of one, yet here I am—enjoying every tummy-twisting minute. The idea of having a true friend had fallen off my vision board; now it's back on, front and center. And capturing the attention of a guy like Trick … well, there are no words.

Wealth doesn't always equate to popularity. Slipping out of a sleek limo says wealthy. I've done that more times than I care to remember since my father married Rachel. Easing my leg over the back of a motorcycle behind a guy that looks like trouble says popular. *At twenty-seven, is it too late to be popular?*

I hand Trick my helmet and shrug off his jacket. "Thanks for dinner." I hug myself, rubbing my arms. It's the middle of summer. Why am I either freezing or burning up in his presence?

He nods, slipping his jacket on.

"We should hang out again." In my head it's a question; in my voice it's a suggestion.

Another nod. "Come by sometime."

"I will." I start to walk away then turn. "Just so you know, I'm not a virgin. So sex on our second date is a good possibility. But since I'm missing the correct anatomy, I'll settle for a private viewing of your sketches." If he weren't gay, I'd still be babbling like the first day we met. But he's unobtainable, so I have nothing to lose by being myself with him. As much as being with Trick feels like a slow drip of adrenaline, he's offered me something I need so much more than physical gratification—friendship.

He puts his bike into gear as my eyes focus on his lips. I wait for it … I think a little part of me even prays for it … there it is, the slight twitch of his lips. I read it that he's pleased, which is perfect because so am I.

THE SWITCH FLIPS. I'd love to chomp my gum and twirl my hair, contemplating the endless possibilities of my relationship with Trick, but I can't. Wasting not another second, I hustle to the ER, get changed, and do what I do best—piece together puzzles.

In spite of the nonstop, grueling hours of the clock ticking one heartbeat at a time, I never question why I'm here doing this. Most days I feel like this is my sole purpose in life—giving more than I take. Even with the nasty smells, which are actually my least favorite part of the job, I still love being here.

"You off?"

I turn to Steven zoned into his cell phone screen. "Just about," I reply, signing my last chart and yawning.

"Breakfast?"

"No way. Bed." I yawn again.

He slips his phone back in his pocket and smirks. "I like the sound of that." He wiggles his brows.

Steven is a lukewarm bath. He has blond curly hair that he normally keeps trimmed short, but today I notice a few wayward curls rebelling around his ears. Blue eyes and dimples, he's textbook cute. It's the wow factor he's missing. Only recently, since I've experienced wow, have I come to that conclusion.

"Let me clarify; I *need* sleep. It's been twenty-four hours and I'm ready to drop."

"Want me to get you a coffee?"

"I don't drink coffee, Steven." He's known me for almost a year and I'm quite certain we've broached this subject before.

"Then black tea, green piss juice, or whatever the hell it is you drink."

I brush past him to go change my clothes. "I don't drink tea either, and I don't want to stay awake so I'll pass on the 'green piss juice' offer too. Bye, Steven."

After freeing my tangled hair from its ponytail and changing out of my scrubs, I dig through my handbag for my key.

"Crap!" I didn't drive.

"Something wrong?" Jade asks from around the corner.

"I forgot I didn't drive in yesterday."

"Bummer. You might have to resort to public transportation like the other ninety-nine percent of us."

Slinging my purse over my shoulder, I pin Jade with an unrelenting glare.

Her eyes slip to her locker. "I'm kidding. Don't look so serious."

I turn and walk to the door, then stop just as I open it. "You do realize this 'wealth' you're referring to belongs to my father's wife and it's securely protected by a mile-long prenup. Aside from the occasional trip I get dragged on or a few designer dresses, I don't benefit from *her* money."

Her locker door slams shut. "Darby I'm—"

"It's fine … I'm used to being judged."

Her weak voice rips through the brief silence. "Really … I'm sorry."

Keeping my back to her, I nod once and leave.

I SHOULD CALL Steven and apologize for blowing him off yesterday, but then he'd want to make plans to meet up—hookup. But that's not what I want to do. For reasons unbeknown to myself at the moment, I want to see Trick again. Maybe it's too soon, but then again, it's not like we're dating so the customary waiting period shouldn't apply.

I need a reason to stop by, like I just happen to be in his area. Honestly, I'm not in his area unless I have an appointment with Gemmie. That's it. I should stop by and get some hair products. My nose wrinkles as I glance at the time. Gemmie will be closing up shop in less than an hour.

"Choose it, Darby." I chastise myself for my expert ability to make hard decisions with ease, yet easy ones debilitate me.

The choice makes itself. I'm in my red beamer heading south before my brain catches up to what my body has already decided. I'm off to see my new friend—my only friend.

"Shoot! Did I forget to put you into my schedule?" Gemmie asks with concern crinkling the corners of her eyes as she mists hairspray over a young blonde's wavy hair.

"No, I just need some…" *Crap!* I have to sell this lie better if I expect always-skeptical Gemmie to buy it. "…conditioner."

Gemmie's not buying it as evidenced by her bullshit squint. I look at the products assembled with perfect precision on the glass shelf by the window.

"Third shelf down on the far right."

I grab the bottle of conditioner.

"Still coming on Saturday?"

I turn, biting my lips together as I nod.

"I'll add it to your bill, sweetie."

"Um … thanks." I submit to the nervous smile revealing my lie as I head out the door.

Her knowing glare pierces my back; I can feel the icy burn of distrust. No sense in hiding my next move, so I throw my shoulders back and saunter across the street. With each step my heart palpates, heating my skin, while long fingers of anxiety strangle my nerves.

The security chime of the front door to Rogue Seduction announces my arrival to both Trick and the raven-haired skeleton in Prada perched on the stool. He's still working and maybe I should have thought of that. Not everyone works the same unpredictable ER hours that I do. The woman stares at me with what I read as an unwelcoming gaze. Trick, however, doesn't so much as flinch in acknowledgement of my arrival. I wait for him to say something, but then again, I'm the one who walked through his door. This is a poorly thought-out plan.

Holding up the bottle of conditioner, I shrug with a slight grin. "I was in the neighborhood, so I thought ..." Either the floor is sinking or I'm having flashbacks of my youth being the unwelcome new kid at school. Either way, I feel an inch tall. "Sorry, I should have called or—"

"Sit," Trick says with a clipped voice, keeping his full attention on Ms. High Cheekbones and pouty lips.

The repressed part of my personality, the defiant part, puffs out its chest. *Maybe I don't want to sit. Maybe I want to stand and wait. Or maybe I don't want to wait at all.*

"Or stand." Trick glances back over his shoulder. There it is— the twitch of his lips. *Cocky shit!* Never did I imagine thinking a guy could look anything but rebellious in makeup, but for the love of all things skin-tingling, breathtaking, and nipple-hardening sexy ... Trick in black guyliner makes me crave friction in my girly parts like nothing and no one before.

I swallow. "I think I'll sit, thank you very much." *Take that!*

Trick lines pouty lips with an orangish-red tint that looks surprisingly good on her. Dark eyes hooded in mile-long lashes look me over. I fight the urge to squirm with insecurity, like when the popular kids rolled their eyes over me with scrutiny.

"Beautiful." I hear a French accent as I look up expecting to see her admiring her reflection. Instead, she's still staring at me.

"She is," Trick replies, just inches from her face.

Embarrassment and *shock* career through my body, obliterating my ability to respond, or think, or ... breathe. These two beautiful people are talking about me ... they're calling *me* beautiful. It's ... crazy!

Interlacing my fingers, I stare down at my hands while I twiddle my thumbs just like Nana does. I bet my mom did it too.

"You're a god," French accent gushes as she stands, leaning into the mirror.

I sneak a peek but look back down as she walks toward the register.

"I'll see you onsite next week, darling,"

Through the corner of my eye I see Trick nod as he takes the wad of bills from the perfectly manicured hand. She flutters her fingers in a dainty wave upon her exit. I return a shy smile.

Trick straightens up his work area as I ease my way over and climb up on the stool.

"She's pretty."

"Thank you," he replies with a smirk while keeping his eyes cast downward on his busy hands reorganizing everything.

"Don't be so arrogant. She may think you're a god, but her beauty is her own. You just enhance it."

Trick turns and steps closer, as in *really* close. If I try to regain my personal space, I'll fall off the stool, so I just pray he doesn't feel my nerves or see my whole body blush with heat. His hand moves and I flinch, but it doesn't deter his motion. Grabbing a few strands of my hair, he runs it through his fingers, teasing it then releasing it at my breast.

Breathe, breathe, breathe!

"If you would have said *he's* pretty, then the compliment would belong to *him*. But you said *she's* pretty, so the compliment belongs to me."

"She—he—*that* was a guy?" The incredulity of my voice trips through the air.

Trick shows me his full-on grin filled with pride. "Don or 'Donna' does cabaret shows." He turns and finishes cleaning up.

"I-I mean—wow!"

"Thank you." He shoots me another smirk.

I roll my eyes. "Stop being so cocky. It doesn't suit you."

"Oh?" He glances up with a raised brow. "Then what suits me?"

With a thoughtful squint, I twist my lips to the side. "I'm not sure yet. I'll let you know when I figure it out."

"Come." He shuts off the lights.

"Where are we going?"

"Grocery shopping."

"Why?" I hop off the stool and follow him out the door.

"I need groceries."

"Want me to drive?"

"Nope, we'll walk." Trick is a good ten steps in front of me.

The guy doesn't wait for anyone or anything. I jog to catch up.

CHAPTER SIX

M Y DISTRACTINGLY SEXY new friend drags me through every aisle, and all the lip-licking glances go unnoticed by him—but not by me. "Women sure do like you."

Trick inspects each apple before adding them to the cart. "Impossible. They don't even know me."

Proving my point, I glare at a lady eye fucking him while her kids cling to the side of her cart like a troop of monkeys. "Let me rephrase, they like your body."

He pushes the cart toward the checkout, glancing over at me. "Do you like my body?"

I swallow hard, grabbing and thumbing through a magazine as we wait in line. "It's … fine. I guess. I haven't paid it much attention."

"No?"

I suck in my lips and shake my head. Ten minutes later we leave with six paper bags of groceries. He carries two in each hand, and I carry the other two.

"If you don't feed me when we get back, I'm going to feel used. You really should consider trading in your motorcycle for something more practical."

The look he gives me misses my jugular by a few millimeters. Warning received. It was a joke, well … sort of.

"If you're hungry you can drink one of the four bottles of fresh pressed juice you stuck in my cart." He gives me a quick sideways glance.

"They were on sale."

He chuckles.

"What? Is something wrong with saving a buck?"

He stops, turns, and bends down so we're at eye level. "*You* didn't pay for them."

My face morphs into a slight grimace. "I'll pay you back."

He shakes his head, continuing on, once again leaving me scurrying to catch up. "I don't want your money."

"I know…" I give him a playful nudge "…that's why I'm letting you be my friend."

"Lucky me." He sets down two bags to open the door.

"Uh … yeah. I'm quite the catch."

He glances back with a questioning brow.

"I don't mean in a romantic way …"

His stare intensifies.

"Not that I'm not romantic, just not with you because you're—"

The one brow raise turns into two. "I'm?"

I sigh. "Ugh! Just … let's go." I kick the heel of his boot.

The signature twitch-smirk filled with a million unsaid words makes an appearance. In such a short amount of time, I've developed a love-hate relationship with it.

We set the groceries on the counter. "I'm going to shower. Feel free to put things away and start dinner." Trick walks toward the glass-walled bathroom. *Wring out my panties and mop up my drool.* He shrugs off his shirt revealing a smoking body marked with various tattoos. "You're staring—*paying attention.*"

"I-I'm … not," I croak. My skin heats to a nice crimson.

"You are," he calls back without looking before disappearing around the wall.

"Smug bastard," I mumble to myself.

"I heard that."

"Whatever and … don't flatter yourself." I start to take the groceries out of the bags, putting things wherever I damn well please.

Serves him right for being so bossy. "You're not my type," I yell over the sound of the shower water.

"Really? So what's your type? Straight-laced?"

No, just straight in general!

"Funny," I yell back.

"So fat clowns?"

I bang the bag of blue corn chips against the counter for the fat clown comment. "Sensitive."

"So pussies?" he yells.

Oops, I just hate it when the gallon jug of milk accidentally gets set on the vulnerable little carton of eggs. I smile in evil revenge as yolk oozes onto the bottom shelf of the refrigerator.

"Intelligent."

"Stuffy." He shuts the water off as I stomp on the package of linguini.

"Sexy." I grind the word through my teeth, determined to not let him get the best of me.

Too late ... holy spontaneous orgasm!

Trick walks out with a gray towel wrapped around his waist, drops of water clinging to his messy hair and rivulets racing down his etched form. "You're staring again."

I clear my throat. "I'm not—what the hell?" My voice screeches to a decibel that even I don't recognize as he drops his towel—revealing his ass. I whip around and squeeze my eyes shut, but his naked body is branded into my brain. I do the only thing I can at this point; I commit it to my deathbed highlight reel.

"Told ya you were staring."

I lean against the counter gripping the edge with my back to him, eyes still squeezed shut.

"Are you standing on my pasta?"

Opening my eyes, I glance down. "It fell."

He bends down, thankfully in jeans but still no shirt, and tugs the package of broken linguine out from under my brown-heeled boot. "It fell *under* your boot?" He stands, tossing the package on the counter while giving me a menacing frown.

I shrug. "Something like that."

"I like breakfast for dinner. How about toast and eggs?" He opens the refrigerator door.

"Works for me." I dig my teeth into my bottom lip.

Trick grunts as he moves the milk off the crushed carton of eggs. Yolk drips on the floor as he brings it to the counter.

I smile in spite of the grinding sound of his teeth and flare of his nostrils. "I'll cook the eggs." I take the carton from him as a sort of peace offering. "You good with scrambled?"

Another grunt, actually it might be a growl. "For your information I like them over easy, but your disturbing 'friendship' skills would indicate that scrambled is my only option at this point."

"You were being mean."

He hands me a skillet after I open every cabinet door except the one with the pots and pans. "I was joking, as in a sense of humor, which I believe was number one on your list of desirable traits."

I spray the pan and pour approximately four eggs into the skillet while choking back my initial response. What he didn't hear was a man who is *straight* is my number one desirable trait. "Yeah, you're a one-man comedy show. I think I've seen your teeth um ... twice. You're ... *icy*."

"Icy?" Trick cocks his head while dropping two slices of bread in the toaster. "How so?"

I season the eggs and stir them. "You have a ... how shall I say it? It's a ... *fuck-off* vibe thing going."

He gives me the stink eye. "Well, you sure didn't get the message."

"Doesn't mean you weren't sending it." I spoon the eggs onto the plates.

Trick sets two pieces of toast on each plate and slides them to the opposite edge by the barstools. Then he gets out butter, jelly, orange juice, and a jar from the spice cabinet.

"So do you still want me to *fuck off?*" I ask, climbing onto the barstool.

He hands me a fork and knife. "I do if you don't stop mutilating my groceries." There's zero humor to his voice, but I'm learning that's just Trick. His emotions are subtle and hard to read, like blurred ink.

I spread butter and strawberry jelly on my toast. "The funny thing is … I'm not usually a vengeful person. At least I never thought so until I met you." I shrug and pile the eggs onto my toast. "I guess you bring out the evil in me. Congratulations, I've been considered a doormat for years, so this is progress for me."

Trick glances over at me then takes a bite of his butter and jellied toast *with eggs piled on top*. He may have militant control over his emotions, but I don't. My grin steals my face. For years my father gave me a disapproving scowl at the breakfast table for my jelly, toast, and egg concoction. But now, I've found my breakfast soul mate.

"What?" he mumbles over a mouthful, squinting at me.

"OMG! It's official; we're BFFs."

He finishes chewing then takes a swig of his juice. "No way…" he shakes his head "…if you ever use OMG and BFF in the same sentence again we're O.V.E.R! Got it?"

My grin has taken up permanent residence on my face. I talk in code all day at work, so I'm not really the ditzy acronym girl; I was just playing with him. However, his growly reaction was so freaking hot, I know I'll end up poking the bear again and again.

Shoving in a big bite, I tap his foot with mine. "We're breakfast soul mates and you know it," I mumble while wiping the corners of my mouth with my fingers. "What are the chances that we both like jellied toast with scrambled eggs on top? Seriously, like one in a gazillion."

He slides over the jar he grabbed from the spice cabinet. "First, I like jellied toast with over easy eggs." He glares at me. "Second, I add cayenne pepper to my eggs. And I'm pretty sure the whole thing is far from an original idea."

Grasping the jar of cayenne like a drawn sword, I accept his challenge. The spicier the better, another OMG-we're-so-meant-to-be-BFFs moment. However, I keep that to myself, *for now*. The idea of us being O.V.E.R terrifies me because this has to be as good as it gets—super squirrel sans shirt, sexy tats, and eating eggs on jellied toast. *Nirvana.*

Trick observes me with a curious look, eyes dilated, lips firm to resist the twitch-smirk. I sprinkle on enough cayenne to permanently burn off my taste buds, then take a bite. Chewing slowly, I grin while savoring the sweet and fiery collision along my tongue and down my throat.

"What are you thinking?" My nerves release the hostage words that have been shackled in my throat since we met. Every look feels like an undecipherable riddle; I'm tired of guessing.

He looks down at his plate then takes another bite before looking at me again. "I'm trying to figure you out."

I almost choke on my laugh. "*Me?* You can't be serious. I'm the epitome of an open book. I've told you just about everything about me. What more could you possibly want to know?"

Trick slides his plate away and rests his folded arms on the counter, closer to me. His eyes flicker over my face and hair, then down my body before meeting mine again. "I want to know why you're here with me?"

Gulp!

He might as well ask me the meaning of life. It's a simple question with an infinitely impossible answer, but I look for it anyway.

His eyes don't hold the answer, his lips are a gateway to something he finds amusing in me, and so I look at the brilliant rainbow of ink along his arms, chest, and back. The stars, small flowers, feathers, symbols, and sanskrit—they could mean nothing; they could mean everything.

I'm attracted to him, but not delusional. He will never look at me the way I look at him ... yet, I'm here. So I shrug realizing the answer is me, not him. "I like *me* with you."

He stares at my lips; he does that a lot. He's probably thinking I could use a Botox injection. *Fat chance!* "Who are *you* with me?" Turning to face me, he pulls my chair closer to his so my legs go between his.

Sucking in a breath, I grab my toast and take another bite to hide my nerves. He has short, dark chest hair that trails downward, disappearing beneath his jeans. On the left side of his abs there are black sanskrit symbols etched to a bold perfection. I love looking at him.

"I'm out of control."

He raises a brow as I grin.

"Nobody's life is in my hands, and I'm not the Senator's daughter. You've seen me without makeup and nearly wetting myself on the back of your bike, yet you still suggested we be friends."

A soft chuckle escapes him as he rests his hands on my knees. The next part I *want* to be one hundred percent true, but it's not—yet. "I don't have to think about sleeping with you or who you're sleeping with when it's not me."

His hands grip tighter on my knees. My breath catches. I hold it, control it, then release it with ease as he releases me.

Grabbing my juice, I suck it down the way he sucks all control out of me. The clink of my glass hitting the counter breaks the eerie, suffocating silence that hovers like a cloud in this large open space. "Tell me about your family."

"Grady and Tamsen are my only family." He pushes my chair back and hops off his stool.

"Tamsen?"

"Grady's sister." Trick rinses off our plates.

"What about your parents?" I climb down and hand him the

skillet.

"What about them?"

"Jesus, Trick! This is such deadweight conversation. It's exhausting dragging information out of you."

He shuts the door to the dishwasher and leans against the counter with his arms folded across his chest, head down. "I think they died."

I shake my head. "What does that mean?"

He looks up. "You work at a hospital but you don't know what it means to die?"

"No, you idiot! I don't understand what it means to not know if your parents are dead or alive."

"Well, lucky you." He walks away, grabs a shirt, and slips on his boots before heading toward the elevator. "Come."

"Where are we going?"

He slides open the gate and steps into the elevator, turning toward me. "I'll walk you out."

"You're kicking me out?" I try to hide the shock in my voice, but I'm sure he can see it in my posture that deflates an inch or two.

"I'm *walking* you out."

I look around the room searching for … something. My pride? Some dignity?

Nothing.

Scuffing my boots across the floor, I sulk to the elevator. Trick shuts the gate.

"You don't have to walk me to my car," I say in a weak voice as he opens the outer door.

He walks out as if he didn't hear me, leaving me to catch up.

When we reach the street he stops. I point to my car on the other side, and he continues toward it. After I unlock it, he opens the driver's door. His mask is back on, not a single twitch, just … stone. I start to get in then stop. Standing straight, I hug him. If it's even possible, his body stiffens more. His arms stay glued to his sides.

"I'm sorry about your parents … wherever they are." Releasing him, I slide into my seat and shut the door. Without looking at him, I pull away from the curb, only risking a glance in my rearview mirror when he's already out of sight. Trick thinks his parents are dead, and maybe they are. Lack of closure can be torture. I wonder if he's given up on any other possibility just to get that closure.

I SHOULD ATTEND yoga classes or something to clear my mind. Psychologically it's probably not in my best interest to submerge myself in a mentally and sometimes emotionally draining job, then engage in the mind fuck that is Trick in my free time.

He radiates an element of mystery and danger. Any attempt to figure him out would be the equivalent of diving head first into the dark abyss. Yet, I'm drawn to him in more than just a physical sense, and I'm not sure it's something I can control. But most disturbing is the realization that I don't want to control it.

Pulling up in front of my nana's place, I look at the time. She's an early riser which means she's usually in bed by eight. It's ten 'til, so hopefully I'll catch her before she sets the alarm and shuts off the lights.

"Yes?" she answers shortly after I press the intercom button.

"It's me, Nana."

The door unlocks.

"Well isn't this a lovely surprise." She opens her arms, sparkling blue eyes that mirror mine crinkle in the corners.

"Hope I didn't wake you." I hug her and feel the warmth of home in her arms—the only arms that have ever felt like what I imagine a mother's love should feel like.

"I don't think that's possible yet. Mary invited me for coffee earlier and I should have skipped the second cup. I think I'll be up for a while yet. So come, sit." A plush, cream bathrobe engulfs her petite frame. The rosy glow of her cheeks and shiny nose indicate she's washed her face, but her ginger and white Peter Pan hair still looks salon perfect. "You have the night off?"

"Yes." I sit in the wing-back chair next to her. "I work in the morning."

"Have you been summoned for the dinner party your father is having this weekend?"

Drawing my knees into my chest, I laugh. "Of course. He's claimed all my weekends until November."

"You could say no. You don't owe him anything."

I shrug. "I know, but I hate conflict." *Usually.* "It's easier to just make an appearance, let him introduce me to some of the most boring people in the world, then sneak out after he ..." Casting my eyes downward, I sigh.

"After he sneaks off to the nearest private room to screw some bimbo?"

"Nana!" My jaw drops.

She smirks knowingly. Nothing gets by her. "Big dicks with too much money and power."

"He's still my father. I know in his own *twisted* way he loves me."

She nods once with pursed lips. "So I know you didn't stop by to talk about your father."

Raising my brows, I pop my lips. "Nope."

"Steven propose?"

"God, no! We're not there yet."

"Yet?" She perks up.

"Ever. He's not the one."

"Oh really? Does that mean someone else has thrown their hat into the ring?"

I bite my lips together.

"Spill, dear. Who is he?"

"He's a makeup artist Gemmie recommended. But he has not, nor ever will be 'throwing his hat into the ring.'"

"Married?" She grins as if the thought of me being someone's mistress pleases her. It's possible all my living relatives are a bit twisted.

I shake my head and smirk. "No, Nana, he's not married. He's ... gay."

She throws her head back and slaps her hand against her chest in a fit of laughter. "Oh my goodness!"

"Why is his sexual preference so hysterical?"

"Oh dear..." she wipes the corners of her eyes "...it's just you have the worst luck in love. When did you find out?"

I reach over and grab a tissue from the sofa table and hand it to her, rolling my eyes. Then I proceed to tell her everything, not leaving out one single detail—including my magnetic attraction to him that shouldn't be sexual but is.

"Well, dear, you've hit the jackpot."

"What? How have you come to that conclusion from everything I've told you?"

"A guy friend who's gay? I hear they're every girl's dream. Except, from the sounds of things, Trick needs to gay up a little more and stop confusing unsuspecting women."

"Gay up? Who are you?"

She snaps her wrist at me. "I read the tabloids you know."

"Yeah? Well then you should know that gay doesn't have a look."

"That's the problem. You used to be able to tell by the ear piercing—right for gay left for straight. Or is it the other way around? Anyway, these days everything gets pierced and so it becomes terribly confusing."

Nana provides nonstop entertainment, and every time I come by to see her I chastise myself for not doing it more often.

"We're friends, period. And maybe you're right. If he would 'gay up' a little more I might feel the jackpot effect."

"Yes, shopping, hair, makeup, and chick flicks without competing hormones or competing for the same men."

"Or wishing he weren't gay," I whisper to myself.

She tilts her head to the side, giving me a soft, sympathetic smile. "Or that too, dear."

CHAPTER SEVEN

GEMMIE IS ONE of my few guilty indulgences. Tonight isn't a gala, and I could wrangle my hair into something presentable for my father's dinner party, but I need an hour in her chair to decompress from the week.

"I talked to Trick earlier. He said you weren't on his schedule this afternoon. Did you forget to book him?"

"It's a dinner party. I think I can manage some mascara and lip gloss for the night. Besides, after you're done working your magic all eyes will be on my hair, not my face." I wink at her reflection in the mirror.

"So ... what were you doing with him the other night?"

I've been waiting for this question.

"We had dinner, just eggs and toast."

"You heard me say he's—"

"Gay. Yes, I know. We're just friends."

"Hmm, that's ... surprising."

I sigh. "Why because I'm not worthy of having friends? Because—"

"Down, girl! Holy hell, what's your deal? I meant Trick. He's very private and not the type to make friends with ..."

"With?"

She pulls my curled hair back into the most elegant ponytail I have ever seen. "Women. They make up ninety percent of his clientele, but I've heard he *tolerates* them ... just barely. However, I don't think it has anything to do with him being gay. I think it's something from his past. So him befriending you is pretty miraculous."

The newly formed knot in my stomach makes me nauseous. I know he doesn't trust women, but I've felt like the exception—until now. Am I Trick's charity case? He's *tolerating* me? I feel like a complete idiot … again. How does this keep happening to me? Is the concept of me finding a genuine friend really that farfetched? *Apparently.*

"What do you think?" Gemmie hands me a mirror to see the back.

"I can't believe you even have to ask." I smirk. "It's fabulous, as always."

She knows she doesn't have to ask, but I don't think she'll ever get tired of clients gushing over her talent.

My eyes cannot help but wander to Rogue Seduction as I leave Gemmie's. The reflection on the window makes it hard to see, but it doesn't look like the lights are on. Trick's probably sticking needles into female voodoo dolls.

RACHEL DIDN'T SEND me a dress this week. That's code for either the dinner party is not receiving media attention that might be free publicity for her brand, or it means she's in New York this weekend. That will make my father's indiscretions easier to hide.

I stare at my strapless, red chiffon dress with silver, open-toed heels that are laid out across my bed as my door intercom buzzes. I slip on my white satin robe and answer the intercom.

"Yes?"

"Hey."

I suck in a nervous breath and tighten the sash on my robe. "Trick?"

"Yes." His word frugality astonishes me.

I buzz him in and hurry down the stairs just as he closes my front door. Faded jeans, black boots, fitted black T-shirt, and exposed tats on his lean, toned arms … he *definitely* needs to gay up.

"Hey."

"Hey." He shoves his hands in his pockets up to his leather wristbands.

"Sorry, I'm getting ready to leave soon—"

He walks up the stairs toward me. "I know." He continues past me, looking left then right at the top of the stairs. Turning right, he proceeds down the hall to my bedroom and on through to my bathroom.

Never in my life have I literally chased after a guy so much— only Trick.

"What are you doing?"

He fumbles through my vanity drawers and makeup bags. "Come." He gestures with his head, without looking at me.

"I've already done my makeup."

He shoves aside the clutter on the vanity top. "Hop up."

Blowing out an exasperated breath, I do as he commands.

"The dress on the bed, is that what you're wearing?"

I nod as he pulls out some different brushes and eyeliner. He takes a step back and looks at me. I don't like this part. My nerves fire with anxiety, and I can feel my skin begin to flush. Trick grips the collar of my robe and eases both sides down over my shoulders, leaving them bared along with some cleavage. My breath hitches.

Lip-twitch. Ass!

He steps forward nudging my legs apart with his, then steps between them so we're so close I don't know if the heat between us is his breath or mine.

"Close your eyes."

Saliva pools in my mouth as the bristles of the brush tickle my skin, each stroke slow and seductive, sending a shivering wave of goose bumps erupting along my skin. Minty warm breath hovers so close to my lips I can almost taste it. I swallow hard again.

"Cold?" That voice. It's a grinding friction against my erect nipples barely covered by my robe.

Another swallow. "A little." I'm not. How can he not see that I'm burning up? His presence always brings a clash of sensations—a chilling sweat.

His left hand rests on my leg, his thumb touching the bare skin on my inner thigh where my robe has fallen away.

Oh my God! It's taking superhuman power to keep my legs from wrapping around his waist. My hands clench my robe, keeping it from falling past my breasts. It's *his* breath ... the heat between us is his breath, because I cannot remember to breathe.

"I'm sorry."

"Huh?" I pant.

Great! I've been reduced to one-syllable noises.

"My parents were—"

"Don't." I find my voice and open my eyes. His brows knit together. "I don't want to be your charity case, or your therapy, or whatever this is between us. Gemmie told me that you basically despise women, so don't torture yourself on my account. I'm sick of disingenuous relationships and—"

He covers my lips with his finger and shakes his head like I'm wearing a straitjacket and speaking in tongues. "As I was saying..." he lifts the brush back to my eye, forcing me to close both of them "...my parents ended up homeless when I was five. I grew up on the streets. Then one day shortly after my fifteenth birthday, I returned from school and they were gone. Over the next several months I checked all the shelters and churches, but there was no sign of them. Nobody had seen them or knew anything about them. It was as if they just vanished."

He blots the corners of my eyes with the edge of a tissue. "Don't. I don't want your pity."

I open my teary eyes and he continues to dab away the moisture. "It's not pity. It's compassion and there is a difference. Okay?"

His lips tighten into a frown. "You're just … *alright*, Darby Carmichael." *A lip twitch!*

Inside my emotions do flips, cartwheels, and fist pumps in the air.

He lines my lips while his purse into frustration as I struggle to keep from grinning, actually beaming!

"I have a vagina, you know?"

Vibrant white teeth peek through his uncontrolled smirk. "I heard that rumor."

"Can you deal with it?"

He glides the gloss over my lips. "I'll deal with you, and you can deal with your vagina."

I laugh as he lifts me off the vanity counter. Reaching the edge of my bed, I stare at my dress then shrug my shoulders. *He's gay … so screw it!* "Will you zip me up?" I ask, dropping my robe to the floor and slipping into my dress with my back to him. "Do you like my body?" I grin.

He zips my dress with slow ease, just the tips of his fingers grazing my skin near the top of the zipper. "It's … fine. I haven't paid it much attention." His voice breaks on the last word.

"Touché." Bending forward, I grab my heels and slip them on. "But it doesn't do it for you, right?" I turn, but he's not here. "Trick?"

"Downstairs," he calls.

I make a cautious descent down the stairs in my heels. "You should come with me. Steven is working and I hate to go alone so—"

"It's not my thing." Trick leans his side against the front door, hands in his pockets.

Grabbing my clutch, I chuckle. "It's not mine either. On a good night I get called into the hospital, but I'm not on call this weekend so I need another excuse to leave early."

"Thanks, but no thanks."

"Oh come on, we'll eat and leave, an hour tops." I close the space between us. He straightens, looking down at me and maybe even a little ... *nervous?* My chest presses against his; I tilt my chin up and bat my eyelashes. "Pretty please." Why I torture myself is beyond me, but I can't stop. Maybe I'm a masochist. Being around Trick and knowing he doesn't want me the way I want him is masturbation without the release.

Trick takes a step back and clears his throat. "I'm not dressed for the occasion."

"There's no dress code. It's at my father's house."

He rubs his fingers across the dark stubble on his chin. "You're dressed pretty fancy for 'no dress code.'"

Slipping off my heels, I race upstairs and change into black skinny jeans, a red Maroon 5 T-shirt, and black boots. "See, no dress code," I announce, bounding down the stairs.

Trick looks me over with a smirk and a head shake. "I didn't take you for the rebel type anymore."

I switch out my handbags again. "What can I say? You're a bad influence. I might even dye my hair black again. *Come.*" I look back and grin as I lead him to the back door. "I'll drive."

We pull out of the garage. "Where does your father live?"

"Barrington Hills."

"Of course he does." Trick stares out his window.

Yes, my father lives on a large sprawling estate in Barrington Hills, but his wife owns it. I live in a single family dwelling in Lincoln Park that my nana bought me. She calls it, and my debt-free college education, a gift from my mother. I live two blocks from her townhome that she downsized to after I left for college. Trick thinks I'm rich ... but I'm not.

However, I could have been.

"Was it Gemmie?"

Trick glances sideways at me.

"Did she mention my plans for the night? I don't remember

telling you, so how'd you know to show up and save me from looking like a peasant?"

He grins and rubs his palms against his thighs, like it's a nervous habit. "Yes, she texted me. Called it a 9-1-1 emergency."

"Oh jeez!"

"I texted her back that you didn't need my help."

I give him a quick glance with wrinkled confusion tugging at my brow. "But you came."

He shrugs. "I did, but she didn't need to know that."

"So peasant girl did need your help?"

"No. I just wanted to see you."

A grand display of fireworks ignite inside then quickly fizzle from the damp thoughts in my head. Is this what having a gay BFF is? All the compliments women dream of their lover saying, but not in a foreplay way. It's spooning and cuddling after sex ... without the sex. *Shit!* Is this what I want?

MY NEW ENIGMATIC friend keeps the conversation focused on me for the forty-five minute drive: my decision to take an ER job instead of joining the Peace Corps like I had originally planned, my love of medicine, my most challenging cases. He doesn't ask me about my family and that thrills me. For forty-five minutes I'm Darby, physician assistant, compassionate humanitarian, recovered misfit—friend to Patrick Roth. Then we cross the black iron gates to the Hart-Carmichael Estate and I become Darby Carmichael, girl who can't even imagine what it's like to grow up homeless on the streets. Trick doesn't say it, but I feel it and see it in his eyes.

"Ms. Carmichael." One of the parking attendants greets me with a warm smile.

"Good evening." I return the smile while a jolt of euphoria zips along my skin as he stares a second too long at my outfit. *Darby – Rebel Child!* It feels good to be back in my old shoes.

If Trick's in any sort of awe from his surroundings he's not letting on. I imagine Grady, salon guru to the stars, has taken Trick to some pretty posh events. Tonight is just a political schmoozing dinner. Trick grabs my hand and leads me to the front door like he owns the place. His sexy confidence has my skin sizzling with heat and my nipples popping out to say *hello*! The crowd at the front door funnels into single file as every guest is marked off the list and taken through security.

"I'm sorry, sir, you're not on the list." The gentleman with the iPad gives Trick a disapproving look without actually checking the list.

Trick squeezes my hand and pulls me in front of him, my back against his chest. *Then he takes a shotgun and blows my mind.* Sliding his arms under mine and resting his hands on my belly, he pulls me closer and *kisses* my neck! There's no longer a distinguishable difference between my red shirt and my skin.

Mr. iPad nearly chokes on his own tongue with a who-the-hell-is-this-tattooed-guy-kissing-the-senator's-daughter look. He clears his throat—of his tongue. "Ms. Carmichael, I'm sorry I didn't see you." A nervous smile pulls at his lips. "Please ..." He gestures for us to go inside.

I slip past security with ease, but they hold Trick back.

"No need. He's with me."

Trick frowns at the security guards; the security guards frown at me, but let him through. My heart jackhammers in my chest and my neck still feels the heat of his lips. *Why did he do that?* Now I know what those lips feel like. I know the way his thick stubble elicits a prickling chill of goose bumps along my skin. And now I can feel his lips *everywhere* and it wrecks me.

"Darby Lucille!" I turn just as Trick grabs my hand again, reminding my nipples that they are out to stay for the evening.

"Nana! What are you doing here?" Trick releases my hand, and I hug Nana dressed to the nines in a *green* lace embroidered dress—a

Rachael Hart original.

"I decided to come for moral support. But it looks like you brought your own." She raises her brow at Trick. "You must be the infamous Trick." She holds out her hand, but not for a handshake.

To my surprise, Trick doesn't hesitate. He takes her hand and presses *those lips* to the back of it. *Lucky hand.* "Trick this is my nana, Grace McDermot."

"It's a pleasure to meet you."

Nana blushes and winks at me. *God!* Could she be any more obvious?

Trick's ego has to be ready to burst: guys love him, girls love him, even elderly ladies go weak in their artificial knees in his presence.

"Where's Daddy Dearest?"

Nana's still batting her eyelashes at Trick. *So that's where I get it.*

"Nana!"

She frowns and looks at me like I'm a four-year-old rudely interrupting the adults. Her gaze falls past my shoulder to the grand split staircase. I turn. My father walks down one side and some 'bimbo' walks down the other side. *Yeah, like that isn't obvious!*

"My lovely daughter looks like she's dressed for a concert in the park. Why is this?" He grits between clenched teeth and a fake smile before kissing me on the cheek.

"I didn't want one of your rich donors to mistake me for one of the expensive call girls you've invited to the brothel." I grit back.

He grabs my wrist and squeezes it so tight tears sting my eyes. "Enough!" He grinds close to my ear. "What has gotten into you?"

I feel Trick's hand take mine, forcing my father to release me.

"Trick, this is my father, Calvin Carmichael."

Trick forces an amicable nod, but my father just gives him a quick glare with a disgusted head shake before turning a cold shoulder to go greet his more important guests.

"Well, shall we?" Nana grins, obviously amused by the power

struggle that's ensued this evening.

We follow her out back to the large white tent sparkling with elegant illuminating chandeliers, round tables adorned with candles and fancy stemware, and an orchestra playing in the far corner. The socialites mingle in their cliquish groups. It's my prom all over again.

"Oh, there's Cynthia Kane. I'll catch up to you two later." Nana grabs a flute of champagne from a server and sashays away.

Trick grabs two flutes off the tray and hands me one. I eye his.

"Don't look at me like that." He's not even staring at me, so how does he know what look I'm giving him? "It's for you when you're finished with that one. Something tells me you're going to need it." Trick continues to survey the crowd and the rest of our surroundings.

I drink on a rare occasion because I'm usually on call. He's right. I might need it tonight. "I'm driving."

"Not anymore, so drink up." He smirks at me while I tip the glass letting the bubbly effervescence tickle my tongue.

We mingle with a handful of people that aren't embarrassed to be seen with the lowly dressed misfits, mainly Nana and a few of the staff members. A cringe-worthy screech silences the room as my father takes the microphone and thanks everyone for coming, then invites them to be seated for dinner. My seating card is always next to my father's, but not tonight. Eventually I find mine and Steven's, which now belongs to Trick, at the very back table—the *escort* table. I'm certain this was a last minute switch since our arrival, but I don't react to my father's shunning.

"Your nana didn't get demoted to the back," Trick whispers in my ear as he seats me in my chair.

"That would never happen. As long as she's alive, she'll always have the best seat in the house."

Trick places his cloth napkin in his lap. "Why is that?"

I take a sip from my—*fourth?*—glass of champagne. Must be why I'm a little loose-lipped right now. "My father thinks Nana controls the purse strings."

Trick gives a polite nod to the bimbo that takes a seat next to him. Then he puts his arm around the back of my chair and leans in closer until his sexy cologne makes my already dizzy head spin on its side. "Purse strings?"

I giggle. "Yes, purse strings. Charles McDermot, my grandfather who died when my mom was sixteen, was quite wealthy. My mom was an only child and was going to inherit a fortune one day. Daddy Dearest was an attorney rotating through the same three cheap suits when he met my mom. My father doesn't need the money as long as he has Rachel, but I think we all know that won't last forever, so he assumes when Nana dies I will inherit the McDermot fortune and of course feel obligated to share it with him." I take another sip of champagne. "So as long as he thinks that, Nana gets rock star treatment. He knows she's my weak spot and I care more about how he treats her than how he treats me."

"*Thinks?* I take it you don't plan on sharing it with him?"

"No, that's not it. After I graduated from college I told Nana I didn't want the money so she donated most of it to various charities. Nana has some money, but she's no longer sitting on the fortune my father thinks she is."

I hiccup in a very unladylike fashion, eliciting snooty looks from the golden pussies seated around us. I can't help the giggle that escapes, so I bury my face into the crook of Trick's neck. "They're ashamed to sit with me too," I say in a voice that's a little louder than a whisper. I inhale his scent. "God, you smell good."

"I think you've had your limit." He grabs my ponytail and gives it a gentle tug.

Whoa! Why did that feel so … hot?

I sit up and squirm in my seat. Visions of him yanking on my ponytail in a more intimate setting drive my train of thought. Our dinner plates are placed in front of us, and I waste no time digging into the artistic concoction that one of the bimbos across the table is taking a picture of with her phone. *Real classy.*

I think they eat three of the julienned carrots, combined, then scowl at me in disgust as I finish my entire meal. "Stop staring. Your now bony asses are going to look like Mac trucks someday when your anorexic deprivation turns into a binge fest. So I hope you have a plan B beyond five-hundred-dollar-an-hour blow jobs."

Trick coughs, maybe masking his laugh, as I'm met with wide eyes and Botox-lipped *O*'s. "Let's go." He wipes his mouth and scoots back in his chair, then helps me out of mine.

"But dessert hasn't been served yet," I whine.

"We'll stop for ice cream on the way home."

"Really?" I perk up.

He doesn't answer as we make a hurried exit. I stumble over my own heavy feet as he pulls me out the door.

"Ms. Carmichael's car, please," he says to the attendant.

I collapse into his chest, feeling a sudden wave of tiredness wash over my numb body. "You got me drunk, Mr. Roth." I giggle. "Now what are you going to do with me?" I nuzzle my nose into his neck again.

"Take you home."

"Boring," I mumble against his skin as my hands slide down his back. I slip them into his back pockets, and he doesn't stop me. "You're my very ... best ... friend ... ever." I sigh, closing my eyes and smiling with warm contentment.

His hands go from static at his sides to resting one on my lower back and the other cupping the back of my head. I'm not certain, but as my car's pulled up I think I feel his lips press to the top of my head.

I SURRENDER TO my heavy eyes within seconds of leaving my father's. Every bump, twist, and turn on our way back to Lincoln Park goes unnoticed by my warm, numb body.

"We're here," a soothing voice whispers in my ear.

"Mmm …" I smile, peeling my leaden eyelids open. "Say that again."

Trick unfastens my seat belt. "Why?"

"Because I like the sound of your voice." I giggle. "Is that weird?"

"Yes." Trick scoops me up and carries me inside. I yelp as he plops me on my bed. "You're right … You are *not* a gentleman."

"Can you manage on your own now?" He shoves his hands in his pockets, looking down at me.

Sighing a sleepy yawn, I let my eyes close again. "You could take off my boots."

He unzips them then pulls them off, peeling my socks off too. "Good?"

"My jeans too." I rub my eyes.

After a few moments, I fight to open my eyes again. An intense stare, that's all I get. I fumble with my button and zipper. "What's your deal? You don't have to like my body, but you also don't have to be frightened or disgusted by it."

He wets his lips, eyes moving down my body. "I'm not disgusted by your body." He shoos my hands away and takes off my pants. "Now are you good?"

"Will you stay?"

"What?"

I roll toward him, grabbing his hand. "Just stay and hold me. Please."

He looks at the ceiling, shaking his head. "You're needy."

I giggle, tugging on his hand. "Only when I drink, and you're the one who got me drunk so you owe me."

"Fine," he grumbles, removing his shirt and pants then slipping under the sheets.

"What are you doing?" I ask as he wads up my throw blanket and wedges it between us from our waists down.

"Protecting myself."

"From what? Me?" I chuckle. "You think I'm going to molest you during the night?"

Lying on his back, he rests his arms at his sides like a cadaver. "You might."

I lift his arm and hug his chest with my nose nuzzled into his neck. His body goes rigid for a moment then melts back into a semi-relaxed state. I sigh against his neck. "Night, BFF."

CHAPTER EIGHT

S HE'S BREAKING ME *down. I need to stay strong. She doesn't know me, I don't know me. Grady will take care of me. I can't complicate things, and she's the ultimate complication.*

CHAPTER NINE

OVER THE NEXT three weeks I spend every non-working moment with Trick. One piece at a time, he's been shedding his emotional armor. He's my friend, a real friend. It feels like we've known each other for much longer than a few weeks.

My giddiness to see him has me counting down the minutes until my shift is over—I've never done that before. I've been avoiding Steven to the point that he has to suspect I'm cheating on him, if you can call it that. We've never labeled our relationship. My dad's campaign has been my excuse for my busyness, but after the election I'm going to have to figure out if Steven and I ever had a relationship, and if so if it's worth trying to salvage.

Trick left for California two days ago to attend a new salon opening with Grady. He invited me to go with him, but I had to work and I knew he needed some private time with Grady. He says he'll stop by to see me on his way home, but he has a late flight so I'm not counting on it. However, I don't set the alarm and he knows my entry code … just in case.

I watch the late night show, the late late night show, and half of the who-the-hell-is-awake-at-this-time show before my body and mind fall victim to sleep.

"God, I missed you." It takes me a moment to figure out that the deep, vibrating voice is not in my head. "I need my Darby fix." I roll over and blink open my eyes to see him sitting on the edge of my bed. He brushes my hair away from my face.

"You're back," I whisper and grin so big he cannot refuse me the same grin in return. I sit up and throw my arms around his neck, pulling him down onto the pillow with me so we're face to face. "I missed you too. How was LA?"

"Insane. You should have come with me."

I nuzzle into his neck. "I'm not sure Grady would have loved you bringing a tagalong when he's not seen you in months."

He rests his palm on the back of my head and strokes my hair. "You haven't met Grady yet, and when you do I'm certain he will love you."

"Not if he thinks he has to share you with me. Does he know we've been sleeping together?" I chuckle because I've stayed over at Trick's several times, and he's stayed with me too since that first night. We sleep together in the most literal sense. At least our complicated situation isn't hindering his ability to still have an intimate, sexual relationship with Grady; although, it's completely snuffing out the flames between me and Steven.

"No, I didn't mention it."

"Would he be mad?"

"No."

I lean back to see his eyes. "Are you sure?"

He smirks. "Positive. Now go back to sleep," he says, pulling my head back into his neck.

"Will you stay?" I murmur in a sleepy voice.

He kisses the top of my head. "I'll stay."

I WAKE EARLY to an empty spot beside me. It's six o'clock and I have to be to work in two hours. Assuming Trick already left, I make my way to the bathroom but stop, hearing the shower and seeing the slit of light escape under the door. As I contemplate waiting for him to finish or going downstairs to make us eggs and jellied toast, I hear what sounds like a moan. My teeth clamp my bottom lips as I grab the handle to the large sliding door. Moving it barely an inch, I peek inside—heart thundering in my chest and pulsing in my throat.

Oh ... my ... God!

Through the steam-blurred glass shower door, I see Trick, tattoo-covered skin taut over tense muscles, head down, one hand against the wall and the other ... wrapped around his cock.

My brain screams at me to shut the door. He's human and humans masturbate. He's a guy with a partner whom he goes months without seeing. It feels like I'm intruding on a private moment that's certainly not meant for my eyes. Yet ... I can't look away. No matter how hard I try I just ... can't ... look ... away.

He's *amazing*—a work of art. And I think I knew it weeks ago, but if not, I know it now. No man will ever compare to Trick. My husband, the father to my children, my earthly cliché of a soul mate will never live up to Trick. He's perfection in my eyes.

I blink away my tears because every time I allow myself to think of him this way, all I feel is grief. It's like I'm mourning the loss of something I never had.

"Fuck ..." he groans as the hand against the wall curls into a fist and the hand holding his cock glides with quicker strokes along his hard length.

Saliva pools in my mouth, and I swallow again and again feeling my heart trying to break free from my chest. Slipping my hand under the waistband of my night shorts and panties, I touch myself, matching the rhythm of my hand to that of his. My fingers are his tongue along my clitoris. Then they become his cock as they slide into my wet channel. He's less than ten feet away and I am desperate to remove my clothes and step into the shower with him. I want to taste him in my mouth and feel him buried inside of me, with nothing between us but wet, naked flesh.

He's close ... *oh God* ... so am I. His hard glutes steel as he pulses into his hand. *Into me.* My fingers, *his cock*, thrusts inside me as I circle my thumb over my clit. He spills out onto the floor of the shower and I melt into my hand, both of us breathless. Closing the inch gap of the door, I lean against the wall next to it—flushed and ashamed.

This one's all mine. I thought Nana and Trick were the perfect combination—what I couldn't tell one I could tell the other. But this … it's mine and as confusing and fucked up as it is, I just have to keep it to myself and hope it *never* happens again.

IT HAPPENS AGAIN. Four more times to be exact! Once more at my house and three times at his. The last being just ten minutes ago. I think he does it every time he showers. Who can blame him? If I had that body and that penis, I'd stroke it every day too. I'm such a perverted Peeping Tom. I'd slit my wrists if he ever found out that I spy on him in the shower and masturbate with him. We're both indulging in pleasure, yet his is normal and mine is stalker psycho.

"Grady's flying in this weekend," Trick announces, walking into his kitchen in jeans, no shirt—just like I like him.

I slide his plate over to him: jellied toast, eggs *over easy*, and juice. "Is that your way of telling me to make myself scarce for a while?"

"Hardly." He kisses the top of my head and sits next to me at the counter. "We're going to a party Saturday night. You should come."

I wipe my mouth and swallow. "I don't think so."

"You working?"

"No, I'm off this weekend, but I don't think I'd fit in."

"You're wrong. It's some exclusive party filled with rich people and celebrities. You'll fit right in unless you threaten to have the escorts fired because they look at you the wrong way."

With a sidelong glance, I glare at him. "Bite me!"

He leans over and bites my neck.

"Ouch!" I squeal and cringe.

His whole face beams with laughter that tapers off as his eyes drift down my face to my chest. A grimace morphs his face, eyes flitting back to mine. I glance down at my chest expecting to see a glob of red jelly on my white T-shirt.

"Oh shit!" I swivel my stool away from him and cup my breasts. I haven't put a bra on yet this morning and my dark nipples came to life with his mouth on my neck. Unfortunately my thin, white shirt hides nothing.

"Sorry—" he starts to say with an apprehension that softens his voice.

"Uh … no … um, it's not your fault. Um … it's just a little chilly in here." I hasten toward his dresser. "Mind if I borrow a sweatshirt or something?"

"Second drawer from the bottom."

I grab a gray hoodie and slip it over my head.

"I didn't mean to—" His forehead tenses.

I wave him off as I hop back up on the bar stool. "Stop, it's not your fault."

"I shouldn't have bit you."

I shove a bite into my mouth. "It's cold in here, that's all," I mumble over my food. "Stop thinking you turned me on or something ridiculous like that. You're gay for heaven's sake."

He purses his lips to the side and nods once slowly. "But you're not."

There they are, the words that make me question this most incredible friendship. He's just acknowledged the part of our relationship that I fear with such heart-wrenching intensity.

Taking in a shaking breath, I release it, feeling the tugging of that knot in my belly. "No … I'm not." I look up at him, completely open and vulnerable, and I wait for him to tell me what this means—what we mean.

He gives me a half smile; it's forced and I know it. "Come with us to the party this weekend and bring a date."

"Like a double date?"

He nods, watching me with reservation in his eyes, like he's watching for me to hesitate or give away something that might say what I'm sure he already suspects—my feelings for him are murky.

"Okay…" I feign confidence "…I'll scrounge a date."

He smiles. "You could always check with your father's escort service."

My face scrunches. "Hardy har har! I don't have to hire a date; thank you very much for your confidence."

Without a doubt I'm going to have to hire a date. Jeez, what is it with the Carmichael family?

"AN ESCORT?" NANA gasps then falls into a fit of laughter.

The waiter at the Local Root, one of my favorite Chicago restaurants, refills our water glasses and simpers at my Nana failing to retain any sort of composure.

I give him a tightlipped apologetic grin.

"Do you have to announce it to everyone in here?" I say in a hushed voice.

"Oh dear! I never thought I'd see the day …"

"It's not for sex and it's not because I can't find a date. It's just short notice and I don't know many guys that would understand my relationship with Trick." *Hell, I don't understand it!*

"So you need a professional?" She takes a drink of her water with a grin still plastered to her face.

I sigh. "I need someone that … ugh! Yes, I need a professional." Resting my elbows on the table, I drop my head into my hands. "How did I get to be so pathetic?"

"Don't fret it, dear. I'll find you someone."

Great. My nana is hiring me a date. It's like she's a pimp or a madam. *No, that's not right either.* This is all so very wrong.

"Is it going to be hard for you to see Trick with Grady?" Nana spears a cherry tomato with her fork and pops it in her mouth.

"Truthfully, yes, but what can I do about it? I have romantic feelings for a gay man, and I'm certain Trick is not gay by choice. I tell myself that if one day he woke up straight I'd be the love of his life."

"Hmm, does that help?"

"No," I mumble in a pouty voice after biting off a piece of warm ciabatta. "But he genuinely wants to be my friend and I his, so the problem is mine to figure out. I don't think the answer is severing ties at this point." I shrug. "I don't know ... maybe seeing him with Grady will bring me out of the infatuated funk I'm in right now."

"Sure, two hot guys touching each other ... that should do it." She winks at me.

There must be a Betty White club Nana belongs to. If she doesn't lose her mind first, I'm certain she will die with her last comment being completely snarky.

"I'm screwed." I sigh.

"Maybe they'll let you watch."

"Nana!"

CHAPTER TEN

WYATT JASPER WILL be picking me up in ten minutes. If he shows up wearing a cowboy hat and a Stetson belt buckle I'm going to murder Nana. I know nothing about him, not even if he's been hired or has willingly volunteered for the role of Darby's date in tonight's double date saga.

My hair is another Gemmie masterpiece, but my makeup is DIY. I spent almost thirty minutes arguing with Trick about it. Grady has him doing makeup for three of the celebrities that will be attending tonight. I know he's a perfectionist who doesn't like to be hurried so I refused to add to his stress today.

I dig a Rachel Hart original out of the back of my closet. It's a strapless olive—*green*—cocktail dress with iridescent beading along the bodice. Oh ... and it's ridiculously short. Before heading downstairs, I wrap a thin black scarf around my neck, slide into my black strappy heels, and take one last glance in the mirror. My volume-enhanced tresses fall in red waves, bangs pinned off to one side, and my makeup is minimal. Trick would be more critical if I tried to be too adventurous with it.

I grab my clutch and silver wrap just as my door buzzes. "Coming!" I yell into the intercom.

Tucking my clutch under my arm, I open the door. *Gulp!* I hold up one finger and smile then go back inside and shut the door. Leaning against it, I dig out my phone and call Nana.

"Hello?"

"What the hell, Nana!" I say in a yelling whisper.

"You like?" she asks with a rolling purr to her voice.

"Where did you find him?"

"My friend Mary; her daughter, Nora, owns a modeling agency. Wyatt is new and Nora thought attending a high-class party like yours would be a good way for him to make some connections. And you needed a date so I thought he was a better choice than an escort. It would be awkward if someone at the party recognized your date as an escort. You know, like showing up in the same dress some other broad's wearing."

"How old is he?"

"Hmm ... can't say for sure, but *young*. Maybe keep his drinks virgin tonight just to play it on the safe side."

"Ugh! Bye, Nana!"

Slipping my phone in my clutch, I rest my head back against the door and roll it slowly side to side. *Unbelievable.* My dress is definitely too short for my date that's probably too young, and I'm off to meet my dream guy's gay lover for the first time. The only thing that might save me tonight is the hospital. They needed an extra person on call and I volunteered. I think my subconscious is looking out for me.

"Hey, sorry about that." I smile, opening the door. "I needed to make a quick phone call. My apologies for keeping you waiting. I'm Darby, by the way." I hold out my hand.

"Wyatt." He takes my hand and kisses it. *Smooth.*

There's probably a million words to describe the flawless figure in front of me wearing black pants with a white shirt unbuttoned at the top and a tailored black jacket, but the first thing that comes to mind is a young Ashton Kutcher look-alike. And I would know because when I was thirteen I had posters of him on my wall, most covered in lipstick marks.

"Nice to meet you. Thanks for *escorting* me tonight." I'm not sure why I feel the need to clarify that this is a mutual arrangement and not a date, but it might have something to do with his age.

He leads me to the town car, undoubtedly arranged by Nana, and the driver opens my door. The party is at an exclusive whisky bar only a ten minute drive away, not long enough to go over everything.

"I'm not sure what you've been told about tonight but—"

He unbuttons his jacket that hangs perfectly from his broad shoulders. "I know everything about you, probably more than I should…" he grins and I blush "…and my story is yours to tell, so what's it going to be."

Damn! He's good.

I fiddle with the fringe of my wrap. "Well, I think we should keep it as close to the truth as possible. I suck at lying, and if you plan on making connections tonight I don't think a made-up job like an intern at the hospital where I work is a good idea. So … you're a model and we recently met through *mutual friends.* Saying your boss's mom and my Nana fixed us up sounds cheesy."

Wyatt grins. "A little."

The car stops and before Wyatt gets out I grab his arm. "By the way, how old are you?"

"Nineteen, but that sounds *cheesy* too, so let's say twenty-one for tonight."

Oh, God, I'm going to hell!

He climbs out with … well, the confidence of a runway model while the driver opens my door. I expect Wyatt to offer his arm, but instead he takes my hand which feels too intimate, but I go with it. As expected I'm on the VIP list with "and guest" and we breeze past the snaking line to a private entrance on the side of the building. The roar of the crowd mixed with music pours out as a muscle-bound bouncer opens the door for us.

"They're in," he says into a bluetooth. "Ms. Carmichael, welcome."

"Thank you." My eyes scan the open two-story room.

"If you'd like, Mel can check your wrap." He nods to the blonde behind the counter on our left.

After checking my wrap, we get drinks from the bar and head upstairs to the VIP lounge. It's wall-to-wall people from the top of the stairs to the back windows and doors leading to a patio with heaters, string lights, and more tables, as well as an outdoor bar.

"Do you see your friends?" Wyatt rests his hand on my lower back, leaning down by my ear.

"No … wait." I lift up on my toes a half inch more than my heels already allow. On the patio I see a circle of people, mostly women, one of whom is teasing her fingers along the nape of a guy's neck … *my* guy's neck! "This way." I attempt to keep my seething to a minimum as I grab Wyatt's hand, worming us through the crowd.

The cool night's air serves as a welcome greeting to my already flush skin. An average height gentleman with a fit-looking body, dressed in light gray pants and a pink, gray, and white striped button-down shirt, spies me through his thin black-framed glasses. It's hard to tell because of his shaved head, but he looks more mature, but definitely handsome. He's standing in front of Trick, who has his back to me and the clingy anorexic bimbo fingering his hair.

"Oh. My. God! You just have to be Darby!" The shaved-head guy yells in a very feminine way. *Grady.*

Trick and bimbo both turn toward me and Wyatt. Bimbo frowns as her eyes make a catty inspection, but Trick's lips twitch, cracking his cool bad-boy façade—but only to me.

"Darby, darling!" Grady saunters toward me with his arms open wide.

Darling—a word I've never heard Trick use and most certainly not in Grady's soprano voice. Trick could take a few gaying-up lessons from Grady. I hug Grady and then he kisses both of my cheeks.

"You are just exquisite. Trick said you were beautiful, but mmm mmm mmm, that's an understatement." Grady brushes his finger down my cheek. "Trick, give this woman her money back. Not even your raw talent could improve on such perfection."

Screw Trick. Grady's my man. *He's* the gay BFF jackpot. I'm talking shopping, manis-pedis, and serious girl talk. And although he is handsome, there's not a cell in my body that's physically attracted to him. "Grady, it's so nice to meet you. Trick has been singing your praises."

Grady looks over his shoulder at Trick. "Reeealy?"

Trick shrugs. "It's true."

"Well, who knew? Anyway, who's your handsome friend?"

I look beside me and smile. "This is Wyatt Jasper."

Wyatt offers his hand to Grady.

"Wyatt Jasper, it's a true pleasure. I'm Grady Cross." Grady is a complete flirt. I glance at Trick who eyes Wyatt as well, but he's not smiling. I imagine he's not too thrilled that Grady's so blatantly drooling over my date.

"So, Wyatt, what do you do?"

"I'm a model."

"Oh my God this just keeps getting better. How did you two meet?" Grady eyes us over the frame of his glasses.

"A mutual friend introduced us," Wyatt responds and I smile in agreement.

Trick pushes off the edge of the patio, leaving bimbo behind, and makes his way closer to us. "Mutual friends, huh?"

And … here we go.

"Yes." Wyatt nods but doesn't elaborate.

"Which friend? As you know, Darby has so many."

I glare at Trick. What's his angle with this? Inviting me to this party was his idea, and me bringing a date was his idea. Now he wants to interrogate Wyatt?

"He's a patient of Darby's so I don't think sharing his name is a good idea. You know, HIPPA and all that privacy stuff."

Holy crap!

My young pretty boy is good … real good.

"I see." Trick looks at me.

"So who's your friend?" I nod my head toward bimbo, changing the subject.

"I did her makeup earlier."

"I see. She seems real *appreciative*." My face wars between a smirk and a scowl.

Trick narrows his eyes at me; it's challenging like he's daring me to say more. Between work and finding a date this week, I haven't seen Trick in five days and I'm a little *agitated*, but I don't know why.

"All the ladies love my Trick." Grady pinches Trick's cheeks together. "But look at this face … why wouldn't they?"

My thoughts exactly as I take in my handsome friend in his usual black attire, tats on display. Grady looks like a fashion queen; I wonder what he thinks of his partner's selection of clothing for the occasion. I notice he's wearing a thin dark guyliner tonight that makes his eyes double in intensity. It's definitely been too long since I've touched him, or myself; I'm feeling too warm on this cool evening.

"Oh, there's Trent! Darby, I must steal your man; he just has to meet Trent." Grady pulls Wyatt away.

I face Trick and we both look each other over then make eye contact again.

"Wyatt's young."

I shrug and take a sip of my drink. "Grady's old."

Trick grins. "Older, yes."

The awkwardness of the moment grates at my nerves. I want to wrap my arms around him, bury my nose into his neck, and feel at home again, but I don't know if that's allowed here with Grady and all their friends.

"Think you'll see him again?" Trick crosses his arms over his chest.

"Wyatt?" My emotions override my commonsense. "I hope so.

Did you get a good look at him?"

The muscle in Trick's jaw twitches. "That dress looks amazing on you."

I gulp back my shock, not expecting that compliment from him. "Thank you. You don't think it's too short?"

Trick's eyes explore my legs. "Depends on the effect you're going for."

I chug down the rest of my martini, needing to numb the nerves that keep firing every time he looks at me. "Well, since you thought I needed a date for the weekend, I suppose I'm going for the spread-me-wide-and-fuck-me-hard effect." *Oh shit! That did not just come out of my mouth.* Sadly, it's not the first time those words have breached the parting of my lips ... it's just been a few years.

Hiding my own shock behind a fake smile, I look up expecting to see Trick's mouth hanging open or him smirking with amusement. Instead, he looks like he could kill something.

The empty martini glass in my hand gets replaced with a full one, but I'm so focused on Trick I don't see who does it. I imagine the staff here know to never let the VIPs mingle with empty glasses.

"Why are you looking at me like that?" I throw back my martini like a cup of water.

Trick grabs my glass and hands me his. "I think you've had enough."

I take a sip of his. "This is awfully watered down, what is it?"

"Water with lime."

Then it hits me. I'm on call tonight. *Shit!* I take down the rest of his and signal to the waiter for another water. "You're distracting me. I'm on call tonight and shouldn't be drinking."

"I'm distracting you?" He laughs, shaking his head which only infuriates me that much more.

"Yes, you're distracting me. You and the women hanging all over you, and Grady acting like it's no big deal. The way you look at Wyatt, the way you look at me ... It's all fucking distracting me!" *Oh god ... where is all this coming from? I'm self-destructing right here, right now. Someone make it stop!*

A pocket of silence surrounds us. My skin burns crimson from the glaring eyes all over me.

Trick's a statue—unreadable eyes, lips set in a firm line.

"Is everything okay?" Wyatt's hand rests on my back.

I clear my throat and blink away the emotions. "Everything's fine. I-I'm not feeling well; I think I should go."

"Oh ... okay, I'll get your wrap." Wyatt takes the empty glass from my hand.

"Wyatt, darling!" Grady calls across the crowded patio.

Wyatt looks at him then back at me. He shrugs with a sad smile, then taking my hand leads me back inside and down the stairs. I make one last glance back at Trick. Still nothing.

"Stay," I say while snaking my wrap around my shoulders.

"What? No, I came here with you."

I shake my head and smile. "Really, I'm going home and going to bed. You should stay ... you've earned it."

Wyatt glances back up the stairs with a tense, contemplative look. "Are you sure?"

"Positive." I kiss him on the cheek. "Thank you, maybe I'll see you around."

I HAVE MY driver stop for electrolyte water and snacks on the way home. The person back at the bar is not me, or maybe it is. *God!* With Trick in my life, everyday feels like a near-death experience— watching myself from outside my own body.

I blame Trick, which is ironic that I'd blame my friend who doesn't drink, on my irresponsible behavior with alcohol. But I do. I blame him for robbing me of my self-control, my ability to see clearly and think clearly. I thought it would get better over time; I thought seeing him with Grady would change everything, but it didn't. The rational part of me wants to make its case for my part in everything too. I knew he was gay, but chose to get involved anyway—the sleeping together, the masturbating. Where did I really imagine this relationship going? But right now, I'm in pain and no amount of rational thinking is going to ease it.

The driver lets me out. "Thank you."

"Have a pleasant evening, Ms. Carmichael."

He pulls away from the curb, but I can't move. My feet are lead and the rest of my body falls victim to the paralyzing heartbreak I feel over the thought I could be losing Trick. Just feet away from my gate, I close my eyes and let the tears fall. It hurts so damn bad. I've fallen in love with my best friend and he can never love me back.

"Don't cry."

I swallow the sob that begins to escape as my body freezes from the sound of that deep voice I love so much. I will my body to turn around.

Trick stands on the edge of the curb with his arms limp at his sides.

"Please … just go away." The words cut through my throat. "I can't do this … I can't be your friend anymore."

"Why not?"

Looking up at the sky, I swipe away more tears and shake my head. "Don't do this…" each word a desperate plea "…please don't do this."

I look at him, my pride too broken to hide my feelings, so I let him see my pain. "You gave me the thing I thought I wanted most in life." Biting together my quivering lips, I taste my salty emotions. "But then you changed everything … and I-I can't breathe when I'm with you…" sniffling, I suck in a shaky breath "…and I can't think without you."

I laugh over my tears, while shaking my head. "God! I'm such a fucked-up mess. I know you can't change, but…" a renewed stream of tears race down my cheeks, and the crippling pain holds my words to a soft whisper "…but neither can I."

I let go of my sob and through the glassy haze of tears I watch him close the distance between us. Fingers weave into my hair, clenching it to bring my lips to his. My world explodes into a million fragments of heaven and hell as I fall limp into his arms. I can't think so I just react to his punishing lips and demanding tongue. My arms fly around his neck—fingers clawing the back of his head. I taste him, smell him, feel him, want him … I fucking *need* him.

He steps forward and I step backward until we're at my gate, then through the door. I'd rather die than lose his touch. He kicks the door shut and jerks off my wrap. A quick draw of my zipper and my dress falls to my ankles. His strong hands cup and squeeze my breasts, thumbs grazing my hard nipples. I moan into his mouth while pushing up his shirt. He grabs it with one hand, breaking our kiss for the first time as he pulls it over his head. Standing inches away, completely breathless, we stare at each other.

His eyes travel from my lips to my bared chest, my white lace panties then to my heels, before meeting my eyes again. And as if it's been chasing us all the way into the house, my brain catches up. I can't read him, but that look … I think it's confusion … Oh my God, it's *regret*. It's not his fault, and I hate that it's happening, but my already red eyes fill with more tears—*shame*. I knew the moment our lips broke, the ugliness of our reality would be waiting, shaking its fingers.

I try to blink my tears away while biting that stupid quivering lower lip. Moving my hands to cover my breasts, I avert my gaze. "It-it's okay. I'm sorry, it's my fault."

His hand cups my jaw, turning my head. My fleeting glance turns into a longing gaze. He brushes his thumb across my wet lips. I close my eyes. Ghosting his mouth up my neck to my ear, he whispers, "It's nobody's fault." Bringing his other hand to cup my face, he kisses me again. If he stops this time … I. Will. Die.

Releasing my breasts, my hands work to unfasten his jeans.

What if he's not hard? What if this is all for me? What if …

Trick grabs the back of my legs, lifting me up, then carries me up the stairs. Dropping to his knees at the top, he lays me on the floor and shoves down his jeans and boxer briefs with his eyes burning into mine.

"Tric—"

His mouth collides with mine again, and before I can comprehend what's happening, he pulls the crotch of my panties to the side and plunges into me. Drawing my knees up, I cry into his mouth. Interlacing our fingers, he slides our hands above our heads and takes me to a place of physical ecstasy … and emotional hell.

CHAPTER ELEVEN

I T'S BEEN TWO days since I've seen or heard from Trick. Without a single word, he picked me up off the floor and carried me to my bed. Dropping a slow kiss on the top of my head, he wiped away a few more of my tears and then ... he left.

I feel complete and empty all at the same time. But mostly I feel like the most irresponsible woman ever. For God's sake I'm a healthcare provider, yet I let a guy with a known history of drug abuse have unprotected sex with me. I'm on birth control, so pregnancy isn't my concern; it's those pesky life-threatening STDs. *I'm an idiot!* I need to call him, since it's apparent he's not going to call me, but I don't know if I can hear his voice and keep it together.

Instead, I take the coward's way out and text him.

Me: *You need to get tested and send me the results.*

I slip my phone in my pocket as the ambulance pulls up, oddly grateful for the distraction. My job keeps me going forward; when I'm here and in the moment I don't have time to look back at the train wreck that happened Saturday night.

The five-year-old boy who fell from a tree goes to X-ray while Jade keeps giving me the eye from the nurses' station.

"What?"

"You're sulking. Is this about Steven and the intern he was caught with in the on-call room?"

Lovely!

I sigh, rolling my eyes. "No, I haven't talked with him in weeks."

"So things are over?"

I laugh. "Well if they weren't, I'm pretty sure they are now."

"Are you mad?"

I sign off on a chart. "No." It's the truth, but I wish I were. It would mean that I had feelings for a guy—a heterosexual guy who's capable of reciprocating my feelings. Instead I get a sympathy fuck from my gay best friend and possibly a nice cocktail of STDs.

THE REST OF the week goes by and not a single reply from Trick. The pain has simmered into a volatile potion of rage. I'm ready to drive over there with a large gauge needle and draw blood from the dorsal vein in his penis!

"Darby, there's a patient in room two that's requesting you." Mary peeks into the lounge and grins. "He said you requested he have blood drawn, but I don't see any notation about it in his chart."

Jade slides through the door past Mary. "Darby, the squirrel's back!"

Dr. Ellis pours a cup of coffee; deep lines draw together on his forehead. "Squirrel?"

Slipping on my lab coat, I smirk. "Jade will explain."

In the twenty steps it takes to get to room two, I give myself a huge pep talk and force ten deep breaths.

Adjusting my ponytail, I throw back my shoulders and open the door. My lungs deflate. Trick's sitting on the table with a black eye, busted lip, and bruised jaw.

"What the hell happened?" I move toward him with cautious steps and lift his chin with my finger to inspect the rest of his face riddled with bruises that look several days old.

"Take what you need." He holds out his arm.

A pang of guilt jabs my stomach, like asking him to get tested shows my lack of trust in him. But I have to start thinking with my head, so I wash my hands, slip on my gloves, and draw his blood. I feel his eyes on me the whole time.

"I'll have someone call you with the results tomorrow." I write on his chart, unable to even look at him.

He hops off the table. "No need. They can call you. I already know the results will be negative."

Guilt. Guilt. Guilt.

He brushes past me to the door.

"Trick." I turn, but he keeps his back to me with his hand gripping the door handle. "Was I your first?"

"First what?"

"Was I the first woman you've ever made love to?"

He doesn't say anything, doesn't move. I'm not sure what I even want his answer to be. And out of all the questions that I should be asking him, this one seems the least relevant, but it's the one I can't get out of my mind.

"Yes," he whispers, and then he's gone.

THE TEST COMES back negative, but I shed the guilt. I have to start being more responsible and sometimes that doesn't make me popular. Nana's meeting me for Sunday brunch. It's the first time I've talked with her in over a week, a record for us. Nana's *the* constant in my life, and if I'm going to have guilt for anything it should be from my lack of contact with her. She's left me several messages but I've been too busy and too scared to call her back until yesterday. I needed the blood test results before I could talk to anyone about last weekend.

"I'm going to cut you out of my will if you pull another stunt like that." She waves a finger at me as she sits down.

"Oh yeah ... the *will*." I roll my eyes.

She gives me the evil stink eye.

"Sorry, I should have called you back."

"Yes, you should have. I was worried."

I laugh. "You know where I live, yet I never saw you."

She shrugs, staring at her menu. "Well, you called me … so spill."

"I had sex with him."

"Wyatt?" Her back pulls to attention.

"Trick."

Her menu slips from her grasp and our waiter has it picked up and back in her hands before she blinks. "How is that even possible?"

I shake my head. "Really, I have to explain the birds and the bees to my seventy-five-year-old nana?"

"Oh, you know what I mean. I thought he's gay."

"He is or was or … I don't know."

"Well, what did he say about it?"

"He didn't. We've only seen each other once since, and all I know is I'm the first woman he's been with."

"What about his partner?"

"I don't know if he's told Grady. When I saw him the other day his face had taken a beating at some point, but he wouldn't tell me about it. There's no way Grady would do that to him so … I … I just don't know. I'm so confused, and angry, and hurt."

Nana clicks her tongue and shakes her head. "So now what?"

"I guess it's over." I tap my finger on the rim of my glass. "But the thing is, I feel like I need some sort of closure. I need him to tell me why he did it, and as much as the words will hurt, I need to know if he regrets it. Without at least that much I don't know how to move on."

She reaches across the table and rests her hand on mine. "I couldn't be more proud of you, and if your mother were here, I know she'd say the same thing. You're a beautiful, smart, and talented young woman. Don't ever let anyone take that away from you. So if you need answers, then go get them. Stand up for yourself; that much I can promise you will never regret."

I nod, feeling the emotions sting my eyes. She wouldn't be so proud if she knew I've been sweating out results of an STD test. "Love you, Nana."

"Love you too, dear."

MY SHOWER AN hour ago was a complete waste. I'm already pitting-out as my clammy palms fist my purse and keys. Although I know Trick's code, I don't feel right letting myself in so I buzz him on his intercom.

"Hello?" *Grady.*

"Hey, Grady. It's Darby."

The door buzzes and I take the elevator up. As if facing Trick isn't enough, I get to face his likely disgruntled lover.

"Hey, sweetie!" Grady greets me with an unexpected enthusiasm. "I was just on my way out." He kisses both of my cheeks. "He's in the bathroom washing off his coverup."

I grimace. "You're not the one who … or you didn't—"

"Rough him up?"

My face twists. "Yeah, that."

"Damn right it was me." He winks then laughs as I inspect him, looking for any signs that Trick landed a punch: broken glasses, bruising, cuts. It's as if he can read my thoughts. "He doesn't fight back about certain things. Have fun." He shuts the elevator gate and waves as it starts to descend.

I will never fully get the weird dynamics of their relationship. I'd say it's a gay thing, but I think it's just a Grady and Trick thing. Stealing my thoughts, Trick rounds the bathroom corner, his movement coming to a sudden halt when he sees me.

As much as I don't want to let my eyes look at his bare chest and arms inked with tattoos of which the meanings I will never get to hear, they have a mind of their own and take a final look anyway. "Hi," I say with weak voice.

"Hey," he responds with equal lack of enthusiasm.

"I won't contact you after today, but I need some answers."

He nods, deep lines sinking into his forehead.

"I just need to know why."

He looks down, lips pulled in a firm line.

"Was it pity?"

His head jerks up. "Why would you say that?"

I press my knuckle to the corner of my eye and swallow past the lump in my throat. "Because I believe that we were truly friends and sometimes friends make sacrifices for each other. And I don't blame you for any of it; I really don't. But now I have all these emotions and I don't know what to do with them. I need some sort of closure to move on. I need you to tell me that it was all for me and that you left because you regretted it ... you regretted us. Just ... please I-I need something ... please, Trick." I wipe my cheeks. The part of me that will always belong to him feels like it's dying. It's not a metaphor; my heart physically hurts right now.

He shakes his head. "I can't." It's barely a whisper, but I hear it.

His words grip my aching heart, threatening to crush it. "Trick, please don't do this. You owe me this much." I walk toward him. "Just say it ... just tell me it was pity. Tell me it was some weird curiosity. Tell me you were confused about your sexuality. Tell me it was nothing ... Tell me *we* were nothing, tell me—"

"I CAN'T!" he roars as his head snaps up, eyes wild, chest heaving. "Because it wasn't nothing! It was fucking *everything!* Don't you get that?"

His words are poison in my veins. This is it, the one puzzle I can't piece together. I know better than to let a man play me the way my father has all these years. I let him see a part of me that no man has ever seen. I did it for Trick, my best friend—only Trick. "I don't understand." I shake my head, confusion distorting my thoughts. He cradles my face. I swallow hard. "But you're gay."

"I'm not."

I continue to shake my head. "B-but I asked you if I was the first woman you've been with."

He shakes his head. "No…" resting his forehead on mine, he closes his eyes "…you asked me if you were the first woman I've *made love* to."

His words slice through me as the sting of deception and lies taints everything I thought we had. I shove him away, leaving him looking defeated, like a wounded animal. "You sick fuck! Why? Who does that? Huh? Is this some bi-sexual game you and Grady play on women? I have feelings! Real. Fucking. Feelings! I shared things with you I've never shared with anyone!" I wipe my watery nose in real ladylike fashion with the back of my hand. "I hate you." I step backwards toward the elevator.

Trick eases forward. "Darby."

"Don't Darby me, you bastard!" I flip the switch to bring the elevator back up. "I *hate* you," I sob.

He backs me into the wall. "Darby …"

"I hate you so much!" My tears feel like acid on my cheeks—my gut punched, my heart crushed.

Trick wipes his thumb along my wet cheek. "Well, I *love* you."

Smack!

He closes his eyes absorbing the impact of my hand on his face.

"Don't say that to me." I glare at him, anger seething from my words.

He opens his eyes. "I love you."

Smack!

He swallows hard and opens his eyes again. "I love you."

Smack! Smack! Smack!

He takes everything I give him as if he needs it. I bang my fists against his bare chest. "You don't deserve to love me! I hate you … I hate you … I hate you.… I-I …" I collapse against his chest, my body heaving in waves of painful, breaking sobs. "I-I love you."

He wraps one arm around me and rests his other hand on the

back of my head, then he kisses the top of it.

SURRENDER. I WILL never love myself for hating him, nor will I ever hate myself for loving him. So there really is only one choice: love him.

The words we've shared have been beautiful, ugly, and the whole universe in between. There's still so much to say, but as Trick takes my hand and leads me into his bathroom, I allow him to say so much more than words ever could.

He turns on the shower, a large rainfall of water cascades from a mammoth rectangular shower head suspended directly above it. Turning back toward me, he pauses, staring into my eyes. They bleed with emotion, and tears would form if I hadn't already let them run dry.

He undresses me with slow, gentle moves as I stand and watch. Then he does the same to himself before leading me into the steamy shower. I close my eyes and melt into his loving touch. Patient hands massage my scalp and caress my body. Occasionally I feel his lips press to my skin and just linger—never demanding, always giving.

On his knees, he touches my body with complete adulation—he *loves* me. With gentle pressure, he curls his fingers into the curve of my butt while resting his forehead against my belly. I move my hands to his head. He looks up at me, blinking away the rivulets of water.

"You scare me, Trick."

He sits down on the floor of the shower and pulls me onto his lap so we're nose to nose. "You scare me too." He grins and I kiss him, diving headfirst into the unknown.

I don't want to need him, but I do. I don't want to love him … but I do. Breaking our kiss, I rise up onto my knees and touch him for the first time. He closes his eyes briefly then opens them, jaw slack. The little part of me that still questions his sexuality evaporates as he kisses my breasts, tickling my sensitive flesh with his bristly face.

He takes my heart so completely; and if he gives it back I know it's the one puzzle I'll never be able to put back together again. I sink onto him, letting him fill me in every way possible.

A SOFT BEAM of moonlight falls on our naked bodies tangled in the sheets. Resting my chin on his chest, I trace the tattooed wings along his shoulder as my mind sorts through the reality of our situation. Maybe I shouldn't have stayed. A smarter woman would have walked out the door, refusing to be played for such a fool.

But Trick's not some guy I dated a few times. We've never dated. He's gone from random stranger to my best friend. I could retrieve my dignity and walk away from the Trick who fucked my body and mind at the top of my stairs. But Trick, my best friend, means too much to me. I stayed for him … I forgave him.

"Trick?"

"Hmm?" His eyes remain closed.

"Why do you want or let people think you're gay?"

A silence falls over us as his words take their time. "I feel … *used* by women. I'm not completely sure why, it's just a feeling about my past. It's given me an *aversion* to them.

"Why do you say it like that? Like you don't know or remember? Is this about your addiction?"

He lifts his shoulders. "Yeah … that's definitely part of it. My past is complicated. I can't really explain it. But for some reason the women I encounter in my line of work don't like taking no for an answer, and I don't like feeling controlled."

"But if you're 'gay' they don't approach you?"

He laughs. "No, if I'm gay I don't lose their business when I turn down their offers. It's accepted as a sexual preference and not rejection."

I rest my cheek against his chest and close my eyes, melting into the beautiful rhythm of his heart. "Trick?"

"Hmm?"

"Will you try to explain your complicated past?"

His Adam's apple bobs as he takes a deep swallow. "I hope so ... someday."

My tears renew as his voice cracks with the last word. Even without knowing what it is, I feel his pain. The part of my mind I can't shut off goes down the road paved with images of abuse or worse.

Scooting up, I bury my face in his neck, pressing my lips to him. "I don't need to know."

CHAPTER TWELVE

Yawn. Stretch.

"Oh shit!" I notice the time, and I have thirty minutes to be walking through the hospital doors. I never oversleep; then again, I never cry like I did yesterday. It's physically draining.

"Oversleep?" I hear Trick, but he's not in bed.

I flail around in the covers trying to untangle. Then I leap out and run to the bathroom, slowing down just enough to do a double take at Trick on a yoga mat in some insane forearm inversion pose. "You're doing yoga *again?*" Trick is one dedicated guy. I don't think he ever skips his morning practice.

He chuckles. "What gave it away?"

Another unforgettable image—Trick shirtless wearing loose fitting drawstring pants, balancing on his forearms causing all his muscles to flex into perfect definition. Yep, there's nothing sexy about that. *Yeah right!* I continue around the glass-walled corner into the bathroom. "Oh, and the yoga mat gave it away."

After throwing on my clothes in just under thirty seconds, I swipe my tongue along my teeth. *Yuck!* "Are we one of those couples that can occasionally share a toothbrush?" I yell.

"That depends."

I jump, not expecting him to be standing in the doorway with his arms crossed over his chest looking completely worthy of playing hooky, which I have never done.

"On?" I'm already squeezing on a glob of toothpaste because it's happening whether he likes it or not.

"On if you need me to send you my dental records first."

I finish scrubbing and spit. "Not funny," I shake my head but grin as I start to brush past him.

He grabs me and pins me to the wall, attacking my neck like a horny vampire. "Well your face says otherwise."

I wriggle out of his hold and grab my purse and keys.

"No breakfast?"

"I'll have my Green Lantern at the hospital."

He pulls on a shirt, shoves his feet into his boots, and follows me onto the elevator. "Green Lantern? Is this something I should know about?" Pulling me into his arms, he kisses me until my knees literally give out.

After walking me to my car he kisses me again, and I'm so going to need a panty change when I get to work.

"Go save the world."

I get in and he shuts my door. Before I pull out, I roll down my window. "Oh, and if you truly love me, then you will most certainly do your homework on the Green Lantern." I blow him a kiss and speed off.

THE NEXT FORTY-EIGHT hours run together in a continuous blur. A nasty string of influenza hits early leaving the ER understaffed. I haven't been home yet, and my intermittent sleep in the on-call room has left me feeling on the borderline of nausea and hallucination.

"You look like shit."

"Thanks, Jade," I say through a big yawn.

"You safe to drive home?"

"Good question, but I think if I roll down a window and blast the radio I should be fine."

Slinging my bag over my shoulder, I glance at my phone. Trick's not a stalker and he's definitely not clingy. I've texted him several times over the past two days just to let him know I wouldn't be leaving the hospital anytime soon. He's replied once with *"That sucks."* I guess it's better than nothing. Right now I'm craving him, but I *need* sleep so I decide to go home; besides it's nine in the morning and he's probably working anyway.

Me: *FINALLY done. Going home to crash. Miss you.*

By the time I stagger into my house twenty minutes later, my phone chimes.

Trick: *Want me to come tuck you in?*

Ugh! Yes, I want to see him, but I look like crap and feel exhausted.

Me: *Yes, BUT I think I'd like it even more if you come wake me in about 6 hrs.*
Trick: *I'll see what I can do.*

I want to swoon over thoughts of him, but the moment my body hits the bed I'm out.

SIX HOURS LATER I force myself to crawl out of bed, straight into the bathroom. Nearly seventy-two hours without showering is all kinds of wrong. Trick missing out on my oily, matted bed head and hairy pits is in everyone's best interest.

After drying my hair, I head down to the kitchen expecting an Old Mother Hubbard moment since I haven't been grocery shopping in over a week. The cupboards are bare, but on the top shelf of my refrigerator is a bottle of Green Lantern with a note attached to it.

I guess this means I love you. Six hours didn't fit my

schedule. Showed up at four—by the way, you snore like a fog horn.

Shaking the bottle of green juice, I roll my eyes. "I don't snore." Not even his snarky humor can take away my over-the-moon high the rest of his note gives me. Turning to grab my phone from its charger, I see another note attached to a DVD.

Just in case I was wrong about the juice.

The DVD is *Green Lantern.* I laugh out loud. A guy who's not afraid to give his girl a Ryan Reynolds movie, how lucky am I? Now I *need* to see him, touch him, taste him, smell him. Instinct takes over and within minutes I'm on my way to Rogue Seduction, juice in hand, enormous grin. I see him in the window working his artistic magic as I park my car and pay with my ParkChicago app on my phone.

I wrangle my hair in one hand as the wind fights to whip it in every direction while I hustle across the street and into the building. The admittedly stunning young blonde on his stool glances over at me while he concentrates on her face, not acknowledging my presence.

"Hi," I call.

"He's in the zone, don't expect him to answer."

I turn, having missed the Gabrielle Union lookalike sitting at the register doing something on the computer. Yep, she fits right in here—flawless mocha skin, dark eyes, brilliant teeth, cheekbones to die for, and long black silk hair.

"Do you have an appointment?" She flashes her beautifully warm and inviting smile.

Between the four of us in the room, without a doubt I'm the one who looks like a troll. Thank God I at least took a shower. "Um, no I don't. I just stopped by to see him."

"Is he expecting you?"

I'm ready to collapse out of site and slither out the door. Why do I feel so out of place?

"I am." Trick's voice heats my skin and does embarrassing things to me in other areas as well.

I turn but his back is still to me.

The beauty at his desk raises a surprised brow and grins. "Can I offer you something to drink? Wine, coffee, tea, water?"

"Thank you, but I'm fine right now."

She nods and motions to the two black leather studio sofas by the window. "Feel free to have a seat while you wait."

I smile and take a seat. Trick never mentioned he has a receptionist and I haven't seen her before. I mentally add her to the million other questions I still have for my mystery man.

Over the next twenty-five minutes I browse through the tabloids on the side table while listening to soft jazz mixed with the occasional blues when his receptionist changes the album on the old turn table. Walking past me she eyes me with a Cheshire cat grin and the blonde offers the occasional feral cat look that says she might scratch my eyes out if I don't stop looking at Trick. *Meow!*

The blonde sashays over to the receptionist while I keep my head down, like I'm in the wrong part of Chicago after dark.

"Come." I look up just as Trick has already passed me, walking toward a door in the back. Glancing around, I wonder if he is talking to me.

"Now, Darby."

Okay, he's talking to me.

I scuttle after him as if I'm sneaking off. I'm met with his stone expression as he holds the door open for me. He flips on the light and shuts the door to a ten-by-ten storage room with shelving along two walls.

"I only have ten minutes," he says with clipped words.

I look around at the stacks of cosmetics and accessories on the shelves and then at him as he moves toward me. "Oh, well then I'll come back la—"

Trick grabs my hair and smashes his mouth to mine giving me an instant case of whisker burn. *The best burn ever!* I grab his biceps for balance. He's hungry and I'm starving. Releasing my lips, he shrugs off his shirt.

"You're going to *come* alright, but it's going to be in the next two minutes."

Fuck. Me! I think I just did.

"B-But your receptionist is out there," I say with a breathy voice as he unfastens my jeans and yanks them down with my panties while I grip his hair for support.

He looks up at me with a quick flash of confusion, then smiles. "She is, so I'd tell you to keep it down, but I'm not sure that's going to be possible."

"Why do you say th-thaaaat!" I *scream* as he simultaneously thrusts two fingers into me and sucks my clitoris, claiming the world's fastest orgasm. *NOT a gentleman!* "Trick! Oh my God … O-oh. My. God!" The choir singing hallelujah echoes in my ears while the ball drops in Times Square with a mind-blowing fireworks display behind my tightly closed eyes, and every nerve in my body cheers in a pandemonium of celebration.

My legs give out, but he has me—my breasts—my neck—my lips. Then he's inside me and my body does what it always does—chases him. I'm … I'm barely coherent. I can't even open my eyes. Every time I start to come down, start to regain consciousness, his hands and lips navigate like magnets to all the erogenous zones on my body and it knocks me out every time.

"Fucking hell! You feel good," he rasps.

I think he just came, but honesty I-I don't know. I-I can't think. He's still for a brief moment, then he's releasing his grip on my ass.

"I'm trying to help you out, sexy, but you have to try. Maybe lock your knees or something."

Stand up. I think I can. *Oh God, he's cleaning me up!* A decade or so passes in my brain, and I'm magically dressed again and sitting in the corner of the supply closet.

"Gotta go. I'll take you to dinner later, okay?" He tosses me a key. "Lock the door when you come out."

Nod. I think I can do that too. He bends down and kisses me, then leaves, shutting the door behind him. Why is he always leaving me behind?

What just happened?

Crazy. There is no other word for what just happened.

FORTY-FIVE MINUTES later—I'm still in the supply closet. Why? I haven't yet gathered the courage to show my face. His receptionist and everyone within a mile radius heard me; I just know it. As good as … well … whatever that was, it doesn't excuse the fact that he's out there with another client and ignoring me stuck in here, paralyzed with humiliation. Kudos to him for walking out like he just came in here to grab a tube of lipstick, but some of us don't have the special ability to hide all emotion.

Damn! I have to pee.

Surely he will be done soon and come rescue me.

Twenty minutes later …

Eye balls floating.

Thirty minutes later …

Time's up!

I have to make a choice: wet my pants or face his perfectly put together receptionist. The fact that I'm even contemplating this decision is a real testament to what my BFF does to me. *I'm going to kill him!*

With a slow turn of the knob, I open the door. The sun has set and it's dark outside and in here too.

What the hell?

No one's at the reception area. I shut the door and grab the key from my pocket to lock it, but there's not a lock on the door.

Seriously ... What. The. HELL?

Tiptoeing forward I peek around the corner. The place is empty. My anger heats to a fiery red that matches my hair. I stomp back to the bathroom that I passed and relieve my bladder. I'm so pissed, in the literal and proverbial sense. After I wash my hands, my phone rings. It's *him!*

"Yes?" I snap.

"Hey, where are you? I figured you'd wait for me at my place."

"I *am* at your place."

"Really? Um ... are you hiding? Because I don't see you."

"Very funny, but guess what? I'm not laughing."

"O-kay ... Am I missing something?"

"You left me in the storage closet!"

"Darby, I had to go. I only had ten minutes to get to my next client. I assumed you needed a few minutes to ... *get it together.*"

"What do you mean get to your next client?"

"It was an on-location job in Streeterville."

"What about your receptionist?"

"My reception—oh, she came with me."

I stare at the key then open the front door and stick it into the lock. *It fits.*

"You're not still in the closet are you?" He laughs and I can tell he's joking because really ... what idiot would still be in the closet?

"Uh ... no, of course not." I lock the door and hustle around the corner to his place.

"I just saw your car still parked on the street and you said you're at my place, so if you're not here then—"

I hear the buzz of his door over the phone as I push the button. "It's me. No more questions. Got it?" I press *End* and proceed inside to the elevator. He opens the gate when I reach the top, sporting the rare million-dollar-white-teeth smile.

"Not another word," I warn.

"Hey, Darby!"

I look past Trick to see his receptionist walking down the stairs in the far corner.

"Sorry I didn't realize who you were when you came in earlier." She has the most angelic smile.

My cheeks flush. So much for avoiding the embarrassing situation. I offer my hand as she approaches, but she goes straight for the hug. Now would be the appropriate time to play a quick game of twenty questions. Starting with *Who are you?*

"Darby, this is Tamsen."

My eyes light up with recognition, then I squint with a bit of confusion. "Grady's sister?"

She laughs. "Same father, different mothers."

I nod. "Very nice to meet you."

"Bye, babe." She leans up and kisses Trick on the cheek.

"It was nice to meet you, Darby." She moves past us to the elevator.

My brain tells me I should be jealous now that I know Patrick Roth is *not* gay. But she has this positive vibe that makes it hard to not like her, and Trick said she's like family. *Like a goddess for a sister.*

"Bye," I say with a few second delay and a kind smile in return.

"Ready?" He pulls on his leather jacket and hands me one too.

I slip my arms through and hold them up, taking notice that it fits me. "Whose jacket is this?"

"Yours."

"What do you mean?"

He flips the lever for the elevator to come back up. "I mean it's yours."

"You bought it for me?" I follow him onto the elevator.

"I did."

"Thank you." I wrap my arms around his neck and kiss him for the jacket. As for the storage room incident, that I'm still pissed about. Unfortunately, I can't express all of my anger without confessing the true amount of time I spent in it.

His eyes search my face for a moment. "You're welcome."

As the large garage door opens, he twists my hair and pulls on a helmet. It too fits perfectly. Two Goldie Locks moments in one night. I stare at him, not even trying to hide my adoration. He will be the hardest puzzle I've ever tried to figure out.

"You're welcome." He grins before bringing his own helmet down over his head.

Two questions dance in my head: What am I doing with this mysterious guy that is curiously unpredictable and completely lovable, and what is he doing with me?

CHAPTER THIRTEEN

S OMETIMES KNOWLEDGE SUCKS, like now, when all I want is to enjoy the ride but images of gurneys with limp bodies being rushed into the ER after motorcycle-car accidents play in my head. As we weave through traffic, I melt into Trick's body allowing a small and irrational part of myself to feel safe. Surrendering to my vulnerability, I let him control my fate.

Trick pulls up along the street by Cantina Laredo. After removing his helmet, he takes mine off and I finger through my hair.

"What?" I question because of his signature stoic expression. "I know, I am a mess with my helmet hair and naked face."

His hands slide up my neck and into my hair, pulling me to him. "You're a beautiful mess." He brushes his lips against mine; it's a mere whisper of a kiss from the docile side of Trick Roth that must have been gagged and tied up by the dominant ego that had his way with me just hours earlier.

On the outside he's a deep canyon with jagged edges, but I've just started to get a glimpse of what most people don't see past the surface ... and it's stunning.

"Come." He grabs my hand and leads me to the restaurant.

"You could say please." I double the speed of my steps to keep up.

"You could say no." He opens the door and like the true gentleman I don't think he really is, he lets me enter first.

"What would you do if I said no?"

"Get a table by the window, order an appetizer, and watch you stand on the sidewalk basking in your independence."

We're seated by a window, ironically. "Someone sure did a number on you." I shake my head.

"Sorry." He looks over the menu. "I'm in uncharted territory with you. *Thank you* for accompanying me into the restaurant." His sly smile steals all sincerity from his words.

Screw it. Trick will be my unsolvable puzzle, and I've just decided I wouldn't want it any other way. He's a take-me-as-I-am-I-don't-give-a-shit guy, stopping on the confidence scale a hair shy of arrogant—aka make-you-beg-for-it sexy. I've met my match. *It's possible I'm actually way out of my league.* No worries, I shall rise to the challenge.

"You're welcome." I roll back my shoulders and smile with confidence, looking at my menu. "Thank you for the mind-blowing orgasm in the supply closet."

"Ah-hem." Our waitress clears her throat.

Great, how'd I miss her sneaking up on us? I retain my cool smile in spite of the hot flash of embarrassment that races along my skin. Trick doesn't flinch, with the exception of his lip twitch. *Cocky bastard!* I'm sure he's thinking, *"That's right ... I'm just that good."* I'm sure she's thinking, *"Could you demonstrate on me?"* Her skin matches mine, so that's exactly what she's thinking.

"It was my pleasure." He smirks, staring at his menu.

Oh hell! Kill me now!

I cannot believe he just said that in front of her.

"We'll have the Top Shelf Guacamole, Camarones Escondidos, and Pescado Del Día. Thank you." I grab Trick's menu and shove it along with mine at our unsuspecting and completely flustered waitress.

She stumbles off. I'll be amazed if she remembers our order.

"You ordered for me?" He leans forward with wide-eyed disbelief.

"Well, she wanted to take our order, but you were too busy

flaunting your afternoon conquest so I ordered for the both of us."

He leans back with a wry grin. "I was simply being polite and engaging in the conversation *you* started."

"What happened to your face?"

"So we're done talking about—"

"Yes, we are." I sip my water. "Why did Grady beat the shit out of you?"

Trick smirks, staring at his silverware he's adjusting. "It was a misunderstanding."

"About?"

"He found something." His eyes look up to meet mine, as if he's daring me to go any further.

Drumming my fingers on the table, I sigh. "What did he find?"

His gaze falters in chagrin. "A couple grams of coke under a Buddha statue of mine."

Don't react. Don't react. Don't react. Oh shit, he's still doing drugs!

"And?" I question in a neutral voice with just a hint of nervous tremble.

"And what?" He shrugs.

I could scream; he's baiting me, waiting for my reaction as if there's a right one versus a wrong one. I'm too old to play games, and I'm too young to get involved in this messed up shit. "*And* nothing, Trick. If you're using again and want help, I'll help you. If you don't want help then I'm out of here. If you have an explanation outside of those two scenarios then now would be the right time to share it. If this is some test of my trust for you, then here's the deal: I'll trust you until you give me a reason not to."

His head moves; it's slight but I see him nod. "I've had it since I stopped going to NA. It's just a reminder." His lips twist into a smirk and then he lets out a small laugh. "I've had it for eight years and have never once been tempted to use it."

"So Grady thought you were going to use it?"

He points to his now yellowish-brown bruises on his face. "I think the answer to that is yes."

"Why didn't you just tell him that you've had it all this time?"

"He knows."

I lean forward, resting my arms on the table. "Then why did he think you were going to use it?"

He averts his eyes, scanning the restaurant as if he's looking for the answer. "Because I had the bag on the counter just ... staring at it when he came home."

A pang of guilt mixed with pain hits me. "When?"

"When what?"

"When did this happen?"

"The morning after the party." His eyes make a slow shift to mine.

I suck in my lips to contain the anger. "You mean the morning after we had sex for the first time—the morning you left me." I laugh, closing my eyes for a brief moment. "Unbelievable. You considered reverting back to a life-threatening addiction after one night with me. God! That makes me feel ..." I shrug my shoulders and blink back the tears.

"Special." He reaches across the table, taking both of my hands.

"Yeah, Trick. That's some real *special* stuff!"

"I was getting rid of it."

I try to pull away. "Sure, up your fucking nose because of your *aversion* to women."

He grips me tighter, not caring if anyone around us is watching. "No!" He grits his teeth. "Because I no longer need a reminder of where I've been ... I have *you* to remind me of where I'm going, and when I'm with you I don't ever want to look back."

I glare at him, feeling overwhelmed by his confession and still a little pissed off about *something*. "Then why did you let him make such a mess of your face?"

Trick releases my hands and sits back with an indifferent grin smeared across his face. "I felt like shit for the lie I let you believe and for leaving you that morning while I sorted myself out. So I figured I deserved it, even if not for the drugs."

Our waitress brings our food; kudos to her, everything's right. I place my napkin on my lap and look at Trick with my face scrunched in disbelief. "That's so messed up. You should have told him."

Trick cuts into his food. "No need to make him feel bad."

We eat our dinner, exchanging very few words. My mind reels trying to process Trick's feelings for me and his unusual sense of self-worth. One minute he's emotionally closed off as if he's protecting himself, and the next he's letting Grady beat the crap out of him because he feels deserving of it. There's such an ambiguity about his actions that leaves me feeling perplexed.

I LET TRICK secure my helmet to his liking, and his admiring eyes don't go unnoticed by me. "You like the jacket, don't you?"

"Yes." He grazes his teeth along his bottom lip. "Leather pants would send the package over the edge." He gets on then I hop on the back, eager to wrap my arms around him.

"So that's what I am to you? A package."

He reaches around cupping my ass and scoots me closer. "You're *the* package."

The engine roars to life; he revs it a few times before we shoot off into the busy stream of traffic.

Nana is going to lose her teeth with grin-baring excitement when she finds out about me and Trick. And when I tell her that I have my own leather riding jacket and helmet it'll probably send her to her grave. Not that she'll worry, just the opposite. She's been telling me my whole life to live it up, take a chance, and fall for a guy that would make my father shudder with disapproval. Done. Done. And SO. VERY. DONE!

We pull into his garage, if you can call it that. The lower level of this warehouse has to be fairly large, but it's always too dark for me to see beyond his bike and a few other covered things which I know have to be warmer, safer automobiles.

"Wait!" I call as the door starts to go down. "I can't stay. I have to work tomorrow."

He pulls off my helmet and sets it on the shelf next to his, then unzips my jacket. When he looks at me with the dark intensity that is only Trick, my breath quickens as a jolt of anticipation zips through me in anticipation of his touch.

"I need my Darby fix first." He slides my jacket off and drapes it over the seat of his motorcycle. That voice is so damn sexy, I swear he could talk me to an orgasm without ever touching me. His hands slide into my hair, fisting it, and bringing me closer until his lips find my neck.

"Trick—"

"Darby," he whispers, sucking my earlobe into his mouth.

"I thought you got your *Darby fix* in the supply closet earlier." My breathy voice makes a weak protest.

Brushing his stubble along my jaw, he seduces me with a feathery touch that elicits a gripping wave of shivers. His lips, pulled into a grin, brush against mine; he knows exactly what he does to me. "I hadn't seen you in two days … touched you in two days … and so I had to devour you. But now…" his tongue teases my upper lip "…I want to *savor* you."

"But Grady and Tamsen—"

"Won't be back for hours … if at all tonight."

Any attempt to deny him would be futile and all in my head—like right now. My thoughts hold strong to my early morning job responsibility; but my hands have already unfastened his jeans, guaranteeing his bike will not be the last thing I ride tonight. I'm such a sex fiend with him.

★

THE SUPPLY CLOSET was lust, sex … a raw need. This—this is love. Trick loves me like it's his sole purpose in life, and being on the receiving end of such a serendipitous love is … *life-changing bliss.*

"I have to go," I whisper into his neck.

Trick makes a slight noise, but I'm not sure he's awake so I ease off his arm and slide out of our tangled mess of sheets. *My God, he's beautiful.* I don't know what this is … what we are, but it's unexpected—a gift. The light fluttering in my chest and the tingling that buzzes along the surface of my skin from his nearness stirring all my nerve endings, it's life. When I'm with Trick I feel everything … I feel completely alive.

I sigh with a pouty frown and get dressed without waking him. It's a little after midnight by the time I get on the elevator. Unfortunately it's a noisy beast, so I'm sure my descent wakes him; but he knows I can't stay so hopefully he'll fall right back to sleep with the same satisfied smile I'm still wearing. As I round the corner of his building, I hear voices. Two guys stand by my car, puffing their cigarettes.

Shit!

I unlock my car, hoping the beeping noise will convince them to step aside. No such luck, instead they're now watching my approach. It's time to make a decision: continue to my car with confidence showing no fear or retreat back to Trick's and hope they don't follow me.

"Excuse me, gentlemen," I say with a polite smile as I approach my driver's door which they're blocking. I leave my thumb hovering over the panic button on my key fob. In this part of town it won't draw that much attention, but it might get Trick's if he did in fact wake as I was leaving.

"This your car, Red?" The younger black kid says as the older white guy, maybe my age, smirks like he's letting his protégé handle me.

"It is. Excuse me please."

"What's a fine thing like you doing in these parts so late?"

Just as I turn to go back to Trick's, the younger kid grabs my arm knocking my key fob from my hand. My blood runs cold.

"Where you going, Red?"

I try to wriggle out, but he grabs my other arm too.

"Darren … uh, let's go." The other guy starts to step away from my car.

"Go is right. I'm going to have a go here at this fine piece of ass."

I grit my teeth. "Get your fucking hands off me!"

"Darren! I'm serious, man, let's get out of here. Just let her go."

"Who the fuck are you?" Darren grips me tighter as he looks over my shoulder.

"I'm the Grim Reaper if you don't do as the lady asks and take your fucking hands off her."

"Trick!" I scream at the sound of his voice behind me.

Darren pulls me into his body, hugging me tight, and that's when I feel the sharp tip of a knife at my back. "What are you gonna do? Shoot me before I cut her?"

I squirm to try and see Trick behind me, but the knife presses harder against me. What the hell is Darren talking about? Does Trick have a *gun*?

"What if you miss?" Darren's face contorts into an ugly smug grin.

"I never miss."

What. The. Fuck?

Darren keeps looking over at his friend.

"Let her go, now!"

Darren relaxes his grip on me and holds up his hands, the knife still in his right one, like he's surrendering.

"Trick!" I cry as I turn and run to him.

He places one hand on the back of my head and kisses the top of it while his other hand keeps the gun pointed at Darren. "Stay right here," he whispers to me.

I let him go and hug my arms around myself as he takes slow calculated steps toward Darren. "If I see you around here again, it'll be the last time you're *ever* seen."

I gasp a jerky breath, covering my mouth with my hand as Trick pistol whips Darren, knocking him to the ground and completely out. In spite of Darren having just threatened me two seconds ago, my instinct is to run and assess his injuries, call for an ambulance, *piece him back together.*

"Don't." Trick grabs my arm, pulling me away from Darren as Darren's friend drags him to the sidewalk and hoists him over his shoulder. "Are you okay?" He slips the gun into the back waistband of his jeans. "Are you okay?" he repeats, framing my face in his hands.

I nod with slow confusion.

"What were you thinking? Why did you leave?" His words carry a sharp edge.

"I-I have to work early."

"I would have taken you or at least walked you to your car. Jesus! Don't *ever* come out here at night by yourself. Do you understand?" His eyes tense with anger as he grips my face tighter.

My wide eyes fix on his in an unsettling mix of fear and confusion. "Why do you have a gun?" I whisper.

He kisses my forehead and sighs. "Because I didn't grow up in Barrington Hills."

CHAPTER FOURTEEN

I *'VE HIT THE point of no fucking return. There's nothing I resent more than the voice in my head saying I don't deserve her. And maybe I don't, but she's color and light, music and laughter, warmth and air. She's breath ... she's life.*

There's nothing as fierce as my instinct to protect her. I would kill for her ... I would die for her.

CHAPTER FIFTEEN

I HAVE TWENTY-TWENTY vision, so it's impossible for me to turn a blind eye to the gun that Trick has. Too many unnecessary casualties cross my path on a daily basis for me to feel that guns are necessary and provide safety in the hands of the average citizen. However, Trick with his gun saved me from being raped or worse. That realization alone gives me pause to re-evaluate the strong beliefs I've held for so long.

We haven't talked about that night since he took me home and held me in his arms until sleep claimed me, settling my shaky nerves. For me, I don't know what I would say about it. Should I apologize for leaving without him escorting me? Should I thank him for owning a gun?

"Tell me about Tamsen," I say, sitting cross-legged on my vanity as Trick applies my makeup for tonight's fundraising gala.

His lip twitches. "Look up," he commands with complete focus.

"She's beautiful."

Another twitch. "Don't blink."

"I talked to Grady about her yesterday while you were in the shower, but he was on his way out again so I didn't get much from him. He said she's a paramedic in New York City and she's not gay nor does she pretend to be."

Trick chuckles which is very uncharacteristic of him when he's working.

"Are she and Grady originally from Chicago?"

Trick pauses and looks into my eyes for a moment as if my question is … *odd?* He shakes his head and continues.

"Does she have a boyfriend?"

He lifts his shoulders. Typical man, of course he doesn't know.

I test the next question in my head a few times and decide it's appropriate if I can keep a nonchalant tone to my voice. "Have you two … been together?"

Trick raises one brow.

I sigh. "Have you … made love?"

He bites my lower lip, dragging it between his teeth for a slow release. "I've made love to you."

I roll my eyes at his semantics. "Have you had sex with her, fucked her?" So much for my attempt to use tact.

He blots along my lips that are wet from him and starts to line them. "No. Would it matter?"

"Of course not. It's just you have such an unhealthy attitude toward women, you know … the despising them and everything … so I'm curious how she ranks so high with you."

"I don't despise *you*." He glosses my lips.

"Well that's a relief." I grab his waistband and start to unfasten his pants.

"Don't start something you can't finish."

"Who says I can't finish?"

"I'll ruin your hair and then Gemmie will be pissed. And then there's your makeup …" He steps back and puts all the makeup and supplies away.

I hop off the vanity and shrug, wearing nothing but my nude strapless bra and panties. "Are you telling me no, Mr. Roth?"

He fastens his pants and leans against the counter with his arms crossed over his chest. "You are truly beautiful."

I look in the mirror. Gemmie has a knack for creating the impossible with my natural waves making them look tamed and free at the same time. And Trick always finds the right shades of eye shadow and liner to bring out a hint of vibrant blue in my eyes. "I'm just a product of some very talented people."

Trick moves behind me so he's looking over my shoulder at our reflection in the mirror. "Darby Carmichael, *you* are beautiful. Gemmie gets a gorgeous head of hair to play with, and I get a perfect canvas." He kisses my neck and my eyelids grow heavy from his touch. "But honestly, my alluring beauty, marking your perfect skin feels sacrilegious."

"Trick … touch me," I whisper with my eyes closed and a fog enveloping my brain.

"If I touch you, neither one of us will be making it to our respective engagements tonight."

My eyes flutter open. "I'm fine with that." I reach behind and grab his hands, placing them on my bare stomach.

He pinches my sides eliciting a squeal and a jump. "That's because your gala is going to be stuffy and boring."

I grab my newest Rachel Hart green dress and step into it. "That's because you're not coming with me."

He zips my dress. "If Tamsen weren't leaving tomorrow, I would be going with you."

"Who's going to sneak off with me to some private corner and remind me how sexy I look tonight?"

He kisses the skin exposed from the plunging back of my dress. "Only someone with a death wish."

I close my eyes, trying to shake the memory of Trick holding that gun like it was an extension of himself—confident, controlled, and deadly serious.

"My driver is probably here." I open my eyes and slip into my heels.

After grabbing my wrap and clutch, Trick escorts me to the car my father sent for me.

He kisses my neck, being careful not to mess up my makeup. "Call me if you need help getting out of your dress later," he whispers in my ear as the driver holds the door open.

He's so mean. "Tell Tamsen goodbye for me."

He nods as I duck into the back of the car.

✪

ENTERING THE GRAND ball room, I recognize the same wealthy crowd. Everything reeks of money and greed. The team of young wannabe politicians that my father sends door to door asking for votes aren't instructed to invite the average citizens of Illinois to these galas and fundraisers. *Why is that?*

Senator Calvin Carmichael flaunts his "relatable" qualities on TV ads, reminding the public that he grew up the son of a hotel parking attendant and social worker. The ads don't mention that he basically disowned his parents after he married my mom and started his first company. My grandma Carmichael died of lung cancer a few years ago, and I love that the decor at Rogue Seduction reminds me of her attic and the many hours I spent listening to her stories of each "collector's" piece she owned. But my grandpa is still alive. Just after my grandma died, he moved to a small house in Watseka, Illinois where he grew up. We weren't that close because he was always working, but I still visit him several times a year.

"There's my girl." My father breaks away from his cronies to greet me with a smile and hug. I hear the click of cameras and squint at the blinding flashes. "No date tonight?" He smiles.

"No. I see that pleases you." I fake my best grin.

"Nonsense, sweetheart. I like Steven."

"Mmm, you like Steven's father."

He ignores my comment as Rachel joins in our little family reunion.

"Darby!" Rachel greets me with feigned enthusiasm that she's perfected over the years. She's a walking billboard for Botox, boobs, and bulimia. "Look at you. Always the belle of the ball." She's complimenting her dress on me because when I'm not wearing one of her designs she never mentions my appearance.

"I just wear whatever arrives at the door."

Rachel flips her pin-straight blond hair back over her shoulder and leans in for her signature air-kiss as the flashes erupt again. "Where's Steven?"

It's obvious how much she and my father communicate. "I'm not seeing Steven anymore."

She looks around the room, giving me a fraction of her attention. "That's too bad. Is there someone new?"

"Yes, my dear granddaughter, *is* there someone new?"

I turn. "Nana!" I hug her because she's the only person here tonight that I'm genuinely happy to see.

"Grace." Rachel steals her for more posed air-kisses. The only reason Rachel tolerates my nana is because she lived with us until I graduated high school. So when my father and Rachel married it was a given that Nana and I were a package deal. I was a junior in high school. We already lived in Barrington Hills, just a "smaller" home. Rachel insisted on buying the largest house she could afford and we all moved in with her. I couldn't wait to graduate and get the hell out of there; neither could Nana.

"Well, if you ladies will excuse me ..." My father's met his three minute quota with his family. I'm sure he has some girl, no older than his own daughter, waiting with her dress up and panties down.

A server offers us champagne. I shake my head forcing a polite smile, while Nana and Rachel each take a glass.

"So, how's your *friend*? You've kept me in the dark."

Rachel raises her brows at Nana's comment. "So there *is* a new guy."

I smooth my palms over my dress, wishing I had taken a glass just to have something to do with my nervous hands. "It's a long story, but Trick is good ... *we're* good." Nana's going to have to wait for the full version when we're alone.

Nana winks at me; she's such a character.

"Trick's a unique name." Rachel's eyebrows furrow, eyes blinking.

"It's short for Patrick."

Her tongue brushes the inside of her lower lip as she gives a slow nod. "How did you meet?"

"He's been doing my makeup for these 'required' events."

"Well, you should bring him to dinner this week before I fly back to New York."

"Yes, dear, you should, and you should pick your nana up on the way." Nana's posture stiffens with an air of readiness.

"Our schedules can be difficult to coordinate…" I glare at Nana for her encouraging this "…but I'll see what I can do."

"Perfect. Text me, darling." Rachel flips her hair and waddles away in her black satin mermaid gown.

"Thanks for that."

Nana wraps her arm around my waist. "It's going to be the highlight of my year. I can't wait to see how your father handles an entire meal with your rebel artist."

"He's not a rebel. That's such a stereotype, Nana."

Okay, the fact that he could show up to dinner packing might qualify him for rebel status.

"He's a gay man banging the Senator's daughter. If that's not a rebel then I don't know what is."

My chest hitches and my skin flushes as I huddle down closer to her ear. "He's *not* gay, Nana!" I grit through my teeth.

Her eyes light up. "Oh my, this just keeps getting better."

I'M SURE IT'S a hundred ways of wrong that I won't vote for my own father in the upcoming election, but I detest the limelight, the deceit, the scandals, and the whole mockery of expectations that has jaded our political system. Everything is so elaborate and so … not me. Nana fits in only because she's lived this life for so long, but she's managed to navigate through it all while keeping a sense of herself.

I can't, not anymore. I'm tired of taking one for the team—a team I no longer want to be on. As our dinner plates are replaced with dessert plates, I push back my chair. The room is mammoth, but I feel so claustrophobic that I want to crawl out of my own skin. The orchestra, the numbing conversation, the eager waiting staff doing everything but wiping my ass—it's too much.

"I'm leaving," I whisper to Nana as she listens to some lady with diarrhea of the mouth go on about the exhausting task of organizing luncheons, tennis matches, dinner parties, and how she hasn't had a mani-pedi in over two weeks.

That's what the wealthy call slumming—pathetic!

Nana nods, squeezing my hand while pretending to be enthralled in what the woman has to say. Nana's a saint.

My driver is summoned to the front of the hotel, and as soon as I get in I call Trick.

"Hey."

"I'm leaving the hotel and I could use help with my zipper."

"Hmm, you didn't stay long." The vibrating edge to his hum lights a fire in my belly as the butterflies take flight.

"Do that again." I squeeze my legs together and close my eyes.

"Do what?"

"That." I moan. "God, Trick. When you talk it feels like you're stripping me with your voice and leaving me naked—begging for just one more word."

"Darby—"

"That's it, keep talking."

He chuckles. "Grady invited a few friends over. Have your driver bring you here, but call me and I'll come get you from the car."

"Trick, I'm physically overdressed, mentally naked, and in desperate need of a Trick fix. I'll go home and you call me when everyone leaves."

"Trick fix? That's my line. You'll be asleep before that happens. Just come here. I'll take care of you."

"What does that mean? You'll have a change of clothes for me or you'll give me what I *need*?"

"Just come."

He ends the call leaving me a puddle on the seat. When the driver pulls up along the street, I text Trick to let him know I'm here.

I open the door before the driver has a chance to get out when I see Trick appear around the corner. He's decked out in black, including his guyliner, with his arm tats on display right down to his leather wristbands. *Perfection!*

Tightening my wrap around my shoulders to block the wind, I clink over to Trick in my heels designed to torture my toes.

"Come." He wraps his arm around me, leading me inside where the warm air greets my chilled body.

Before we get to the elevator I hear laughter and voices from above. "How many people did Grady invite over?"

"Fifty or so."

"Fifty? Ten is inviting a few friends over. Fifty is a party."

He shuts the gate to the elevator, grabs my hands pinning them behind my back, and pushes me into the wall, my chest pressed against his. "So tell me about this *fix* you need." The elevator jerks into motion as his lips hover achingly close over mine.

I swallow hard then lunge for his lips, but he pulls his head back, denying me.

"Tell me." He ducks his head, lips ghosting over the swell of my breasts. "Tell me what you need," he whispers.

"I-I—"

We jolt to a stop and someone slides open the gate, but my eyes don't leave his. And there it is—the lip twitch.

"Too late." He winks.

"Darby!" Grady yells.

Trick steps back dragging his eyes the full length of my body— tempting me, teasing me, torturing me. A mob of people I've never seen pull him off in one direction while Grady kisses my cheeks.

"Well look who just walked off the cover of *Vogue*!" He holds me at arm's length. "Remember, Trick's mine tonight," Grady leans in and whispers into my ear. "Now, get a drink and mingle." He pushes me into the crowd toward the kitchen.

Trick's mine tonight?

I catch a lot of interesting looks, some a little creepy, as I navigate to the kitchen. This eclectic gathering has it all: goth, runway model, tattoos, piercings, shaved heads, fancy hats, and even the beanie-cap-saggy-pant-rapper look. The only thing missing is an over-dressed Senator's daughter.

Here! Let the fun begin.

"Don't mind Grady…" I turn to a friendly smile from Tamsen "…the gay masquerade has been a symbiotic relationship between Trick and him for years. So even if Trick decides he's ready to come out of the reverse gay closet, Grady still needs his favorite decoy."

"Decoy?" I laugh because there's nothing normal about Grady and Trick.

"Grady's my brother and I love him, but he's a man's man-whore."

I look around for Grady and Trick and to see who else is listening to Tamsen. "So what does that have to do with Trick?"

Tamsen loops her arm around mine, pulling me out of the congregation of people and off to the side. "Grady has a knack for falling for married men, usually ones who have lots of money and a reputation to protect."

"Married men?" I'm feeling dense, completely incapable of following what she's saying.

Tamsen laughs. "Yes, married men who live two lives. The socially acceptable one with the wife, three kids, and a dog, and the one that involves Grady booking fancy hotel rooms for the weekend so they can be who they really are."

"But Trick—"

She holds up one finger. "I'm getting there. Trick … well look at him; who cheats on a guy that looks like that?" Tamsen winks at me. "So nobody ever suspects that Grady is a home wrecker and Trick gladly vouches for him whenever he gets into a sticky situation. He's the perfect decoy and always willing to offer Grady an alibi because Trick's fine with people thinking he's gay, especially women." She giggles. "However, it's quite fun to see guys hit on him."

"I-I don't know what to say …"

"Well, you've swooped in and turned Trick completely inside-out so Grady knows their mutual agreement is about to expire. He's just buying time, that's all."

"So I'm supposed to pretend that I'm not with Trick?"

Tamsen shrugs. "No." Lifting up on her tiptoes, she looks around the room and grins as her eyes fix on something or someone. "As you can see, the women are all over Trick. They always are, like they think they can convert him, but he ignores them like any gay guy would." She purses her lips to contain her smirk. "However, if it were me, I would play it up to my advantage." Looking me over, her grin widens. "You look hot tonight and there's not a straight guy in this room who hasn't noticed you, so I'd find my own group of attention. At least if it were my man, I'd make him sweat it out for a while."

"You think I should flirt with other guys?"

"Flirt, no. Trick's not flirting. In fact, if you asked him he'd say he's just not *making waves*. So you should wade through the pond, and if you catch a few fish along the way, so be it. Just don't *make waves*."

I love Tamsen. She's the girlfriend I never had but have always wanted. "You're evil … but brilliant." I grin.

She hands me a glass of wine and nudges me toward the crowd. "Nope, just experienced. Now go get 'em."

Squeezing through the crowd, I look for a friendly face.

"Hey there."

I turn. *Bingo!* I'm not proud of the fact that I'm quite familiar with knowing when a guy's interested. After I grew out of my nerd girl phase in high school, I rebelled ... really rebelled. I lost my virginity in the restroom of a pub on campus to a guy I met two hours earlier—not my proudest moment. I never saw him again after that night. With rebellion comes the stubborn attitude that all your bad decisions are someone else's fault. Those first two years, everything was my father's fault.

"I don't believe I've had the pleasure yet. I'm Drake"

I grin inside. Drake has a few too many piercings for my taste, but the tats on his brawny arms and up his thick neck rival Trick's. His head is shaved, but his blue eyes mirror mine and so does his friendly smile.

"I'm Darby."

Drake plays into Tamsen's plan as if he's been hired to do so. Placing his hand on my *bare* lower back he pulls me closer to his side. "Phil, Bradley, Todd, meet Darby." The skinheads circle me with greedy eyes.

"Darby, your dress is the shit!" Todd licks his lips while his eyes take liberty with my body.

"Thanks, I just came from another *event* so I feel a little over-dressed."

Bradley shakes his head, eyes glassy. "Nope you're fucking perfect."

"She is isn't she?" Drake's hand slips an inch lower.

Don't make waves. Don't make waves.

"How do you know Grady and Trick?" Drake lightly teases circles on my skin.

I look around and spot Trick among a crowd of women, but his eyes are fixed on me. The petite brunette on his right teases the tips of her fingers along Trick's waistband just under his shirt.

Yeah, this is bullshit!

"I'm a client of Trick's," I mumble, keeping my eyes on Trick.

"I see. Well, have you seen the upstairs? If not I could give you a private tour."

Drake's words are a distant echo over my mind's attention on Trick. "Um … will you excuse me for a moment?"

I step away from the pack and head straight to Trick, who is leaning on the back of the couch acting like a llama at a petting zoo. There are so many women around him he's untouchable to me. It's like he's some rock star and I can't see over his groupies.

"Pardon me. Excuse me. Step aside please." I elbow my way through the women, earning a slew of nasty looks and catty hisses. As I steal the position directly in front of Trick, he crosses his arms over his chest. I cross my arms mirroring him, like we're seconds away from a showdown.

I don't know if it's the little bit of wine I've had, my worn nerves from the gala, or my need to be alone with Trick, but something snaps and my mind forgets all reason and my words escape all censorship. "I think Drake wants to take me upstairs for a quick fuck. What do you think about that?"

Our small circle of spectators falls silent with the exception of a few gasps and whispers. Trick has dominant control over his emotions, but I can see in the slight tensing of his jaw that it's wavering.

I purse my lips, tilting my head to the side. "So you don't have any thoughts on the matter?" I raise my shoulders. "Okay then, he seems like a nice enough guy and I'm horny as hell right now so have a pleasant evening, Mr. Roth." Turning on my heels, the crowd of women part like the Red Sea and I strut my stuff straight toward Drake.

"Come!" A strong hand with a painful grip clasps my arm, jerking me in the opposite direction.

Practically dragging me onto the elevator, Trick slams the gate shut and flips the switch down. I try to free myself from his hold, but he tightens it, yanking me into his chest. Releasing my hand, he grabs my head and kisses this life and maybe my next out of me. His tongue demands all of my mouth and his lips possess mine in a frenzy of emotion that's filled with such passion my whole world spins on *his* axis.

The elevator stops. His mouth and unforgiving stubble make a punishing trip down my neck as his hands clench my ass so tight I can already feel my skin bruising. "Don't ever fuck with me like that again," he warns, each word feels like lightening cracking through the air sending chills along my spine.

I take two fists full of his hair and jerk his head away from my neck. "Don't ever let another fucking woman touch you like that again." I grit each word through clenched teeth, chest heaving, eyes wild.

He leers at me with such intensity I swear he's seeing more than I see in myself. Then his expression surrenders: lips soften, jaw relaxes, eyes come to life. His hands cover mine until I release his hair, and he guides them to his face, closing his eyes like he's feeling my touch in his soul. He nods. "These hands ... only these hands ..."

CHAPTER SIXTEEN

D ARBY CARMICHAEL DOES what I swore no woman would ever do—she owns me. Period. I offered nothing, yet she took everything, and I don't fucking ever want it back.

"Let me," she whispers as I start to remove my shirt.

I raise my arms, surrendering to her as the dark material is pulled from my body. Her eyes explore my marked flesh, and when her pink tongue slides out to wet those perfect cherry lips ... dear God, I want to fall to my knees right here in her bedroom and beg for redemption. I'll worship her until the day I die because only her touch can take away the sins that plague my jaded soul.

I clench my fists as she pulls down my pants. She wants this ... me. She wants to see all of me. My control wavers on the edge of insanity because all I want is to touch her, taste her ... inhale her like the addict I never knew I was. *The addict I ... Never. Knew. I. Was.*

For a brief moment I squeeze my eyes shut, fighting to remember, dying to forget.

She's clueless to the depths of her own beauty. I've hidden myself behind ink and makeup just like I've done for so many other people. But Darby has the purest, unmarked skin I've ever seen. Her auburn hair pulls the most incredible hues of blue from her eyes. She's ... stunning.

When she reaches behind and unzips her dress, letting it pool at her feet, I die a little. Subtle curves with definition and purpose exemplify the essence of female beauty exactly how it was meant to be. Stepping out of her dress, she moves behind me. I suck in a breath as her lips press to my back, fingertips tracing the ink all the way to my shoulder.

"This ..." she whispers "...the colors are exquisite..." she moves her lips along my tattoo, "...but why a vulture?"

Pump, pump, pump.

I continue to clench my fists, feeling all my muscles go rigid in response. My God, the need to touch her is excruciating. "Unconventionality ... destruction ... death, but also patience..." I swallow "...renewal ... protection."

Her fingers ghost down my arm as she moves in front of me again. The softest gaze follows her touch over my diverse palate of feathers, flowers, and a river of flowing black letters and symbols all the way to my hand.

How will I ever tell her that I don't know what half of them mean? How will I show her what I can't see?

"I love you, Trick." Soft eyes find mine, then fall to her finger tracing over the wide black sanskrit from my lower abs around to my back. "What does this mean?"

"Don't look back in anger," I whisper.

Her delicate brows tense as she moves her head in a slow single nod. "You and I ..." she presses her lips to my chest "...we're not a game. No more pretending." She looks up at me.

"No more pretending," I confirm.

Turning her back to me, she removes her panties then draws her long hair over her shoulder. I kiss her neck and die a little more as her body shudders from my touch. Unhooking her bra, I whisper in her ear, "Do you wonder what you're doing with me?"

Her breath catches in her chest as she turns to me. "Sometimes ..." Her eyes flit between my eyes and my mouth.

I devour the lips I crave while laying her on her bed. Her fingers make a deep claim into my back while her legs clasp around my ass, drawing me inside. Heavy eyelids surrender; she moans my name. Resisting the urge to move, my jaw relaxes to release my labored breath as I wait for her to look at me again.

Opening her eyes she moves her hands to my face. "But most of the time..." she kisses me and I rock my hips into her beautiful body "...I wonder what I'd ever do without you."

CHAPTER SEVENTEEN

T RICK PLAYS EVERY part of my body with the expert precision of a concert pianist playing ten sheets of Bach—soft, hard, fast, slow, and an infinity of beautiful in between.

"Trick … please …. oh please … I-I'm so close … oh … God … there, right … there …" I arch my back, sitting astride him as our bodies sync in rhythm, seeking the pinnacle of sexual pleasure.

He sits up with nothing between us but sweat and flesh. Our mouths absorb every guttural moan and cry, and when he releases with a vibrating groan, I climax into another world. Never … and I mean *never, ever* have I experienced anything like it. In every look, every touch, every breath there's friendship, love, and a feeling bigger than words—an unexplainable synergy.

We collapse onto the sweat-soaked sheets looking like we just finished a marathon. I don't sweat this much when I bike.

"What was that?" I say through labored breaths, staring at the ceiling.

Trick chuckles with his hand resting over the wet smattering of fine dark hair on his chest. "Fucking mind-blowing."

"Yeah…" I laugh "…that sums it up pretty good. I mean, that wasn't normal."

He rolls on his side with his head propped up on his elbow. "Superhuman sex?"

I giggle. "Yes. Like in the movies when two immortals have sex you know it's just … transcendental."

"You're the sexy superhero, I'm merely the immortal." Leaning forward he sucks my nipple into his mouth and drags his teeth along it with a wicked grin.

I shove him on his back and roll onto him, biting his salty, wet neck. "It was all you. I was playing catch up the whole time, like I always do with you."

He gathers my hair into a ponytail and twists it one direction and then the other. "As I recall I let you go first, and I think you went second too. You're welcome."

I laugh into his neck. "You and your recollections are a real handful."

He kisses my head. "As I *recall,* you proved I'm easily two hands full."

I sit up and smack him with my pillow. "What is it with you men and your penises? Yes, you're ginormous and what you do with it is legendary. Is that what your ego needs?"

Trick grabs my pillow and hugs it to his chest. "Legendary huh?"

Jerking my pillow from him, I flop back onto the bed with my back to him. "Ugh! Goodnight."

Hooking his arm around my waist, he pulls me into him, nuzzling his whiskery face along the back of my neck. "Goodnight, sexy."

NOTHING BEATS BUTTERED toast, strawberry jelly, and eggs with your breakfast soul mate. Of course I don't say this to Trick because he's not a fan of gushy things like OMG BFF stuff. The only things he despises more are Emojis in texts so of course all of my texts to him are filled with them and some are all Emojis. My love for him may be a bit sick and twisted.

"Rachel wants us to come for dinner this week when our schedules allow, aka tomorrow night because that's the only night my father doesn't already have plans."

Trick walks up behind me, shirtless, and cups my ass while brushing his scruff along my neck.

"Down boy, or your over-easy eggs are going to collide with my scrambled," I warn, holding up the spatula.

He smacks my ass then hops up on the counter. "I'm surprised your father wants to see me again."

"That would be a surprise." I grin bringing the spoon from the jelly toward my mouth.

Trick grabs my wrist and leans down licking the jelly off *my* spoon. "You're crossing the line, buddy."

"Lines?" He hops down and carries our plates to the table. "Are there lines between us?"

"Yes, jelly ones. Rule number one … at my place I lick the jelly off the spoon."

He rubs his barefoot across mine under the table. "Well if you want to lick jelly off something—"

I glare at him in spite of the fact that I would love to lick strawberry jelly off any part of his body. "Rachel wants to meet you."

"Why?" He takes a bite of his toast.

"Because she's nosy and controlling."

"Sounds like fun, but I think I'll pass."

"What?" My eyes grow big. "You can't say no."

He finishes his bite and presses a napkin to his mouth. "Yes, I can. I don't need their approval and neither do you."

I deflate, at least on the inside. My father has very few redeeming qualities, but he's still my father. And Rachel … well she's tolerable—barely. I didn't expect Trick to do flips over the idea of dinner with them, but I also didn't expect him to flat out refuse.

We both finish eating, the air void of conversation. Grabbing our plates I take them to the kitchen. "I need a shower. I have to go into work for rounds."

He follows me up the stairs. "You're mad."

I keep walking. "I'm not."

"Then look at me."

Stopping at my bathroom door, I sigh before turning around. He stops a few feet away with his arms crossed over his chest.

"I'll go."

"No." I pivot and drop my robe to the floor then turn on the water to the shower. "You don't want to go."

"True, but I'll go for you if that's what you want."

I step in the shower and roll my eyes. Of course that's what I want, that's why I asked, but now his initial decline has changed everything. Now I want him to *want* to go. *Shit!* I've never been this way with any other guy—a needy head case. "No. It's too late. Now I don't want you to go. I'll take Nana because she enjoys my company."

Shut up, Darby!

With every word I become more pathetic. Closing my eyes, I let the water wash away the puffy-chested ego that's trying to cling to me. I still when Trick's arms snake around my waist, pulling my back into his chest.

"Did you just disinvite me to dinner?"

I smile, closing my eyes briefly while releasing a sigh, then turn in his arms and look up at him with a half grin and a nod. Pressing my lips to his chest, I wrap my arms around his waist. "I want you to come ... for me."

He tilts my chin up with his finger. "I know and that's why I'll be there for *you*. Someone has to pick up the pieces when they disappoint you."

I open my mouth to argue, but Trick stops me with his sexy lips. Just as well, my argument is feeble. He's right. I'll leave disappointed like I always do. When will I learn?

A STORM OF anxiety rips through my body leaving every last nerve frayed by the end of the day. Since the little dispute I had with Trick over dinner with my father and Rachel, the pressure for everything to go as smooth as possible weighs on me like a collapsed building.

"Big plans tonight?" Dr. Creepy Creighton asks as I finish signing my last chart.

"Dinner with family."

"Sounds exciting," he responds with an unusual interest in my plans.

"Yep, real exciting." I slip my pen in my pocket and turn to go get changed.

"You have plans for the weekend?"

Making a slow turn, my eyes narrow at him. "Why?"

He slides his hands in his coat pockets. "I heard you and Ashby are no longer together, so I thought we could get dinner or drinks."

Ew!

I feel invisible spiders creeping along my skin. Every cell in my body rejects even the thought of dinner with him. I was young and stupid, slept with a few too many guys during my rebel phase, but Dr. Creighton has slept with nearly every single female on the hospital's payroll. He's no longer young, now he's just stupid. *There is a difference.* He's the same coffee cup everyone's been drinking out of for the past two years. I have to choke back the "hell no" and force out a much more polite version.

"I'm seeing someone."

"Wow, that was quick."

Really? The hospital whore is judging me?

"Not that it should matter, but Steven and I have been over for a while."

He steps closer, eyes licking me like a salivating dog as he lowers his head. "Well if this new guy doesn't work out ... you know what they say about yours truly."

I move my head to the side, brows pulled tight in a wrinkled-nose expression.

"Yes, to a night with me is epic. No, to a night with me is tragic."

And people entrust their lives to this guy. I turn and walk away. "I can live with tragedy." *You disgusting piece of shit!*

After a quick change, I text Trick with a minimum of five Emojis to let him know I'm on my way home and will pick him up in an hour. I'm a planner so I run through topics of conversation that will be acceptable during dinner tonight, and by the time I'm home I have nothing. Trick will be on trial tonight, and although my father hasn't practiced law in years, his hard-core-cross-examination personality is still alive and ready to attack at a moment's notice. Unfortunately, he's had much longer than a moment's notice to prepare for tonight.

Rummaging through my closet takes far too long. I'm already running twenty minutes late to pick up Nana.

"All right, give me all the highlights before we get to Trick's," Nana insists the moment she gets in my car.

"The highlights?" I laugh.

"Well, not the hanky-panky stuff ... unless you want to tell me. It might surprise you to know that your nana was quite the little minx in her day."

The genuine laughter and heartfelt love that bubbles out of my chest for my nana is the truest thing I've ever known. "Nana, nothing you could say would surprise me. You know you're a rock star in my eyes."

"And Trick?"

I sigh. "He's ... *something*."

"But not really gay?"

I laugh. "Definitely not gay." A warm tingle settles between my legs just thinking about all the ways Trick has demonstrated his heterosexuality to me. "He has a troubled past which has given him an *aversion* to women, so he and his home-wrecking friend, Grady, have been pretending to be partners to stave off unwanted attention. It's complicated, weird, and even a little disturbing. I still haven't wrapped my head around it."

"He sounds like the trouble you need." Nana rests her hand on my leg, giving a teasing squeeze.

"He's trouble all right—troubled, dark, and sexy. I don't recognize myself when I'm with him. He brings out my wild side..." Nana's eyes perk up along with her wide grin "...and also a jealous side. I don't like that side."

"Jealousy, huh?"

Glancing sideways, I frown. "Yes, it's toxic like the flu. I feel like crap when I allow it to sink its nasty claws into me. It's so different with Trick. Not that I haven't been in relationships before, I've just never felt the pangs of jealousy or *neediness.*"

"Neediness? Oh, dear child, you're in deep. I never dreamed I'd see the day when my independent girl would feel needy."

"I know! That's just it. I almost had an emotional meltdown when Trick said he didn't want to come to dinner. And then when he finally agreed to it, I sulked because I wanted him to *want* to go. What is that? Talk about messed up. I swore I'd never be that girl who plays mind games and gets her feelings hurt by the slightest confrontation, but that's who I've become."

"It's called vulnerability, and it's not always a bad thing. We have to open our hearts to allow love to find us and with that comes vulnerability, jealousy, and even your dreaded neediness. It's all a front to protect us from our ultimate fear."

"That being?"

"Pain."

Do I think Trick can cause me pain? *Yes.*

"I'll text him we're here." I look down at my phone as Nana clears her throat.

"I don't think that's necessary."

I look up and sure enough ... he's killing me. Who is this guy and what did he do with my Trick?

"Your boy cleans up real nice."

That's just it. I don't want Trick "cleaned up" and looking like an imposter. I want tight short-sleeved T-shirts with lots of tattoos on display, badass leather wristbands, worn jeans, and black biker boots. I step out of the car as he approaches in his black suit and tie.

Fucking hell! He's wearing a suit?

My capris, red halter top, and sandals feel way too casual in his presence.

"Hey, sexy." He hugs me, lifting me off my feet.

"What are you doing?"

He sets me down. "Last I knew we were having dinner with your family."

"I'm talking about your *suit*." I gesture with my hand.

"I was underdressed the last time we went to your father's for dinner, so I thought I'd step it up a notch. You don't approve?"

I sigh and pull him to me by his jacket lapels. "I just want you to feel comfortable in your own skin around my family."

He kisses me, soft and slow. "It's a suit. My skin is the same underneath." He bends closer to my ear. "I'll show you all of it later."

Lovely, there goes my dry panties!

We both turn to the tapping sound on the window. Nana smiles, pointing to her watch.

"We'd better get going."

Trick opens my door and then gets in the backseat.

"Hello, young man. I can sit in back if you'd like to sit up front." Nana works her charming smile even though she has no intention of getting in back.

"Hello again, Grace. Thank you for the offer, but I'm fine back here."

"Suit yourself."

I choke on my own laughter as I glance at Trick in the rearview mirror. He might not see the humor, but all I can think about are the numerous occasions he has told me to "suit yourself."

"I heard you're not gay after all."

"Nana!" I grip the wheel and grit my teeth.

. Trick's lips twitch when I glance back, completely horrified. "I heard that too." He's a damn glacier back there while I'm self-combusting one Nana comment at a time. This is going to be ... One. Long. Ride.

CHAPTER EIGHTEEN

A S TRICK OPENS my door, I expect to see blood dripping down his neck. Nana talked both of his ears off the whole way here. Aside from the sexual orientation clarification, it was mostly about how she and my grandfather met and how hard he worked right up until he died.

Nana marches off toward the front door then turns around. "Don't forget to ask Darby about her first kiss."

For the love of God, Nana!

"So tell me—"

"No." I sidestep him.

He grabs my arm. "Spill."

I grumble, nothing in particular, as I turn with a sour face. "My first kiss was the day I graduated from high school. My father and Rachel had a party for me." I stare down at my feet, rocking back on my heels while tapping the toes of my sandals together. "No kids from my class came, just friends of my father and Rachel. One of the neighbors ... well, their *child* was home from college and kissed me out back in the rose garden."

Trick chuckles. "An older guy, huh?"

I risk a glance up at him with a sheepish grin. "An older *girl.*"

Lip twitch. I'm impressed by his control. "You kissed a girl?"

"She kissed me."

"Did you like it?"

"Shut up. I had a shitty childhood, not that you would—"

Oh. Fuck!

"Trick, I'm—"

"Don't." He kisses me, resting his forehead against mine.

"But you grew up with nothing—"

"And you grew up with everything." He kisses me again. "I'm glad it was that way and not the other way around."

"Trick—"

He shakes his head, probably seeing the tears of regret in my eyes. "Come." Taking my hand he pulls me toward the front door.

As soon as we enter, we're greeted by the cloying tone of Rachel's voice because seriously ... God wasn't cruel enough to actually give someone that as their natural voice. "We're in here."

Trick starts to pull me toward the voice like he lived here, not me. I love everything about him, even the things that drive me crazy. He has a sexy bad-boy appearance with a reserved demeanor, but he's confident and dominant as hell when he wants to be.

"Hey..." I tug on his hand and wrap my arms around him before we reach the formal living room "...thank you for this."

He leans down toward my neck and I tilt my head, begging for his mouth to claim my skin. "You can thank me in a more proper way later." He sucks and bites at my sensitive flesh.

"Ah hem ..."

I start to move, but Trick takes his time, not even flinching before he gives me one last nip.

"Good evening, Rachel."

Trick lifts his mouth from my neck with his back still to Rachel. He wets his lips then rubs them together; I swear he fucks me with his eyes and a smirk that says I-don't-give-a-damn-who-just-walked-in-if-I-want-you-I'm-going-to-take-you. God, I've never wanted to be bent over that wooden banister so bad in my life. Desire used to be an afterthought, a luxury. Now it's a rash that I can't stop scratching.

"Trick this is Rachel Hart, my father's ... *wife*." I fake a grin.

Trick turns and offers his hand. "Nice to meet you."

Rachel looks like she could pass out, the color draining from her face and her chest rising and falling with rapid, shallow breaths. It's the Trick effect. Her wide eyes dart back and forth between his face and his hand. Trick glances over at me with his hand still held out and gives me the knitted eyebrow look.

I roll my eyes and shake my head because I don't know what her problem is. She has a peculiar personality. "Rachel?" I say in two slow syllables.

She swallows then clears her throat. "Uh ... yes, sorry. It's nice to meet you too." Accepting his hand with hesitation, she eyes him as if she's waiting for him to say something more.

Trick releases her hand and looks at me with a subtle squint that shows lingering confusion in his eyes.

"Well, shall we?" Rachel motions with a head nod to the living room. Even her Botox brow doesn't hide her tension as she forces a tight-lipped smile while blinking as if she just got contacts.

"There's my girl." My father holds out his arms.

I release Trick's hand and hug my father. Nana winks at me with a sly smile stealing her lips. "Father." I step back, grabbing Trick's hand again. "You remember Trick."

My father nods once as his face falls sour. "*Yes*, I remember. How nice of you to indulge my wife's thirsty curiosity by joining us for dinner."

"I'm indulging your daughter, not your wife."

"Maybe for now. Let's eat." My father plasters on his politician's smile while everyone drudges through the thick tension, making our way to the dining room.

I recognize that look in my father's eyes. It's his way of saying, "See you in court." Tonight the dining room will serve as the courtroom, and Trick will be on trial for the duration of dinner.

Trick pulls my chair out, but I don't think his faux gentlemanly manners are going to earn him points with my father. He sits next to me and leans over to my ear as I take a sip of water. "The only thing that's going to get me through tonight is knowing that when it's over I'll be fucking you into the middle of next week."

I choke, searching with desperation for my next breath. A wry grin slides up Trick's face as he pats my back.

"Are you okay?" Nana and my father chime at the same time while Rachel scowls at me, as if choking at the dinner table is just another example of my poor etiquette.

Pressing my hand to my chest, I nod. "F-fine."

"So, Trick, are you originally from Chicago?" My dad wastes no time.

"Darling, we just sat down. Must you start with the interrogation?" Rachel sips her wine, avoiding eye contact with everyone.

Nana peers at me as if I have the answer to Rachel's uncharacteristic behavior. I expected my father and Rachel to tag team the interrogation.

"Asking him where he's from is hardly an interrogation. Do you feel interrogated, Trick?" My father loves putting people in the hot seat then daring them to admit they feel the heat.

"I'm from Queens."

I look over at Trick. This is news to me. Admittedly, I never asked where he was from. Somehow I made the assumption that he grew up homeless on the streets of Chicago. He looks at everyone except me, as if gauging their reaction is more relevant than the wide-eyed shock on my face.

"I see. Do your parents still live there?"

"They're dead." Trick takes a bite of his salad.

"Siblings?" My father doesn't even have the decency to offer his condolences before moving on to the next question.

"No."

"What brought you to Chicago?" He just keeps firing away.

"Cal, really can you let the boy enjoy his dinner?" Rachel swoops in to save the day, but hell if I know why.

"Job offer." Trick ignores everyone but my father, except for giving Rachel the occasional glance.

"And what is it you do?"

"I'm a makeup artist."

My dad chuckles and takes his first bite of food, as if he's made his case and is ready to dismiss the witness from the stand.

"I started out doing sketches and selling them on the street and at local art festivals."

Food has to be hanging out of my mouth. I can't believe Trick is volunteering information he's never shared with me—information I've been too afraid to ask about.

What's his angle?

"If you'll excuse me, I need to check on something with Susie in the kitchen." Rachel leaves the table.

"Darby, what's new with work?" Nana breaks the silence.

I smile at her then look over at Trick who seems to be in deep thought with his eyes fixed to his food as he chews each bite with slow concentration. He seems a million miles away.

RACHEL NEVER RETURNS to the table and nobody goes to check on her. What does that say about her? What does that say about us? My father takes an "important" call before dessert is served and never returns either. Nana and I end up having a conversation about her friend's recent diabetes diagnosis. Trick says nothing, just a nod or two whenever we try to engage him in our conversation.

We leave without a single goodbye from Rachel or my father. I'm usually the one being shunned for my poor etiquette, but right now I'm so embarrassed by the way they just left as if we weren't worth their time.

Nana nods off on the way home while Trick stares out the back window. I feel like a cab driver, and eventually I turn on the radio to drown out the monotonous silence.

"Nana," I whisper, giving her a gentle nudge but she still startles.

"Oh dear! Did I doze off?"

"Yes, I believe you did." I chuckle.

Trick gets out and opens her door.

"Thank you. You're quite the gentleman."

He's not.

"I'll walk you to your door."

She pats his chest. "No need. I've got it, but thank you. Night, dear." She waves to me as she heads up her walk.

"Goodnight, Nana."

Trick gets in the passenger seat and shuts the door. "I have an early morning tomorrow." He gives me a weak smile. It's more than a lip twitch and less than the full on grin so I know it's forced.

"I do too, but I was still going let you *fuck me into the middle of next week.*"

He moves his hand behind my head rest and looks me over before meeting my gaze again. "Maybe tomorrow."

"What's wrong?"

"Nothing. I just have an early morning tomorrow. I'm doing onsite work for a photoshoot." He looks ahead.

My shoulders slump. "Okay. Tomorrow, *maybe.*" I pull away from the curb. "Why didn't you tell me you were from New York?"

"It never came up, I guess."

"And the sketches … you sold your art?"

"Uh-huh."

It's a little jarring that he's never shown me his sketches and the only mention he makes about them since the first night at his place is to my father and Rachel who couldn't care less. I don't even know where everything is. He's moved it all completely out of sight.

"You must have intimidated Rachel … which is hard to do."

"Why do you say that?" he asks, glancing sideways.

"She insists on knowing everything about everyone, and not only did she not ask you, well … anything, she actually tried to prevent my father from probing. It was…" I shake my head "…weird."

It's not that I didn't feel a little intimidated by Trick when we first met, but Rachel Hart is cutthroat; backing down from anyone is not her style.

"Yeah, that is weird."

As I pull up along Trick's street, he unfastens his seat belt. "Drive safe." He brushes his knuckles across my cheek then starts to get out.

What the hell?

"Are you serious?" I can't hide the pain in my voice.

He ducks down looking back in at me.

"Drive safe? That's it? What the hell happened since *fucking me into the middle of next week?* Did I do something wrong? Is this about my family because I-I don't understand?"

He sighs, closing his eyes for a brief moment. "I'm just ... *off* tonight. I'll..." he pauses with another sigh "...I'll be fine tomorrow."

I want to get out and hug him into some sort of submission, but I feel this wall between us right now. And as much as I love him, I really don't know him well enough yet to anticipate how he might react to being pushed into opening up to me. The part of Trick I don't understand feels dark, and it scares me more than I could ever admit to him.

Pressing my lips together, I nod and he shuts the door. As I pull away, I look in my rearview mirror and see him raking his hands through his hair.

CHAPTER NINETEEN

I THINK *I fucked Rachel Hart ... or maybe she fucked me. I don't know because I can't remember, but she does ... she knows me ... she remembers.*

CHAPTER TWENTY

S LEEP EVADES ME at every turn. I've brought up Trick's number on my phone at least a half a dozen times, but my finger won't press *Send*. After hours of restlessness and pent-up anxiety, I ignore the clock reading 3:30 a.m. and throw on my shorts and sports bra.

An hour later I'm drenched in sweat, and my legs feel like jelly from spinning the hell out of them. The only thing more exhausted than my legs is my mind. I've replayed the evening so many times trying to figure out what went wrong. Why does Trick feel *off* and what does that mean? It's as if it has something to do with Rachel, but that really doesn't make sense either. He watched her with a tense look of confusion even when she wasn't looking at him. Maybe he was pissed that she was so insistent on dinner then completely avoided all topics of conversation that involved him.

Ugh!

I wish I could figure it out. Instead, I'm showered and ready for work two hours early. Hunger hasn't hit, and exhaustion is lurking but not ready to overtake my incessant stream of thoughts. A quick text might ease my mind. He'll get it when he wakes and maybe text me back so I can focus on work today without obsessing over last night.

> **Me:** *Sorry about dinner. You were right, we shouldn't have gone. Couldn't sleep well without you ... missing you. Hope your day isn't so "off."*

After I send it, I force down my last Green Lantern and head into work early. It's sad that I hope some emergency comes along that will require an extra set of hands. I need to preoccupy my mind until I can see Trick again.

THE UNUSUALLY SLOW day in the ER drags on, but I'm off now and headed to Trick's. He never texted me back, which is surprising since I was nice enough to send my earlier message Emoji-free. The lights are off at Rogue Seduction, so I park and head up to his place. When I reach the top floor and open the gate, I'm greeted with him in just a pair of shorts doing another funky yoga pose that brings shades of crimson to my skin. His name alone turns me on; everything else is an erotic bonus.

"Hey." I smile as he lowers to his feet.

"Hey." He wipes his face with a towel. "I didn't know you were coming by."

I stop my forward motion that's intended to put my body in his arms—the place I'm so desperate to be right now. "Uh … well, I'm sorry. Guess I should have called."

He gulps down a glass of water, wiping his lips with the back of his hand. "So what's up?"

I'm not the foremost expert on relationships, at least ones that mean anything, but the thick, tight knot in my stomach gives me the uneasy feeling that he's trying to blow me off. *Holy shit, is he dumping me?* Trick's not saying the words, but his actions speak volumes. He didn't kiss me goodnight; he didn't return my text; he's not welcoming me with any sort of affection … He's not making me feel welcome at all.

Pushing the words past the lump in my throat, I muster a weak smile. "Nothing's up. I thought we could get some dinner or something—"

"I already ate." He sets his glass down and looks at me like I'm the equivalent of a neighbor coming by to ask for a cup of sugar …

and he doesn't have any.

An embarrassing mess of emotions threatens to overtake my composure. "Okay, well…" I step back toward the elevator "…I guess I'll see you around."

He stares at me … no words, yet his silence says everything.

I shut the gate and flip the switch. With just one shaky breath my heart overflows with suffocating pain pushing a flood of emotions to the surface. Cupping my hand over my mouth, I hold my breath, my tears, and my sobs inside until a gush of air hits me as I emerge from his building.

The door slams shut and I lean against the side of the brick building and fall to pieces. I know the anger will hit at some point, and I'll say the words to him that will give me back some dignity and help rebuild my confidence; but right now … I just need to cry.

Not being able to make sense of it just intensifies the pain. Was it my father? Rachel? The wealth that surrounds me? Wiping away the tears, I push off the side of the building and adjust my scarf so it covers most of my tear-stained face as I take shaky steps toward my car.

"Darby." Trick's voice at my back twists the knife a little deeper.

I stop, but I can't turn and look at him.

"Come."

Closing my eyes, a few more painful tears fall down my cheeks as I shake my head. Opening them I take in a breath of courage and continue walking to my car.

"Darby!"

My legs move faster until I'm jogging. With each pounding step I rush my heart to safety. Strong arms grab me from behind, and as he hugs me I completely shatter. My brain screams for him to let me go, but my words are buried under too many emotions. When love and anger collide, it rains down a flood of heartache. I *hate* feeling vulnerable; it hurts so fucking bad.

"I'm sorry. I'm so fucking sorry, just come back."

"I-I don't understand …"

Trick turns me around; the stoic face that I'm used to seeing has been replaced with dark eyebrows gathered in a pained expression. "I'm messed up and I should …" He squeezes his eyes shut.

Clenching my fingers into his shirt, I jerk at it. "What? You should what? Let me go?" Rage builds with each word, each breath.

He opens his eyes—regret. God, it's so thick in his expression.

"If you try and give me the 'it's not you it's me' or 'I should let you go' bullshit story, I swear I will never forgive you." I release a sob. "So fucking make up your mind…" I shake my head, emotions surging out of control "…because you're *killing* me."

Trick grabs my head, and fisting my hair he kisses me so hard it feels like he's taking my very last breath. My tongue fights with his for control as desire turns into an insatiable need that can no longer be ignored. As he starts to ease up, I grab his face, holding his mouth to mine. Stopping or even slowing down feels impossible.

Grabbing my ass with a bruising grip, he lifts me up and I clench my legs around him as he moves toward the alley. He pushes my back against the unforgiving brick wall a few feet from his door and rips off my scarf. The friction from his rough face burns my sensitive skin as he sucks and drags his teeth over my flesh.

"Trick …" I grind my hips into him, feeling the head of his erection through his shorts. My mind flashes to 'what if someone looks down the alley?' but that's all the further that thought goes. "Fuck me, Trick …"

His hands move under my blouse, and with the impatience I'm craving, he jerks down my bra and cups my breasts so hard I cry out in pain. Sliding one hand around, he palms my ass and stumbles the last few feet to the door. He types in the code while I reach between us, sliding my hand into his shorts.

"Fuck!" He throws open the door, staggering inside until my back hits the metal lattice elevator gate.

My grip on his cock hardens and so does he as I stroke him,

grazing my thumb over the wet tip. Pulling my hand away, he sets me on my feet. Before he can slide the gate open, I hunch down taking his shorts and briefs with me.

"Darby—"

I take him in my mouth and suck until he falls forward with a clanging rattle of the gate, leaning his forehead against it and gripping it with his hands.

"Shit! St-stop …" His words come out desperation and broken as he clenches his teeth, sucking in a hissing breath.

Releasing him, I kiss my way up his torso, pushing his shirt up until he grabs it with one hand and shrugs it off. Pressing my lips to his hard pectoral muscle, I bite down on it relishing the salty taste of his sweat.

He growls and grabs my face, smashing our mouths together. I dig what little nails I have into his hard ass with one hand and stroke him with my other. One minute I have my shirt on, the next he's tearing it open; the clink of the buttons flittering across the floor barely audible over our moans.

My breasts tingle, heavy in his hands as he kneads them with a firm, rough grip, circling his thumbs over my nipples. "Trick—" My head falls back against the gate, jaw slack.

He tortures my neck all the way to my collarbone with nipping kisses; sometimes sucking so hard I swear he's marking me. When his mouth finds my breasts, I grab two fists full of his hair and hold him to me while arching my back. Pressing one hand to the small of my back, he slips his other down the front of my leggings.

"Oh … God …" My chin falls to my chest, he looks up at me with his mouth covering my nipple, sucking and teasing as he slides two fingers into me, pressing his palm against my clit.

"You're so fucking wet." He releases my nipple and groans while holding my gaze.

Trick hypnotizes me with his eyes. I cup his sexy face, running my thumb across his lips as my breaths come quicker. His tongue darts out and I slip my thumb into his mouth. Closing his eyes he sucks on it, matching the slow thrusting rhythm of his fingers.

"N-now ... I-I need it *now*," I beg with a weak, breathy voice.

I whimper from the loss of his touch, but then he pulls off my boots and removes my leggings and drenched panties. He wets his lips and grabs my hips. I know where he's going, but the instant his touch breaches my folds I know I'm going to explode, and I *need* this to last.

"Don't!"

He looks up at me with a slight squint of confusion. My heart still aches, and I want him to take that feeling away. I need to feel him crawl under my skin and possess me ... claim me ... own me.

"Just *fuck* me ... I *need* you to fuck me until the only thing I *feel* is how *hard* you're fucking me."

In an instant, a storm rolls into his eyes and everything goes dark. I see the color of his past and feel intensity radiating from his body as he comes to standing. I look up and I. Just. Need.

"As you wish." No smile, not even a twitch.

Grabbing my hips, he turns me toward the gate. My heart pounds against my ribs, my breath the only sound slicing the eerie silence. I gulp down any fear that tries to work its way up my throat as Trick ghosts his hands down my arms, leaving a prickling of bumps in their wake. With a firm grip he takes my hands and places them on the metal lattice.

"Hold on *tight*," he rasps in my ear.

Wedging his leg between both of mine, he spreads me wide, clenches my hips until I suck in a seething breath of air between my teeth, and then he slams into me. My piercing cry doesn't stop him. He pulls back and does it over and over again. My knees threaten to buckle as the intensity builds. Trick grabs my hair and pulls my head back with a slow but very firm tug.

"Stay standing," he demands through labored breaths.

My numb fingers curl into the unforgiving metal of the gate

that's slipping from my sweaty grip. "Trick!" I cry his name as his fingers press to my clit. "I'm ... I-I'm ... close ..."

And then ... he pulls out.

"No!" The orgasm that's sitting on the edge waiting to be released blurs my vision.

Whipping my disoriented body around, he assaults my breasts and neck with his lips, teeth, and tongue. Mission accomplished, my heart feels nothing but its own galloping beat. Now I *need* the release so I move my hand between my legs and my drunken eyes start to roll back in my head.

"Not happening." Trick grabs my wrist and moves both of my hands around his neck.

"T-Trick ..."

He lifts me up and eases me down onto him. I drop my head to his shoulder, but he doesn't move, even when I try to rock my pelvis into him, our chests ebbing and flowing together. The split second of reprieve ends and he finishes me.

My back hits the gate and the metal bites my skin as he shows no mercy fucking me not into next week, but the next century. Even after my orgasm rips me apart and his warm release invades me, he continues to grind into me as if he's making sure I have absolutely nothing left to feel, like each thrust is an exclamation point at the end of the most profound sentence.

When our bodies come to rest, he licks a slow path up my sweat-covered neck and whispers in my ear, "Hard enough for you?"

Chasing my breath that's just too far gone to ever catch, I nod.

Wrapped around his body, we take the elevator up and he lays me on his bed. Somewhere between that first punishing kiss and my incredible, *hard*-earned orgasm, the pain evaporated and now I'm ... *better*.

CONFUSION? PAIN? REGRET? I wonder what's going through Trick's mind as he sits on the edge of the bed with his back to me, head bowed. I sit up and press a soft kiss to his shoulder while wrapping my arms around him.

"When I was twenty I was hit by a car."

My grip on him stiffens. I rest my cheek against his back, waiting idle for his next word.

"The trauma to my head involved some memory loss. They said it could be permanent or temporary … it feels permanent."

Holding my breath, I remain paralyzed by his words.

"When I think about my past it's … it's like I can't remember and I can't forget. Sometimes I'm so lost I can't find my own reality."

Tracing my finger along the sanskrit that wraps around to his back, I blink through the tears … the raw empathy I feel for him. *Don't look back in anger.*

"What's the last thing you remember?"

He lets out a small breath of a laugh. "Sketching my father playing his harmonica at the subway station. He made twenty-one dollars and fifty-two cents that night. I sold the sketch to a commuter for thirty."

I stop my tracing motion. "But you told me about the day your parents *disappeared*." I can't bring myself to concede that they're dead. "That had to be after you sketched your dad."

"I've been gifted bits and pieces of my lost past from people who knew me. A pastor from an inner city church was one of those people. He visited me in the hospital every day after the accident. When I was ready to face the reality of my memory loss, he told me about the weeks I spent looking for my parents." Trick turns and looks at me but only for a moment before he casts his eyes downward. "So sometimes I take those pieces and fill in the gaps to give myself a story … a past."

Of course I can't fathom what he's really been through, but in a small way I understand what's it's like to take pieces of something and give it a life again. I do it every day. "Is that what happened last night? Were you giving yourself a past for my father and Rachel ... for me?"

His eyes find mine again, and there they are—those million unspoken emotions. "Sort of."

"I still don't understand why you tried to shut me out."

With a slight shake of his head, he sighs. "It was too much. Last night I wanted so bad to remember; I *needed* to remember, but I couldn't. Five years of my life—gone, erased. What if I remember? What if I wasn't a nice person? What if I did bad things?" He rests his palm against my cheek. "Will you still choose to love me?"

Placing my hand over his, I close my eyes. A world where I'm not loving Trick seems unimaginable and cruel. But since he snuck into my life and claimed my emotions, I have no idea how I would react. He's good at keeping secrets, he owns a gun, and an hour ago I thought he was dumping me. Predicting my reaction to the shitload of unknown that happened in five missing years of a drug addict's life is astronomically impossible.

Opening my eyes, all I can do is speak what my heart shares with his. "If you remember who you were, will you still choose to love *me?*"

He answers with a slow kiss. It may be a yes or it may be a no ... or it may just be that in love and life certainty is never more than a breath away.

CHAPTER TWENTY-ONE

MY PHONE ALARM screams at me, an unwelcome reminder that vampire season is here—I will go to work in the dark and come home in the dark. Leaving a naked Trick behind in bed is not an easy feat. Of course I love my job and the worthwhile feeling I get from helping others, but right now I want to help myself to a naked Trick. Indulge in the physical bliss of him inside me, possessing every single atom of my being.

"Shit," I whisper to myself in realization that my clothes are downstairs strewn along the entry.

After padding across the floor, I cringe as the gate rattles shut, but Trick doesn't stir. The elevator screeches to a jerky halt. I frown at the scattered buttons on the floor as I gather up my belongings.

"Fucking hell! Darby!"

I flinch with a white-knuckled grip on my wad of clothes. It's possible he thinks I left … alone again in the dark. As the elevator ascends, I see black leather boots first, then jeans, a bared chest, clenched jaw, and finally steam seething from his nostrils. Opening the gate with caution, I press my lips together with a grimace as my stomach roils. With a hesitant step toward him, I gulp down my nerves and lift onto my toes, brushing my lips against his before depositing a small peck.

"I was just getting my clothes."

Drawing in a breath and holding it, his gaze flicks upward as his head turns in a minute shake. "You should have woke me."

Sidestepping past him, a sarcastic chuckle escapes me. "To ride down the elevator with me?" I pull on my leggings then steal a shirt from his dresser.

Trick turns. "Were you going to wake me before you left?"

"*Yes.*"

Maybe.

"I'm going to program the garage door code into your car and from now on you'll park inside."

After tying back my hair, I shove the ruins of my shirt into my handbag. "Mr. Roth, are you giving me unrestricted access to your place?" My brows peak.

Trick tugs his shirt down over his head. "I'm giving you unrestricted access to *me*. And I'm keeping you safe."

"You think you're my protector?" I ask while shoving my feet into my boots.

"Come," he calls, heading to the elevator while leaving me ... as always ... scurrying after him.

TRICK IS AN extreme emotional roller coaster. I've been up and down and whipped in every direction, feeling scared, nervous, sick, and a whole lot of tummy twisting, adrenaline surging desire for more.

"Oh my God! What the hell happened to you?" Jade's shrill startles me as I pull my scrub top over my head.

"What are you talking about?" I cock my head to the side.

"Your back." She stares at me with cow eyes.

I walk over to the mirror and pull up my shirt, looking over my shoulder.

Crap!

I slide my shirt back down over my red welts. Ironically, they don't hurt too badly. It's hard to tell because I have a general soreness in most of my muscles, a few hickeys on my chest, as well as some bite marks. That's what I get for asking to be fucked *hard*.

The "I fell," or "I got mugged," scenarios won't work with Jade. She's too smart.

"I got shoved up against an old elevator gate." I sit on the bench and tie my shoes.

"Were you being mugged?"

I stand corrected.

"No ... I wouldn't say that." Looking up, I wince, feeling a flush creep across my cheeks.

Her jaw plunges to the floor. "Sex? Are those marks from sex?"

My ego throws up its dukes at the incredulity in Jade's voice. "Would that be so hard to believe?" I'm a miserable failure at keeping a straight face.

Jade laughs as I tighten my lips to hold back my own shit-eating grin. "Yes, it would be hard to believe, but you're too honest to lie, so ..."

I pull on my lab coat and adjust my badge. "So what?"

"So who's the guy and where can I get me one?"

"He's the squirrel."

Jade finishes getting dressed. "A squirrel, huh?"

"No not *a* squirrel, I said *the* squirrel."

She freezes, mid tie of her scrub pants. "I knew it! I could feel the sexual tension in the room that day. Oh my, he must be a real machine. Is he? Does he like it kinky? Oh God ... I bet he does. Did he tie you up? Handcuffs? Let me see your wrists."

"I'm not even going there, Jade." I shake my head and walk out the door.

Yes, he's a machine.

The sharp edge to his voice, a proverbial knife to my throat, Trick doesn't need to use restraints ... he paralyzes me with a look, ties me up with words, and controls me with his body.

THE DAY STARTS with such a high, but as the laws of gravity kick in I have nowhere to go but down. Around noon, I receive a text from Trick.

Trick: *Catching a flight to LA in 2 hrs. Call you later.*

I start my slow deflate for the rest of the afternoon. As I walk to my car, I receive another text.

Rachel: *We need to talk. ASAP!*

Lovely.

Me: *On my way home. I'll call you later.*

Rachel doesn't respond. She's used to working with a team of dogs following her around, tails wagging, just waiting for her to give a command. I'm not that obedient. I can already see her squinting at her phone wondering where my father went wrong with me.

I spy a black Escalade along the street in front of my house as I turn to pull in back. It would seem that Rachel just happened to already be in the city. *Stalking me.*

My front door buzzes at the exact moment I walk in though my back door. I should rush to let her in; it's starting to rain outside. Instead, I change into my workout clothes while the door continues to buzz at annoying intervals.

"Rachel." I greet her with an innocent smile as if I just now heard the door buzz.

"Darby." She ushers past me without an invite inside. "We need to talk."

"So you said in your text." I shut the door and follow her into the formal living room.

Rachel makes herself at home on the love seat, legs off to the side, crossed at the ankles, and hands folded on her lap. "I ... well, Cal and I don't want you to see Trick anymore."

Damn! She's got a big-ass pair of balls under that black pencil skirt of hers.

My eyelashes flutter a bit as I smile. I'm buying time for my brain to formulate a thought-out response that doesn't involve the words *fuck you*. "Wow, that's a mighty big request." I step to the couch, resting my hands on the back of it opposite her, fingers digging into the mustard fabric.

"You're too smart, Darby, to play dumb with me. This isn't Cal's first election, and you know that rogue family members can end a political career."

My neck and jaw stiffen; my temperature soars. "*Rogue?* Really, you're going with that?"

"Don't be so defensive. Everything was how it should be when you were with Steven, but now you've dragged this guy home whom we know nothing about. He could have a real disaster of career-ending skeletons in his closet."

"Wow!" I jerk my head back. "Don't worry about Darby's happiness. God! That's been the story of my life, but not anymore." I shove my feet into my tennis shoes and bend down to tie them. "You can tell *Cal* that he doesn't even have my vote, so he sure as hell doesn't have a say in who I choose to love. Half my genes, that's all he has, and most days I wish he didn't even have that." I straighten my posture, crossing my arms over my chest.

Rachel stands, rubbing her hands over the front of her skirt. Her lips curl into Satan's smile, then it slips. "*Love?*" she jeers, pinning me with a piercing look. "You're going to get your heart crushed, little girl." She inches closer. "Guys like Trick aren't capable of love. You have no idea what you're getting yourself into." Pulling on her coat, she walks to the front door then turns as she buttons the last button. "Cut him loose, Darby. I'm not *asking*."

My muscles quiver with anger. She's judging Trick without merit the way people have judged me my whole life.

Fuck her!

Darby the *doormat*, no longer. Rogue? They haven't seen anything yet.

I turn up the music so I can actually feel it, then I hop on my bike and ride until my heart threatens to collapse along with the rest of my body.

MY TAKEOUT ARRIVES just as I finish drying my hair. A hard hour of cycling leaves me ready to pass out on the sofa. Fixing my own dinner? Not happening.

My phone chimes the minute I plunk my tired ass down with my Chinese box in hand.

Ugh!

I lumber to my feet again and grab my phone before plopping back down in my seat. "Hey!" I feel guilty for scowling at my phone when I see Trick's photo on my screen.

"Hey, sexy. Miss me?"

"I do, and why is that? Grady says jump and you say how high?" New bolder Darby emerges with a sassy attitude after my earlier confrontation with Rachel. It wasn't that long ago that I was a conformist in the Don't Make Waves Club.

"His *friend* is short a makeup artist for a movie that they're film-ing. She went into labor yesterday. Anyway, her assistant was going to step in since she's been mentored for almost a year, but I guess she wasn't as ready as they had hoped. So I'm here filling in."

I pick at my lo mein noodles with chopsticks. "You're trying to tell me that in all of Los Angeles, there wasn't another person who could fill in?"

"And still allow Grady to be the one who 'saved the day?' No."

"He's doing this to impresses his *friend*, by which I assume you mean lover."

Trick laughs. "You're sharp."

"How long?"

"A week, maybe two. They're almost done filming."

"What about your clients?"

"Grady took care of my schedule."

"He's like your makeup pimp."

"It's a job. With Grady I always have a job."

"Yeah, Grady's a real peach. By the way, I never did ask you why Tamsen was working with you when she came here to visit. She's a paramedic, correct?"

"Grady asked her to come and deal with me."

"What does that mean?"

"Tamsen got me into rehab after I recovered from my accident. Aside from her EMT training, she has experience with drug rehab, so anytime Grady thinks I might be ready to fall off the wagon he calls Tamsen. She shadows me for a few days, and when she's satisfied that I'm not losing my shit again, she goes back home."

"You sound like a real handful."

"Sexy, I think you know from experience that I'm way more than just a *handful*."

"Jeez, here we go again. Don't flatter yourself. I have small hands."

He snickers. I can just see his lips twisting into a devilish smirk. "Think you're pretty brave when you're two thousand miles away from me, huh?"

"I'd say the same thing if you were here. What would you do about it anyway? Fuck me into the elevator gate until I have welts on my back?"

The devil laughs again. "I saw those this morning."

Whoosh!

He just stole my gusto. "You did? Why didn't you say anything?"

"I didn't see the need to get you all worked up."

"I have marks all over my back! My nurse walked in this morning while I was changing and thought I'd been mugged!"

"And your point is?"

My jaw drops but no words escape. How can he ask me that?

"As I recall … let me think … Oh yes, your words were 'fuck

me until the only thing I *feel* is how *hard* you're fucking me.' Does that sound familiar?"

I raise and lower my jaw like a damn puppet, but still no words.

"Well, this morning when I saw your back, it looked like you must have *felt* how *hard* I was fucking you. Like a … a stamp or seal of approval."

"Wh—a—are—are you *serious*?" The shock in my voice reaches opera pitch.

"Were you not?"

"Yes … no … I don't know."

"You could have told me to stop. Did you want me to stop?" That voice … my God it cracks with iciness then drips confidence from his smoldering ego.

"Trick …" I sigh with frustration.

"Darby …" He goads me.

"So what type of movie are they shooting?"

He breathes out a small snickering. "Pornographic, BDSM … nothing too exciting. Just a bunch of naked people grinding on each other."

I set my box of noodles on the coffee table and sit up straight, taking a deep swallow. "Oh, that's … well, does that require a lot of makeup."

"Darby?"

"Hmm?" I hum past the nerves of insecurity.

"I'm just bullshitting you. It's a paranormal film based on a book."

I grab my takeout container like I'm going to throw it at him. Damn! I wish I could beam him in the head with it or knee him in the gut. "I hate you!"

He chuckles. "You don't, but my God you're so gullible. I can just see you biting your lips together until they turn white. I bet your hands are fisted like you want to beat the shit out of me."

I'm nearly crushing the box of noodles and my hand holding the phone is white-knuckled. *Ass!*

"You're just mean."

"You're beautiful."

Melt ...

He manipulates my emotions with mastery.

"I do miss you." I submit to his hold on me—the hold he has, *two thousand* miles away.

"I gotta go. Grady's rolling his eyes and tapping his foot."

"Hi, sweetie! I'm taking our guy out tonight. Kiss. Kiss. Love you!" Grady yells from the background.

"Okay, well ... bye."

"Darby?"

"Yeah?"

"Love you."

"Love you too."

AFTER TWO MORE long days of work and only a short "Good morning, sexy," and a "Goodnight, sexy," text from Trick, I decide to invite Nana over for dinner and cards. She likes Bridge and I like Go Fish so we settle for Cribbage and a bottle of wine with the box of truffles she brought.

"Rachel visited me the other day."

Nana looks up from her cards. "Lucky you."

I sip my wine. "Yeah, lucky me. She basically told me to end things with Trick."

Her brows pull together. "Why would she do that?"

I shrug. "I'm not sure. Some crap about skeletons in his closet and *rogue* family members ending political careers."

She snorts with laughter. "You saw her the other night at dinner. She's bat-shit crazy."

I glance up from my cards, attempting a poker face. "I'm sure she thinks the same thing about you."

Nana pops a truffle into her mouth, eyes rolling back in her head. I think she's of the belief that chocolate is better than sex. I love chocolate, but if Trick came in bite-sized portions wrapped in fancy foil, he'd bankrupt the chocolate industry.

"I am bat-shit crazy, but since I've acknowledged it I'm no longer a danger." She winks. "But Rachel is oblivious to her craziness, which makes her a liability to everyone around her."

"Well her craziness was in overdrive the other day. Before she left she let me know that she's not *asking*. My love life is none of her damn business."

Nana refills our wine glasses. "Is it?"

"Her business?" I squint.

"Love. Is Trick love?"

I sigh with a dreamy grin that appears at just the mention of his name. "Did I tell you he bought me my own helmet and jacket for riding on the back of his *motorcycle*?"

Nana's posture inflates at least six inches until her whole body beams with pride.

My cheeks heat and I feel like a thirteen-year-old girl with my first crush—captain of the football team type crush. The one where all the other girls are catty-bitch jealous that the most popular guy in school only has eyes for the shy girl with pale skin and unruly red hair.

I sip more wine, fading back into my chair, allowing myself to really think about Trick with unguarded feelings and nonjudgemental eyes. "He was the guy I never imagined myself with ... now he's the guy I can't imagine myself without."

Nana's expression softens. "I'm happy for you, dear."

I nod and smile with a few tears in my eyes. "I love him; I'm not even sure it's a choice anymore." I laugh and shake my head. "The truth is he may have a closet full of skeletons, but I wouldn't know and ... I'm not sure he does either."

Nana tilts her head to the side.

"He was in an accident, hit by a car. Now he has partial memory loss, about five years of his life just … gone."

"Oh, Darby …"

I give her a sad smile. "He has trust issues and I think a lot of it stems from the memory loss … well that and the fact he grew up homeless."

Her face contorts into a sad grimace.

"He was homeless at five and orphaned by fifteen. Can you image? A fifteen year old coming home…" I shake my head "…wherever 'home' is when you're homeless, to discover his parents have just vanished. He assumes they're dead and maybe they are, but what if they're not?" I sip my wine. "I don't know what to think, but I do know I love him, even the part he can't share with me. Can you believe he owns a gun?"

Nana shakes her head. "Doesn't mean he's done anything bad with it. A lot of people own guns for protection. I have one in my bedside stand."

WTF?

"Close your mouth, dear. It's not very ladylike."

"Nana—I-I don't know what to say. *You* have a gun?"

She sorts her cards like we're really going to finish this game. "Of course, Bridge club is Tuesday Thursday, Wednesday Friday I go to lunch and shopping with friends, but on Mondays Mary and I go to the shooting range. How'd you think I've managed to keep such muscle definition in these old lady arms?"

"Pilates, Nana. You go to Pilates, not the shooting range."

She snaps her wrist at me with a dismissive *pfft*. "I haven't done Pilates in almost six months, not since Mary had surgery on her knee."

Resting my elbows on the table, I rub my temples, but it doesn't help. This conversation is happening. It's not a dream or *nightmare*.

"My point is that Trick is a smart guy. He didn't grow up under the same circumstances that you did, and he doesn't live in the best neighborhood. You should have him teach you how to use a gun."

I shake my head. "No way. The night he pistol whipped my attacker I was reminded of the violence I clean up after every day and—"

"Darby! You were attacked?"

I grimace. "Sorry, no that's not what I meant. I wasn't attacked. There were these two thugs trying to scare me one night when I left Trick's place. But he came out with a gun and ... it was fine. I'm fine."

She leans forward and rests her hand on my arm. "You should have told me, and you're fine because Trick had a gun with him."

"I don't think the gun mattered. They would have left me alone even if he wouldn't have had a gun." I speak the words, but I have yet to one hundred percent convince myself.

"I think I love him too." She pats my arm, a coy smile tugging at her lips. "Steven wouldn't have known what to do in that same situation. He might have run them over with his canary mobile, but even that wouldn't be too likely. The impact would leave a dent."

"Oh, Nana! Steven's not a bad guy."

"I know, but the more your father liked him the less I did. We have to be suspicious of anyone your father likes too much."

"You know it was Steven's dad, not really Steven."

She tips the wine bottle toward her glass only to discover that it's empty. "Humpf. Well you know what they say, the apple doesn't fall far from the tree."

I sigh. "Then what does that say about me?"

"It says you're your mother's daughter, and believe it or not when she met your father he was a better man. Lucy had impeccable taste in everything. Calvin didn't deserve her, but she made him a better man, until ..." She swallows back uncharacteristic emotion. Nana is a rock, but my mother, Lucille, is an unprotected part of her heart that always elicits a flicker of raw emotion in her eyes.

"Until me," I whisper.

Nana reaches across the table, and grabbing both of my hands she squeezes them tightly. "She chose you, Darby ... we all did."

I let a tear escape. "Is it crazy to miss someone you never knew?"

She reaches up, catching my tear with her thumb. "You know her. I swear she gave you her soul when she died. You're so kind, loving, and forgiving. It's why despite the million reasons your father's given you to disown him, you still love him. That's Lucy in you. I adore you, Darby, and I think it's beautiful the way you love my Lucy, because she sure loved you. For nine months, you owned her heart."

And then she gave me her last heartbeat as I took my first breath.

I blink back more tears. "Thank you, Nana, for giving me a mother's love."

She stands, walks around the table, and hugs me to her chest.

CHAPTER TWENTY-TWO

THERE MUST BE a set amount of time that justifies my missing Trick—desperately missing him. It's probably longer than five days, and if I'm honest with myself, I started to feel it within twenty-four hours of his departure. Pathetic? Yes, but so what.

"Miss me, sexy?"

I sneak into an empty exam room and lean against the door, pressing my phone to my ear, eyes closed. Just for a few moments, I *need* to be seduced by his voice. "I'm a basket case, *and* don't you dare gloat. Just tell me you miss me even half as much as I miss you."

He chuckles and my nipples wake up and scream to my vagina, "Trick's on the phone!" My vagina blushes, a slow drool flows across her lips. "Missing you is worse than rehab. I've got the shakes; I need my Darby fix so fucking bad."

A knock at the door shakes me from my dreamy state. I crack it open.

"Sorry, I didn't know this room was occupied." Jade looks askance at me. "What patient do you have?"

"Nobody, I'm on the phone ... with a ... pharmacist."

"Sorry, I need the room and you have sutures waiting in room two."

I smile against gritted teeth. "One minute, give me one minute."

Jade rolls her eyes. "Fine. One minute."

Bringing the phone back to my ear, I sigh.

"You have to go," Trick says.

"Yes, unfortunately."

"I need to get back to work anyway. The porn stars are coming back to the set."

"You're not funny."

"I'm a little funny."

"Bye."

"Later."

I open the door and Jade stumbles toward my feet. "Were you eavesdropping?"

She rights her step with a quick recovery. "No, I was just getting ready to open the door and tell you your minute's up just as you opened it."

I look at my watch. "I still have thirty seconds." I scowl at her. "You ... were *eavesdropping*."

"Was that Patrick?" She follows me out the door and to the nurses' station like a yippie little dog.

"I told you I was talking to a pharmacist." I grab the chart and start to read over it.

She sidles next to me, nudging me with her shoulder. "I know what you *told* me; now I'm asking for the truth."

Keeping my head down, I grin. "Oh, Jade, Jade, Jade ... if only it were any of your business."

"Oh come on, Darby! Throw me a bone."

I slide the chart over to her. "Okay, Mr. Howard, room four. Possible fractured pelvis ... if I remember correctly that's a bone. Why don't you get me an X-ray?"

She sticks out her tongue. A couple of the other nurses snicker. "You're no fun."

I head toward sutures in two. "Oh, I'm a barrel of fun; you've just never taken the time to get to know my fun side."

This amazing thing has happened since I met Trick. My neediness for acceptance—inclusion—has started to vanish. I don't mean it in a gruff or snobby way; I'd love to be friends with Jade outside of work, but I don't crave it like I did every day of my life before I met him. Trick … he's my best friend. He gave me that before he stole my heart. Then again, I don't think he really stole my heart. I think I gave it to him when I still thought he was Grady's. It's a testament of what his friendship means to me—everything.

✪

DAY ONE MILLION without trick. *Aka day 10.* My heart keeps different time. The good news: I survived the political fundraiser tonight alone. It helped that Rachel's back in New York and my father was too busy to chat about my personal life. The bad news: I have the day off tomorrow and little to take my mind off Trick.

I flip through the channels, read a few chapters in my book, and call it a night. No need to stay awake any longer when Trick awaits in my dreams. In the darkness of night I see him with such vivid-ness—intense blazing eyes and a strong jaw covered in a thick stubble. I rub my hands over it and his lips twitch, my twitch. It's the smallest smirk; the one that says he knows how much I love everything about him. I smell him; it's soap, a rugged sandalwood and pine cologne and those pheromones I could recognize in a room full of men with my eyes closed. My nose nuzzles into his neck; his hands thread through my hair, clenching, bringing me to him. God, I love the way he always fists my hair like I'm his lifeline.

"Trick …"

"I need my Darby fix."

My heart leaps into my throat capturing my breath while I open my eyes because that voice … it's not in my dream.

He's here!

I put my palms on that sexy stubble with slow apprehension, like he could vanish under my touch. The street light filtering through my sheer curtains illuminates life in those amazing eyes. "You're here."

"I'm here." He kisses me and it's a breath of air filling my lungs, feeding my heart, and awakening every cell in my body.

That taste, it's a quenching drink of water with a splash of mint. A warm inviting tongue greets mine with slow but firm strokes—a controlled desperation. Releasing my lips he kisses my cheek while cradling my face. I pull back, just to stare at him. My eyes blink in a rapid flutter.

He gives me what he doesn't give anyone else ... that roguish grin with perfect white teeth while he shrugs off his shirt. The beautiful terrain of muscles and tattoos indulge my eyes. Then he pushes down his jeans and boxer briefs, grin growing as I pull my eyes away from *him* to his eyes ... Dear God, he's his own finest masterpiece. I don't care, he can wear that cocky grin all he wants. After ten days I'm going to unabashedly gawk at every inch of him.

A statue, he stands at the edge of my bed. I drag my drunken gaze back to his eyes again. "Miss me, sexy?"

I dig my teeth into my lower lip to contain my exuberance while I give him a slow nod. He reaches down and pulls my T-shirt over my head. I lie back. He pulls off my panties and kisses a slow trail up my body; my eyelids leaden from his touch.

"Darby ..." he whispers over my lips.

I open my eyes and press my palms to his face.

"I love you." He takes my right leg and pulls it up as he sinks into me.

I fight to keep my eyes open as my breath catches. "I love you too ... so damn much." I breathe out, pulling his face to mine, bending my other knee, and allowing his body to completely claim mine.

BRRR ...

I haven't even thought about turning on the furnace yet because summer is not over. However, fall has made a hail mary and landed two surprisingly cold days into the end of summer. Last night it fell into the forties with rain and gusty winds and now my place is *freezing!* Trick's passed out, and as much as it kills me to leave his warm, naked body, I have to get the heat going in this place just to take the chill off.

"Eek!" The icy floor shocks my toasty toes. Making a mad dash for the thermostat in the hall, I wrap a chenille throw around my naked body. Flipping on the heat, I scurry on the balls of my feet back to the bedroom. An amused face propped up on a tattooed arm greets me.

"What are you doing?" He lifts the covers as I sprint the rest of the way, tossing the throw to the floor and leaping into bed.

I bear hug his warm body, cold nose nuzzled in his neck. "I can't believe I have to turn on my furnace, but it's a cool sixty degrees in here."

He kisses the top of my head. "You seemed plenty warm last night. In fact, I think you were sweating."

I giggle, kissing my way down his chest under the covers. "I was just giving you your Darby fix."

He lifts the covers, tilting his chin to look down at me. "And what are you doing now?" That voice is an acoustic vibrator; it makes every conversation foreplay for me.

I inch my way down, kissing below his navel then licking along the tip of his erection. His hips jerk up. I grin. "Now I'm getting my Trick fix."

He moans as I take him into my mouth. His hands fist my hair and the covers fall back over my head, leaving me in a darkness of pleasure. This has never been my thing ... until Trick. Everything about him is officially *my thing.*

Everything about him leaves me in the most incredible sensory overload. I'm so drunk on him. He moans and tugs at my hair, driving me insane with need. Trick unleashes some untamed part of myself ... I could fucking devour him.

"Darby ... stop ..."

Not happening.

I feel the conflict in his grip on my hair. He starts to pull me away, but his hips pulse toward me, begging for more.

"Fuck ... Darby ... I-I'm ... serious ..."

I ghost my hand over his hip and slide it under his ass, digging my fingers into his tight muscles. For just a few minutes I want to control his body the way he does mine. I want to feel him lose his mind, helpless to my touch.

"Shit ... Darby!" His body goes rigid as I swallow every last drop of his salty essence.

My trip back up his body is just as leisurely as it was going down. Best. Trick. Fix. Ever!

He flips the cover off my head and the smile on his face ... no words, just no ... words.

"Good morning, Mr. Roth." I grin, running my tongue in a seductive circle over my lips.

He shakes his head. "I think it's time for me to return the favor."

Rubbing my lips together, I feel the warm tingle of rosiness spread along my cheeks. "Um, yeah about that..." my nose wrinkles "...I sort of took care of that too..." I dig my teeth into my lip and shrug "...you know, since I had a free hand."

"Jesus, Darby!" Trick squirms under me. I feel him start to come back to life. "Do you have any idea what the thought of you touching yourself with my cock in your mouth does to me?"

I kiss the corner of his mouth then sit up, wrapping the sheet around me. "I have an idea."

"Where are you going?" I've never heard Trick sound anything but raw and masculine, but I detect a hint of a whine in his voice.

I laugh. "Eggs and jellied toast. I'm hungry."

He tugs at my sheet. "But you just ate."

Twisting my body, I free myself from his grip. "Yes, I had my morning dose of zinc, calcium, potassium, fructose, and protein, but it wasn't very filling."

"There's more where that *came* from."

I snort. "I'm sure there is." Standing, I hustle into my closet and pull on a pair of pink plaid flannel lounge pants and a sweatshirt.

He slips into his jeans and tugs his shirt over his head. "I don't think the average woman knows the nutritional composition of semen."

Wrapping my arms around him, I slip my cold hands into his back pockets. He brushes my hair away from my face as I gaze up at him. "I've never been that good at average."

He kisses me, then brushes his nose against mine. "Thank God for that."

✪

"SO WHAT'S MY BFF have planned for us today?" I flip my hair up, shutting off my hair dryer.

Trick leans against the vanity, arms crossed over his bare chest. A few rivulets of water still cling to his messy post-shower hair. "You know I don't respond to your text talk."

I reach up on my toes and kiss the corner of his jaw. "You sure did in the shower. Every time I OMG'd, you gave me more hashtag wowza!" I bat my eyelashes at him. "Emoji winking face. Emoji face blowing a kiss."

I think he growls, but it's so subtle I can't say for sure. The scowl ... that I can't miss. "If your *oral* skills weren't so refined, we'd no longer be friends."

Shoving my dryer in the bottom drawer, I laugh. "Yes, we would be." I hop up on my vanity next to him. "So, Mr. Artistic God to the Stars, what's my face need today?"

Trick stands, turning toward me. I don't know if the day will ever come that I don't feel a twinge of nerves under his expert, scrutinizing gaze. He feathers the back of his hand across my cheek bone, then brushes his thumb along my bottom lip. "You're with me today. Your face doesn't need anything." He slides his hand behind my neck and presses his lips below my ear.

"It doesn't have to be a lot. Maybe some mascara or lip gloss?"

He straightens shaking his head, then turns, sauntering out of the bathroom. "I only hide your perfection from other people. Come."

I'm beginning to lose track of how many times he says something that feels like a defibrillator to my static heart. Trick doesn't claim to be a gentleman, and truthfully he's not, but when it comes to sweeping me off my feet he has the biggest fucking broom I've ever seen.

"Where are we going?" I brush past him to my closet as he slips on his shirt.

"My place. I want to show you something."

"If it's your arsenal of weapons, I don't want to see it, but Nana might."

He leans into my closet doorway, resting his hands on either side. "I don't have an arsenal. I have a gun … or two."

I glance up at him while tugging on my boots.

"Your nana's into weaponry?"

"I don't know if she has a machete or a grenade belt, but she has a handgun in her nightstand."

Trick's eyes crinkle in the corners as a smirk plays across his face.

I duck under his arm and grab my phone off the nightstand. "That's only half of it. She and her friend, Mary, go to the shooting range every Monday."

"That's … awesome." He turns.

"Awesome?" I shake my head, heading toward the stairs. "I don't think senior citizens with arthritic hands, glaucoma, dementia, and a slew of other issues should be packing."

"They probably offer an AARP discount at the shooting range."

"I also don't think you should be allowed to have a handicap parking permit *and* a gun permit." I pull on my jacket.

"Now that's not true and you know it. In fact, it's just the opposite; people with disabilities can feel vulnerable and they definitely need a way to protect themselves."

"Brilliant. Before long I'll be writing prescriptions for handguns."

"Well, if it bothers you, maybe you should write your senator about it."

I give Trick the stink eye before he walks past me to the back door. He slips on his socks and black boots that are sitting by his suitcase. "You're driving. I took a cab here from the airport."

My heart swells at the thought of him coming to my place straight from the airport. If he weren't still here, I'd blow up his phone with chat acronyms and Emojis.

CHAPTER TWENTY-THREE

SEVERAL PHOTOGRAPHERS GREET us with flashes and coy smiles while I back my car out the garage.

"What the hell?" Trick jerks his head away from their intrusive lenses just inches from my windows.

"Countdown to the polls. The campaigns are making their official shift from throwing sand at the playground to digging their opponent's grave."

"Why take our picture? What are we?"

I give Trick a sidelong glance. "Dirt."

"Am I going to be an *issue?*"

I chuckle. "God, I hope so."

"Why would you say that?" There's an iciness to his words. "Are you using me to rebel? Slumming with the homeless guy?"

He's taking the defensive like he did shortly after we met. I was ten percent angry and ninety percent turned on then, but now it flat out pisses me off that he would think that about me. I get he has trust issues, but I'd hoped by now they wouldn't be with me.

"Thanks for the trust, but no, I'm not using you to rebel." I sigh. "Rachel visited me the other day and basically told me to stop seeing you. She fears you have too many 'skeletons' in your closet that could destroy my father's chance for re-election."

Trick's eyes stay focused on the road ahead.

"She also thinks you're going to crush my heart and that you're incapable of loving me." I expect a response. I need a response, but he's still a statue—no response, no emotion.

"So if you define rebelling as giving my father and his wife the proverbial finger by not allowing them to decide who I choose to love, then maybe I am a rebel. But if the issue here is you not *trusting* me, then maybe Rachel's right. Maybe you're going to crush my heart."

Still nothing.

My heart knows him, of that much I am certain—my head, not so much. Trick would never hurt me on purpose, but broken is broken. This heart of mine won't care how it happened; the pain will feel the same.

His door opens as I push my newly programmed button. I put my car in park but I don't shut off the engine.

I will not be Darby the Doormat!

He reaches over, shutting off the car. I stare at him, waiting, because he's going to have to give me a good reason to open my door. I fight the urge to melt into his hand as he caresses his palm against my cheek.

"I'd never forgive myself if I crushed your heart." Releasing a slow breath, he closes his eyes for a moment. "I'm sorry for what I said. You might be the *only* person I completely trust ... including myself."

My lips pull into a sad smile as I cover his hand with mine and lean into his touch. "That's what BFFs are for."

That earns me a lip twitch, but I know he's fighting the full-on smile.

"Come." He gets out and so do I—because I want to, not because he told me.

He pushes the button to lower the door and then flips several other switches. I'd suspected this garage or warehouse space expanded farther than what I've ever been able to see with the limited lighting from the one set of fluorescents or the natural light from the large door. What I didn't expect was the massive amount of *stuff*.

"What is all this? Is it yours?" There's more than just the one covered automobile, four to be exact. At a quick glance I see three more motorcycles, a set of jet skis, stacks of boxes, and at the very back there are more covered objects that look like his artwork that had been upstairs.

"This…" he points to the partially covered black Audi SUV "…is Grady's. But the rest is supposedly mine." He shoves his hands into his pockets and watches me as I take slow steps deeper into the maze of everything.

"It's from your missing past?"

"Yes."

"Where was it?" I lift the edge of another car cover. It's a lime green Lamborghini.

"A warehouse in Queens, much like this one."

"Your place?"

"Yes. I don't remember living there, but it was the address on my license and the building was purchased in my name and completely paid for just like everything in it … everything here."

"Did you have a roommate?" I flip open the lid to a box. It's filled with gaming equipment.

"Not that I know of. Word on the street was that I lived alone."

"Were you a dealer?"

"I don't think so, yet it's the only logical explanation. Nobody I talked to knew me as a dealer, just an addict."

I knock on the top of a safe that's had the lock busted on it. "What was in here?"

"Money."

"How much?"

"Enough."

"Where is it now?"

"I donated most of it to an outreach program for the homeless."

I nod. "So why keep everything else? Why transfer it to a similar warehouse here in Chicago?"

"I couldn't stay in New York for a number of reasons, but Grady and Tamsen thought recreating my living environment, including all of my stuff, might help bring back my memory. The upstairs is almost identical as well, same furniture, lighting, even the appliances are identical."

"Why couldn't you stay in New York?" I peek in another large box. It's filled with framed artwork. No one I recognize; they're all numbered prints.

"Grady needed me in Chicago, but also it wasn't safe for me to stay. I was at a disadvantage; there were too many people who knew me, but I didn't know them. I didn't know who I could trust, and apparently I didn't hang with the crowd that was welcoming me with open arms ready to fill in the blanks of my past."

Taking my time, peeking in a few more boxes here and there, I worm my way to the far end. Trick follows me, keeping a consistent distance between us. It's as if he's giving me space … space to look through everything … space to process everything.

The mix of belongings is odd. I'm not sure I can see Trick having purchased all this stuff with drug money. Something tells me these things were gifts. I want to ask him if he's sure his parents were his real parents, but that's a subject I don't think I can broach. It's just that everything around me feels *familiar*, not the stuff itself, more the *feeling* of it all. I grew up with people giving me stuff; for wealthy people it's easier to give money than it is time. My father showered me with gifts, but never his attention. Even Nana did it on a rare occasion.

Was someone giving Trick one thing because they couldn't give him another?

I stop where there feels like an invisible line. Everything before here is randomly scattered around. What I assume to be Trick's artwork is organized and carefully draped. I think I have his unspoken permission to continue, but this feels personal. Before I was browsing at things like I would at an auction, but touching what's in front of me would feel like snooping, an invasion of his privacy.

I look back at him. He leans against a steel support beam, hands crossed over his chest. "Go ahead." He nods.

My gaze falters for a moment before meeting his again. "Will *you* show me?"

Pushing off the beam, he moves without hesitation, like he knows exactly what he wants to show me first. As he pulls away the sheet, my heart surges upward, strangling my throat. I can't breathe. It's a photograph of a homeless couple slouched against each other sleeping. They're dressed in tattered layers, sitting on flattened cardboard boxes against a brick building backdrop. Their hands are gloved but their fingers are intertwined. It's heartbreaking and heartwarming at the same time.

"My parents."

I nod, biting my lips together while taking in a shaky breath. "You took this picture?"

Trick shakes his head. "I drew it."

What?

Squinting, I step closer, leaning so my face is within inches of it. The shadows, the exactness of detail, every wrinkle, every eyelash, skin peeling from their dry lips ... my God it's not possible. The realism is indescribable. I was brought to my knees in awe when I thought it was a photograph, but this ... "Trick, where did you learn to do this?"

"I don't know, I mean ... I didn't. I've never been able to explain it other than my hands are good at recreating what my eyes have seen." He removes another sheet, and another, and another until I feel dizzy. My head cannot make sense of this. They're all people or parts of their body. Hands holding a book, toes curling in grass, lips sipping from a drinking fountain. *Unbelievable!* The water from the fountain looks so real I swear it would feel wet if I touched it.

"Has it ever occurred to you that maybe your money came from selling your art?"

He chuckles. "Maybe when I've been dead for a century."

"I'm serious, Trick. These could easily go for thousands of dollars—conservatively."

"So you think during the five missing years of my life, at least some of which I was strung out on drugs, I was selling my sketches, which can take up to two hundred hours to complete one, for..." he gestures to everything else in the room "...hundreds of thousands of dollars?"

I shrug. "Maybe you have a rich uncle ... maybe you won the lottery. How much money was in your checking account after the accident?"

"Less than two hundred dollars." He nods toward the safe. "Apparently I paid for things in cash."

"So aside from the pastor, you didn't question friends, neighbors ... anyone?"

"Just like here, I didn't have neighbors to question. The only friends I can remember are from high school but they were long gone by then, and according to my bills, I owned a cell phone but it was never found. I'm sure the numbers under a contact list would have been helpful. Grady had a friend check into my phone records, but most of the calls were to private numbers. Probably drug dealers. I don't know." He sighs, running his hands through his hair. "It's all so fucked-up."

"Do you want to know?"

His brow tenses. "What do you mean?"

"I mean, you had all that cash. Why didn't you hire a private investigator to dig into your past, fill in the blanks?"

He shrugs. "Once Grady and Tamsen got me through rehab, they convinced me to leave that part of my life behind. I don't know, like my memory loss was a blessing of sorts. It's not that they didn't want my memory to come back. Obviously they went to a lot of work to make this place a reminder of my past. They just want it to be all or nothing. They want me to remember it … not figure it out."

"Is that what you want? Do you believe it's a blessing that you don't remember?"

He scratches his neck, eyes fixed in contemplation. "I think it's a blessing that I'm clean and sober because I'm not sure I would be had I not lost my memory. But feeling like something or someone from those missing five years could come back to haunt me is the part that feels more like a curse.

"What could haunt you?"

Trick takes slow steps toward me; a wrinkling of worry distorts his handsome face. "Anything that could take you away from me." With a whisper touch he glides his fingers along my cheeks and down my neck.

I rest my hands on his forearms, closing my eyes. "I'm not going anywhere."

"What if I've fathered a dozen children?"

I smile, fluttering my eyes open, a laugh escaping. "Then you'll have to sell some of this stuff to get paid up on child support."

"I'm serious. You're not the first woman I've been with."

I laugh again. "Well, you're not the first man I've been with … not even close." I pull away from him and start covering up his sketches.

"What if I killed someone?"

I swallow hard but keep my hands busy so he doesn't see me flinch. "Then I'll hope the court grants us conjugal visits." I reply, controlling my nerves and censoring my reaction.

"You're saying this because you don't think it's true. But what if it were?" It's not always a look, with Trick it's often just a feeling. Maybe it's something only I can feel. I used to think it was a challenge, part of his take-me-or-leave-me personality. But as of lately that *feeling* holds a hint of fear … insecurity.

"What if I die tomorrow? What if you do? What if terrorists

attack our city?" I deflate; there really are no words of comfort. "I choose to love you now because there's no future in what ifs, there's *only* now."

Eyes. On. Me. God, he has the most commanding gaze, a predatory look, that hunted feeling of being cornered where surrender is the only way to survive. "Come."

✪

NAKED UNDER A blanket on the couch with Trick, sipping cocoa after incredible sex, it can't possibly get any better than this.

"When did you first realize your talent?" I lean back against his chest and sip my chocolate bliss.

"The beginning of my sophomore year in high school. Alicia Watson, she was a senior and had the biggest rack I'd ever seen. She was *experienced* and I told her I was too, but it was actually my first time. Rumors of my *skills,* all true of course, spread like wild fire within days."

I twist my body toward him. "What are you talking about?"

He takes a sip, using his mug to hide his smirk. "My talent. After what just happened ... you know, the screaming and begging ... I assumed you were referring to my sexual talent."

"Oh my God!" I turn back around and elbow him in the gut, almost spilling my cocoa. "The only thing that could have spread like *wild fire* is your ego. And they're *breasts* not a rack!"

He continues to chuckle as his free hand slides up to my breast. "These are breasts..." he circles his thumb over my nipple "...Alicia had a rack, and for the record, I'm a breast guy." I feel his erection push against my back.

My eyelids grow heavy as Trick sets his drink down and mine next to it. He uses both hands to caress my breasts, bringing my nipples to firm peaks. Arching my back to his touch, I moan. My eyes flutter open. "What is that?" I squint.

He sucks my earlobe into his mouth, teasing it with his teeth.

"What's what?" he mumbles, dragging his tongue down my neck.

I place my hands over his, stopping his motion. "Attached to the electrical conduit pipe. Is that a ..."

"Camera." He starts to squeeze my breasts again, his breath hot in my ear.

"Camera?"

"For security. Don't worry, I'm the only one who can look at the footage."

"Oh my God! Is it always recording?"

"It's motion-activated." He nips and sucks at my neck some more while his right hand slides down my abdomen.

He moans and I feel a bead of moisture against my back as his hips rock up, his firm erection sliding against my skin. "Fuck, Darby ... your body is so damn sexy." His middle finger pushes over my clit between my slick folds.

Everything is such a blur when he touches me, but it doesn't stop my eyes from trying to focus on the camera. We have a blanket over us, but is it really masking our movements?

Are we being recorded? Do I care? Oh hell!

Trick tosses the blanket off us with one hand while his other slides down farther. An uncontrolled moan escapes as his finger slides into me. "I want to see you come, sexy."

The camera ...

"Spread your legs wider ..."

I spread them and his finger slides the rest of the way in.

"That's it." His words ... his voice ... it turns me on as much as his touch. "Look at yourself ... every peak..." he pinches my nipple "...every valley..." he rubs his palm against my clit as he finger fucks me into oblivion "...every curve..." his hand slides from my breast to my hip, and clenching it hard he pulls me back against him, his erection finding more friction against my back "...you're just. So. Fucking. Beautiful."

I rock my pelvis into his hand, arch my back, and reach behind, clenching his hair. "Trick, oh my God …"

The camera …

"I'm so close, d-don't stop …"

The camera … the camera … Oh FUCK! The camera!

It hits me so hard I could die right here on the spot. The camera has been haunting me, but not because it's recording what's happening now or even the numerous times we've had sex before today.

"Oh God!"

"Let it go, sexy." Trick's voice grits next to my ear.

Shoving his hand away while thrashing my body like a trapped animal, I leap from the couch with frantic urgency. I grab the blanket off the floor and wrap it around my body.

"What the hell?" Trick yells with wide-eyed confusion.

"You have to erase everything that's been recorded on the camera since you met me. *Please*, I'm begging you. Don't ask questions, don't watch it, just erase it. Promise me, Trick, promise me you'll just do this for me. If you love me, you'll just say yes. Okay?" I don't think I've ever felt so desperate in my life. My heart pounds with anxiety, fueled by every nerve in my body firing with blood curdling fear.

Trick looks at me like I've transformed into an alien and maybe I have.

"PLEASE!" I drop to my knees. I *actually* … Drop. To. My. Knees.

Trick sits up and leans forward with his elbows on his knees. The cockiest smirk I have ever seen pulls at his lips. "Darby Lucille Carmichael, what the fuck has got you worked up into such a frenzy?" His gaze drops to my hands and so does mine.

I didn't think it was possible to look or sound any more pathetic. I was wrong. My fingers are interlaced and white knuckled at my chest. I've been stripped of my dignity, robbed of my self-respect, and put on display in the town square with a noose around my neck.

At this point I don't know if I prefer the stay of execution or the floor to fall out from under my feet.

My phone rings and I manage to deflate even more. I crawl, *yes crawl*, over to the table because I'm not done begging. I answer it, keeping my eyes on Trick's as one of the nurses from the hospital informs me of a multiple injury accident requiring extra staff. After a clipped response, I press *End*.

Sitting back on my heels, blanket lost along the way, I rub my hands over my face.

"You have to go?" Trick asks.

I nod, blown away by the timing. Some idiot was probably pre-occupied on their cell phone causing a huge accident riddled with casualties. I should take this opportunity to count my blessings and realize my issue is nothing compared to the victims on their way to the hospital. But I'm human and a very selfish part of me feels like one of the casualties today.

"We can continue this *intriguing* conversation later." Trick stands, pulling on a gray pair of sweat pants while I dress with swift moves.

"If you don't erase it or if you watch it, we're over." I pull on my shirt and shove my phone into my handbag.

Trick grabs my waist and jerks me into his bare chest. "We're never over." He nips at my pouty bottom lip.

I shove his chest and head to the elevator. "We are if you don't do what I ask. If you watch that I swear I will hate you forever!"

I turn and shut the elevator gate, a stern warning on my face.

"Yeah, well I've been the recipient of your so-called *hate* before, and I think it's kinda hot." He wets his lips. "Besides, I was here. Is there a particular performance you're not proud of?"

I press the down button, scowling as he disappears.

Yes, Trick! I'm not particularly proud of the "performance" where I mas-turbated while watching you shower ... more than once!

CHAPTER TWENTY-FOUR

THIRTEEN PEOPLE WERE involved in the accident, eight survived ... for now, and two of the eight survivors are children. Their parents were both casualties. A younger version of Trick flashes in my head. One day your parents are here, the next day they're gone. Yet, I still can't piece that part of his past together. It doesn't make any sense.

It's nearly eleven at night by the time I get home and my next shift is in the morning. Trick hasn't tried calling or texting. I have to hope for the small silver lining to this emotional day—he erased the recordings *without* watching them first. Trick may be introverted, but I bring out his cocky side and I know he wouldn't wait one second to call me about my 'performance' so I don't think he's watched it.

The faster we can forget about all my performances, including my meltdown this afternoon, the better. I take the lead by sending off a quick text as if nothing happened.

Me: *Just got home. Sooo tired. Dinner tomorrow? Love you <3*

I don't wait for a response. Instead, I jump in the shower then dry my hair and collapse into bed. The instant I shut off my light, my phone chimes.

Trick: *Yes to dinner. Sleep well. Love you.*

I sigh, closing my eyes. Trick has earned my trust big time. If it weren't for the fact that I don't want to ever mention it again, I would send him a candy land of Emojis thanking him for respecting my wishes. Trick's the best … the very, very best!

JUST A FEW short months ago I met my best friend; then my dreams came true. I was a caterpillar until the metamorphosis of his love set me free, and now I fly high … so high on every thought of him.

Point A to point B … It's all bliss racing across town from a job I love to the man I love. Does one person deserve to be this happy? I park in the garage, *my* garage spot, and take the elevator upstairs. It's dark and silent, so I assume Trick is still working. Maybe I should get naked on the bed and wait for him. Then again, he'll be hungry and so am I. Maybe sex can wait.

Drumming my nails on the kitchen counter I contemplate making dinner for us. I'm sure Trick thinks my only useful skills are sex and sutures. Inspecting the cabinets and refrigerator, I realize my options are minute. A trip to the grocery store is in order, so I decide to pop down and let Trick know my plans.

As I walk by the window, I see him in his zone. The sexy intensity on his face when he works does all sorts of crazy stuff to my body. Opening the door, the curly-haired brunette shifts her gaze to me, but mine goes to her hand, fingers slipped inside Trick's front pocket. He, as usual, doesn't acknowledge me. I glare at her while assessing the situation. For a split second I give her the benefit; maybe she's unstable on the stool and using him for balance. But when her knee begins to rub along the inside of his leg the balance excuse vanishes.

"I'm sure he'd appreciate you keeping your hands and *legs* to yourself." I lean against the checkout counter.

Trick doesn't turn in my direction, or even flinch to acknowledge that I've just spoken. The brunette smirks. *The fucking bitch actually smirks!* And because she's just that stupid, she sits up straighter, arching her back and shoving her silicon balloons within an inch of Trick's chest. I don't need an Urban Dictionary from Jade to know that *this bitch is gonna die!*

I push off the counter and march up next to Trick. "I'm going to get a few groceries," I say through gritted teeth while wrapping my hand around stupid's wrist and removing it from Trick's pocket.

"You did *not* just touch me?" She raises her brows like I've committed a crime.

Trick finally looks over at me then down at my hand clenched around her wrist. "Darby," he warns.

I release her wrist. "Yes," I smile, batting my lashes at him.

"I don't know who she thinks she is, but if she touches me again—"

Trick holds up his finger to her while looking at me. "Darby was just leaving."

My eyes go wide while cocking my head to the side. "I was?"

"Groceries … go."

Trick may not want to make waves, but if he doesn't put an end to this I'm going to be the goddamn tsunami that does.

The brunette smirks and … *No way!* How many shades of stupid is this broad? Her hand goes back to his pocket.

"If you want all your fingers to work when you walk out of here, I suggest you keep your *hands*. To. Yourself!" I grab her hand with a little more force.

"Hands off, bitch!" she yells, yanking her wrist from my grasp.

"Darby!" Trick growls.

"You get *your* hands off, *bitch*!" I try to wedge myself between her and Trick, getting up in her face.

Trick wraps his arms around me from behind, lifting me off my feet.

"Let me go!" I yell.

"Quiet!" he grinds in my ears while hauling me off toward the back. Opening the infamous storage closet door, he drops me and slams the door behind us.

I whip around, hands fisted, jaw clenched. "She's groping you!"

"You're making a scene." He leans forward toward my face.

I stand by my original claim. "She's. Groping. You!"

"She's a fly on my ass. When I'm working I don't notice so it doesn't matter."

I shove his chest, forcing him to step back until his back hits the door. "It matters to me!"

He shakes his head. "I've got to get back out there. We'll discuss this later."

"Don't you *dare* walk away from me!" I warn as he turns to open the door.

"Or what?"

I draw in a shaky breath. "Or you'll break my fucking heart. Because somewhere over the past few months I got the impression that you love me."

His shoulders slump, back still to me.

"And when Grady invited all those people over you said *these hands*, only *these hands*. Was that a lie?"

His hand moves back, clasping mine. I close my eyes. As frustrating as Trick can be, it will never go unnoticed by me just how much he gives of himself to me. Sometimes it's more than I think he really has to give. But even for him, I will not be a doormat.

He opens the door and leads me out to an obviously perturbed brunette. Pulling up another stool off to his right, he keeps hold of my hand while I climb up on it. Brunette tries to burn a hole in my skull with her evil eyes as Trick brings his mouth to my ear.

"I *do* love you."

He releases my hand and gives his focus back to her. My heart stands idle in my chest as her hand reaches for his pocket.

"Hands off," Trick says while rouging her cheeks.

He resuscitates my heart. Her whole body goes rigid as all the color drains from her shocked face. I don't give her another glance. There's only one person in this room worthy of my attention— Trick ... only Trick.

He finishes up, takes her money, and locks the door after she leaves. When he turns, my lips turn up into a sheepish smile. He walks back to me with that damn unreadable look. Hands go straight to my hair as he leans down and rubs his nose against mine. I slip my hands under his shirt, and he steps closer as I slide them up his back, digging my fingers into him. A silent claim that he is in fact *mine*.

"Darby?"

Here comes the lecture.

I close my eyes as his lips ghost over mine. "Hmm?"

"Marry me."

CHAPTER TWENTY-FIVE

3 Days Earlier

I'M NOT PROUD of looking through Darby's phone contacts, but I need something I can't ask her for—answers. Right now, there's only one person who I *know* has them.

"Rachel Hart," she answers her phone in an exasperated voice.

"How do you know me?"

Her silence confirms my suspicions.

"Who is this?"

"How did we meet?"

"I don't know what you're—"

"Stop lying to me!"

She sighs with impatience. "I met you when my *stepdaughter* brought you to dinner."

"You knew I wouldn't recognize you, but you were still nervous ... *that's* what I recognized."

"You're delusional."

"I fucked you."

She snickers, unable to hide her nerves. "Don't flatter yourself. I'm a married woman."

"I love Darby."

"You don't know what love is." The piercing edge to her voice unmasks her façade. "If you have a working cell left in your brain, you'll walk away and never contact me or Darby ever again."

"Because I fucked you?"

"Get. This. You pathetic waste of space, I am a self-made woman and I can guarantee you no man has ever *fucked* me!" She hangs up.

Just what I was afraid of … *she* fucked *me*.

CHAPTER TWENTY-SIX

"W HAT DID YOU just say?" My fingers dig deeper into his back.

Trick closes his eyes and brushes his lips across my forehead, down my cheek, finding home at my mouth. "Marry me, Darby Carmichael." He opens his eyes to mine ... my eyes that ... Can. Not. Blink. "You're the only memory I ever want. So can you do that? Can you give *me ... you ...* forever?"

Oh my God! Oh my God! Oh my God!

Tears. So many tears for a friendship I never imagined, a love only found in dreams, and a man that has captured my heart so completely I can only breathe when I'm in his arms.

Trick brushes the back of his hand over my cheek and kisses me with beautiful patience and fragility. "Say yes, Darby," he whispers with a vulnerability that pulls at every one of my heartstrings.

The mind speaks with reason and logic. The heart ... it doesn't speak, it just *feels*. But here's the thing about feelings ... they are the unspoken truth.

"Yes."

He wipes my tears. "Yes ..." That smile, those white teeth, they're for *me*!

Now he kisses me like I'm his, *forever*.

Logic wants in so bad, but I'm not ready to share this moment with anyone or anything other than Trick.

"Come." He takes my hand and leads me out the door.

"Where are we going?" I ask as he pulls me in the opposite direction of his place.

"Grocery shopping. Wasn't that the real reason for your visit?"

I suppose some guys might suggest a trip to Tiffany's or to the nearest bed to celebrate, but my guy's taking me grocery shopping. The perfect part ... I wouldn't have it any other way.

"I LIKE LINGUINE," Trick announces as I grab a box of spaghetti.

I purse my lips to the side and exchange the box for fettuccine. Trick smirks. We spend the next forty-five minutes making compromises and learning about each other's food preferences beyond eggs, strawberry jelly, and multigrain bread. We haven't mentioned the words engagement, wedding, or marriage since leaving Rogue Seduction, yet our shopping says it all. We're planning forever and sometimes forever starts with something as simple as pasta.

We walk back to his place, both hands loaded with sacks of food. Words are sparse, but the sidelong glances with sexy smiles are plentiful. Bliss. It's pure bliss.

"I'm going to take a quick shower," Trick announces as I put the salmon, that we agreed on, in the oven.

"Okay."

"I'll be about ten minutes if that helps you gauge the time."

I wash my hands and grab a towel. "The salmon will take about twenty, so you should be fine."

He shrugs off his shirt on the way to the bathroom. "I wasn't talking about the fish. I just didn't know if ten minutes would be enough time for you to do *your thing* while I'm in the shower."

I squint in confusion. He attempts to hide his grin by biting his bottom lip. And then it hits me.

"Oh my God!" My skin flames with embarrassment and anger. "You watched that?"

I throw the towel at him, but it only makes it a couple feet. Then I grab my purse and stomp toward the elevator. He hooks his arm around my waist and hauls me over to the bed.

"Let me down!"

Tossing me on the bed he straddles me, pinning my flailing arms above my head. With my eyes squeezed shut, I thrash my head side to side. "Let me go! I trusted you!"

"Darby ..."

"We're over. Don't Darby me!"

He holds me in place but doesn't say anymore. After all my resistance siphons the last drop of energy from my body, I open my eyes. "I'm so embarrassed," I whisper between labored breaths, averting my gaze.

"I'm so in love."

Damn him!

I look at him and he kisses me. Our tongues slide against each other, soft moans vibrating between our mouths. Releasing my hands and my lips, he sits up and undresses me with hungry eyes but patient hands. My tongue eases out, wetting my lips as he stands to remove his pants.

"Never stop looking at me this way," he says with vulnerable emotion in his deep voice.

I move my gaze up his body until I meet his eyes. "Never stop loving me this way."

He takes my foot, pressing his lips to my arch. "Never," he whispers.

IT TAKES US both a few seconds to realize the smoke and fire alarm going off is not from our steamy lovemaking.

"Shit!" Trick jumps out of bed and runs to the kitchen.

With hot pads on his hands, he takes the salmon out of the oven, naked. *You don't see that every day.* I wrap a blanket around myself and tiptoe behind him. "It was supposed to be lemon-pepper, but blackened is fine too."

He gives me a wry look, then glances up to the ceiling. As if on cue, the alarm stops. He pulls off the hot pads then tugs my blanket away. "Where was I?"

I giggle and grab the blanket. Wrapping it around my back, I hold it open in the front. Trick hugs my naked body while hoisting me up and carrying me back to bed, blanket wrapped around both of us. He lays us down, me on top of him, our faces hidden under a curtain of unruly red hair.

"I can't believe you said yes."

Hours later, and here it is, the first acknowledgement that what I think happened wasn't just a dream.

I smile. "I can't believe you asked."

For one rare moment, there's translucency to his emotions; right now I feel his thoughts. They're the ones that can't imagine why I'd agree to marry someone after only a few months—someone with a troubled, unknown past.

"I know you're wondering why I would say yes to the dark part of your life that you don't even understand yourself." I kiss the corner of his mouth. "But I don't think you have any idea how honored I feel to be invited into the parts of you that can't be seen. And tonight…" I tear up "…you chose me. Every time I hold my breath … hoping, praying, *needing* you to choose me … you do. You chose me and the last time someone chose me was the day I was born … and then she died."

Trick kisses my tear-stained cheeks while his hand cups the back of my head—the loving gesture I've come to know, expect, and cherish. "I'll always choose you."

IT'S AFTER NINE o'clock before we manage to separate long enough to make a new dinner—cold cereal with bananas. So much for showing off my culinary skills. I think his place is going to smell like burnt salmon for the next six months.

"Can we talk about the video?" Trick nudges my leg as we eat our cereal, sitting on the sofa at opposite ends, legs in the middle.

"No." I scowl.

"It was when you still thought I was gay."

I spoon around the last few floating wheat squares and bobbing bananas in my bowl, keeping my head down. What I'm not doing is engaging in this conversation.

"Want to know what I thought when I saw it?"

"No."

"I was so fucking turned on."

I roll my eyes. Apparently he doesn't know what "no" means.

"Because you have to know I was thinking of you. God, since the first day I met you, it's all I could do. Seeing you, touching you, smelling you, fucking *sleeping* with you and your hands all over me, face in my neck. If I wasn't touching myself fantasizing about you, I was drowning in ice water."

I risk a timid glance up, face still red. His impish grin does nothing to help my embarrassment.

"Okay…" I sit up and start to stand "…I think that's enough."

He grabs my waist, pulling me back to the sofa. "*But…*" he waits for me to look at him "…but then I felt guilty, like a complete asshole for ever letting you believe anything but the truth, because when it was over … when you had *finished* … "

I shake my head and try to pull away again, but his firm hold prevents my escape. "Look at me."

I feel more exposed than I have ever felt in my life.

"After the fact, I saw the pain in your face—the shame, the guilt, the agony of probably thinking *we* would never be. And a little part of me died in that moment." He sets our bowls down on the table and kneels in front of me, nose to nose. "I'm sorry, Darby. I'm just so fucking sorry."

I nod and he kisses me. My hands frame his stubbly face. "So you erased the video?"

His head jerks back. "No fucking way! It may be sad, but it's still the hottest fucking porn I've ever seen."

My hand makes its way to slap the shit out of him, but he intercepts and pins me to the back of the couch. "God I love your feistiness." He attacks my neck. "And I can't wait for you to touch yourself for me."

I wriggle in his grasp. "*That* will *never* happen."

He bites my nipple through my T-shirt. "Oh ... mark my word ... it'll happen."

THE GIRL WHO doesn't trust men is marrying the boy who doesn't trust women. What. Are. The. Chances?

There was no getting down on one knee and there was no ring, yet it was the most unexpected and beautiful proposal. I'm dying to tell someone. Jade is a possibility, but I know she'd never keep it to herself, and I'm not ready to tell the world. This is where that BFF since kindergarten that I never had would come in handy. Nana will find out as soon as I leave work, but it has to be in person; that's why I can't tell her yet.

I have to tell someone!

> **Me:** I need to tell my BFF something. Can you be my BFF and ONLY my BFF for a few moments?
>
> **Trick:** Yes, I can be your "friend" – what's up?
>
> **Me:** Last night the man that gives my heart complete purpose asked me to marry him. It was breathtakingly unexpected and utterly insane ... but I said yes anyway because he's the dream that all other dreams dream of being. Do you think I'm crazy?
>
> **Trick:** Yes. But I think he's one lucky bastard!

I text him back five heart and kiss Emojis—he doesn't reply.

On the way to Nana's it occurs to me that I have no idea how my father proposed to my mother. He, of course, has never talked about it and neither has Nana. I can imagine it being a big production in front of a lot of people, an expensive ring and scripted emotions. Maybe in another life I'll be the girl who wants to marry someone just like her father, but it's not this one.

"Hey, Nana it's me, open up."

The door buzzes and I bounce up the stairs with exuberance.

"Well, this is an unexpected surprise. I thought we were having lunch tomorrow."

I hug her. "We are, but I have something to tell you and it can't wait."

She holds me at arm's length, looking at me with narrowed eyes. "Rachel and your father are parting ways?"

"What? No! I mean, that would be some amazing news too, but no."

She deflates a little and walks into her kitchen. "Wine?"

"No. I just need to say this, Nana!"

She grabs a wine glass and pours herself a generous serving of Merlot. "I'm all ears, dear."

Warmth radiates through my body as my heart drums in my chest. "I'm getting married!"

Nana stops mid sip, swallows, and gasps. "What did you say?"

Internally, I laugh. I said those same words to Trick.

"I'm getting married. Trick proposed last night."

"Oh, sweetie, that's—" She hugs me.

"Crazy, insane, out of the blue, too soon, unexpected … I know, but I said yes anyway."

"Wonderful … I was going to say wonderful." She kisses my cheek and gestures for me to sit next to her at the table. "I assume you haven't told your father? Or did Trick ask for his *blessing.*"

I snort. "No, I haven't told anyone but you. And Trick's still alive, so it's safe to assume he didn't' ask for my father's blessing."

"So when are you going to tell him?"

I shrug. "I don't know … never."

"I hope you both have current passports because when he finds out you're going to have to flee the country." She wiggles her eyebrows while sipping her wine, then swallows, followed by a dreamy sigh. "But forbidden love is so romantic."

"You make it sound so tragic."

She grabs my left hand. "Where's the ring?"

"He didn't give me one. Honestly, I don't think he planned it. It was as if in that exact moment he decided he wanted to marry me. I love that he didn't even have to think about it; he just … knew. And I did too."

Nana's smile spread across her petite facial features. I've been waiting all day with impatient anticipation to share this with her and this is why—she's genuinely happy for me.

"So when's the big day going to be?"

I drum my fingers on the table. "I don't know. I mean, one minute he's proposing and the next we're walking to the grocery store like any other ordinary day. We haven't really talked about it. I don't know if he's thinking a month from now or a year. But it doesn't matter. I just want to be with him. Hell, I'd go down to the Justice of Peace and marry him tomorrow."

Truth.

I'd gamble on him and his unknown past without so much as a blink. I'm willing to say "screw it" and just figure it out as we go.

CHAPTER TWENTY-SEVEN

"**G**RADY, GO."

"My God you sure do try to sound important." I shake my head, boots propped up on the counter, waiting for my next client.

"Says my swoon-worthy God of all things color. I'm shopping for suits. You never call me, what's up?"

"I asked Darby to marry me and I think her stepmom fucked me."

"Out, out ... everyone out. This is an emergency." Grady's in panic mode, and everyone around him should be too. He's unpredictable when he feels like he's losing control over me. "Have you gone mad?"

"I'm not asking for your permission or even your advice. But you and Tamsen are the closest people I have to family, and I'll never be able to repay you for what you've done, so out of respect I wanted to let you know."

"I'll be on the first flight out of LAX."

"Grady! I don't need you to come rescue me."

"I'm not *even* ready to address you proposing to Senator Carmichael's daughter. I'm sure no doubt without his consent, but her stepmom? Where did you ever come up with such a ridiculous accusation?"

"You told me the only information you found out about my past from so called 'people on the street' was that I was a junkie and screwed older women. Well Rachel Hart is older and she's from

New York—"

"Christ, Trick! That's not a fucking connection that means any-thing—"

"I saw it … it was a look. The way she looked at me, she wasn't seeing me for the first time. She was nervous with a subtle mix of pain and anger. I knew it that night, but I had to be sure so I called her."

"You did what?"

"I had to know."

"And did she confess some lurid affair to you?"

"Of course not, but she was on the defensive and warned me to stay away from both her and Darby. You said you suspected these 'older women' took advantage of me. She told me men never fuck her; she fucks them."

"So your brilliant solution to all of this is to propose to Darby?" Grady's voice takes on a soprano pitch.

"I love her."

Grady laughs. "You love her. Well that's great, Trick. Tell me, did she accept your proposal before or after your dick had this vague memory of being up her stepmom's pussy?"

"Fuck you! I haven't said anything to her. I don't have any proof … yet."

"So you're going to start out your life with her while this epic epiphany that you fucked her stepmom weighs on your conscience?"

"Rachel's scared that I might remember something. I can tell. She's not going to say anything. Hell, she doesn't want to admit it to me, why would she ever say anything to Darby?"

"Does she know you've proposed to the Senator's daughter?"

"No."

"And what are you going to do if you're right. What if you were with her and someday she decides to tell Darby? Some people will slit their own throat in the name of revenge."

"Darby loves me."

Grady gives me another cynical laugh. "Well, there ya go, kid, I guess you two lovebirds have it all figured out. Good luck with that."

I press *End* and swipe my arm across the counter, sending makeup flying everywhere. "Goddammit!"

Who. The. Fuck. Was. I?

CHAPTER TWENTY-EIGHT

"**H**EY."

Trick turns at the sound of my voice, clenched jaw, heaving chest, and a mess of makeup all over the floor.

Rubbing the back of his neck, he closes his eyes and dips his chin.

I tiptoe through the mess until I stand in front of him, looking up at the last face I ever want to see. "So my day was good. How was yours?"

He opens his eyes. "I've had better."

Biting the inside of my cheek, I nod. "I can see that. Want to talk about it?"

He searches my face with pain and intensity in his eyes. "Not really."

I step back and manage to hop up on the stool without smashing anything under my feet. "Well, if you don't want to tell your lover…" I shy away from fiancée for now "…maybe you should tell your BFF. It usually works for me."

Planting his hands on his hips, he glances at me, and that lip twitches. *He's mine now.*

"I would tell my *friend* that if I hadn't already lost my mind, I'd swear it was happening now. I would tell my friend that all I know for sure about my past is that I was seriously fucked-up. I would tell my friend that *all* I want to do right now is take my lover to bed and fuck her until the world makes sense again, and then I want to pack our bags and get the hell out of here … and never return."

Uhh …

All I can do is hold my breath. Just … no words.

Trick lifts his shoulders then drops them in defeat as he bends down, tossing some things in the garbage and others back on the counter. "But I would never tell my lover that because I wouldn't want her running for the hills. So to her I would say that I had an argument with Grady and I let him crawl under my skin. Then I would suggest to her that we grab an early dinner and hang out … maybe play Battleship or Scrabble."

His defeated tone takes all the humor out of those last words.

I slide off the stool. "Will you be okay for a little while? I need to do something. I'll be back later."

Trick nods without looking up from the mess in front of him.

IN THE CAR I call my supervising physician and then I call Nana. As the gates open I expect my heart to start racing in my chest, but it doesn't. It's as if I don't care anymore. I'm not here for permission or approval.

"Ms. Carmichael, how nice to see you."

"I'm still Darby." I hug Susie, the housekeeper who's known me since I was born.

She smiles, a soft crinkling around her eyes and lips shows the years. "He's in his office."

"Thanks."

I nod and smile at the extra security stationed around the house. The place I called home for two years before college has become a fortress over the past few months. I knock on the solid wood door.

"Not now."

I roll my eyes and open the door.

"I said not—" My father looks up from his desk, reading glasses low on his nose, gray hair combed over Donald Trump style. "Darby."

I step in, closing the door behind me.

"Did I know you were coming?"

I chuckle. "No, sorry did I need to make an appointment?"

He removes his reading glasses, tossing them on his desk, and leans back in his chair. "Have a seat." He nods to the chair opposite him.

"I'm leaving town." I sit on the edge of the chair, not planning on staying very long.

My father folds his hands and rests them in his lap. "You made the trip here to tell me you're going on vacation?"

"No, I made the trip here to tell you I'm leaving indefinitely."

"That thug break your heart?"

I wish there were some compassion in his voice, like a father should have if his daughter did in fact get her heart broken, but my father is devoid of that.

"No, he stole it."

"You're too good for him. You were raised better than that."

"Better than what? Homeless? You don't even know him."

"I've seen all I need to know."

"You've *seen* all you need to know. And what is that? His tattoos? His address?"

"You're not leaving. With two months left before voters go to the polls, the last thing I need is you making a scene."

I spring from my chair, gripping the edge of his desk, leaning forward. "A scene? Falling in love and living my own goddamn life is *not* making a scene! Fucking anything with tits and a skirt is making a scene!"

"That's enough!"

"I don't know what my mother ever saw in you."

"I said that's enough!"

"Fuck you, *father!*"

Whack!

Stomach acid gurgles up my throat, but I swallow it back down.

With my hand cupping my cheek, I taste the salty metallic mix of blood on my tongue as the tip of it traces the gash on my lip.

"Now look at what you made me do." He grabs a handkerchief from his pocket and wipes the blood … *my blood* from his hand.

I suck in my bloodied, quivering lip as hot tears bleed down my cheeks. "Nana said my mom saw something special in you … but I've never *ever* seen it." Turning, I make my way to the door with wavering steps.

The biting sound of hate in his voice stops me as I turn the knob. "That's because it's gone. It died with her … the day you *killed* her."

Swallowing back the sobs, I run straight to my car. Susie's voice echoes in the distance, but I don't stop. The wad of tissue sticks to my lip as I blot the blood and wipe my face in the visor mirror. I wasn't an abused child. I can count on one hand how many times my father has hit me. Tonight was number four. Justified? Absolutely not. Provoked? Always.

The pain he doles out makes it easy to walk away, but it also makes it easy to come back. Four—the number of times I've seen the pain … the *love* he must have had for my mom. Twenty-seven— the number of birthdays I've celebrated without my father. He's always left a gift or money, but I've never once seen him *on* my birthday. That line between love and hate is so fine it's nearly invisible. I thought it would get better, but as the years progress his "love" for me has been engulfed by pain, and now all I see is his anger.

IT TAKES ME less than fifteen minutes to pack my suitcase. The moment I pull into Trick's garage, I feel the heaviness in my heart lift and nearly vanish. He is my home, my safe haven. Before the elevator comes to a complete stop, I see Trick sitting at his kitchen counter eating a sandwich.

"I was going to wait for you to eat, but my stomach overrul—" Trick gets his first unobstructed look at me as I tug my suitcase off the elevator. "What the fuck!" He stands with a jerk, sending the stool crashing over against the concrete. He cradles my face before I can utter a word. I flinch as his thumb grazes my cut lip. "Darby, what the fuck happened?"

With a shaky breath I swallow past the lump in my throat, but my tears don't get the memo that no more are needed. "We can l-leave in the m-morning..." my lower lip begins to quiver again "...go an-anywhere you w-want to go."

"Darby! Who did this to you?" The last time I saw this look on Trick's face, he had a gun pointed at my attacker.

I shake my head and sniffle. "I s-said something I-I shouldn't have."

"Who?" he seethes.

"My father."

He releases me and starts to walk past me.

"Trick!" I grab his arm. "Don't ... let it go. Please, I need you."

He stops, his bicep steel in my hand.

"I *need* you."

When he turns back to me, I place my hands flat on his chest. His heart pounds against the rise and fall of each angry breath. Looking down, I slide my hands to the button of his pants.

"No." He grabs my hands.

Closing my eyes, the tears spill over. I open them and look up. "If you say no ... it will hurt worse than anything he said or did to me."

His brow furrows. I don't mean to cause him pain, I just need him to take mine away. I need to feel physically and emotionally loved more than I ever have before.

He releases my hands and shrugs off his shirt. His hand cups the back of my head while his lips press to my cheek. The tip of his tongue grazes my skin, dissolving my tears. He consumes my pain with his touch, one tiny drop at a time.

Scooping me up in his strong arms, he carries me to the bed and sets me on the edge. A final shaky breath ricochets through my body. He undresses me with *love*. Every touch, every look takes away a little more pain.

Then he finishes undressing himself and lets me just look at him. It's not arrogant, or cocky—no lip twitch. He's giving me what I need. I *need* to take all of him in—let him flow into all the cracks and crevices of my heart, replacing all the missing pieces. His love stitches me up ... holds me together.

Kneeling on the floor, he wraps his arms around my waist and rests his head on my legs. "My BFF texted me today. She's getting married. OMG, like ... WTF can you believe that? Heart Emoji, kiss Emoji, smiley Emoji, ring Emoji, thumbs up Emoji, and applause Emoji."

A laughing sob escapes from my chest. More tears, but now they're tears of joy and love ... my God, so much love. I run my fingers through his hair and he lifts his head giving me a breathtaking smile. My palms press to his stubbly face. "Your BFF sounds like the luckiest woman in the entire world."

His gaze slips and he nods. "God, I hope so."

I scoot back on the bed. "Come."

He smirks, and we both know I can use *his* command, but the control will always be his. "You first." He presses his hands to my inner thighs, spreading me open. When the heat of his mouth and the brush of his stubble find my sensitive flesh, I moan, letting my heavy eyelids drift shut.

"Trick ..." With one hand fisting the sheet and my other clenching his hair, I let him take me to that other world—a world where light and darkness collide, emotions vanish, and all that's left is the most incredible out of body experience.

After I melt into a pool of bliss in the middle of his bed, he still doesn't take ... he continues to give. His hands glide over every curve with such patience it feels like he's sculpting me. Lips breathe love over my skin, eliciting a chilling shiver as I arch my back into his touch. His hands slide up, drawing mine above my head. Our fingers intertwine; I cry out as his tongue teases my sensitive nipple.

"Darby ..." he whispers over my skin while sinking into me, filling every last physical and emotional void.

Our hands clench together like they're holding on to something greater than this moment. He rocks into me; hovering over my face, we just stare until ... *the world makes sense again.*

THE EIGHT-HUNDRED MILLIGRAMS of Ibuprofen I took before going to bed numbed the pain and allowed me to collapse into a coma-like state. I don't think I moved an inch the entire night. I wake feeling rested, but my face is sore again.

"Trick?" my croaky morning voice calls out.

He walks around the corner in black boxer briefs, rubbing a towel through his wet hair. "Good morning." He smiles and leans down, pressing a feathery kiss to my swollen lip. "You were out."

I nod. "Yeah, I must have been exhausted."

He sits on the edge of the bed with one leg propped up. His gaze focuses across the room at my suitcase. "I scheduled us flights this morning." He looks at me. "Are you sure about this?"

I nod, tracing the script under his arm. *Don't look back in anger.* "I'm sure."

Trick rests his hand on my thigh. "Don't you want to know where we're going?"

Sitting up, I climb out of bed, loving the way he unapologetically stares at my naked figure when the sheet falls from my body. "I'll go anywhere with you," I say, walking to the bathroom.

CHAPTER TWENTY-NINE

ARRIVING AT O'HARE three hours before our flight, a jittery mix of nerves and excitement churn in my belly. *What are we doing? Running away? Starting over?*

"I assume you have your passport?" Trick glances over at me as we get out of the cab.

"Yes." I grin because he still hasn't told me where we're going, and I haven't asked.

We check in and snake our way through the snail-paced security line. I've now discovered we're headed to Los Cabos, but Trick assures me it's not our final destination.

"Lunch?"

I nod as we walk to a bar and grill down from our terminal. It's now after noon so the place is packed. We opt to eat at the bar to save time.

"Two lemonades." Trick orders for us while we look over the menu.

As I glance from the cob salad on one page to the grilled portobello sandwich on the next page, something familiar catches my attention on the TV behind the bar. My eyes flit side to side over the words of the closed caption.

My father.

I grip Trick's arm and he follows my gaze. My father's being escorted from the hospital through a crowd of reporters and photographers, arm in a sling and his face banged up. It's hard to tell to what extent because of the bandages and his sunglasses.

The words on the screen flash across too fast. I can't make sense of it all.

"... *home invasion ... Senator Carmichael was assaulted in his sleep ... suspicious malfunction in the security recordings ... no one knows how the intruder made it past the guards ...*"

"Oh my God," I whisper.

Trick looks back at his menu. "I think I'm going to get the turkey club. What are you getting?"

My breath catches in my throat as I inch my head to the side, eyes wide. His gaze eases from the menu to me. He knows the question, and the longer he stares at me, emotionless, I know the answer. My eyes slip to his throat. His Adam's apple bobs with a deep swallow, then my eyes go back to his.

"I'm only going to say this once." He pauses as if to make sure I hear the serious depth of his voice, or maybe to make sure I hear the unwavering tone of it.

I nod once with slow apprehension.

"*No one* will ever get away with hurting you. Understood?"

My blood turns to ice; my mind reels. I was so out of it last night. That's how he managed to sneak away without me knowing. My God, he thinks this is tit for tat. He broke into the home of a U.S. senator and assaulted him in his sleep and—

"Darby?"

My eyes focus again. Trick gestures to the bartender waiting to take my order.

"Um ... cob salad, Italian dressing."

He smiles then turns to put our order into the computer.

"Hey," Trick calls to the bartender. "Can you change the channel?"

The bartender grabs a remote under the counter and flips the channel to some daytime talk show.

"Thanks," Trick says. Turning toward me, he scoots my stool closer to his and cups the back of my head, bringing my face a breath away from his. "What he did to you is *not* okay. I don't even want to know if it was the first time he laid his fucking hands on you. But I can promise you, it was the last." He presses his lips to my forehead.

"But you could go to jail," I whisper with a shaky voice.

Trick releases my head and sits back, chuckling. "Did you see my picture on the TV?"

"He probably doesn't know who did it."

Trick takes a drink and crushes a piece of ice between his teeth. "Oh, he knows, but he also received a photo of you sleeping last night, with your face looking the way it does." He looks at my face. "Well, before I covered it up for you this morning."

"You're blackmailing my father," I whisper, looking around us.

Trick rubs the back of his fingers under his chin. "Absolutely not. I just sent him the photo. Whatever conclusions he makes are all his own."

I pull my phone out of my handbag. The battery went dead last night and I don't remember turning it back on after charging it. There has to be a message from my father or Nana. But when I turn it on and check, there's nothing.

"I should call him."

Trick shakes his head and laughs. "And say what? That you're sorry someone *hit* him?"

"He's my father."

"He's a sperm donor."

I flinch. His comment stings … the truth can do that.

Trick leans in, squeezing my leg with his hand. "If you want to stay, just say so."

As my tongue brushes my lip, I rest my hand on his. This isn't a question that should have to be answered. "I want to be with you."

"You can be with me if we stay."

I shake my head. "I don't want to stay."

Trick skims my cheek with his thumb, an ease to his facial expression. "Me neither."

WE LAND IN Los Cabos and Trick informs me we're renting a car to drive to Todos Santos, our final destination. Then he informs me we'll only use the rental until he arranges to have his motorcycle shipped down here. In this moment the reality of what we're doing hits me. I told Nana I didn't know how long I'd be gone, but I told my work I needed an extended leave for personal reasons—I didn't actually quit. But … I'm still in. Wherever Trick goes, I go.

"Let's get a cab to the nearest car dealership."

Trick takes our luggage from the carousel. "We're not buying a car."

"Well maybe *we're* not, but I am. It rains in Mexico too."

"That's why we either stay in or wear our rain gear for the bike. Come." He takes off toward the doors.

"We can't have sex on the back of your motorcycle."

He stops, allowing me to catch up. Pursing his lips, his eyes trail down my body. "I beg to differ, but if that's why you want a car, then…" he turns and continues through the doors "…suit yourself."

"Typical guy."

"What's that?" he asks, hoisting our luggage into the back of the taxi.

I smile. "Nothing."

TRICK STARES AT my new purchase with his hands resting on his hips. "It's a chick mobile and a bait and switch. There's no way we'll be having sex in the back of that thing. You should have bought the Escalade."

I hand him the keys to my little red Saab. "Yeah, well we'll give it a go once we get out of town a ways."

He snatches the keys and slips on his sunglasses. "If we're out of town, no need to cram in the back. I'll just fuck you on the hood."

I open the passenger door and look at him over the frames of my sunglasses. "The hood will be too hot from the engine."

We both say "trunk" in unison and hop in the car.

He starts the car and puts his hand on the gear shift. I put my hand over his. He looks at me.

"Thank you."

"For what?"

I lean over and kiss him. It's slow, our tongues making lazy strokes together. His hand moves from the gear shift to my face and when I start to pull away he holds me to him, dropping the softest kiss ever to the corner of my fat lip. "For wanting to make memories with me." I smile.

"I love you, Darby Roth."

My brows peak. "I'm not your wife, yet."

He puts the car in gear and pulls out. "You will be … soon."

My initial grin snaps into a grimace as my enthusiasm grows so big it pulls at my lip. Every ounce of my being does a happy dance. If this is karma for all the years I tried to find friends, tried to fit in with no avail, then I love her. Karma and I are BFFs … well, after Trick of course.

We roll down the windows and let in the warm breeze. I'm in paradise and it has nothing to do with Mexico.

"Why Todos Santos?"

"Have you been?" He gives me a quick sidelong glance.

"Nope, have you?"

He shakes his head with a mega-watt-just-for-Darby grin. "My parents met in Todos Santos."

"Seriously?"

He nods, eyes on the road ahead. "Christmas break their senior year of high school. Their parents rented places next door to each other on the beach. His family was from Utah, her family lived in

Minnesota. They both told the story the same way … love at first sight." He chuckles. "I hated hearing it over and over again. Now I'd give anything to see their eyes light up as they narrate every word, both sharing parts of the story like lines of a play."

"So how'd they end up …" I hate even saying the word. The thought of Trick and his family homeless cuts so deep, especially after seeing that picture he drew of them. It was them having everything and nothing at the same time.

"Homeless?"

I nod.

"They wrote letters and talked on the phone until after they both graduated in the spring. My dad even switched his college plans to attend school with my mom. So the summer before their freshman year of college they met up in Colorado to camp for four weeks in the mountains. Neither set of parents approved, but they were both adults so there wasn't much they could do."

Trick pauses and I want to ask more questions but I know he's not done with the story. He works his lower lip between his teeth, so I wait.

"A week after they started college my mom found out she was pregnant with me. Her parents campaigned for an abortion, and his basically disowned him. His parents found religion…" he glances over at me "…and I say that because had they actually found God there's no way they would have disowned their own child over the creation of a life."

"I take it they decided to keep the baby." I grin and he does too.

"Yes, I'm here." He sighs as if the story has only just begun. "My dad had planned on majoring in business and working on Wall Street, and my mom was studying music and had dreams of attending Juilliard. So with both parents against them and having basically nothing except a baby on the way, they moved to New York. My dad got an entry level job on Wall Street, aka as a janitor, and my mom taught piano lessons through a music outreach program in the city. They had a one room apartment…" another glance over at me "…not as in one bedroom, as in one room. Even making rent on it was a struggle for them. Then I came along and with no insurance they brought home a baby and a truckload of hospital bills. By the time I was five the outreach program had shut down and three weeks later my dad lost his job … I guess when Wall Street isn't doing well even the janitorial staff is affected. Neither one could find work and eventually they were evicted."

I hate hearing this because there's such a misconception about the homeless, as if all of the people who end up on the street are addicts and lazy people with no work ethic. I will never look at a homeless person the same way again.

"So why didn't they go home?"

Trick shrugs. "Neither one had talked to their parents since they left for New York. Five years later I don't think they felt like they still had family. I'm sure pride was a big factor too. My dad was a proud man, even with nothing but the clothes on his back, he was still a proud man. He was never a panhandler and hated it when he saw my mom doing it. She had a child to feed and would toss her pride aside and beg for money to buy food. I admired them both for what they believed in. My dad never let the circumstances define him, and my mother … I think she would have asked family for help, but she loved my dad too much to ever do that to him."

I wipe away a few tears. I'm sure it would never get made into a movie, but right now I feel the story of Trick's parents, the forbidden, unstoppable love, and the way they truly lived out their "for better or worse," was just … beautiful. Maybe the most beautiful love story I have ever heard.

THERE'S A CLOUD of somberness over the rest of our drive to Todos Santos. I imagine Trick's mind stays with his past, maybe the times he remembers, maybe trying to figure out the parts he doesn't. I think about my own life and what different paths we both took to get here. I would never say it out loud, but a part of me envies what he had growing up. It sounds crazy, I know it does, but he had two parents who loved each other and adored him. I had everything I needed and plenty I didn't, and thankfully, so very thankfully, I had my nana. But I am the poster child for money can't buy happiness.

Everything about Trick's past spirals back to his parents. How did they both just disappear? He was still a child, fifteen, but still a child—their only child. It doesn't make sense that they would leave him without a single word. But it also doesn't make sense that they would both just vanish or die without a trace. But every time I mention my suspicion or lack of understanding to Trick, his pain makes me feel like I'm stomping on their graves.

"What do you think?" Trick asks as we pull up and stop on a dirt drive.

I hop out and scuff my flip-flopped feet across the hard dirt to an old wooden gate painted rustic red.

"It's all I could come up with on short notice…" Trick walks up behind me "…we're just renting it. I know it's nothing huge—"

"I love it." I turn and throw my arms around his neck. He hugs me back, lifting me off the ground. "I love it … it's *perfect.*"

He chuckles. "You haven't even seen the inside, and it's dark. You can't see much out here either."

Releasing him, I practically bust through the gate to see more. The house is authentic Mexican architecture, with arched doors and windows, adobe exterior painted what looks like a muted sand color, and traditional tile roof. I walk a few more steps then turn a complete circle in awe of the lush gardens and fruit trees.

"Don't act impressed. I know you've seen places much fancier than this." Trick hangs back a few steps and his rare moment of insecurity saddens me.

I shake my head. "I'm in awe of the moment … this moment in my life." Retreating, I place my palms on his cheeks. "It's everything.

It's the house, these gardens, and *us*. I don't ever want to leave." My mind registers what I just said, but it only takes a moment to realize … it's the truth.

Trick grabs the back of my legs and lifts me up. My hands in his hair, his lips on mine, and this world—*our* world—it's paradise. He moves to my neck and I moan. "What are we going to christen first?" he mumbles along my skin.

I giggle. "If you don't stop, I think the dirt beneath our feet will be first."

"Suit yourself."

My stomach flips as he starts to lower us to the ground. "Trick! I'm not serious."

He sets me on my feet and nips my neck, followed by a smack on my ass. "Get inside. Between this and the backseat sex that never happened you're being a tease today."

I try to turn the knob. "It's locked."

"The owner said he'd leave a key under the planter."

Bingo!

We walk through the doorway and find the light switch. It's surprisingly spacious with modern appliances, handcrafted stone-work, and Mexican tile.

"There's no furniture."

"It's a rental, not a vacation home. I'll grab our luggage."

I walk out to the covered courtyard, welcomed by the rhythmic, lapping waves of the Pacific and the glassy reflection of the moon off its dark surface.

"Well, it's our lucky night. Someone left a lounge chair." Trick sets down our luggage and hugs me from behind, resting his chin on my shoulder.

I glance off to the right at the wicker chaise lounge with a weathered blue cushion. "We're going to sleep on that?"

"We'll pull it inside. It's just for one night. At least it's a roof over our heads."

Ouch!

I turn in his arms. "Absolutely." I grin, not wanting to seem like a spoiled little rich girl for a single second. "Let's check out the rest of *our* place."

He kisses me. "Mmm ... *our* ... I like that."

We take our luggage upstairs to the master bedroom. A full wall of windows and double doors opening to a private terrace and a picturesque view of the ocean greets us.

"Wow!"

Trick's lip twitches when I look over at him. He's pleased and so am I.

He sets down our suitcases. "We're never leaving."

I laugh. "Uh yeah, ... *never.*"

I HAVE A small glimpse of the magic Trick's parents had between them as Trick holds me in his arms on our gifted lounge chair, surrounded by darkness. It really doesn't matter where we are ... it only matters that we're together.

"Trick?"

"Hmm?"

"Why do you have such an aversion to women?"

His neck stiffens as he takes a deep swallow. "My past."

"The part you remember?"

"The part I don't."

"How can that be, if you don't remember?"

He sighs. "After my accident, Grady talked with people who either lived near my building or worked in the area. One guy who owned a food truck that he parked on the corner of my building told Grady he occasionally saw me coming and going, usually with a woman, but not always the same one and they were definitely older than me. Grady said everything about it seemed off. He thinks those women were taking advantage of me in some way, probably something to do with the drugs. So between dealing with my memory loss and trying to stay clean, I've found it in my best interest to avoid women outside of a professional capacity."

He laughs. "The truth is my female clientele *were* a bunch of rich bitches that always wanted more than what I was willing to give them. They'd fuck a gay man just to prove they could. It's laughable; it didn't matter how much makeup I painted on their face, the ugly on the inside always seeped through. So the makeup on my face, the 'icy' fuck-off attitude you felt, it was my defense—my way of protecting the part of me I don't know. The less connection women feel with me the better. That's the thing with memory loss, it makes you feel vulnerable."

"So why me? I mean, obviously you lumped me into the same group as the rich bitches at first, but then you had a change of heart. Why?"

"You slapped me that night." He chuckles. "I don't know if a woman has ever hit me like that before and at first I thought you were just offended. I've seen that look too many times … it doesn't phase me. But the way you stood up to me … stood up for yourself, it was just so fucking … hot."

"Hot?" I laugh.

"Yes, hot. As in gloves are off let's go eight rounds in the ring."

I bite my tongue. That night after I slammed the door in his face, I was so turned on I could barely think. The tension between us that night, it *was* sexual. I thought it was just me.

After a few minutes of silence, I lean up, kissing the angle of his jaw. "The women, in New York, maybe you were sketching them. Did you ever think of that?"

"Grady did, but I've never sketched anyone for money, so that wouldn't make sense. I mean, I sold my art, but I never did 'special requests.'"

"Well maybe you did and you just don't *remember*."

He kisses the top of my head. "Maybe. Goodnight, sexy."

I nuzzle into his neck. "Goodnight, I love you."

CHAPTER THIRTY

DISORIENTED. IT TAKES me a few minutes to piece together where I am and how I got here. Stretching out of my fetal position, I get a whiff of the musty smelling cushion to our make-shift bed. What I'm not seeing, feeling, or smelling is Trick. However, I hear the most inviting sound ever—the ocean. I glance back at the opened door to the veranda, and there he is ... inverted on his yoga mat and shirtless. All I can do is stare. The urge to say something or touch him ... my God, the urge to touch that body is torturous, but I don't. This is his time, his thing. Maybe he needs his meditative practice to make sense of the chaos in his life. As I turn toward the kitchen, I see several mangos and bananas on the counter that weren't there last night. I peel back the skin to the mango, sinking my teeth into its juicy flesh. *Amazing!*

"Are you wondering what the hell we've done?"

That voice ... my nipples respond first. I turn, wiping my chin and sucking juice off my finger.

"Lucky finger."

Sliding it out of my mouth, I grin, struggling to keep my eyes off his bare chest—muscles, tattoos, and that dark happy trail that in fact makes me *very* happy.

"I feel self-conscious under your scrutinizing gaze." He pinches nothing but muscle and skin at his waist. "Am I starting to get love handles?"

I giggle. "Yes."

"What?" He looks up in wide-eyed shock.

I shake my head. "No, not yes to your love handles, yes to what the hell have we done. I didn't think this was me. I love Chicago … I love my job. Then you came along and everything changed. I left my home and my job with barely a moment's notice to get on a plane with a guy that I've known two seconds. And now we're here and talking about staying … *forever.*" I laugh. "I still have food in my refrigerator and stuff in my locker at work. This is insane."

Trick moves toward me with a predatory look in those dark eyes. "How did I change everything?" he asks, pushing me up against the counter, sending me into sensory overload that he does so well.

I wet my lips, craving his touch, his taste … craving *him* in *me.* "You showed me real love. "

"And now?" He grabs my wrist, bringing my mango to his mouth, taking a bite and licking his lips.

My breath quickens. "And now my favorite place to live is in your arms and my favorite *job* is …" I purse my lips to the side and rub my hand over his erection that's pressed to my belly.

He smirks, his brow pulling up. "Yeah?"

I nod.

Trick looks at his wrist. "Well, you better get going, sexy. I'd hate for you to be late for work."

I laugh, pressing my lips to his bare chest and easing my way down to *work.*

WE SHOWER SINCE my *job* got a little messy, especially after adding the fruit into the mix, which I found out he picked from our front yard. We're growing mangos and bananas in our front yard! *Yeah, this girl from the Midwest hasn't wrapped her head around that one yet.*

I call Nana and let her know my whereabouts. She asks if I heard about my father's attack, and I hate myself for lying but I play dumb anyway. I'm still trying to deal with it myself. What am I supposed to say? *Yeah, he busted up my face so Trick paid him a little visit, and I saw the news about it at the airport, but I still chose to leave the country without so much as a phone call to see if he's okay.*

Truthfully, Nana wouldn't blame me. If she knew she'd probably hire her own hit man to beat the shit out of him. Maybe she'd do it herself. It's possible she has a black belt in some martial art that I don't know about. Nana's not privy to any of the *four* incidents between me and my father. I managed to avoid her after the first two until the evidence was gone from my face, and the third I blamed on falling down the stairs. I cringed after saying those words to her. It's confusing; I was eighteen when he first hit me so none of it was ever "child abuse." What was I supposed to do? Have my father arrested for assault because I have a knack for pushing his buttons?

"Does your Nana hate me?" Trick asks as we head to town for ... everything.

"Hate you? Why would you ask that?" I glance over at him.

"For stealing you away."

"I'm sure she's going to miss me as I will her, but her dream has always been for me to live outside of the box, take chances, do something unexpected. Basically send my father to his early grave."

Trick stiffens with my last words.

I clear my throat. "And speaking of sending him to an early grave. I have to know ... I mean, I didn't want to at first, but now I do. The gun, the violence, the security cameras you must have disabled ... where did you learn all of that?"

"You really want to know?" He glances sideways with peaked brows.

"Yes, well no ... I think I *need* to know. Don't you?"

He shrugs.

"Were you a hit man?"

Trick laughs. "No."

"Have you ever killed anyone?"

"No ... well, I hope not."

Yeah, that wasn't a fair question.

"Have you ever shot someone?"

"Yes, but it was self-defense. I just kneecapped him."

My eyes grow wide. "But were you trying to kill him?"

His head jerks back. "No. I was trying to kneecap him. If I would have been trying to kill him, he'd be dead."

"So you're a good shot?" I think I know this from the words that were shared the night I was assaulted outside Trick's place, but I want to hear it from him.

"Yes." He sighs like he's not proud of it. "I joined a gang when I was twelve. The kids were older and taught me a lot. We'd target shoot under the train tracks and in old abandoned buildings. From the moment they put a gun in my hand I could hit any target. I don't know … I'm gifted in the eye-hand coordination department or something. I think that's why I can sketch with such accuracy."

That's a reality check. While I was in girl scouts learning to tie a fisherman's knot, Trick was shooting guns with his gang members.

"And the fighting?"

"Survival. It wasn't really instinctive at first. I got the crap beat out of me on numerous occasions until something inside of me snapped. Then it ended. Never again was I the kid on the bottom getting his face smashed into the ground."

I did take a self-defense class my freshman year of college, but I was screwing the instructor so I'm not sure I learned much more than he likes it doggie-style every time.

Might keep that bit of information to myself.

"Why a gang? I get the desire to fit in. Lord knows I had it in spades, but weren't you worried about getting into a situation that could land you in jail or worse?"

Trick pulls into a shopping area. "For me it was safer to belong to a gang than not. Jail wasn't a concern. At the time it would have meant a bed and three warm meals a day. I'm not saying I never broke the law. Sometimes we stole things to survive, but I didn't do anything that would have meant years in prison. The guy I knee-capped was trying to steal my parents' stuff, which wasn't much, and he had a gun too." He shuts the car off and looks at me.

I pull my hair back into a ponytail. "I get it. My senior year of high school Tammy Sievers stole my purse from the locker room. I could never prove it, but the bitch did it so I keyed her car ... both sides."

The lip twitches as humor dances in his eyes. "You were a real badass."

I grab my purse and open the door. "Damn right I was. Now *come.*"

WE'VE LANDED OURSELVES in an art lover's oasis. Trick lights up every time we pass an art gallery or a shop with local handcrafted goods. *Job? What job? Chicago? Where's that?* This sleepy town nestled amongst desert, mountains, and ocean makes Chicago seem like a social migraine. I hear no sirens or honking horns and the people here move at a snail's pace, because really ... what's the hurry?

"Okay, so we've ordered furniture, our mattress will be delivered later today—"

"And we will test it out immediately," Trick interrupts.

I tug his hand toward a small shop that looks like it carries linens. "Yes, all this shopping has tuckered me. We'll need a nap for sure."

Trick jerks me back into his arms. My sundress rides up my legs as he palms my ass. "We'd better stop for some caffeine, then, because we won't be sleeping on that mattress anytime soon." He rubs his nose against mine then nips at my bottom lip with a low growl.

"Down, boy. Tourists are watching."

"Well then let's give them a show."

I shove my hands in the back pockets of his ripped, frayed jeans and kiss the line of his jaw. "So should we do it against the side of the building or on the trunk of our new car?"

With one hand he holds me as a shield to him while he adjusts himself with his other hand. "Fuck, stop! You're giving me a hard-on."

I continue to kiss along his jaw and down his neck. "Last I knew that's a requirement for public fornication."

"Get in the store and stop teasing me." He grabs my arms, turns me around, and nudges me forward.

"You started it."

After we get towels and sheets, we decide to head back *home*. Another jolt to my brain, *home*. We're going to live here together for … well, as long as we want. Insane.

CHAPTER THIRTY-ONE

WITHIN A WEEK we have a fully furnished home, a stocked kitchen, and our marriage license. Trick breaks the news to a very grumpy Grady about our move and plans to stay here indefinitely. Since he's in LA I wouldn't put it past him driving down here and personally strangling Trick. Rogue Seduction is closed until Trick's replacement can be "discovered" as Grady puts it.

As for my place, Nana agrees to take care of the necessities. I tell her to sell it; I really don't care, but she insists on keeping it in case I decide to come "home." My work on the other hand, not so pleased. I told them I was taking personal time, not quitting. But it only took two days here to make the call that I wasn't coming back. I think the marriage license pushed any doubt out of my head.

This feels like a honeymoon, although we're not technically married yet. It's easy to walk out from our veranda and gasp at the incredible beach that is our backyard to paradise. I keep thinking I should start packing my bag because vacation is almost over. But it's not, so I'm going to keep my ass planted in the sand until life pulls me out.

"You really should start coming with me. There were twelve of us today." Trick stands in front of me blocking the sun. I can't complain. He's in his shorts, no shirt, and gripping a towel draped around his neck. He missed a few beads of sweat trickling down the bumpy terrain of his chest.

"I'm not that great at yoga. I'm more of a cycle girl."

"Tomorrow you'll come with me." Trick's words have a finality to them.

"Hey, neighbors."

Trick turns and I lean to the side to see past him. A young guy with a surfboard makes casual strides through the sinking sand over to us. A stark white smile graces his face that gives way to a lean bronzed body that's been perfected by hours of sun and surf. He runs a lazy hand through his wind tossed mess of copper-blond hair then offers his hand to Trick.

"Hey, I'm Declan. You must be the new neighbors Martin said we have."

Martin Cruz, our landlord, owns four homes along this stretch of beach.

"Trick and Darby Roth," Trick squeezes his hand and my jaw comes unhinged.

"Nice to meet you."

I stand, brushing the sticky sand from my legs. "Darby *Carmichael.*" I offer my hand without missing the twitch of frustration in Trick's stone face. "We're not actually married yet."

Declan takes my hand. "Oh, well when's the big day?"

"Today," Trick announces as my eyes bug out at him.

Lip twitch. Arrogant fucker!

Trick snakes his arm around my waist, pulling me into his side and forcing me to release Declan's hand.

"Congratulations! That's awesome! You doing a beach wedding? Lots of family or just a few friends?"

My tongue remains thick and numb as I wait with anticipation for these answers right along with Declan.

"It's just us. We're getting married not having a wedding."

His words steep in my mind. Do I get a say in any of this?

"Ah man, you guys should have it on the beach. It's going to be killer weather today and Martin can do the ceremony. He did three just last month."

Trick looks around and shrugs. "Sunset?"

Declan grins and nods. "Now we're talking. I'll handle every-thing. See you back here in about six hours." He jogs off and turns with a final wave. "Nice to meet you, neighbors!"

Trick pulls me into his chest, an unavoidable smirk curling his lips.

Drawing my head back and cocking it to the side, I squint my eyes. "Oh. My. God! Did you just plan *my wedding* with a complete stranger right in front of me?"

Trick cups my neck and pulls me closer until my head tips back to look up at him. "A marriage ceremony, not a wedding." His lips press to mine as his other hand tugs at the tie to my bikini top while he moans into my mouth.

"No." I push away leaving him panting with an insatiable hunger in his mischievous eyes. "If I don't get a say in my *ceremony,* then you don't get this…" I shake my head while retying my top "…until I legally bear your name."

His eyes stretch wider. "Are you refusing to have sex with me?"

"Yes." Pivoting in the sand, I grab my towel and walk to the house with my shoulders back and an extra sway in my hips.

As I pour a cup of juice, the veranda door opens and Trick walks in *completely naked.*

The glass jug clanks to the counter as my grip weakens.

"I'll be in the shower, in case you want to watch."

I gulp down the juice in my mouth. "No need. I already pleas-ured myself while you were doing yoga," I lie, because damn his arrogance.

I hear a *thud* and "fuck," presumably my cocky, soon-to-be hus-band literally tripping over my words on his way up the stairs.

I FEEL LIKE I'm in a car with the top down, the warm love of the sun on my face, the breeze dancing with my hair, the radio breathing an endless serenade, and the man of my dreams driving with one hand on the steering wheel and the other on my leg—the occasional gentle squeeze to remind me this perfect dream is my life.

"Where did you go?" I ask as Trick walks up behind me while I attempt to add a few purposeful curls to my hair.

He wraps his arms around my waist and nuzzles his lips into my neck, eyes on our reflection in the mirror. "You'll see."

I frown in the mirror.

"Why the face, sexy?"

"I need Gemmie. It's my wed—I mean my *ceremony* day…" I roll my eyes at him "…and my hair's going to look like a damn bird's nest."

"You look perfect." He nibbles the sensitive skin below my ear.

I sigh. Tossing aside my curling iron, I shrug out of his grip to go get my phone.

"Where are you going?" he calls, but I ignore him.

Grabbing my phone off the kitchen counter, I do what any girl in my shoes would do. I text my BFF.

Me: *Dear BFF – I need you … I can't tell my fiancé this, but it's my wedding day and I want to look amazing for him. He doesn't understand that for one day I want to feel as beautiful as he says I am. My hair is rebelling and my skin looks blotchy from the sun. Can you help me?*

I tap the screen of my phone for a few moments until it chimes.

Trick: *Come.*

My smile grows … my heart overflows.

When I stop in the doorway to the bathroom, Trick crooks his finger at me. Tears sting the back of my eyes as I walk to him and he lifts me up on the vanity. "My *friend* is going to be the envy of the ocean and chase away the sunset with her beauty. Then she's going to marry a guy completely undeserving of her love."

I try to swallow back emotion as he catches my tear with his thumb. "You're not going to stop until you've claimed *every single piece* of my heart, are you?" I whisper.

He ghosts his fingers along my jaw, tilting his head to the side with a gripping intensity to his eyes. "I'm not going to stop until I feel your soul take my last breath."

I think his just took mine.

★

THERE'S NOTHING he can't do. Sometimes I actually hope he'll choke on his food or twist an ankle just so I can be the one with the skills. Even chatty Gemmie would fall speechless if she could see how Trick has transformed my stubborn flames into a controlled fire—stunning and mesmerizing. My make-up—a work of art.

After applying lotion to every inch of my body, I emerge from the bathroom. Trick looks out our windows with his hands resting in the pockets of his dark denim jeans, fitted white button down dress shirt hugging his every curve with the sleeves rolled up, tats on show. *Melt* ...

"Come."

Melt some more ...

I follow him into the closet.

"Trick ..." I hold back the tears because I will not mess up his hard work.

He eases my robe back over my shoulders until it slinks to the floor at my feet. Then he takes the white strapless sundress with a lacy overlay off the hanger. I step into it as he holds it. While he zips the back I run my hands over the delicate material. "Where did you get this?"

"In town, the shop owner made it. She had it in back for a 'special occasion.' I convinced her it wouldn't get any more special than today, gracing your beautiful body."

"How can this..." I shake my head in amazement "...this day with no friends and family feel so ... perfect." I turn to him and press my palms to his dark bristly face. "Because it is ..." I whisper, "... it's perfect."

His eyes, usually so dark, sparkle with life ... our life. "Come." He takes my hand and leads me to our sandy backyard with a handful of complete strangers in casual beach attire. They've lit an enchanted pathway of glowing lanterns from our veranda to the beach where the setting sun casts heavenly shades of violet, yellow, and orange on the end of our day and the beginning of our forever.

Martin Cruz, our landlord slash ordained minister, grins behind his scraggly salt and pepper beard. He's exchanged his crazy-colored island shirt for a soft yellow collared linen and white shorts. In our bare feet we make a casual stroll hand in hand to our gracious group of witnesses. We both smile at Martin and turn toward each other. He says a few words about love, life, and commitment. I hear none of it. All that my mind can think is "How did he choose me?"

"Trick, what would you like to say to Darby?"

Trick smiles—my smile. "This is all I have to give you—me." He lifts his shoulders and his vulnerability rips away a little piece of my heart. "A book with blank pages, weathered edges, and eraser marks, that's what I am. I need you to paint my future, write my story in permanent marker, just like the mark you left on my heart the day we met. Your touch is the only thing I feel, your voice the only thing I hear, your face the only thing I see, but your love ... your love, my beauty, is the only thing I *need*." He squeezes my hands and my eyes respond with a few tears. "Memories are mortal emotions, but love ... what the heart feels, it never forgets. I'll *never* forget you, so be my wife, Darby. Write a story with me that never ends."

I press the pads of my middle fingers to the corners of my eyes then take Trick's hands again.

"Darby, what would you like to say to Trick?"

I laugh and blink back the impending emotions. "There's twenty-six letters in the alphabet that can be arranged to express an infinity of emotions." I shake my head. "But not mine, not for you.

There are no words to express the way my whole world falls at your feet, staring up in awe at my best friend, my lover … my forever. The river of love for you that runs through me is deep and all consuming. I came alive for you. With the soft stroke of your brush, you painted my life a million shades of amazing and now my heart finds its rhythm from your love … our love … forever. So be my husband, Trick. Let our story be the only one that matters."

Martin clears his throat and grins. "Do you Trick take Darby to be your wife?"

"I do."

I release a small sob disguised as a laugh.

"Do you Darby take Trick to be your husband?"

"I do." My words are but a whisper, caught in a knot of emotion.

"Then with the power vested in me, I pronounce you husband and wife. Trick, you may kiss your bride."

Our small gathering of witnesses clap and holler as Trick holds my face and kisses me, not letting the onlookers interfere with our moment. It's slow and patient as our tongues make languid strokes against each other.

"I love you," he whispers over my lips, releasing me.

"I love you." I say it but I'm sure he and everyone else can already see it in my ridiculously large grin that is on my face to stay.

"Congratulations!" Declan slaps his hand on Trick's shoulder and gives him a manly squeeze of approval. Then he holds out his arms and I smile while he embraces me like we've known each other far longer than eight hours. "Come meet the rest of your neighbors."

Trick pulls me into his side as the rest of the small group closes in on us.

"This is Colby. He's taking a year off college to *find* himself." Everyone laughs. "So if you see his ghost or twin, let us know."

Colby rolls his hazel eyes, flipping his carefree, dark surfer hair off to the side. "Says the guy who's *still* not been accepted to medical school."

Declan shrugs. "I'm just struggling with a few classes that's all."

"Med school, huh?" I smile. "Let me know if you need help with anything. I was a physician's assistant in Chicago."

"Really? That'd be awesome. Thanks."

"It's the least I can do for our wed—I mean, *ceremony* planner."

Trick digs his fingers into my side showing his lack of appreciation for my mocking him. "Originally, I thought we'd make love tonight, but you seem to be asking for me to fuck you *hard*," he whispers in my ear.

I hope the dark blanket of night covers my red face as everyone stares at us, probably thinking my doting husband just whispered sweet nothings into my ear. They have no idea he's not always a gentleman.

"Ahem …" The guy next to Colby clears his throat.

"Sorry, dude. This is Wes. He's a marine biology student and he'll be here for the next few months to observe the whales, aka get college credit for surfing."

Wes smacks Declan in the back of the head, and we laugh. "Nice to meet you and congratulations." Wes is stocky with cropped blond hair, not the typical surfer look.

"Thanks." Trick and I both smile.

"And last but definitely not least, this is Mallory, Colby's girlfriend."

"Fiancée." She corrects him holding up her ring finger.

Declan rolls his eyes. "Whatever, you've had that ring for two years and still no wedding so I'm no longer sure it's really an engagement ring."

She sticks out a pouty lip and flips back her long dark hair revealing some serious silicon pouring out of her small halter top sundress, then elbows Colby in the gut. "We'd have a date set if a certain someone would hurry up and find himself. Anyway, Trick and I met this morning. I did yoga with him."

I make a quick glance at Trick, who keeps an impassive look to her comment. Then I look to see if his eyes are tempted by the large *rack*. Just in case old habits die hard. *Yep, he's staring.*

I snuggle into him pretending to nuzzle his neck. "If you don't stop gawking at her *rack,* the only thing you'll be fucking tonight is your hand." I smile at everyone as they look at us like we're the poster couple for happily ever after, and we are ... or we will be after we get a few things straight.

Trick's fingers dig yet a little deeper into my side, but I don't know why. I'm not the one staring.

"Well, we should let the newlyweds have some alone time," Martin interrupts. "And it is a Wednesday so some of us have to get up early tomorrow."

"Who might that be?" Declan jokes.

"Well, we really appreciate this. It was so kind of all of you to befriend us and make this such a special day. We should hangout this weekend or something ... if you want." I hate the never-been-accepted-school-girl insecurity that bleeds from me. They don't know me and I have no reason to think they wouldn't want to be friends, but my confidence has been beaten down too many times.

"Absolutely!" Declan replies. "We live right over there." He points to the house down the beach a little ways. "Martin rents it out to my parents but they're over in China for the next six months so we decided not to let a perfectly good beach house sit vacant."

I nod and smile.

Everyone exchanges hugs and I hate the way I watch Trick to see how his body responds to Mallory and her cleavage. I was jealous and possessive when I thought he was gay. Marriage could push my limits past the boundaries of all reason.

As the small group trudges off through the sand we watch them in silence for a few long seconds; then Trick turns and pulls me into his arms. "Don't."

I lift my shoulders, avoiding eye contact.

"Mrs. Roth, look at me."

I can't hide my faint smile as I look up.

"Have you ever seen the Oscar Mayer Wienermobile?"

I laugh at the words I never imagined coming out of his mouth. "Yes, why?"

"Does it catch your attention when you see it?"

"Yes, why?"

"Is it because you wish you could drive it or you wish you had one?"

Another laugh and a head shake. "No."

Trick jabs his thumb in the direction of our neighbor's house. "That *rack* was the Wienermobile." His hands slide to the zipper of my dress. I close my eyes as he drags it down with seductive patience, eliciting a flood of prickly goose bumps across my skin. "You, my sexy, beautiful wife … you are a Ducati." My dress falls to the sand.

My heavy eyelids flutter open as his mouth claims my neck, his hands feathering down my arms. "A Ducati?"

"Mmm hmm." He works the buttons of his shirt, letting his lips hold me submissive to his touch. "My bike is a Ducati."

"You love your bike?"

"Very much." He tosses his shirt to the side and my hands claim the tat-covered skin I crave. He's so damn sexy; my body feels on the constant edge of convulsion just from the heat of his skin.

"More than me?"

Trick stills, his mouth a breath away from mine. He stares at my lips and then flits his eyes to mine. *A lip twitch.* "No." He moves to capture my kiss, but I pull away.

"Oh my God! Did you have to think about it?"

In the darkness his teeth shine white. He grabs my waist, stealing my breath as he lifts me to him. I wrap my legs around his waist, and he carries me to the house.

"You hesitated!" I clench his hair and tug it, making him look at me.

He tries to dip his head down to my neck.

"You hesitated!"

As he carries me up the stairs to our bedroom, I keep a firm grip on his hair.

"I married *you*."

"Because they wouldn't give you a marriage license to marry your stupid bike."

Plopping me down on the bed, he straddles me. His face so close to mine our noses touch. "Now there's no need for name calling, and I hesitated because I couldn't believe you even asked." He drops slow kisses on my face. "My bike makes me feel good about my hard work. It's the nicest thing I've purchased with my own money." He slides his hand behind my head. "*You* make me feel good about myself. You're not my possession..." he presses his lips to mine, our tongues colliding in an explosion of need "...but I still want to possess ... every ... inch ... of ... you."

I close my eyes. His mouth skims down my neck to my shoulder, across my collarbone, and down to my breast.

"Possess me ..." I breathe out.

My husband ... *dear God* ... my *husband* stands and removes the rest of his clothes and pulls off my lace panties. "I have the most beautiful *wife*." Trick kisses the inside of my ankle and makes the moment an eternity ... an infinity of love. Lips, breath, tongue, hands, and every other inch of his body worships mine like I'm his religion and this bed is our church. And I swear his love is God sent and his touch is a glimpse of Heaven here on Earth.

"Trick ... it's too much," I plead as he brings me to the precipice over and over. Buried inside me, he drives me to ecstasy and then pulls out and tortures my sensitive nipples, my neck, my lips, and the occasional swipe of his tongue along my swollen sex. I am a feather's touch away from orgasm or death ... it could go either way at this point. The tangled sweaty mess of bed sheets has become typical of our love making that's really a marathon or sexual torture, depending on the night.

He flips me so I'm on top of him, sweaty and dizzy with so much need I can barely sit up. Grabbing my hips he guides me until he's lined up to my entrance, and then he brings me down onto him so hard we both cry out as I collapse onto his chest. Our mouths absorb our moans stirred by his last few deep strokes into me.

"S-so good…" I pant into his neck "…that was … so … good."

"Agreed." Trick chuckles with his hands still tangled in my hair. He rolls us to the side and grins. "Wife."

I grin. "Husband."

After long minutes of post-coital bliss, Trick rubs a few strands of my hair between his fingers with a glazed look in his eyes. "Why'd you say yes?"

I stare at my finger tracing the sanskrit on his abs. I've done it so many times every symbol has found its own etching in my mind. "Because you asked."

He laughs. "But you didn't have to say yes."

"You're wrong."

"How's that?" His muscles contract under my touch.

"Because anything else would have been a lie." I glance up at him.

He nods. It's subtle, but I see it. I'm attuned to a million little things about this man that I'm certain nobody else sees. Each little twitch, flinch, slow nod, or drawn out blink holds significance. These are the times I *feel* his thoughts. These undefined emotions mean so much.

"Why did you ask me to marry you?"

"I wanted you to know that I belong to you." Leaning forward he kisses me.

The profoundness of his words steals my breath. He didn't marry me to *take* anything; he did it to *give* me everything.

He yanks the knotted sheet loose and covers our naked bodies, pulling me closer until my nose finds home in its favorite spot at the crook of his neck.

"Goodnight, wife."

"Goodnight, husband."

CHAPTER THIRTY-TWO

O UR SHEER SHADES invite nature's alarm—the sun. I roll to nuzzle, but my nose finds nothing but pillow. There should be a law against waking up alone after your *marriage ceremony* night. I reach for the sheet that has drifted down my naked body, needing to erase the goose bumps from the chilly morning air.

"Leave it. I'm not done looking at your tits."

I bolt up, of course grabbing the sheet and covering my *tits*. Trick smirks, handing me a glass of juice, then yanks the sheet away. My eyes rove across his body, stumbling over a bump of aggravation when they hit his exercise shorts.

"It's our honeymoon. Why are you up and *dressed*?" I take a sip of juice.

He bends down, sucking the skin along my neck. "We're going to yoga, then we'll come back and I'll work on getting my wife broken in good."

I cough on my juice, half of it landing on his chest. He shakes his head while wiping it away with the sheet. Everything that comes out of his mouth is either words of romantic poetry or a dirty sailor beckoning his wench—rarely anything in between.

"Break me in?"

"Yes. But first we should get you limbered up. Come." He waltzes out of the room like we just finished discussing our grocery list.

I swing my legs over the side of the bed. Maybe I do need to limber up. Trick woke me in the middle of the night with his head buried between my legs. I was convulsing in under sixty seconds. Then he plunged his steel cock in me and made a relentless sprint to his finish as well. Afterward he pressed a soft kiss to my lips and said one word, "wife," before spooning me into his body and drifting off to sleep. I question if he was even awake. It felt like he was acting out a dream. Some people sleep walk or raid the refrigerator in their sleep; maybe Trick's thing is going to be sleep sex—spontaneously waking in the night and pounding his wife. *Hmm …*

TRICK WAITS FOR me with an extra towel and yoga mat. I fill my water bottle and step out into the cool morning breeze.

"Wife," he says with his back to me.

"Husband." I snuggle into his bare back, wrapping my arms around him.

He grabs my water and takes a swig. "Ready?"

I slide around to his front, lifting on my toes to kiss him. He denies me nothing, cupping the back of my head and holding me to his lips for a long kiss. "I'm going to embarrass you."

He laughs. "Come."

I follow him down the stairs to the beach where we head north.

"Yoga is not a competitive sport. You do it for yourself without worrying about what other people around you are doing."

"This coming from the guy who decided to marry me yesterday to make his claim in front of our neighbor. I'm not sure if I should feel wed or marked."

He glances back at me. "I'm spontaneous."

"You're incorrigible. So is there an instructor or does everyone just do their own thing?" I jog to keep up with his long strides. *Damn! Why is he always in such a hurry?*

"Bridget and Courtney take turns leading the group. Courtney led yesterday so I assume Bridget will lead today."

"Are you the only guy?"

"Nope. Stuart was there yesterday."

We make our way around a small inlet and there are about ten people stretching out on their mats in the sand with the rising sun to their backs and the breathtaking expanse of the Pacific in front of them.

"Trick and Darby!" Mallory waves jumping up and down. She's in danger of a black eye if she doesn't take it down a notch with her silicon punching bags bouncing all over the place. "Hey, everyone, Trick and Darby got married yesterday."

We're greeted with smiles and congratulations as Mallory introduces me to everyone else. The group is basically all perfect bodied twenty-somethings with shameless eyes all over my husband. Then, yes, there is Stuart and his wife Leona, both probably in their fifties. We spread out our mats as Bridget has everyone face east for several Sun Salutations. As we progress through more poses, I watch Trick to make sure I'm doing them right, but I'm not the only one watching him. *Everyone* else watches him too, with the exception of Stuart. Even his wife sneaks a peek every chance she gets.

Trick seems oblivious to the wandering eyes or maybe he's in his "go with the flow" mode that Grady taught him. Massive muffins Mallory is going to pull something in her neck if she doesn't keep her head down during Down Dog. Trick has got to see her staring at his ass. Bridget keeps reminding everyone to breathe with each stroke. Well, I'm seething and everyone else is panting, maybe even drooling a little. Trick and Stuart are the only ones controlling their breath to sync it with their movements.

"Everyone look at Trick."

I whip my head around, nearly toppling over in the sand, to see Bridget has walked over to Trick.

"See how his shoulders are strong but relaxed, pulled away from his ears." She rests her hands on his shoulders. "His abs are pulled in…" she slides her fingers down to his abs "… and he's low in his stance, front knee open and he's firming his butt." Her hand starts to move toward his butt. *Bitch thinks she's going to touch my man's ass!*

"Ahem!" I clear my throat loud enough to startle Bridget from her demonstration.

She gives me a fake grin and moves back to her mat. Trick? Well, his lip twitches. That cocky bastard is going to pay for it later!

We finish an hour's worth of contortionist training and then lie flat on our mats in Savasana or Corpse Pose to calm our central nervous systems and clear our minds. Not happening here. I'm worked up into a jealous frenzy that I'm not the least bit proud of and my mind is thinking murderous thoughts. After our final cleansing breaths, Bridget salutes everyone with a slow bow and a "namaste." *The light in me honors the light in you.* Aka, everyone else is in a peaceful loving place, but I've fallen victim to the bitch monster.

"See you tomorrow!" Bridget calls as we walk back down the beach.

No you won't!

My anger unleashes a superpower in my legs allowing me to keep a few strides ahead of Trick.

"You're sexy when you're jealous."

"Shut up."

He chuckles and it's fuel to my fire. "This is going to be fun."

I whip around and he stops within inches of bowling me over. "Fun?" I scowl, looking up at him. "We haven't been married for twenty-four hours and I'm already pissed at you. You think that's fun?"

"I think we're going to fuck *hard.*" The grit to his voice leaves no room for question. He's turned on by my anger. This is his foreplay. It's possible since the elevator gate incident he's made the assumption I like a good pounding. I do, but I like it on my terms. There's a very specific frame of mind that goes with the pain slash pleasure scenario that we've done a few times. As my feet sink into the sand with him towering over me, eyes burning into my flesh, I don't feel like this is going to be on my terms.

Squeezing my legs together, I'm able to hide the way my sex melts to the sound of his voice. My hardened nipples, however, need to practice more self-control, a pokerface of sorts. "I hate the way you let women touch you." I force some backbone into my words.

"I can see that." He steps so close my chest touches his.

"So. Why. Do. You. Let. Them. Do. It?"

"On a scale of one to ten, how wet are you for me right now."

What?!

"Did you know I wake up in the middle of the night with the most fucking uncontrollable craving for you?"

Gulp ... I did gather that last night.

He leans down, the heat from his skin, his breath, and his smell invading my personal space in every way possible. "I bet you're a ten and dripping over the fucking edges of the scale right now."

With my heart slamming against my chest, I smack the yoga mats out of his hand and run. There's no time to look back. I keep going until I reach the back door and rush through without shutting it. Skidding into our bedroom, I grab my phone off the dresser and scurry to the guest bedroom. With a quick look around I dive into the closet and shut the door, hiding behind a slew of his art supplies that showed up yesterday.

Now I decide to practice my controlled yoga breathing, fearing he'll hear my labored breaths from downstairs. Then it hits me. I'm hiding from my husband ... in a closet. *What the hell?* This can't be normal. I can't hear anything so after a few minutes I turn on my phone.

Me: *BFF, I need your help. I'm hiding from my husband.*
Trick: *Why is that?*

I swallow hard.

Me: *Because he's intimidating.*
Trick: *What are you afraid of?*

Trick: *Having your nipples sucked so hard you orgasm the moment he sinks his teeth into them.*

Trick: *Having his cock so full in your mouth you can't help but touch yourself?*

Trick: *Feeling his fingers curling inside you as his tongue flicks over your clit while your hands are restrained and you're helpless to his touch?*

Trick: *Or just a good old-fashioned fucking bent over the back of the sofa?*

Umm ... uhh ...

"Ahh!" I scream as the closet door opens. My heart explodes and I nearly wet myself. I shuffle my feet against the floor, scooting as far in the corner as I can, hugging my knees to my chest.

"Come."

I shake my head, holding my breath.

His lip twitches. Then, with what can only be described as a scene from a horror movie, he grabs my ankles and drags ... he fucking *drags* me out of the closet. "Trick!"

Hoisting me over his shoulder, he smacks my ass so hard I yelp. "I'm thinking sofa."

"Trick! Stop!" I scream, kicking and flailing as he carries me downstairs. As I pound my fists against his back, something catches my eyes. He has the ties to both my satin and terrycloth robes partially tucked into the waistband of his shorts along with one of his belts.

OH SHIT!

He sets me down with my ass backed up to the sofa, my chest heaving, eyes wide.

"Do you love me?"

I swallow and nod.

"Do you trust me?"

My gaze falters.

"Darby?" He lifts my chin with his finger.

"Do. You. Trust. Me?"

Another swallow, another nod.

"Good." He lifts my yoga top over my head, wetting his lips as he stares at my breasts. Then he pulls down my pants, leaving me naked. His lips skim up my legs, stopping at my sex, but all he does is just breathe out causing my legs to pinch closer together. Then he inhales. Standing, he watches me—daring me to run again. "It's my job as your husband to bring you unfathomable pleasure. Understood?"

A slow nod.

"Good." He takes the belt and binds my hands in front of me.

I've been tied up before, but he doesn't know that, and I'm a little surprised he doesn't ask me if it's okay.

"Turn."

I stare at him for a moment. Then I slowly turn. He ties the robe belts around the back legs of the sofa.

"Spread 'em."

I glance over my shoulder at him. He looks up with a don't-make-me-ask-you-again look. Sighing, I spread my legs and he ties them with the opposite ends of the anchored belts. Placing his palm flat on my back, he pushes me forward.

"Bend over."

I bend over.

"Fucking perfect."

"Trick!" I yell as two of his fingers plunge into me with unexpected surprise.

"Do you have any idea how beautiful you are?"

"Trick ..." I try to tip my pelvis into his touch.

He pumps his fingers into me a few times then removes them. "Just as I suspected ... an overflowing ten."

I can't see him, but I feel his cocky grin and if I know my dirty husband, he's sucking my juices off his fingers this very moment.

But my body doesn't have time to relish in his kinkiness because there's a knock at the door.

"Trick—"

He leans over me, running his tongue along my shoulder. "Shh ... Don't. Move," he whispers. Is he blind to the fact that I'm *tied up!* Where the hell am I going to go?

I'll admit, this isn't how I imagined our day going when we made love last night for the first time as husband and wife. If this is day two of our marriage, what's he leaving on the Spice Things Up list twenty years from now?

There's a chattering of muffled voices. I assume Trick's getting rid of a neighbor or something, but he's taking his leisurely time. I think I'm going to tie him naked to the couch later then leave to go shopping.

My body goes rigid as the voices get closer.

"Wait!" I hear Trick yell.

No! No! No!

"Well, what do we have here?"

Grady.

I close my eyes and die with zero dignity.

"Trick, now aren't you a boy after my own heart. Looks like we both like 'em tied to the sofa, bare ass up."

"Out!" Trick grinds through clenched teeth as he releases my legs with quick hands.

An animal cut loose from a trap, I sprint upstairs not bothering to let him release my wrists. Collapsing on our bed, I bury my head in my pillow; emotions warring between screaming or crying. So I do both.

"Shh ..." The side of the bed dips as gentle hands release my wrists. Trick pulls me up onto his lap, and I bury my face into his bare chest.

"I want a divorce."

He kisses my hair and chuckles. "Never."

"I'm so embarrassed."

"I'm sorry. I share the blame."

My head snaps back. "You *share* the blame?"

Trick's lips twist to the side and he nods. "Had I not had your ankles tied so tight you would have been able to escape before they came in."

"*They?*"

"Grady and Tamsen."

"Tamsen was downstairs? She saw me like—ahh!" I pound my fists against his chest. "We are over … over … over … over …"

He hugs me tight, pinning my arms between us. "Tamsen's a girl. You're being modest for no good reason."

I try to twist and wriggle out of his hold. "It's not modesty, you idiot! They didn't just see me naked, they saw me tied to the sofa. They saw my ass crack spread open. THEY SAW MY ASS CRACK SPREAD OPEN!"

He releases me from his grip with my final outburst and I stumble to a stand.

"But it was a beautiful ass crack, sweetie! Like a breathtaking eclipse!" Grady calls from downstairs.

"Oh my God!" I close my eyes and let my head fall into my hands.

"Get dressed. I'll meet you downstairs."

"I hate you!"

"You love me." He kisses the top of my head then walks out the door."

"I hate you!" I call a little louder.

"You love me!"

CHAPTER THIRTY-THREE

THIS BEATS THE sex in the supply closet humiliation tenfold. I throw on some clothes and walk to the top of the stairs then back to our bedroom a half dozen times, but I can't make myself go downstairs. So I'm going to sit on our bed and wait for them to leave, whether it's in an hour or a week.

"Darby?" Tamsen calls with a knock at the door. *So much for avoidance.*

"Come in." The heat and flames of crimson saturate my skin.

"Trick asked me to come up here."

I roll my eyes to the ceiling and sigh as she closes the door behind her. "You must think I'm nothing but a sex-crazed hussy after the supply closet incident and now this."

She laughs. "Hardly. I think you love a man that's been celibate for a long time and now he can't get enough of ... you." Her smile, as always, feels comforting and genuine.

"He's intense, that's for sure." As I say the words, I'm reminded that Jade said the same thing the first time Trick came into the ER.

Tamsen nods. "That's a good word." She sits next to me on the bed.

"How does a guy like Trick go so many years without being with a woman? I get that he somehow felt taken advantage of, but if he can't remember the details then how has that feeling stuck so long?"

"Grady. He's Trick's constant reminder of where he's been and why he never wants to go back."

I scoot sideways so I'm looking at her. "Does Grady know more about Trick's past than what he's told him?"

Tamsen stares at me and it's the same look Trick has given me so many times. The look that says a thousand emotions but only a few words will be spoken. "Yes."

"I don't understand. Why doesn't he tell him?"

"He won't know what to do with the information. It's possible it could trigger his memory, but if it doesn't then he's left with knowledge of a man he might not recognize..." she narrows her eyes a fraction "...especially if his actions were *questionable*."

"Questionable?"

Tamsen rests her hand on mine. "You're happy. Trick is ... like I've never seen him before. So maybe some things don't matter."

"Does this have something to do with him owning a gun?"

"Trick owns a gun because it makes him feel safe, not because he's a wanted criminal."

I sigh. "One moment I wish his memory would come back and the next ... I just don't know. But last night everything changed—" I close my eyes.

"What happened last night?"

I open them. Warmth radiates through my body and a bubbling grin takes over my face. "We got married."

"What?" Tamsen squeals, eyes wide and glowing. She bounces up and down on the edge of the bed then pulls me in for an exuberant hug. "Oh my gosh! Grady said he proposed, but I had no idea it would happen so fast." She pushes me back to arm's length. "You're not—" She grimaces.

I laugh and shake my head. "I'm not pregnant."

Tamsen's body melts. "Good ... I mean not that you having a baby would be bad it's just—"

"Stop. There's no need, I get it." I wave a dismissive hand.

Her smile surges back. "Trick got married." She shakes her head. "Never in my wildest dreams did I think I'd see the day. You, my dear, have worked some serious magic on his heart."

I bite my lips together. "That's a good thing, right?"

"It's the best. Well, Grady might not think so, but he'll get over it. He adores you."

"He does?" I cock my head to the side.

"Of course. In spite of their twisted fake 'partnership,' Grady really does want Trick to find happiness, even if it throws a wrench into Grady's immediate plans. And you, my dear, are definitely Trick's happiness."

I blink back a few tears. "I love him."

Tamsen hugs me. "I know you do, and he loves you ... probably more than you'll ever know. I just hope that if his memory ever comes back you'll remember the Trick downstairs is not the same man he was then."

I swallow past the lump in my throat. I don't want to look back, but I'd be lying if I said it doesn't scare me.

"I don't even know what to say." I sit back, showing a tight smile of guilt. "He asked me to marry him less than two weeks ago and then we just took off. I don't have a job and neither does he. I mean ... is this epically romantic, a real carpe diem moment, or catastrophically stupid?"

Tamsen laughs. "Epic ... it's undoubtedly epic."

I squint one eye. "So what are you and Grady doing here? I'm glad you are, well ... a phone call would have been nice." I feel that crimson creeping up again at the thought of what they saw when they walked in the door.

"Yeah, I don't think we'll pull the surprise thing again." She winks. "Grady flew back to Chicago to interview someone for Trick's position. Then he came on out to New York. Grady feels like he's Trick's big brother and he worries about him. So after you two flew the coop, Grady thought the two of us should pop down to Mexico to make sure our 'little brother' is doing okay. We'll only be here for a few days, and don't worry we're staying at a hotel—"

"Oh my gosh, no way. You'll both stay here. We have a spare

bed and a very comfy sofa."

If they can shake the vision of my naked ass bent over it.

"You're newlyweds, we wouldn't dream—"

"I'm not taking no for an answer." I stand. "Let's go inform the gay guys."

Tamsen giggles and stands. "I already love you, Darby. We're going to be *very* good friends."

I smile and head to the stairs before the emotions rack my body. I'm sure Tamsen has a million friends. With her kind demeanor and glowing smile, I don't know how she couldn't. What she doesn't know is she's my second official friend *ever;* and I'm just speechless.

THE SOUND OF Trick and Grady laughing about something as we walk downstairs swells my heart. I love the sound of Trick laughing. Maybe because he shares it with such reservation to a very small and exclusive few people.

"Darby!" Grady stands, arresting me with a breathtaking hug. "I want to hate you for taking my boy, but I just can't."

Tamsen walks past us with an I-told-you look.

"Please forgive us for the intrusion."

I stiffen. "It's fine. Just forget about it … as in *really* forget about it."

Grady chuckles. "Forget … never, but my lips are officially sealed." He releases me, kissing both cheeks.

Trick smirks, reclined on the sofa with one ankle resting on the opposing knee. "Wife."

I squint my eyes and shake my head. We were minutes away from having the shortest marriage ever after this morning's incidents. But one look and I'm his again … I always was.

"Husband." I plop on his lap as he uncrosses his legs.

As if we're the only two people in the room, his hands dive into my hair, pulling me in for a slow, deep kiss. It's his reminder that while he may not own me, he will always possess me.

"Forgive me?" he whispers over my lips while releasing me.

"Eventually." I grin.

We look over at two sets of eyes looking at us with such adoration it makes me want to freeze this moment, this *feeling*, in time forever.

"Damn!" Grady shakes his head. "I can't believe we missed the wedding by a day."

"It wasn't a wedding. It was a marriage ceremony." I grin, batting my lashes at Trick.

"What?" Tamsen asks with confusion etched on her face.

"We met one of our neighbors yesterday morning, a young surfer. He was being friendly, *neighborly*, and that's when Trick announced we were getting married … that day. *Then* he proceeded to plan the 'ceremony' with said neighbor right in front of me."

"Way to claim your woman." Grady winks at Trick.

"Way to be an ass." Tamsen elbows Grady in the gut while scowling at Trick. "No wonder we weren't invited or that neither of you are wearing rings. Let me guess … your neighbor looked at Darby like she's the beautiful woman that she is and you couldn't waste another day before claiming her … marking her like an animal."

"I didn't treat her like an animal." Trick sighs with a slight shake of his head.

"Well, you did have her tied to the—"

"Grady!" both Trick and Tamsen yell.

Grady shrugs. "Well you did."

"Are you drawing?" Tamsen asks. She's taking the spotlight off me and visions of my tethered naked body.

"Not yet, but I'm going to start again. Darby swears my work is worth thousands of dollars, so I figure it'll pay the rent."

Grady laughs. "As I recall, you were paid quite well at your last job. You can't possibly be hurting for money already."

"No, but Darby insisted on furnishing the joint as soon as we moved in and that wasn't cheap."

My jaw unhinges, eyes bulging from my head. "I tried to pay for *everything* but you wouldn't let me!"

A lip twitch. *Ass!*

My eyelids tighten to a squint. "You're sadistic. You play me all the time. I'm in limbo between bruising your ego and stepping on your toes. Either I'm flaunting my money or taking advantage of you."

"Did you have her sign a prenup?" Grady makes a serious face but I see wicked delight dancing in his eyes.

"Nope. My bad. She's already threatened to divorce me and I'm sure she'll take my Ducati and my computer with my video surveillance recordings."

I borrow Tamsen's move and shove my elbow into Trick's gut. He feigns injury.

"Tamsen and I are having a slumber party tonight in *my* bedroom while you two boys flip for the sofa and spare bedroom."

Tamsen stands and leans in for a fist bump. "Word, girlfriend."

"Since when are we staying here?" Grady asks.

"Since Darby insisted we stay with them."

"Mmm, mmm, mmm … Oh dear, Trick. I do believe you've already lost your pants in this relationship. Has it even been twenty-four hours?" Grady shakes his head.

I know what's coming because there's one part of Trick that is always predictable—his cocky side.

"Darby likes me best without my pants."

Sometimes it's not worth the fight. I shrug. "It's true, I do."

Grady and Tamsen fall into a fit of laughter, clearly not expecting my admission. I lean back and kiss Trick's jaw and whisper in his ear. "I like you like a Greek statue—sculpted, naked, and *hard.*"

From my mouth to his cock, I feel him come to life under my butt as he grabs my hips and adjusts my position on him. If anyone's keeping score, I think I just took the lead.

"So what about you, Darby, are you going to look for a job too?"

I frown at Grady. "Yes, but it won't be in my chosen field. I'm not licensed to practice in Mexico."

"Aren't you going to miss your job?" Tamsen looks at me with a hint of sympathy.

I look at Trick and smile in spite of the concern lining his face. He, too, is waiting for my answer. "That's the funny thing ... I always imagined finding my purpose and I thought I had. Then my real purpose found me and being with *him* is all that matters. So I'll find some job to feel like I'm making a contribution and to make my share of the rent of course." I wink at Trick. "But for now, I'm just living in the moment ... and it's a pretty damn good one."

My statement earns me another we're-the-only-ones-in-the-room kiss.

"I fucking love you."

"You'd better, because I moved to sunny Mexico with you and in case you haven't noticed, I'm a redhead with fair skin."

"You must be adapting ... I noticed you have a nice bikini tan line already—hipster-boyshorts, nice!" Grady grins.

Being around Grady, I'm not sure how I ever believed Trick was gay. What guy can identify the correct bikini bottom name from a tan line? Then again, I hate even thinking such stereotypical thoughts. That's Nana's thing. I also hate that he's actually seen my tan line.

"Grady, it's okay to not speak every thought that pops in your head." Tamsen pinches his lips together.

"We should grab an early dinner. What do you think?" I once again veer the conversation in a direction suitable for me.

"I'm in!" Tamsen hops up. "Let me go change out of my travel clothes.

"Ditto, sister." Grady follows her upstairs with their suitcases.

I pivot my body so I'm facing Trick, straddling his lap. "You are in a shitload of trouble, mister."

He sucks in my bottom lip and drags it through his teeth while gripping my hips. "You can take it out on me in bed later."

"Tamsen's sleeping with me, remember?"

Trick assaults my neck. "Like hell ..." he mumbles against my skin.

"I CAN'T BELIEVE we're going to the Hotel California for dinner." Tamsen laughs as we ride in the backseat of my red Saab.

"We're in Todos Santos, of course we're going to the Hotel California. It's historic and I've heard the chef at the restaurant is amazing!" Grady wipes clean his sunglasses and slips them on. "Did you know the hotel was founded by Mr. Wong, a Chinese immigrant? He wanted the locals to think he was Mexican so he changed his name to Don Antonio Tabasco. However, he was eventually called 'El Chino,' which means 'The Chinese Man.' He brought ice from La Paz to his restaurant making him the first and only place at the time that served cold beer."

Tamsen rests her hand on my arm. "Grady is an encyclopedia of useless information."

"Don't be catty, little sis."

Through the rear view mirror I see Trick holding tight to his smirk.

"So it wasn't owned by the Eagles?" I wink at Tamsen.

Grady shakes his head and flips his wrist back at me. "No, of course not, silly girl. Did you know there have been many firsthand accounts of spirits and ghosts in the courtyard of the hotel?"

Both Tamsen and I snicker.

"Let me repeat ... useless information."

Grady scowls at his sister, trying to hide his own grin.

Our early dinner guarantees us immediate seating and the next couple of hours fill with crazy laughter about Trick and Grady's gay charade that has put them both in the worst situations over the years. Tamsen and I find ourselves giggling just to giggle by the time Grady orders a third bottle of wine. Trick watches me with a curious mix of amusement and caution as I down another glass of red wine. He's the only sober one at our table.

"Darby, did they catch whoever assaulted your father?"

Grady's words try to pull at my conscience, but it's been drowned in wine. Yet, I still have plenty of snickering available. "I don't think so." I rest my hand on Trick's leg. "What do you think, sweetie? Do you think they caught the guy that broke into a U.S. senator's secured estate, disabled the security cameras, and assaulted him while he was still in his monogrammed Zimmerli pajamas."

He rests his hand on mine, giving it a circulation-seizing squeeze. "How would I know?"

"Did they figure out motive?" Tamsen asks.

Trick cuts me off just as I start to speak. "What do you think, Darby? What would motivate someone to assault your father? Any ideas?" He rests his arm on the back of my chair, fisting my hair just enough to make it taut—to make his point.

It's amazing how the right words can have a more sobering effect than a strong cup of coffee. "How would I know?" I grin through clenched teeth.

"Well you two sure don't know much." Tamsen snickers, and it is laughable because we're the *only* two aside from my father who know what really happened.

"That's why we're here, to escape all the crap that was interfering." Trick's words hold a finality to them as he releases his grip on my hair, but I don't want him to release me. From the first time he grabbed my ponytail at the political dinner, my body has recognized that tug and its connection to a bundle of nerves between my legs. I start to giggle, covering my mouth with my hand as my skin flushes. My last three large gulps of wine have caught up with me, leaving a warm, tingling, and slightly numbing sensation hugging my body.

"What's so funny?" Tamsen asks and starts to laugh too ... just because.

I lean toward Trick's ear and cup my hands around my mouth. "I just realized how much I love it when you pull my hair. It messes with my vagina ... in a good way." I giggle. "I even liked being tied up and I *love* it when you fuck me *hard*. Does that make me a naughty girl?"

I sit back in my chair and adjust the napkin on my lap. A smug smile steals my face as I glance up at Tamsen and Grady. The wide-eyed look of curiosity on their faces is priceless. I bet they'd love to know what I just whispered in Trick's ear.

As if on cue, both of them erupt into a bellowing of laughter, Tamsen covering her face with her hands and Grady hugging his stomach as he leans forward, barely breathing.

Scrunching my nose, I look at Trick for insight into their odd behavior.

He grimaces while digging his teeth into his lower lip. "I think it's time to cut you off."

"Why?" I look at Grady and Tamsen again. They're both wiping tears from their eyes. "What's so funny?" I start to laugh too, because it must be something really good. Although I'm not sure how I missed it.

Grady cups his hands around his mouth and leans toward Tamsen, mimicking what I did to Trick. "You got in whisper position but you forgot to actually whisper." He cracks up again, letting his forehead fall to Tamsen's shoulder.

Turning, my face pulls into a tight, painful smile, looking for confirmation that I should crawl under the table and stay there until closing. Trick nods and I close my eyes, sinking down into my chair as the floor calls to me.

"The answer to your question, sweetie, is yes. That might make you a naughty girl."

"Oh my God!" I cover my face before Grady finishes speaking. The room spins as embarrassment burns the surface of my skin.

"Check please!" Grady hollers to the waiter with an impish grin.

CHAPTER THIRTY-FOUR

IT'S CHILDISH, BUT necessary. I pretend to fall asleep as soon as Trick shuts the door to the car. I'm buzzed and relaxed but not tired ... not yet. Right now I want to avoid any more embarrassment in front of Grady and Tamsen.

Trick carries me into the house. Tamsen offers, with a giggle and hiccup, to forego our girls' slumber party until tomorrow night. Trick doesn't respond, but I imagine the look on his face could kill on contact. He takes me upstairs and sets me down on our bed. The moment I hear the lock to our bedroom door click, my eyes open. They're heavy drunk with alcohol and *lust*.

I. *Need*. Him.

Sitting up, our eyes meet. He shrugs off his shirt. My intoxicated gaze drags over every inch of his sculpted, ink-etched, sexy as hell body. His wild animal eyes feed my addiction. Holding my gaze with an unwavering dominance, he continues removing his clothes. Piercing glare, controlled moves, and the most incredible body seduce me. *Only* Trick can bring me to my knees ... *begging* ... without a single touch.

He sits on the bed, his back against the headboard. "Come." One word, it vibrates over my skin sending chills up my spine and stealing a beat from my heart as something inside explodes. A million shards of desire ricochet to my very essence.

Standing, I step out of my heels and release the halter tie to my dress. He fucking eats me alive with his eyes as I slide down my panties. Crawling up the bed, I fall victim to his compelling gaze. It says the only thing that needs to be said ... *there will be no more words.*

Straddling him, I grab his hair and cry out as his mouth seizes my breast. His flat palm slides up my back. Fisting my hair, he tugs it—hard. My head falls back and I collapse onto him. Another cry passing my lips as he impales me ... *possessing* me.

THAT LOVE ... THE one that's too good to be true, and that passion ... the one that feels like a wild animal's trying to escape from within—I have that with Trick. The intensity we share, the sweat, the urgency, it's righting all the wrong from our past—one look, one touch, one breath at a time.

"Don't move," a rough, groggy voice warns as I wiggle under the blanket of his body.

"It's after eight and I have to pee."

"It can wait." Trick rubs his sandpaper face over my chest, kissing the swell of my breasts. His hands slide up my sides and I feel the instant reminder of his insatiability.

"My bladder disagrees. Besides we have guests and we should try to be hospitable."

"I need to be inside you."

I wriggle my way out. "I'll urinate on you and even if you're into golden showers, I'm not." I walk to the bathroom.

Trick buries his face in the pillow and groans. "Darby ..."

I smile, looking back at my inked pile of perfection, naked on our messy sheets. He's mine—a truth I'll never really get used to. A quick pee and a much needed tooth brushing gets interrupted with my husband's morning *need* that will not be dismissed. He needs this release as much as I needed my bladder relief. I think it may have something to do with the mouthful of toothpaste I haven't yet expectorated or the cold vanity top against my bare ass, but my orgasm doesn't make an appearance. However, by the time we get out of the shower I'm more than sated.

✪

"Mmm, what's that smell?" I whisper to Trick as we make our way downstairs an hour after waking.

"That would be Grady."

"Good morning, newlyweds," Grady says with naughty suggestion in his tone.

"It is." Trick palms my ass with no discretion. I don't even care at this point. Grady and Tamsen have to know by now that we're either having sex, talking about it, or thinking about it. I'm not a drunk that suffers amnesia the morning after; my memory from the restaurant is all too clear. I'm a dirty girl that likes to be man-handled and dominated in the bedroom. Who knew? *I did.*

"What are you two boys going to do today while Darby and I flaunt our stuff on the beach, watching the hot surfer guys?"

"Excuse me?" Grady rests his fist on his hip, flipping it out with sass.

"Okay … Trick, what are you going to do today while Darby, *Grady*, and I flaunt our stuff on the beach, watching the hot surfer guys?"

"According to your description, it would appear I'm surfing today."

Co-cky!

"You surf?" I raise a brow, cutting into my pancakes.

Trick shoves a bite into his mouth, shaking his head.

"The boy lived in New York then moved to Chicago. But I'm sure he could walk down the beach in board shorts while holding a surf board and the women won't give a shit if he can surf or not."

Trick rolls his eyes at Grady, but his smile contradicts his feigned annoyance.

✪

TRICK FOREGOES THE beach scene, opting to dig out his sketch pad and graphites instead. Grady puts on his own show for onlookers strolling down the beach. He may be in his forties, but his body is holding tight to its early thirties. Tamsen looks amazing in her string bikini with Brazilian bottoms, and the sun loves her skin as much as Grady's. The sun and I? Not friends yet. My only beach friends are SPF fifty and a wide-brimmed hat, but I love the salty ocean breeze, and the rhythmic lulling sound of the waves crashing into shore, and the way the white sand massages my toes every time I curl them into the cool grittiness.

"Tell me, Darby … why did Trick assault your father?"

I tilt the rim of my hat and look at Grady reclined with his eyes closed. "What are you talking about?"

"I can read Trick better than anyone, honey. Your father must have done something unforgivable. Trick's not a hair trigger. Everything he does has purpose and control, but maybe not with you. I'm beginning to think you bring out a Trick I haven't seen before."

With little consideration, I dismiss any idea of trying to deny Grady's accusation, instead focusing on his interesting observation. "Is that a bad thing?"

"In Grady's book it is. He's been Trick's mentor for said 'purpose and control.'" Tamsen laughs.

"Shows what you know. I think Darby is exactly what Trick needs—a distraction."

"A distraction?" I look over again at Grady, but he remains statuesque.

"At first I was pissed that he was leaving Chicago, but now I realize being here with you is the distraction from his past that he needs. An official letting go and starting over."

"I'm not trying to be a distraction. What if one day he wakes up and remembers everything? There's nothing predictable about memory loss from head injuries. Anything could trigger his memory."

"Well let's hope for your sake he doesn't."

I sit up, turning to face him. "Why? What will I learn that will change us?"

For the first time Grady rolls his head to the side, and peeks open one eye. "It's hard to say, but what I do know is he was high most of the time and *reckless*."

"Where did all the expensive stuff in his garage come from?"

Grady shrugs, aiming his face at the sun again. "Honey, you're looking for the wrong answers."

"What does that mean? What are the questions to the right answers?"

"There's only one question."

"Which is?"

"Which is ... does it matter?"

"It matters if Trick could be in danger! What if he owes someone something? Is he supposed to go through the rest of his life looking over his shoulder?"

Grady moves his hand to my arm, eyes closed, lips smirked. "This much I can assure you. Trick's past isn't trying to catch up to him; it's running away from him with the fear of God in its eyes."

CHAPTER THIRTY-FIVE

WHO THE FUCK *is this?*

I've tried to sketch Darby but my hand makes all the wrong lines and angles. It's as if the shadows of this image in my head are fighting to come into the light. With each stroke of my hand, she reveals a little more of herself.

Who the fuck is this?

There's an unexplainable driving force inside that can't be held back. I need to get her out. I need to see her. She's the answer to a thousand questions, yet I fear her. What if I bring her to life and she steps off this paper and takes mine away?

Who. The. Fuck. Is. This?

CHAPTER THIRTY-SIX

CHRISTMAS ARRIVES EARLY in Todos Santos for Trick. His motorcycle has been delivered and I'm not sure, but I swear he gets tears in his eyes. Grady declares he's riding bitch before Tamsen or I can slip a single word into the conversation. A quick peck on the lips and they're off.

"You have the makings for margaritas?" Tamsen asks.

Blocking the sun with my hand above my eyes as I watch the guys ride off, I shake my head. "Sorry, I married an addict."

"Well then, it looks like it's time to introduce me to your neighbors."

I raise a brow at Tamsen. "You think it's a good idea to ask neighbors I barely know if they have ingredients for margaritas we can borrow?"

She loops her arm around mine, tugging me in the direction of Declan's. "They were at your wedding; they're practically family." She giggles.

Thirty minutes later, we're back home sipping margaritas on the veranda.

"I can't believe you agreed to go out with Wes in exchange for drink ingredients." I shake my head.

Tamsen shrugs. "It's just breakfast, and Grady and I are leaving the next day anyway." She takes another sip. "Mmm, and these are so good. It's totally worth it."

I nod in agreement. "Can I ask you something?"

"Sure."

"What's the connection between you, Grady, and Trick? I mean, Trick thinks of you as family and I know you got him into rehab, but surprisingly he's never told me, and I've never asked how you three came to be so close."

Tamsen flips up her glasses. "Really? You don't know?"

I shake my head.

"I was part of the team that responded to the accident the night he was hit."

"Oh..." I twist my glass by the stem "...so how did that lead to everything else? You were just doing your job. Doesn't that end after you make the transfer to the hospital?"

Tamsen takes a drink then rubs her lips together with a slow nod. "Yes, it does, but that night was an exception."

"How so?"

"Grady was driving the car that hit Trick."

"What?" I set my glass down and sit up straight.

"Grady said Trick was like an animal running out into the street. There wasn't enough time to stop. Alcohol, drugs ... it was all in his system. It was also the dead of winter and he had on a T-shirt, pants unfastened, and bare feet."

My forehead tightens. This is painful to hear. It doesn't feel like she's talking about my Trick.

"Grady knew it wasn't his fault, but he still felt responsible in some way. He wanted to talk to Trick's family and let them know what happened, but when he discovered there was no family, he couldn't walk away and leave him. Grady had to know he was going to be okay."

Tamsen stares down at her glass. "Grady is the one who took Trick home after he was released from the hospital. That's when he discovered Trick's world—the art, the drugs, the very expensive 'stuff.' I'm still not sure why, but he took it upon himself to make sure Trick got it together. I helped him into drug rehab while Grady was relentless with trying to piece together the mystery of Patrick

Roth." Tamsen laughs. "Grady knew Trick was officially 'his' when he brought him a slew of makeup and told Trick to make him look like a woman."

I smile, remembering the Don and Donna incident.

"Deep down my brother has a heart of gold, but he's always jumped at opportunities that are mutually beneficial."

Tamsen sits up and turns toward me, resting her feet on the ground. "Truthfully, it was easy for both of us to want to help Trick. He was so lost and helpless, like a child. Beneath the addiction and questionable actions, he's a good guy, and in some ways we've felt like the memory loss was his chance to start over. I know it sounds crazy, but I can't help but wonder if it was fate that he and Grady's paths crossed that night."

THE BIKER BOYS return and Trick heads straight upstairs to draw. I've been spoiled having all of his attention, but now that his bike is here and he's started drawing again, I'm going to have to learn to share. By six I check on him to see if he plans on joining us for dinner. What I don't expect is for the door to the spare bedroom to be locked.

"Trick?"

"Hmm?"

"Can I come in?"

"Just a sec."

Really?

"Whatcha need?" He smiles, opening the door, but just a crack.

I bob my head side to side to see past him. "What are you drawing?"

He scrapes his teeth over his bottom lip. "Well, I've been trying to draw you."

"Me?" My eyes go wide to match my grin. "Let me see." I step forward, but he blocks me.

"You can't. Not until it's done."

"Why not?"

"I don't like people looking at my work before it's finished."

I never took Trick to be the self-conscious type. He's as cocky as they come with everything else, but with the one thing he has every right to be cocky about he shows vulnerability.

"Am I naked in the picture?" I raise a single brow.

"Sleeping."

"Oh … that's … interesting."

He nods.

"Well, we're going to dinner. Are you ready?"

He grimaces. "Would you be too mad if I skipped out tonight? I'm at real critical point and I don't want to lose my focus by leaving."

I shrug. "Okay, I guess. You must be in the zone?"

He nods.

"Can we bring you back something?"

"Nah, I'll grab a snack later."

I feel my lips pulling into a frown, but I make a quick recovery so he doesn't see my disappointment. "Well, I'll see you later then." I lean forward for a kiss just as he shuts the door … In. My. Face!

"Have a good time," he hollers from the other side of the door.

It would appear as if the honeymoon is over.

"Trick's not going," I announce at the bottom of the stairs.

"Come on, we don't need him. Besides I think it's great that he's engulfed in his art again." Grady offers me his arm and I take it with a forced smile.

"What's he working on?" Tamsen asks.

"Me."

"He's drawing you?" Grady gasps.

"That's what he said."

"God, this love-hate relationship I have with you just keeps getting more intense."

I squint at Tamsen as we get in my car.

"Grady's been trying to get Trick to sketch him for years … nude, I'm sure." We laugh but Grady slumps into the backseat with a pouty face. "But Trick won't do it."

I pull out of the drive. "Don't feel too bad, Grady. Trick's not sketching me nude either. He's sketching me sleeping."

"Yeah, but probably in the nude," Grady grumbles.

I'M SAD TO see Grady and Tamsen leave. They're starting to feel like my family as well. Yesterday, Tamsen kept to her promise and had brunch with Wes while Grady and I took an eco-tour of Todos Santos. Trick? Well, he's been locked up in the guest bedroom, including sleeping in it. He insisted Tamsen and I have our girls' slumber party—for two nights.

"Take care of our boy." Grady hugs me and I feel like he's my "big brother" too. "Wander up the coast and see me sometime. It's a fantastic drive."

"We will."

Tamsen pulls me in for a hug. "Love you, sweetie. I'm sure you're missing Trick, but our girl time the past couple days has been the absolute best."

"I couldn't agree more. Are you sure you don't want to move down here with us?"

Tamsen laughs. "Maybe when my prince charming sweeps me off my feet. Besides, I'm going to text you every day; you'll be glad I'm not here so at least you can shut off your phone when you get tired of hearing from me."

"Okay, ladies. Enough already. I've got a plane to catch."

"Did Trick open the door when you went up to tell him good-bye?"

Both Grady and Tamsen shake their heads. "He just hollered 'thanks for coming.'"

Tamsen laughs. "At least you can't be mad at him; he's still sort of spending time with you."

"Or he's cheating on you with you." Grady snickers as they walk out the door.

The house takes on an immediate silence ... loneliness. All I keep thinking about is the approximate two hundred hours that it can take Trick to complete a drawing. I have no idea how much he's been sleeping, but I doubt it's that much. Maybe if I'm lucky I might get to see him in another week or two.

JELLIED TOAST WITH eggs and cayenne gets me a kiss on the cheek as he opens the door just enough to accommodate the diameter of the plate. Catch of the day from a restaurant near the shopping district gets me a wink as he grabs the sack and shuts the door. But dinner ... okay, I skip dinner and offer him dessert instead.

I knock on the door.

"Hmm?" It's become the usual response.

"Hungry?"

"A little. What did you bring?"

I shake my head at the fact that we're having this conversation through the locked door. "I brought what used to be your favorite."

The lock clicks and the door opens a fraction. Trick's lips part as his eyes roam over my *naked* body. "Our bedroom, five minutes," he says, shutting the door.

Five minutes turns into fifteen, but I don't complain because all that matters is he's in our bed giving the real Darby, not a sketch, his full attention. Foreplay doesn't make an appearance tonight. There is no sipping the martini; it's a shot glass of sex ... bottoms up— literally. I have to concede, although it's quick, Trick's precision is g-spot-on.

Damn him!

He kisses my forehead, slips on his jeans without fastening them, and walks out of our bedroom. Just as soon as my body floats back down to Earth, I am going to be really pissed at him—for something. I'm sure when my brain begins to form coherent thoughts again I'll know what that something is.

IT'S BECOME QUITE clear that Trick has found a way to feel productive again. I suppose it's unrealistic to think our most worthwhile contribution to society is mind-blowing sex. After a lonely night in bed and leaving Trick's breakfast by the guest bedroom door, I get ready to find my non-Trick purpose. As I open the front door I'm greeted by Declan in shorts and a muscle shirt with his hand fisted like he was just about to knock.

"Hey." I smile.

"Hey. Sorry, are you on your way out?"

"Yes, I was just getting ready to …" *Find my new purpose?* "… run some errands. What's up?"

"I didn't know if you were serious about helping me with some of my online classes, but if you were—"

"I'd love to!" I grimace at my own eagerness. I'm a newlywed; I shouldn't be jumping at the opportunity to get out of my house and hangout with the neighbor guy, but I am because I'm just that bored.

Declan's eyes grow big. "Really?"

"Sure."

He nods. "Okay, great. When's the best time for you?"

I shrug. "Now works."

His head jerks back. "Now? Weren't you needing to run some errands?"

I wave a dismissive hand, closing the door behind me. "It's nothing important. Your place?"

"Yeah, sure." He gestures with his head toward his house. "So what's Trick doing today?"

I slip on my sunglasses. "He's drawing."

"Drawing?"

"Yes, he's an artist."

"Wow, that's awesome. What's he draw?"

"People."

"Well he's come to the right place. Todos Santos is an artist's paradise. Is he going to sell his sketches?"

"I think so. Although he's working on a drawing of me right now. I don't think he's planning on selling it, but honestly I haven't asked."

When we reach Declan's, he gets us drinks and snacks, grabs his laptop, and takes us out back. "So what made you want to become a PA?"

Slipping off my sandals, I curl up on the chaise lounge. "I job shadowed one my senior year of high school. She did basically the same procedures, diagnosing, and treating that the physician did but she worked three days a week. You don't see too many part-time physicians. I don't know if I'll ever have children, but if I do I'd like to have the option of working part-time. Then there's the option to change specialties without going back to school. Physicians can't jump from surgery to dermatology without going back to school but PAs can."

"What was your specialty?"

"I worked in the ER." I grin. "An adrenaline junkie of sorts, but for me it was the challenge of putting together the broken puzzles."

"You must be good under pressure."

I nod. "Yes, in my job I was. No one makes the right decision one hundred percent of the time, but I've been good at going with my instincts."

"Confident?"

"Yes. It's hard though. Sometimes you can be overly confident. I work with some people who think they can do no wrong. For myself, I try to find that balance."

"You ever kill anyone?"

I laugh. "Looks like we need to work on your medical nomenclature. Have patients *died* under my care? Yes. It's unavoidable if you work in the ER long enough."

After another half hour of small talk, we start working on his school work. I shoot off a quick text to Trick so he doesn't wonder why my car is still at home but I'm not.

Me: Helping Declan with his school. If you decide to take a break, I'll run home!

A half hour later I get a response.

Trick: OK

By the time Colby, Wes, and Mallory show up, we've put in almost four hours of tutoring. They invite me and Trick to dinner, but I decline this time, knowing that Trick will not be socializing until he's completed his project. The eerie silence drowns me as I open our front door. A little part of me was hoping he'd been making dinner, watching TV, or even doing yoga, which he hasn't done in days.

"Trick?"

No answer.

I go upstairs and knock on the door.

"Hmm?"

I sigh. "Let's go out for dinner."

"Not tonight. Maybe tomorrow."

I lean my forehead against the door. "Please."

"Tomorrow." His voice is absent of emotion.

"Well I'm going."

"Ok."

Clawing at my scalp, I shake my head. This sucks. I don't give a shit how fabulous this picture of me is; the resentment is going to take away from my full appreciation of it.

"Oh, and I'm taking your Ducati. Any special instructions before

I leave?" I call on my way down the stairs.

The bang upstairs sounds like the doorknob impaling the wall.

"What did you say?" Trick stands at the top of the stairs in his jeans, no shirt—eyes wild.

Mentally willing the smirk on my face to hide, I turn around. "Welcome to the world again."

"You're not taking my bike."

I shrug. "Who's going to stop me?"

"Darby." He squints his eyes.

I grab my purse and his key from the counter then sprint outside and around the corner to the carport.

"Darby!" Trick yells, chasing me in his bare feet.

I yank off the cover and grab my helmet. He jerks my helmet from my grip along with the key and picks up the cover from the ground.

"Not happening."

"Take me for a ride, please."

"Tomorrow." He walks off toward the house while I fight back the tears.

CHAPTER THIRTY-SEVEN

THE BRAIN IS complex and some things just can't be explained, such as the woman I'm drawing. I have to remember her. For God's sake, I'm drawing her! It's effortless for my hands to keep adding details; they know every single one. But what I really want to do is bang my head against the wall because she's so familiar. I know her, but how? Is my memory coming back or just fucking with me?

I'm pissed, and paranoid, and … confused. Then there's Darby. I can hardly look at her. What would I tell her? I'm drawing a woman sleeping who's *naked*. I don't make shit up. I don't draw things I haven't seen. My sketches aren't imagination, they're recollection. I've been with this woman. *Fuck!* I can even hear her voice, but not her words.

I need a trigger—a name, a location … something. It's not finished, but as is the case with most of my work, I'm not sure it ever will be. I find details run to infinity. Eventually I just have to move on to something else. Sliding my phone from my pocket, I take a picture of my drawing and send it to Grady with a message.

Me: Recognize her?

Grady: Should I?

Me: I fucked her.

Grady: I hope not recently ;)

Me: Cut the crap. I drew her but I don't know why. I know her but I don't know how. I'm fucking miserable.

Grady: You have a beautiful wife and a promising future. Forget *about the woman.*

Me: *That's just it! I can't forget what I can't remember.*

Grady: *Thought you were drawing YOUR WIFE!*

I don't respond. There's nothing left to say. I'm an asshole now and I'm pretty sure I was back then too.

CHAPTER THIRTY-EIGHT

SOMETHING IS WRONG with Trick, but I don't know what. His obsession with sketching me is going too far. He won't let me see it. He won't come out of that damn bedroom except to shower and go to the bathroom. He's even slept in there for the past five nights. I've turned into his personal maid—doing laundry and catering food to "his" room. The motorcycle ride? Never happened. Sex? Haven't had that either, and I refuse to stand outside his door naked again looking like I'm begging for it.

I still haven't looked for a job. Declan keeps me busy in the afternoons tutoring him. He insists on paying me, and although I try to refuse, he won't take no for an answer. I value his friendship along with Wes, Colby, and even Mallory's to a certain extent. I've had dinner with them now two different nights, without my husband, and I've spent several mornings watching them surf. They're all really good at it. I enjoy feeling like their equal and I know telling Declan that it's ridiculous to pay me because I don't need the money would taint that. So I conveniently use the money to buy more snacks and drinks and contribute to the meals we have together.

This morning I have to do a double take when Trick comes down the stairs before I have a chance to finish making breakfast and leave a plate outside his door.

"Morning." He smiles and kisses me on the top of my head.

"Good morning. Breakfast?" I hold out his plate.

"Nah, I'll eat when I get back."

"Back?"

He grabs the key to his motorcycle. "I need a few supplies."

"O-kay." I set the plate down. "Trick?"

He stops with his back to me.

"What's going on?"

"Noth—"

"And don't say nothing! That's all I've heard over the past week!"

"We'll talk later." He continues out the door.

My appetite dissolves, engulfed by my anger. As soon as I hear him speed off, I run upstairs and turn the knob. It's locked. *Of course it is.*

I hurry to my bathroom and find a hairpin. It's a simple push lock so it easily opens. I expect to see an easel, sketch pad, or something, but there's nothing. Opening the closet, I rummage through everything.

Nothing.

I sigh with my hands fisted on my hips. Dropping on all fours I look under the bed.

Nothing.

Sitting back on my heels, I feel a pang of defeat mixed with anger, until my eyes focus on the corner of something sticking out between the mattress and box springs. I tug on the corner, sliding out a large sketch pad. The first page is blank, and the second, and the third. My frustration grows as I flip through each empty page with impatience.

Oh. My. God.

On the back page is a sketch of a woman … a *naked* woman and it's not me. My breaths come quicker as panic and anger overtake my entire body. He lied to me. Why would he lie to me? Who is this woman? This. *Naked.* Woman.

I'm not sure how much time passes, but I can't even stand up. My legs feel numb from sitting on them for so long and my eyes are glued to her. The jealousy of knowing he's been spending every waking hour, and many while I've been sleeping, drawing her ... thinking about her ... fantasizing about her. I think I would feel less cheated on if he'd spent an hour in a cheap hotel with a hooker.

"Darby ..." His normal, strong voice floats through the air with an edge of caution—a hint of vulnerability.

I don't turn to look at him. I can't. "Who is she?"

"I don't know."

I laugh—the alternative is too painful. "Brilliant. You don't know. She's pretty fucking detailed for you to *not know*."

"I'm sorry."

Two words that are supposed to be a white flag, a concession of wrong doing, the catalyst to a truce—those two words unnerve me. They are the last two words I want to hear. We haven't even come close to a surrender. I hate him for thinking he can throw out those two fucking words! One of the worst feelings is when "I'm sorry" feels like a slap in the face.

I glare at him. "What are you sorry for? Lying to me? Ignoring me? Fucking cheating on me!" I heave the sketch pad in his direction.

"I didn't lie." His gaze slips.

My eyes widen. "You told me you were drawing *me*!"

He shakes his head. "I told you I was *trying* to draw you."

"You and your stupid semantics." I stand, blood relieving the tingling in my legs as I point to the sketch pad by his feet. "Has it ever occurred to you that what you *don't* say says a hell of a lot more than what you *do* say?"

"I didn't mean to hurt you."

"Then why did you? Why have you spent all this time drawing her instead of being with me? Are you going to sell this? Is this our rent money?"

He shakes his head, defeat written all over his face, slumped posture. "I had to draw her."

"Why?" I whisper, defeat pulling me under.

"Because she's part of my past that my subconscious is sharing with my hands. I feel like my brain is trying to remember, but ... I just can't."

I wipe away a few tears. "Why is she naked?"

He shrugs. "It's just the image I have of her," he whispers, head bowed, no eye contact.

I step past him.

"Darby?"

I don't stop. He can't say anything that will make this right, not now. When things start to crumble they can't be put back together until the debris settles. Right now ... I'm still crumbling.

I walk up the beach until I see our neighbors catching their morning waves. Declan wades to shore and holds up a friendly hand, heading toward me.

"Good morning."

I force a smile. "Hey. How's the water?"

"Amazing. When am I going to get you out here?"

"I don't surf."

"Well, there's always a first time."

"Maybe."

"Are we still on for today?"

I nod. "Yeah, same time?"

"Sure, or you can come a little early and we can grill out lunch."

"We'd love to."

I freeze from the sound of Trick's voice as Declan focuses his attention behind me.

"Hey, Trick! Finally came out of your cave, huh?"

"I did." His words are clipped.

Declan's forehead wrinkles with confusion. I'm sure he can feel the iciness between me and Trick even with the sun shining on us. "So ... lunch for six today?"

I force yet another smile and give him a slow nod.

"Great, see you in about an hour." He jogs off toward the rest of the group.

"Come."

I dig my feet farther into the sand. "I'll *come* when I'm damn good and ready."

"You'll see your boyfriend soon enough. For now you need to come home with your husband."

I find my feet in seconds, toe to toe with him. "I'm going to forget you said that because I. Love. You. I've been helping Declan study. Period! The difference between us is I would rather be with you. I choose you, even when you break my fucking heart." I pivot, trudging my way back to the house.

I LOCK MYSELF in our room for the next hour and thankfully Trick lets me be. The visit to the beach was to once again lay claim to me … another pissing contest, only Declan doesn't get it. He acknowledges I'm a married woman and shows no interest in me beyond friendship. Why my egomaniac husband can't see that is beyond me. For someone who shows insane talent for recognizing detail, he only sees what he wants to see when it comes to me.

When my hour is up, I breeze past Trick in the kitchen and head out the front door. He catches up to me before I reach the path to Declan's. Without saying anything, he takes my hand. I don't squeeze back; instead, I let my fingers fall limp in his, like a child not wanting to hold their parent's hand across the street.

"Welcome!" Colby says with a huge grin as we walk up the back stairs.

Declan and Wes flip the fish on the grill and Mallory jumps up, still wearing her bikini.

"Hey, Trick. Haven't seen you at yoga lately." She adjusts the ties to her top, hiking up her cleavage.

"I'll be there tomorrow." He smiles, and I don't look at him long enough to see if he's focused in on the Weiner Mobile. Mallory's rack will probably be the next thing his hand just has to draw.

"You finish the picture of Darby?" Wes asks while cracking open a beer.

"Yes, I'm done with my drawing."

Drawing. More of his sneaky semantics.

"So what do you think, Darby?" Colby asks.

There's no need to look at Trick. I can feel his body go rigid next to mine.

"It's ... unexpected." I plaster on a fake smile.

"Can't wait to see it." Wes adds.

"It's a nude." My plastered smile doesn't flinch. I shrug. "But it's really amazing, incredible detail. I wouldn't mind you having a look if it's okay with Trick."

All eyes shift to Trick. "It's personal." The slipping of control vibrates in his tone.

"That's cool." Colby pats Trick on the shoulder. "Well, we're just glad you finished up and could join the party."

We eat lunch and listen to our neighbors chat about surfing, drinking, and occasionally school. I act engaged with their conversation, but Trick has more trouble playing the part. What we don't do is acknowledge each other. Mallory seems to be the only one with suspicion in her eyes. Probably because she's so in tune to every move Trick makes. I can see why she and Colby are still in the engagement stage—he's oblivious to her blatant, wandering eyes.

"If you two want to spend the afternoon together I'm pretty much caught up on studying so ..."

I say, "I'll stay." At the same time Trick says, "We would." The awkwardness thickens to the point of suffocation.

Declan's eyes pinball between us. If there was any uncertainty if the newlyweds are getting along, there isn't now. I drop my façade and walk down the beach, slipping off my sandals.

"Thanks for lunch. I'll check with you tomorrow, Declan."

The rest of the group hollers their goodbyes. I don't have to look back to know Trick is making quick strides to catch up.

He grabs my hand. "How nice of you to choose your husband over your student."

I yank my hand from his. "Really? Are you sure that's what you're going with? The husband card? Well guess what? The husband card has been denied, just like the wife card was denied for the past week. I'm tired of you pissing on me to prove a point to Declan. He's not trying to get into my pants. He's not trying to steal me away from you, and he's definitely not locked up in his room drawing me NAKED!"

Another out-of-my-skin moment. There should be a sense of pride from not playing the Darby the Doormat role, but I'm not confrontational by nature, except occasionally with my father. I love Trick, and I even love his protective side, but I don't care for the side that doesn't trust me.

"I'm not cheating on you," he says with an unsteady defeat in his voice.

"Yeah? Well I'm not cheating on you either, and I'm not shutting you out of my life. I haven't done anything to lose your trust."

"I trust you I just don't trust—"

"No! Declan has done *nothing* wrong. When you act crazy jealous for no good reason, all it says to me is that you don't trust *me*, not Declan!" I continue stomping my way home.

I know he doesn't see the difference. All that's probably going on in his head is the jealousy I've shown when women have groped him. But Declan has never once said or done anything inappropriate. If he did then Trick would have my blessing to put him in his place.

As I WALK in our back door my phone rings.

"Hello?"

"Hey, sweetie. Is … everything okay?" Tamsen's soothing voice dampers my temper.

"Fine." Then it hits me. "Why do you ask?"

"No reason. Just checking in that's all." She's doing a terrible job at feigning innocence.

"You must know about the picture, huh?"

Silence.

Just as Tamsen starts to speak, Trick walks in the back door, watching me with cautious apprehension.

"Um … yes, I did hear about it." I can envision the grimace on her face.

"I just saw it this morning. He's very talented." I don't back down from Trick's gaze. He obviously told her and or Grady about it, so we might as well all have a discussion about it.

"You're upset and you have every right to be. I haven't seen it. Grady told me about it and I can't believe Trick lied to you."

"Oh he didn't. It was me. It's always me misunderstanding what he's saying. He was *trying* to draw me." I cock my head to the side, glaring at him. "Now that I think about it, he's not that talented after all, because the drawing doesn't look anything like me. I guess we should consider it an epic failure."

"He loves *you*. I'm not condoning his behavior, but I know he loves you and his biggest fear is losing you to the reality of his past. He's lost everything that's mattered to him, including part of his memory."

I hear her words, I really do. More than that, I feel her words. I know in time I'll realize my reaction is more from pain than anger, but I'm not there yet. I'm still crumbling.

"I know."

"He's there, isn't he?"

"Yes."

"I'll let you go. I love you, sweetie. I love you both, and I know you'll get past this. Okay?"

"Thanks, Tamsen. Love you too."

I press *End* and set my phone down, letting my eyes follow it. Trick rests his hand over mine. Just his touch squeezes my heart to the point of pain.

"I don't want to talk about it. I need to be angry, and hurt, and irrational ... just for a while." I look up at him with tears in my eyes. "Can you give me that much?"

There's so much pain in his eyes as he nods. "Come." He grabs our shoes and leads me outside to the carport. He does his signature hair twist, pulls on my helmet, and I nearly cry from his touch as he palms my ass bringing me closer.

God, I need his touch.

We sail off into the warm breeze and this is exactly what I need—no words, just the comfort of his nearness that I've been so lonely without over the past week. With each passing mile, my arms tighten around him and I begin to feel the heaviness in my heart lifting, falling behind with the wind. Our connection is indisputable. My love for him is haunting ... I've crossed this line and there's no going back. We ride for what seems like hours, and I wonder if he fears the loss of my touch when we get home the way I do his.

Eventually we arrive home; we can't run forever. Trick shuts off the engine. He removes his helmet then takes mine. As I begin to walk toward the house, he grabs my arm with a gentle hold, turning me around. His hands go straight into my hair. I close my eyes and feel his breath over my face.

"Wife."

I release a breath and the last of my anger because I no longer need it. "Husband," I whisper just as his lips touch mine.

CHAPTER THIRTY-NINE

I WAKE ALONE in our bed, nothing new. Trick held me last night. It wasn't sexual, it was just love. We didn't say much and *that* was the apology I needed. I asked for time and he gave it to me. Now I feel alone, and the threads that mended my heart last night threaten to break at the thought of him back in that room drawing *her*.

I close my eyes and draw in a shaky breath.

"My wife's favorite."

Opening my eyes, Trick walks through the door with eggs and jellied toast. A genuine, I-love-this-man grin steals my face and it feels like forever since it's been there. Sitting up, I take the plate from him.

Swiping my finger through the jelly running off the edge of the toast, I wink at him. "*You're* my favorite." I lick the jelly off.

He sits in bed next to me, both of us with our backs against the headboard. "So we're still friends?" He takes a bite of his toast.

"No. We're BFFs and breakfast soul mates."

He nods with a grin, and instead of the usual head shake and eye roll that accompanies my acronyms, his body relaxes. I think he needs my words as much as I needed him to bring me this breakfast in bed instead of being in the other room drawing.

"I love the way you hum when you eat your eggs and jellied toast."

I furrow my brow. "What are you talking about?"

He chuckles. "That fact that you don't even know you do it makes me love it that much more."

I roll my eyes. "I don't hum when I eat." Taking a bite, the strangest thing happens. I hum. *Holy crap! I hum when I eat.* How have I never noticed?

Trick laughs. "My God, I love you."

I grin, but as quickly as the moment happened it ends and our smiles fade. It's the memory of yesterday haunting today. Our laughter only covers the pain that's still there. After a few minutes of silence, Trick leaves the room. I continue eating my breakfast trying not to hum. My phone chimes.

Trick: BFF?

Me: Always

Trick: I hurt my wife yesterday and I feel gutted inside.

I suck in a shaky breath as my eyes fill with tears.

Me: Why?

Trick: I wanted to protect her from my past, from the vision that has haunted me for the past week. I had to get the vision out of my head and the only way to do it was to put it on paper. I thought the woman I drew would bring it back.

Me: Bring what back?

Trick: My memory.

I wipe a few stray tears for him, for the demons that must haunt him. And then I shed a few more for the guilt I feel. He needed me to do what I do best—show compassion, Instead ... I gut him.

Me: Come.

He stops in the doorway. I wipe my cheeks and set my plate aside. "Tell me about her."

His teeth dig into his bottom lip. "I don't know how I drew her ... I just did. She's so familiar, yet I don't remember her."

I nod and take a deep swallow. "Why did you draw her naked?"

I whisper. The words hurt.

His face pulls tight into a pained expression. "It's just the vision I had. I couldn't put clothes on her … she wasn't wearing any." His eyes meet mine. "I know how painful this must be for you. It means I was with her … like that."

I laugh, eyes still dripping a few tears. "It's so stupid. I'm jealous of a drawing." Shaking my head, I continue to laugh at the absurdity of my jealousy. "She had you when I wanted you. She took away my time with you. Hell, I was jealous of myself when I thought you were spending all that time drawing me."

Trick moves to the bed and pulls me on his lap so I'm straddling his legs. "I wasn't lying when I said I wanted to draw you." He rubs his nose against mine, sliding his hands up the back of my satin nightgown. "I'll always *want* you." He kisses my lips with reverence. "I want you now." His hands slide around until his thumbs brush over my nipples. "Can I have my wife … now?"

My heavy eyelids close as I nod.

TWO DAYS LATER my BFF texts me. He says he's too afraid to ask his wife for an hour to finish his drawing, but if she agrees to it he promises to take it into town and sell it. Less than an hour later my BFF texts me, thanking me for putting in a good word with his wife. He's finished and ready to take it into town.

"What price do you want to put on it?" The guy at the gallery asks after he tears his eyes away from the drawing.

I see Trick getting ready to put a ridiculously low price on it.

"How about you display it for a week and take bids on it. Then sell it to the highest bidder when the week is up."

The guy looks back down at the drawing, shaking his head. "You really drew this?"

Trick chuckles. "Yes." He points to the corner. "And that's my signature."

The guy nods once.

"Five hundred, tops," Trick says as we get in the car.

I fasten my seatbelt. "Five grand, minimum."

He raises an eyebrow at me. "Shall we make it interesting?"

I slide my sunglasses down my nose, looking at him over the frames. "What did you have in mind?"

"I win, you watch *the* video with me … naked."

"The security video?" My eyes go wide.

He nods with a devilish grin.

I stare, actually glare, at him then slide my glasses back up my nose. "Fine. But *when* I win you're going to erase the footage in front of me … naked."

Trick lets out a roaring laugh. "Deal, sexy."

NORMALCY … WE FALL into it again even though we both know with Trick's memory and his past lurking at every turn, our lives could change without warning. I've resumed my tutoring with Declan, but it's now at our place—a compromise. Trick has started a new drawing and while he still doesn't like to show his work until he's done, he's agreed to leave the door to the spare bedroom open and work on it no more than forty hours a week, equivalent to a normal job.

"The gallery just called," I say with a soft voice as Trick concentrates on his drawing that's facing away from me.

He glances up. "Oh yeah?"

I nod.

"And?"

"I told him I didn't want him to tell me what it went for so we can find out together when we go pick up your payment."

He covers his drawing and rubs his palms together with greedy friction. "I should get the video on standby."

"No, you should get ready to delete it."

"We'll see. Come."

We take his bike to the gallery. Of course I'm hoping I win, not just because I want that embarrassing video of me deleted, but also because I want to prove to him that his talent is rare and worth so much more than he thinks.

"My cock's hard just thinking about watching that video with you." He adjusts himself as we get off the bike.

I rub my fingers along my shirt over my breasts. "My nipples are getting hard just thinking about you pressing that delete button."

He smacks my backside. "Get in there."

The gallery owner smiles as we walk in the door. "Bueno días!"

"Hi, we left a sketch—"

"Si, I know, I know ..." he cuts me off. "I feel terrible. I really wish you would have given me longer than a week. I just know I could have gotten so much more."

Trick bends down by my ear. "I can just see your hand slowly slipping beneath your underwear," he whispers.

I jerk my elbow back into his stomach and smile at the owner. "It's fine. Next time we'll give you longer. So what did you get off this one?"

He wrinkles his nose. "Sorry, only thirty."

I try not to deflate completely right here in front of him, but I'm just so disappointed and shocked. I assumed with Todos Santos being an artist's haven that people around here would have a greater appreciation for something as artistically brilliant as Trick's work.

"Now, I usually take fifty percent commission, but since I feel bad about not getting more for you, I'm only keeping forty percent this time." He hands us an envelope.

It's thick. I open it and count the money. "What the hell?"

"I'm sorry, señorita. I needed more time."

"There's eighteen thousand dollars in here!"

"Si."

Trick grabs the envelope from me and counts the money.

"You sold his drawing for thirty *thousand* dollars?"

"Si. That's what I said." He looks at me with confusion etched along his forehead.

I turn and look up at Trick, wearing the smuggest grin my face has ever had. "He sold your drawing for Thirty. *Thousand.* Dollars!"

Trick looks equal parts confused and shocked, his forehead wrinkled, jaw slack, and nothing to say.

I turn back around. "Must have been a pretty wealthy person who came in. What are the chances?"

"Oh, no. I didn't sell it here. I sold it online. That's where most everything sells. It shipped out this morning.

"Lucky me ... I mean, lucky us." I smile. "Thank you so much. Have a nice day." I turn and practically have to push Trick out of the gallery. He still hasn't said one word.

"My hero." I wrap my arm around him as we walk to the car. "I do believe you just paid our rent, utilities, grocery, and gas bills for several months or more."

He slips on his helmet still in a daze, leaving me to put mine on by myself this time. "I can't believe it," he says with an edge of sorrow or disappointment to his words.

"How can you say that? You didn't think you'd get more than five hundred dollars for it."

He shakes his head, throwing his leg over the bike. "I'm not talking about the money. I can't believe I have to erase the video."

"Oh my God!" I get on behind him and dig my fingers into his sides until he jumps, bringing his elbows in to stop me.

"Do it." I plant my hands on my hips looking over Trick's naked shoulder ... actually his naked body.

"This can't be undone. Are you sure you don't want to think about—"

"Do it!"

He grimaces, pressing his finger to the *delete* key, like he's about to end all life on Earth.

And … it's gone!

"Happy now?" He grumbles, closing his laptop.

"Yes."

He turns, holding his arms out to the side, palms up. "So why did I have to be naked for this? *My* request made sense, but this doesn't. The least you could have done was suck my cock to ease the pain of my loss."

"Yeah, the way you eased my embarrassment by watching the video in the first place, and the way you've been talking about it ever since."

He moves his hand to his cock and starts stroking himself.

"What the hell are you doing?"

"You like?"

I can't look and yet I can't not look … so of course I'm looking.

"Stop it!"

His length grows in his hand with each stroke. "Feel free to touch yourself too."

"Stop it!" My words are stern, but damn I cannot stop staring at him.

"At what point when you used to watch me did you decide you wanted to slip your hand inside your panties?"

"Put your clothes back on." I force myself to turn my back to him.

"I will when I finish. Touch yourself, sexy."

I turn back around. A cocky smile slides up his face as he strokes himself with more intensity. My lips part as I watch him; then my tongue circles over them.

"Take off your clothes …" he grits between his heavy breaths.

With slow seduction, I remove my clothes. It feels like his eyes are licking my flesh.

"Do you … want … to touch … yourself?" He pants out each

word.

"Yes," I breathe, sliding my hand down my belly, then turning, I flash up the stairs.

"Darby!" Trick yells with a grinding displeasure to his voice.

I slam the door to our room and lock it. Resting my back against it, I widen my stance and ... touch myself. "Oh ... God ..."

"Darby!"

Bang! Bang! Bang!

The door vibrating from his fists pounding on it only intensifies my pleasure.

"Fuck!" He yells with a final punch. "Are you touching yourself?"

My fingers speed up, easily sliding along my wet sex, thanks to Trick. "Feels ... so ... good ..."

"Stop!"

"I'm ... close ... oh God ... right there ... yes ... Yes ... YES!" I melt down the door as my orgasm sucks the life right out of me.

He growls a few expletives. "I want a divorce." Then I hear his grumbling fade as he stomps down the stairs.

As far as self-induced orgasms go, that one was the best. He had me so worked up when he was stroking himself; then that voice, that damn sexy voice does it to me every time. It was torturous for me too. I wanted his body pressed to mine, filling me, more than almost anything, except how much I wanted to show him that I won the bet and he was not going to steal my victory.

CHAPTER FORTY

I N SPITE OF Trick's claim of "sexual torture," we're still married. I explain to him there were no witnesses, whereas I have two witnesses that saw me tied up and bound to the back of the sofa, naked. Memories like that make me a little envious of Trick's amnesia.

Trick looks up from his work as I lean against the door frame to the guest bedroom.

"Can I interest you in lunch?"

"You?"

I laugh. "I was breakfast. I'm thinking actual food. Maybe you could take a break. We could throw on our helmets and go someplace."

He grins. "Great idea, there's something we need to get while we're out."

"What's that?"

He moves toward me with sexy mischief in his eyes. Laying a soft kiss on my lips, he whispers, "You'll see."

We stop for lunch and enjoy our meal and the great weather on the rooftop patio. I wonder when the day will come that I stop pinching myself for this life. Even with all the uncertainty of Trick's past, it doesn't take away from the craziness that brought us to this point in such a short amount of time. We are proof that certainty is only in the now and the future is nothing more than a random guess.

"I'm crazy in love with you." I grin, sipping my margarita.

Trick leans back in his chair, stirring his soda with his straw.

"Well, the first is definitely a requirement for the second."

"Maybe." I nudge his foot with mine. "How did you get into yoga?"

His lips purse to the side. "Tamsen suggested it as part of my drug rehab. A friend of hers is an instructor. It works well with the twelve-step program. It taught me new coping mechanisms."

"And when you do it you look insanely fuckable."

Trick chuckles while shaking his head at my crass comment that was meant to elicit this exact reaction. "Yes, of course, that's the *main* reason I do it."

His eyes tense as he stares at his glass. Those hidden emotions of his are running rampant; I can see it in the way his smile slips. "Why did your father hit you?"

In spite of us being outside, it feels like there's a lack of oxygen in the air around us. I did not see that question coming. "I suppose a psychiatrist would say because he's never properly dealt with the loss of my mom, and I'm a reminder of her. I'm here and she's not. So when I anger him, all those pent up emotions cause him to lash out at me."

"But why do *you* think he hit you?"

My eyes find Trick's. "Because he's a coward and an asshole, and he knows it. He just doesn't like it when I remind him of it."

"He hit you because you told him you were leaving with me."

"No. He hit me because my mom died and I lived."

"That's fucked-up."

I shrug.

Trick leans forward, taking my hand. "I owe your mom *every-thing.*"

Tears.

I swallow the lump of emotions in my throat. "Did I mention I'm crazy in love with you?"

A lip twitch.

★

WE END UP down in Cabo ... at a tattoo parlor.

"What are you getting now?" I ask as he takes off my helmet. "Have you made sure this is a reputable place? Tattoo removal isn't a fun process, and you also need to make sure you're not going to end up with an infection."

He cups my face, laying a sound kiss on my lips. "I've checked everything out. We'll be fine."

"*We'll?*"

"Yes."

"I don't need a tattoo."

"Yes, you do. Come."

I *don't* come. I stand rooted to the ground by the motorcycle.

Trick looks back. "What?" He sighs.

"I've never thought about getting a tattoo before."

"Then don't think about it now. Come." He gestures with his head to the door.

With lead in my shoes, I make my way to him. He takes my hand and drags me inside.

After an hour wait it's our turn. I've been informed I don't get to pick out my tattoo. *Figures.* Trick negotiates with the artist while I observe our surroundings, inspecting the sanitary conditions.

"Do you want to go first or do you want me to?" Trick asks.

Does he really have to ask?

A smirk and head shake. "I'll go first."

I give him a slow you-bet-your-ass-you-will nod.

Thirty minutes later and we're on our way home. Left ring fingers bandaged over the date we got married tattooed in sanskrit. I nearly cried at just how romantic of a gesture it was ... That and getting a tattoo on the sensitive skin of my finger hurt like hell. Trick didn't even flinch. *Cocky showoff!*

"Wife." Trick opens the door to the house.

"Husband." I grin, holding up my bandaged finger while walking past him.

"What are you doing?" He asks as I send a text to Tamsen.

"I'm telling Tamsen you bought me a wedding band today … or…" I glance up with an annoyed smirk "…a *marriage* band."

He bends down, burying his stubbly face in the crook of my neck. "You can call it a wedding … a marriage … a ceremony … getting hitched." He skims his hands up my sides, dropping his mouth to my cleavage exposed with my V-neck top. "You said 'I do.' That's all that matters to me."

Trick is anything but conventional. I was a little surprised that marriage mattered to him, but then he brought me to the place where his parents met and I saw a side to Trick I'm quite certain very few have ever seen—the boy who grew up a witness to the most beautiful, yet tragic love story ever.

"Show me … show me how much it matters." Each one of my words comes out a breathy slur as I set my phone on the counter.

He straightens, that sexy gaze a slow lick up the center of my sex as I melt with need for his touch. Wasting no time, he gives me what he knows I want—he removes his shirt. I grin and remove mine. We make haste with ridding our bodies of the rest of our clothes.

"Bed or counter?" He presses his naked body to mine, tangling his hands in my hair, tugging my head back until I'm looking up into his eyes.

"Counter."

He kisses me and lifts me up.

"Ooo! Bed!" I squeal, clamping my legs around his waist as the cold tile meets my bottom.

He laughs and carries me upstairs. "You just got your first tattoo but the counter is too cold?"

"Shut up." I kiss him as he lays us down on the bed. Pressing my palms to his face, I push him back just far enough to look into his eyes. "Counter says quickie. I don't want anything about this to be quick." I brush my thumb over his bottom lip. "Show me your *wedding* vows."

He does ... he shows me that the memories we make will be filled with long motorcycle rides, lazy, long lunches at little restaurants in town, and plenty of quickies on cold tile. But at the end of every day we'll remember that our memories are all chapters to a love story ... our love story.

I LOVE THAT we're the couple that stays tangled in each other's bodies all night. I love the way he fists my hair like he's holding a security blanket when I bury my face in his neck. I love that he still wakes up most nights with his head wedged between my legs, like I'm a midnight snack, and that less than ten minutes later were both sated and right back to sleep, not feeling the least bit exhausted from it in the morning.

Slipping out of bed, I try to sneak out before he wakes.

"Darby," his groggy voice calls.

"Go back to sleep. You're not supposed to be awake. I'm going to surprise you with breakfast in bed. Just pretend this conversation never took place."

His lips pull into a barely detectable grin, but he doesn't open his eyes. I make quick work of toast and eggs while noticing on my phone I have thirteen missed calls from Tamsen and one message and another missed call from Jade. She's probably wondering what to do with the stuff in my locker. I smile as I listen to Tamsen's message while I butter and jelly our toast. I bet she's dying to see my ring. I didn't mention it's a tattoo.

"Sweetie it's me. I've been trying to reach you and Trick. Darby ... I don't know if you've heard or had the TV on ..." The shakiness in her voice sends chills down my spine and when she pauses I hold my breath. "There's been an accident. And since I haven't heard from either you or Trick, I assume you haven't been contacted yet. Your family's been in a car accident. I don't know all the details yet or their conditions, but it's all over the news and it appears to be pretty serious. So call me and let me know when you get this message. Grady and I are both getting flights to Chicago; we'll probably be there before you and Trick. I'm so sorry ... I didn't want to leave a message but I don't know what else to do. Call me."

With shaky hands and my heart in my throat, I listen to the message from Jade.

"Darby, it's Jade. Your family's been in an accident. I need you to call me as soon as you get this message."

My phone crashes to the ground. "Oh my God ..." The words are barely a whisper. I can't speak; I can't breathe. Thankfully my legs work without my brain, taking me up the stairs and straight into the closet to get my suitcase.

"Darby?" Trick calls but I'm still at a loss for words. "What are you doing?" He stands at the door, watching me toss random items into my suitcase. "Darby!"

I jump and look up, with one blink the flood gates open.

"Baby, what is it?" He hunches next to where I'm kneeling on the floor and pulls me into his body.

"The-there's b-been an a-accident," I sob. "I n-n-need to g-get home."

"What happened?"

"C-car accident. I-I have to g-go." I wriggle out of his hold.

He stands, lifting me to my feet. Then he bends down to look in my eyes. "Get dressed. I'll pack our stuff and get our tickets. Okay?"

I nod, my lower lip trembling.

EVERYTHING'S A BLUR until we land at O'Hare. I'm certain Trick has had to drag me everywhere until this point. I've seen him on his cell phone and mine too, but I haven't been able to formulate the words to ask who he's talking to, and there's been this eerie silence in my ears. I see people's lips moving, but it's as if someone hit the mute button.

When we get to the hospital, I don't wait for Trick or help him with our luggage. I fly through the emergency room doors, straight to the nurses' station.

"Darby." Jade sees me before I reach the counter. She pulls me into her arms "I'm so sorry."

I pull back, confused by her somberness.

She looks at me then something over my shoulder catches her eye and she gives a small nod. I turn.

Trick takes my hand and pulls me aside so we're not standing in the middle of the normal chaos. He cradles my face and takes a deep swallow. "Darby ..."

I blink releasing tears because he's scaring me.

"Your father didn't make it."

I swallow and just ... stare. The voices around me are nothing more than distant echoes. "Where's Nana?"

Trick furrows his brow. "She's upstairs. Her injuries were minor."

I turn and head for the elevators.

Trick catches up to me just as the elevator doors close.

"Darby, look at me." He grabs my arms. "Did you hear what I said?"

I nod as the elevator doors open. "What room is she in?"

Trick shakes his head as I once again pull away from his grip. I get Nana's room number and run down the hall. Her friend, Mary, is sitting in the chair next to her bed.

"Darby." Mary frowns with sympathy in her eyes.

"How is she?"

"She's fine, just a concussion and a few minor cuts and bruises. Doctor said she can go home tomorrow morning."

Mary rests her hand on my back as I watch Nana sleep. "Sweetie, I'm so very sorry about your father."

"When was she last awake?"

"What?" Mary asks looking at me and then at Trick.

"Has she eaten anything today?"

"Uh … well, yes."

Trick's hand slides up my back underneath my hair, and with gentle strokes he massages my neck.

"You must be Trick?"

"Yes," he answers.

"Hi, I'm Mary."

"Nice to meet you."

Mary steps back. "I'm going to go get some coffee. Can I get either of you anything?"

I don't respond.

"We're fine, thanks," Trick replies.

"What happened?" I whisper.

Mary stops at the door. "They were on their way to dinner and a driver ran a red light. They hit the back half of the vehicle on your father's side."

"Nana must have been sitting upfront with the driver. She always sits upfront." I smile and squeeze her hand, so grateful that she was in a safer spot.

"Grady and Tamsen are on their way." Trick kisses the top of my head.

I nod. "You should go back with them. I'm going to stay here with Nana tonight. You can come get us in the morning."

"I'll stay with you."

"No, Grady and Tamsen are here to see you."

Trick leans down, kissing the top of my head. "They're here for *you*, Darby. We're all here for you."

"Nana's going to be fine. Grady and Tamsen didn't need to fly in for a concussion."

Trick starts to say something just as Nana's eyes creep open.

"Nana!" I squeeze her hand again.

"Darby, dear." Her voice is rough and weak.

"I was so worried about you."

She moves her head from side to side. "I'm sorry—"

"No, it's fine, Nana. I'm just glad you're okay."

"It was my idea … to go to dinner … he didn't want to go."

I shake my head. "Shh … it's fine, you're fine. The doctor said you can go home tomorrow. I'm staying with you tonight."

She narrows her eyes, looking past me to Trick.

"Hi, Grace. Glad to see you're doing well."

I turn to look at Trick. His expression is hard to read. It's like the two of them are saying something that they're not actually saying.

"We'll get you home tomorrow and you and Darby can spend some more time alone… *talking*."

Nana nods, squeezing my hand, her eyes glassy with tears. "Yes, dear, tomorrow we'll talk."

CHAPTER FORTY-ONE

G RADY TEXTS ME that he and Tamsen are in the waiting room, so I excuse myself. Turning the corner from Grace's room I'm greeted with Rachel. She freezes, all color draining from her face. Just as quickly as it disappears it comes back. She glares at me. I don't think she's waiting for me to give my condolences.

"Visitors are restricted to family only," she sneers.

"I was visiting my *wife's* grandmother." I hold up my left hand and point to the tattoo on my ring finger.

The color leaves her face again as she averts her eyes, brushing past me.

"By the way ..." I turn. Her jaw's clenched, eyes squinted at me. "I know what you're doing and you'd better knock it off or I'll bury you. Got it?"

I don't "got it" or "get it" for that matter, but I'm not going to let her know it. "Darby's in there. I don't think she wants to see you. Besides, I think I'm actually considered family more than you are, given recent events."

Her jaw drops.

There's your fucking condolences, bitch!

"HEY ..." TAMSEN HUGS me. "How's Darby?"

"In denial."

"What?" Grady hugs me too.

"I told her about her father and several other people have tried to comfort her, but she won't even acknowledge that anything about him is being said, let alone that he's dead. Her only focus is Grace."

"That's not good," Grady grimaces.

"No, but Grace goes home tomorrow and I'm hoping if they spend some time together Grace will be able to help her acknowledge and accept what has happened."

"She's in shock, that's all." Tamsen hands me a bottle of water.

"Yeah, I suppose."

"We saw Rachel Hart walk that way, then she left as quickly as she came." Grady sips his coffee. "We met years back, but I'm sure she doesn't remember me, otherwise I would have given her my condolences."

I shrug, gulping down the remainder of my water. "Don't sweat it. I gave her condolences from all of us."

Grady raises a suspicious brow. "Must have been why she was leaving so fast."

"Hmm ... I hadn't noticed."

CHAPTER FORTY-TWO

I INSIST TRICK go home with Grady and Tamsen. They all look me over with a careful eye. I glance down at myself. I got dressed in a hurry, it's possible my clothes don't match.

"What?"

Both Grady and Tamsen hug me before walking out of the room.

"Nothing, baby." Trick pulls me into his arms, leaning down to nuzzle his nose in my hair. "I love you. Call me if you need anything. Okay?"

I nod, then he presses a soft kiss to my lips. "Goodnight."

"Night." I smile.

Nana eats her dinner while I sip a Green Lantern, compliments of Jade.

"So what do you want to talk about?" Nana asks.

I shrug, then hold up my left hand with a smile. "Trick decided to forego the traditional diamond and permanently mark me instead."

Nana grabs my hand and laughs. "My Darby has a tattoo. Never thought I'd see that day." She winks. "But I'm glad I did."

"Todos Santos is amazing. You have to come visit soon. We're right on the beach and it's such a paradise."

"So that's an official invite?"

"Yes. Although you never need one. Trick's been drawing ... he sold one for thirty grand in only a week. The gallery owner said he could have gotten so much more had he more time."

"What did he draw?"

My heart sinks. In all of my enthusiasm I sort of forgot that would be a natural follow-up question, but this is Nana and she'll know I'm lying if I try to tell her anything but the truth.

"A woman from his past." I frown.

Her eyes go wide. "From his past that he forgot?"

I nod.

"So he remembers?"

"Not really. All he has is the image. He doesn't know why he has it. I think he drew her hoping it would trigger the rest of his memory, but it hasn't."

"Is she pretty?"

"Yes, older looking … well, at least older than he would have been at the time he last saw her."

"What was she doing in the picture?"

I grimace. "Lying on a bed … *naked.*"

Nana's brows form two tall peaks. "And what did you do when you saw it?"

"I kinda freaked out. It's such a long story, but we're good now and the fact that he made so much money off it somehow made everything better."

"Because you two needed the money?" Nana has trouble keeping a straight face.

I roll my eyes. "Yes, we did. We have rent and other expenses, and aside from the little bit of money that I've made tutoring our neighbor, neither one of us have had a reliable form of income until he sold that drawing."

Nana pushes away her tray of food. "I could give you money, dear."

"I don't want it."

"It's not as much as it could have been, but it's rightfully yours.

I'm not going to live forever and your grandfather worked hard for it. He would want you to have it."

"He never knew me."

"But he would have adored you."

I smile. "Thank you for saying that." I take her hand. "But I have money. I've never made a rent or house payment until now." I give her the you-should-know-why look. "And I've worked full time ever since I graduated from college, without student loans to pay back. And I've made decent money with my job."

Nana smiles. "I'm so proud of you. You're a shimmering gem, Darby. You have such a big heart and you know what's important in life. All those girls in school missed out on being friends with you. Shame on them. I bet not a single one of them grew up to be half the woman you are today."

"You mean Darby the Doormat?"

"No!" Nana scowls. "If everyone were a hard ass like me, the world would be in trouble. Never apologize for being compassionate. It's who you are and the recipients of that compassion are some of the luckiest people in the world, and I can guarantee they will never forget you."

"Love you, Nana. Now…" I pull her blankets up and smooth them over her "…get some rest."

AS SOON AS Nana's asleep, I head down to the cafeteria. Everywhere I look I'm met with watchful eyes and sad expressions. I get a bag of pretzels and a bottled water then take a seat at an empty table. First I feel it, then I look around to confirm it—the glances that make a quick diversion every time I look up, followed by whispering and subtle gestures in my direction. I pop a mini pretzel into my mouth and chew it in slow motion as I glance up at the TV in the corner.

Senator Carmichael was pronounced dead after four

hours of surgery in attempts to repair massive internal bleeding sustained from a car accident last night. There has been no official details released in regards to his funeral arrangements ...

I shake my head slowly.

"Your father didn't make it."

"I'm so sorry ..."

"So sorry about your father ..."

"We're all here for you."

"It was my idea ... he didn't want to go ..."

"No!" I scream the word, silencing the room. My heart is ready to explode. I can't breathe as my mind tries to make sense of everything. A surge of nausea has me buckling over. Grabbing my purse, I rush past the heads all turned in my direction to get to the bathroom. I barely make it to the toilet before I expel what little is in my stomach. "Oh God!" I continue to dry heave.

Sitting back on the dirty floor of the stall, I hug my knees to my chest and shiver through a cold sweat. Fumbling for my purse, I manage to retrieve my phone and send off a text with only four letters.

Me: *help*

I drop my phone in my bag and lay my forehead on my knees, praying for *help*.

"Miss? Are you okay?" A voice calls from outside my stall.

I shiver, shaking my head some more.

"Can I get or call someone for you?"

"T-T-Trick."

"Trick?"

I nod, squeezing my eyes shut.

"Did you say Trick?"

I nod, but cannot speak.

"Do you have a number?"

I open my mouth to speak but all that comes out are sobs, painful emotion being wrung from my heart.

"Um ... I'll see what I can do."

CHAPTER FORTY-THREE

I'D RATHER TEAR my own fucking heart out of my chest than know that she needs me and I can't find her. She won't text me back or answer her phone. Grace is asleep so Grady, Tamsen, and I split up to look for Darby.

"Hey!" I call seeing a familiar face.

The nurse that worked with Darby turns.

"Have you seen Darby?"

"No. Isn't she with Grace?"

I shake my head and jog to the elevator.

"Maybe she's in the cafeteria!"

I don't acknowledge her, but I'm heading there. I rip through the crowd of people on the elevator when the doors open on the lower level. Looking right then left I don't see her, but I spot both Grady and Tamsen.

"No luck?"

They both shake their heads. I fist my hair and growl in anger. "Dammit! Why won't she answer her phone?"

"Are you looking for someone?" An older woman with an ID badge asks.

"Yes," Tamsen answers then describes what Darby looks like.

"She ran to the bathroom about an hour ago. Another lady went in to check on her. All she said was 'Trick.'"

"Trick, you can't just barge into the women's bathroom!" Tamsen calls, chasing after me.

Like hell I can't!

"Darby!" I slam the door open so hard it makes a crashing sound against the back wall.

All the stalls are unoccupied except one.

"Darby!" I bang on it and look underneath. "Open the door."

She releases a strangled sob, and I don't wait another second before yanking the door open sending the metal latch clattering to the ground.

"Shh ... I'm here." I pick her up, cradling her in my arms as her face buries into my chest with gut-wrenching cries. Tamsen grabs her purse and Grady holds the door open for us.

"H-he's d-d-dead ..."

I press my lips to her head while carrying her to the elevator. "I know, baby ... I know," I whisper.

Grady drives us home, and I carry her to bed and just hold her. It doesn't matter what I thought of her father. In spite of everything, I know she loved him. That's just her, always giving more than he deserved and settling for so much less than she needed from the ungrateful bastard.

I'm not sure what time it is when her body finally quiets and stills. Tamsen slips off Darby's shoes and mine then spreads a blanket over us. "I'll be on the couch if you need anything," she whispers.

I nod and mouth "thank you."

There will never be enough time left in my life to repay Tamsen and Grady. They are without exception always here for me when I need them, but what's most amazing is they have a way of knowing I need them even before I do.

My life's circumstances have never been ideal, but this I know. I've been loved more than most people are in a dozen lifetimes. My parents had nothing and yet I felt like I had everything ... everything that mattered. Grady and I might not always agree on things, but he picked me up, dusted me off, and gave me purpose again. Tamsen ... well Tamsen is an angel if there's such a thing. She healed me from the inside out and *sinceriously* gave me back my sense of self-worth. Then there's the woman in my arms. She's my future … my whole world … my lover … my wife … my BFF.

CHAPTER FORTY-FOUR

OH. MY. HEAD. I think my eyes are swollen shut. As I try to shift, strong arms tighten around me.

"Pee ... I need to pee," I whisper. Before I can say another word, I'm being carried to the bathroom. "I can walk." I squint up at Trick through the slit beneath my puffy eyelids as he sets me on my feet. He crosses his arms over his chest. Sure, like I want him to stand here and watch me pee. "I could use a drink of water."

"Tamsen, Darby needs some water!"

I sigh. "I need my purse too."

"Grab her purse too!"

"Okay, if you must know I don't need water or my purse. I need thirty seconds by myself to tinkle without you watching me."

Trick smirks. "We're married."

"And I'd like to keep it that way. So let's not make a point of watching each other shit and piss, okay?"

He chuckles. "Suit yourself." Just as Tamsen turns the corner to the bathroom, he signals for her to leave and follows her out.

After washing my hands and splashing cold water on my face, I get ready to turn the corner to what I know will be three very sad faces looking at me.

"Hey, sunshine. I've got pancakes and eggs, but I could do toast and jelly for you instead," Grady calls from the stove.

"Pancakes are great, thanks."

Tamsen hands me a glass of orange juice, giving me her genuine smile, not the one everyone was giving me yesterday.

"Thank you."

"Come." Trick pats the barstool next to him.

It's the word I want to hear. I was worried when he felt the need to carry me to the bathroom. Coddling is not my thing. Last night was my breakdown; now it's passed. I'm sensitive and compassionate, and in spite of what some mean, catty bitches have thought over the years, that doesn't equate to weak. I had a weak moment, but I am not a weak person.

"When do you want to go get your nana?"

I scoot up on the stool. "Just as soon as we're done eating. She'll be itching to leave. Besides, I feel awful for abandoning her last night when I told her I would stay."

"No need, honey. I talked with the nurses on her floor and told them you weren't feeling well and to tell your nana when she woke that you'd pick her up in the morning." Grady winks at me, setting a stack of three pancakes on my plate, two more than I'm going to be able to eat this morning.

"You're the best."

Grady gives Trick an I-told-you-so look.

Trick rests his hand on my leg, giving it a gentle squeeze. I expect him to make some snide comment to Grady, putting him in his place the way they both seem to do, but he doesn't. It makes me wonder if Trick shares my gratitude for what our friends, our *family*, have done.

WE ARRIVE AT the hospital, greeted by anxious Nana dressed and sitting in a guest chair looking more like a visitor than a patient. The doctor discharged her a half an hour ago.

"There's my dear girl." She stands holding open her arms.

"Good morning, Nana. Sorry we would have been here earlier, but I overslept and then Grady made breakfast."

"No worries, dear. As long as we stop for some real coffee on the way home, I'll be happy."

Trick lets me drive and Nana sits in the front seat. Once again, allowing me to be strong, not over-coddling me, and allowing Nana to have her favorite spot in the vehicle.

"So ... how are you today, dear?" Nana breaks the silence, giving a quick glance back to Trick.

"She knows." He gives her a sad smile then meets my gaze in the rearview mirror.

"Well in that case I'll break more bad news to you. Rachel came by the hospital this morning before you arrived, and now she's planning on meeting us at my place around noon to discuss funeral arrangements."

"I'm sure he has it all specified in his will. What's to discuss?"

"Day, time ... I don't know."

We pull up in front of Nana's and Trick gets out to open her door.

"Thank you, handsome." She winks and he grins.

"You can stay if you'd like or you can pick me up later." I wrap my arms around him.

"I'll give you two some time alone." He kisses me.

"Thank you ... for everything," I whisper against his lips.

"There's nothing I wouldn't do for my wife ... my *life.*"

I smile. "I'll call you later." I hand him the keys and take Nana's *real* coffee so she doesn't have to maneuver the stairs with it in her hand.

After I get her settled on the couch with her feet up, a blanket over her lap, and her coffee, I curl up on the love seat across from her. "I never asked. Was Rachel in the car too?"

"No. She had a holiday fashion show rehearsal. That's why I invited your father to dinner. It was..." she forces a sad smile "...your mom's birthday. We were on our way to her favorite restaurant—the place is still open after all these years. I bet you never knew we did this every year, just the two of us. It's the only day of the year that I see a glimpse of the man he used to be with Lucy. But this year, for the first time since she died, he tried to skip out. Said he had too much to do with the election just around the corner."

Nana shakes her head, an intent gaze focused at the lid on her cup. "I insisted he come, just for an hour or two. I wouldn't take no for an answer." She draws in a slow, controlled breath. "Nobody saw it coming."

"What happened to the drivers?"

"The driver of the vehicle that hit us died. She wasn't wearing her seatbelt, at least that's what Mary said. Our driver suffered a broken arm but he's fine." Nana's pained face meets my gaze. "Now, dear, how are you handling this?"

I feel the emotions sting my eyes as I chuckle. "Not so good last night. That's why I didn't stay with you. But now I just don't know. I'm sad, hurt, and angry. Whether he deserved it or not, 1 loved him. I think a child is programmed to love their parents and it makes me sick to think of how long I waited for him to show me love." I roll my eyes to the ceiling and swallow. "I mean … it goes both ways, right? Parents should be programmed to love their children, no matter what." I wipe a single tear from my cheek. "You've always told me that he loved my mom, so I kept thinking that eventually he'd let go of her loss and embrace me like I was the only precious part of her he had left."

"My sweet girl, he loved you even if he didn't know how to show it."

I shrug. "Well, it's too late now." There's a part of me that wants to tell her about the times he hit me, but I think Nana needs to believe something good about my father. She needs it to make sense of his relationship with my mom. "That's what hit me the hardest. It wasn't the loss of the man that he was; it was the loss of the man I'd hoped one day he'd be."

The door buzzes. I hold up my hand to Nana. "I got it."

"Darby." Rachel says with a slight huff as she brushes past me. Her eyes don't look the least bit puffy and her usual bitch mask is firmly in place. I'm sure when she heard the news of my father she probably popped a few Xanax and continued on with her day after putting a reminder in her phone to stop by the hospital to pick up his personal belongings.

"Let's hurry up and get through this. I'm way behind on work, not to mention I have to be back in New York by Saturday." Rachel slips her gloves into her handbag and shrugs off her full-length coat.

Nana and I share the same expression. *What the fuck?* Okay, Nana's might be "Who the hell does she think she is?" but mine is definitely "What the fuck?"

"By all means, Rachel, we'd hate to dawdle too long over something as trifling as my father's death."

Rachel could freeze fire with her scowl and medusa eyes, but lucky for me, I'm immune to her evil glare.

"Life goes on for the living."

Nana purses her lips, but I can see the smirk she's trying to hide. This might be very inappropriate timing, but I can't blame her. If we don't laugh at Rachel, we'll end up strangling her.

"That it does. So what do you need from us?" Nana sips her coffee.

"As I'm sure you both already know, Cal left detailed instructions with regards to his funeral. However, one of his wishes was to have a closed casket."

Nana and I share another look, this one says: *Who really gives a shit?* Okay, that may be mine, but Nana's is at least "get on with it, bitch, you're wasting our time."

Rachel stands looking at us with her hands on her hips like she's waiting for us to what? *Gasp? Scream in protest?*

"Christ! Would you get to the point?" Nana sighs in exasperation.

I cough to hide my amusement. Nana's just too funny.

Rachel's Botox lips make a sorry attempt to pull into a firm line. "My point is I'm coming out with a men's line of formal wear in less than a month and it would be absurd to not have Cal wearing one of my designs!"

"So dress him in your suit. You don't need our permission for that." I roll my eyes, even if it is disrespectful and rude.

"That's my point!" She grinds out the words, but no matter how growly she sounds, her point is still out of my radar of comprehension. "I'm not going to have him wear my new design if nobody's going to see him!"

My stomach and chest ache from holding in the impending laughter dying to escape. Nana's right, Rachel is batshit crazy.

"Well … dear … then leave the lid up," Nana says with admirable control as I bite my lips together.

"I can't, not without consent from both of you. Changes can only be made if there's unanimous agreement among the three of us."

"You have our blessing." Nana has donned her kid gloves to talk motherese with Rachel and it's laugh-out-loud hysterical.

Rachel grabs her coat and marches to the front door. "Fine, then. Duncan will be calling you both for your consent. The funeral is Thursday at eleven."

She slams the front door and we fall into a fit of laughter. I'll give Duncan, my father's attorney, my consent on this deathly important matter, but it won't be without conflict. I'm stuck in the middle. Part of me wants to piss off my father, wherever he may be, by letting his wife dress his corpse like a mannequin and put it on display against his wishes. Then there's the other part of me that wants to deny Rachel this, just because it's so much fun watching her have her little tantrums.

WEDNESDAY EVENING WE spend at the visitation where I try to

channel a few of the emotions I had the night we arrived so I can play the part of the grieving daughter. The problem is I already used up my initial shock and now I'm settled into the orphaned child role that I'd become accustomed to over the years.

If anything, my biggest challenge is fighting off an untimely case of the giggles as I have to listen to Rachel describe to everyone how the suit my father's wearing brings out the natural warm hues of his skin. Maybe it's my medical background, but I'd always assumed once all the blood was drained from the human body the skin no longer had "warm natural hues."

"Can I get you anything?" Trick whispers in my ear, pressing his body to my back.

"Aside from out of here?" I say through clenched teeth behind my fake smile that's just big enough to say thank you for coming but not too big to overshadow my expected grief.

"I love you." He kisses the top of my head and steps back. I don't think he's as immune to Rachel's icy glare as I am. And for whatever she's-so-damn-bat-shit-crazy reason, she keeps looking behind us to make sure he's in the shadows and not lurking too close to her.

"Hey, Darby."

I look left to a familiar voice and smile when I see Jade and several other ER nurses waiting to pay their respects. For the first time all evening I tear up and it has nothing to do with my father. I'm just beside myself with emotion that they came here for me.

"Hey." I hug each one of them and wipe my tears … tears they'll never know are for their kindness.

By the end of the night at least a dozen other nurses, PAs, and doctors come through the line. Maybe I was wrong. Maybe I have become so paranoid of judgment in my life that I act preemptively and judge other people first.

Life lesson learned.

⭐

THERE'S A SOMBERNESS in the air when we arrive home from the visitation. I think the exhaustion of traveling, dealing with the adrenaline of the events at the hospital, and now a long visitation is catching up with us.

"Tamsen and I are going out for a drink." Grady winks at me and Trick as we get out of the back of his car. "We'll be back in let's say … two hours?"

Trick nods to Grady, and Tamsen grins, waving at me through the passenger window.

"Come." Trick takes my hand, pulling me toward the elevator while Grady and Tamsen back out of the garage.

"Did you tell them to give us time alone? For sex?"

Trick chuckles as we step off the elevator. Then he takes my jacket. "Grady's itching to go out so he's using us as his excuse." He pulls me into his arms. "Don't worry, we're not going to have sex."

I nod once, wrapping my arms around him. We did just get back from my father's visitation, and I haven't slept that well. Exhaustion is an understatement, but do I like that Trick's taking sex off the table? *No!*

"I'm going to change and brush my teeth." He releases me and walks toward the bathroom.

I watch him, admiring the way his white dress shirt hugs his shoulders. I slip out of my dress and walk around the corner into the bathroom wearing just my black panties and strapless bra. Trick spits toothpaste into the sink and wipes his mouth as I start brushing my teeth. Glancing up at his reflection in the mirror, I catch his eyes perusing the length of my body as he unbuttons his shirt. When he shrugs it off his shoulders, I make a quick spit before I either choke on it or swallow it down.

Turning, I rest my hands on the edge of the vanity and lean back against them. Trick unfastens his dress pants, letting them fall to the floor before stepping out of them and removing his socks. I wet my lips. My eyes take in the artistic terrain I've come to love and *crave*. It takes a few moments for me to realize he's standing still. I shift my eyes to his face.

He's trying not to look cocky, but failing. "You're staring."

"I am." I grin.

"Because?" He moves closer.

I stand straight, resting my hands on his chest. "Because I can."

His hands slide up my sides and around my back, unclasping my bra. It falls to our feet.

"What are you doing?" I whisper.

"Admiring my beautiful wife…" his lips brush along my jaw to my ear "…because I can."

CHAPTER FORTY-FIVE

I BURIED MY father today—no tears, no pain. Even now, the only emotion I recognize is guilt. I must have had an allotted number of tears for him, and I used them all up the other night. The pathetic part ... I actually tried to think of something sadder than my father's death to draw out a few. My lack of emotion garnered more attention than Rachel's Hollywood worthy act of grief. I'm pretty certain she squirted something in her eyes to get them to water so damn much.

"Nana?" Trick asks as my phone chimes with a text.

"Nope. Rachel." I shake my head then stare back out the window, entranced by the mesmerizing sparkle of Chicago's skyline coming into view against the descending darkness. "We left her, the grieving widow, thirty minutes ago and she's already demanding I find time to get my father's stuff from the house we just left *and* her penthouse in New York." I laugh. "Unbelievable. He was her husband. Why doesn't she deal with his shit? Does she honestly think I'm going to find some precious, sentimental memento that I can't live without?"

"Tell her to go fuck herself."

I chuckle. Maybe I'm not Darby the Doormat anymore, but I'm not quite Fuck Off Trick Roth either. "If I'm honest with myself, I have to admit that there's a part of me that's curious what my father has hidden in his closets. Even one picture of my mom that I haven't seen before would make it worth my time, so..." I glance over at Trick "...looks like I'm going to New York."

He sucks in a slow breath and releases it with equal control.

"I don't expect you to go. You can stay here or go back to To-dos Santos. I would understand."

He nods, twisting his lips to the side. "When are you going?"

"Well, I don't want to drag this out, so I'll probably go through his stuff here tomorrow then fly out on Saturday, then either back here or home on Sunday depending on where you're going to be."

"Where do you want me to be?" he asks as we pull into the garage.

With me.

I shrug. "I know you were in the middle of a drawing before we left for Chicago, so if Grady and Tamsen are leaving in the morning, maybe you should head home too," I say while opening the door.

Trick takes my heels that I slipped off in the car, my coat, and purse in one hand then helps me out with his other. In spite of his constant reminders that he is not a sweep-you-off-your-feet prince charming with refined manners and censored speech, everyday he does something … the smallest gesture … that shows me he's becoming *my* gentleman. And right now he's doing it—carrying my belongings in one hand and leading me with his other. I feel loved, cherished, and utterly adored. *Best. Feeling. Ever!*

WHEN TAMSEN FINDS out about my trip to New York, she changes her flight to go back with me on Saturday. Then she offers to go with me to Barrington Hills to sort through my father's personal items while Trick takes Grady to the airport.

"So you're going to pack up all of his suits and *things*…" Tamsen holds up a Cubs Jersey like it's going to bite her "…and do what with it?"

I riffle through the drawers in his walk-in closet. "I'm not packing up shit. Rachel can deal with his clothes. I'm just looking for anything from my past or my mother's—photos, jewelry, sentimental items. Although I'm not holding out much hope that we'll find anything like that. I don't think Calvin Carmichael was into scrapbooking or had a cedar chest filled with ancestral relics."

Tamsen dives into drawers on the opposite side, even checking coat and jacket pockets hanging above her. "What's this?"

I turn as she holds up a necklace with a heart pendant, diamond letters "LC" in the middle. "Where'd you find this?" I take it from her, running my thumb across the diamonds.

"It was under these silk handkerchiefs." She points to the drawer. "Do you recognize it?"

I nod. "From the picture of my mom on her wedding day. She was wearing it. Nana said my father gave it to her as a wedding gift."

"LC?"

"Lucille Carmichael," I whisper.

"I'm surprised he didn't give it to you."

I shake my head in slow disbelief. "After he and Rachel got married, I asked him for it, but he said it got lost in the move."

"So he lied?"

"Yes, but … I don't understand why. Maybe he did misplace it and later found it, but forgot to say something."

Tamsen laughs. "God, I love your innocence."

I slip it in my pocket. "You mean my ignorance or naïveté." I shake my head. "I just keep trying to see what my mom must have seen in him."

We spend the next two hours going through his stuff, but end up leaving everything behind except the necklace.

AS SOON AS we get back, Tamsen leaves to meet an old friend from college for a few drinks since deciding to stay in Chicago for another night. She invites me to go, and as tempting as a girls' night out is for *this* girl, I decline.

"Giving up on a night with Tamsen for me, huh?" Trick grins, looking up from his computer screen at the counter.

"Yes, so don't make me regret it." I slip off my boots and hug his back. "Did you decide to stay or fly home?"

"Home. I'll dive into my work…" he turns to me "…then when you get there I'll take a couple days off to get a long wife fix."

I tease my fingers through the nape of his hair. "So your Darby fix has turned into a wife fix, huh?"

"Yes. It's pathetic, I can never get enough."

I nod, rubbing my lips together, eyes perusing my badass, tatted husband. "Take your shirt off."

He raises a single brow. "Yeah?"

"Yeah." I grin.

And then it begins with that single, barely noticeable *lip twitch*. Now that he's mine, I welcome that cocky as fuck arrogance. Tonight it's all I want.

He shrugs off his shirt and I stare, just waiting for the words I want to hear. I can *feel* his ego swelling, and as much as my hands ache to touch his painted skin … I wait.

"Enjoying the view?"

There it is … that voice I swear vibrates the most intimate parts of my body. Biting my thumbnail, I meet his gaze and nod.

"Anything else I can do for you?"

God! It just keeps getting better.

Another nod.

He smirks.

"Pants off."

He stands, unfastening his jeans. "As you wish."

I don't instruct him to take off his briefs, but I don't complain when he does. I'm too mesmerized by his arousal.

"Now what, sexy?" He's so comfortable in his skin, confidence dripping from every inch of his flesh.

I twist my lips to the side, a slight squint to my eyes. Holding up a "wait" finger, I retrieve my robe tie from the bathroom. As I walk back out to the kitchen, Trick's eyes home in on the tie in my hand.

"Husband." I give him a wicked grin.

"Wife," he says with slow apprehension in his voice, eyes flitting between mine and the tie.

"Ever been tied up, Mr. Roth?" I tilt my head to the side.

Fucking lip twitch. I love it!

"Not … that I recall."

"You *up* for a little fun?"

"Bring it on, sexy."

"Come." I turn and drag the rug by his bed over to the large steel beam in the middle of the room. "Lie down."

Trick grins and obeys.

I bring his arms above his head and tie them together, then secure them to the beam.

"My wife's a kinky little temptress."

I nod slowly while stripping for him. "Do you have any idea how much I appreciate you taking care of me over the past few days?"

His eyes fall to my breasts that spring free as I remove my bra, but I leave on my pink lace panties. "I think so." He swallows.

Kneeling, I straddle his legs. "Well, tell me when you *know* how much I appreciate you." I lean forward, running my tongue up the entire length of his erection.

"Fuck, Darby …"

I grin just before taking him in my mouth, teasing him until his hips begin to jerk off the floor.

I look up as he looks down, lips parted, eyes squinted, and arm muscles flexed, tugging against the restraint. No warning needed, he knows by now that I'll take everything he gives me. After a few long minutes of my mouth, lips, and tongue paying homage to the best husband ever, he grunts, "Fuck!" releasing into my mouth.

After taking every last drop, I smile, licking my lips. "Do you feel *appreciated*, husband?"

Breathless, he nods with a relaxed grin. There's a couple seconds of unmistakable vulnerability in a guy's eyes right after he loses control from the touch of a woman. *Priceless!*

I sit up, crawling to the top of his body. "Good. Now, I'm feeling a little neglected. Think you could help a girl out?" Straddling his face, he wets his lips as I lean forward, grabbing the steel beam with my hands while lowering to his mouth. I moan just from the feel of his hot breath against my lace panties. Making him work for it is half the pleasure as he licks and sucks the wet crotch of my panties.

"I'm so fucking hungry for you." The deep voice takes me from wet to drenched.

"Trick …" I breath out his name as my heart rate escalates. Circling my hips as his teeth tug the thin material to the side, I drop my chin and watch his tongue lap a slow stroke up my bare sex. "Oh. My. God …" I swallow hard as his eyes meet mine, a grin pulling at his lips.

"Shit!" I hug the beam for support, pulling up to my feet, knees weak. "Tamsen! She's coming!" I whisper with panic as the clank of the elevator sounds on its assent. I race to the bathroom to grab my robe, that won't stay closed because my tie is being used for—*shit!* My naked husband, still tied up and sprawled out on the rug doesn't so much as show a flinch of concern for his state of exposure.

"You pulled too tight, I can't get the knot undone," I whisper, hands shaking.

"And that's my fault?" Trick raises one smug eyebrow.

"Crap!" I grab a blanket from the couch and cover his body with it just as the elevator screeches to a halt. "You're back early?" I smile, holding my robe closed as Tamsen steps off the elevator.

Her brow wrinkles as she looks me over then glances around. "Yeah, my friend, Debra, her husband called because their daughter was running a fever so we ended it early. Uh … where's Trick."

"Naked under this blanket and tied to the beam." My skin flushes at the sound of Trick's unwelcome voice.

Tamsen cups her mouth with her hand and tries to hold back

her laughter but fails. "You two are ... quite the pair."

I grimace. "I'm so sorry I didn't think you'd—"

Tamsen shakes her head, holding up her hand. "It's fine. I'm just going to..." she points to the stairs" ...go sleep in Grady's bed. Goodnight."

I close my eyes, releasing a heavy sigh. She must think we're the kinkiest couple ever.

"Am I done being your dirty little secret?"

My eyes pop open. In coping with my embarrassment, Trick still naked and restrained somehow slipped my mind. "Not one more word." I flip the blanket off his head and work to get the knots undone.

"What did I do?" He rubs his wrists while I slip the tie through my robe loops.

"You—you got me all..." I wave my hand in the air "...worked up and then I wasn't thinking clearly. Then you just had to let Tamsen know where you were—"

Trick slips on his jeans, no underwear. "Really?" he whispers, leaning toward me while making a quick glance at the stairs. "You think she was just going to walk past me on the rug with my feet sticking out one end of the blanket and my hands tied to the beam at the other end?"

I cross my arms over my chest. "Well ... I guess we'll never know, will we?" I march off to the bathroom like I have a purpose—but I don't. After a quick pee and a long hand washing, just to buy time and save face, I emerge with my dignity barely being held together by my stubbornness.

Trick rests against the counter with his legs crossed at his ankles, looking down at his phone. Mine chimes in my handbag on the bed.

Trick: *Friend, my wife just tied me to a pole and did things to me I will NEVER forget. She is so fucking hot!*

I glance up and grin because he's still looking down at his phone as if he's waiting for his "friend" to respond.

> **Me:** *BFF, hope your wife knows she hit the jackpot with you.*
> **Trick:** *Breakfast for dinner?*

I look up and smile at him still looking at his phone. "I love the hell out of you."

Lip twitch.

> **Trick:** *I know you do.*

He glances up and I giggle while shaking my head. With the sexiest gait ever, he makes his way over to me and kisses me like he hasn't done it a million times before, and in turn my body reacts like it's the first time. Leaving me breathless and dizzy, he kisses the tip of my nose.

"I'll start the eggs and dibs on the jelly spoon." He smirks.

I roll my eyes. "Hand me my jeans."

He swipes them off the floor and tosses them at me.

"Thanks." I step into them.

"What's this?" He bends down where my jeans had been. "Where did you get this?" He holds up my mother's necklace, staring at the dangling pendant.

"It was my mother's." I take it from him and slip it in my purse. "My father gave it to her on their wedding day. Tamsen found it in one of his drawers today." I pull on my shirt. "It was the only thing I took. I have a feeling New York is going to be a wasted trip. I can't imagine finding anything there when he spent most of his time here, but I suppose I should go, just in case I'm wrong."

CHAPTER FORTY-SIX

F *UCK!*
　　　The necklace. I remember it ... I remember *everything*.

CHAPTER FORTY-SEVEN

TAMSEN ENDS UP coming down to eat Trick's dinner, although she skips the jelly and has her eggs on the side, totally proving my point that Trick and I are breakfast soul mates. However, we're not tonight. Something came on fast because one minute he's texting me with a smirk on his face and the next he's huddled in fetal position on the bed and has been for the past two hours.

I shower and try to get him to let me check him over, but he doesn't want to be touched or moved, so I cover him up with the blanket and eventually fall asleep next to him after my worry settles. By morning, he's in the same position.

"Hey, sweetie. Our flight leaves in three hours, but I can cancel." I sit on the edge of the bed, pressing my palm to his cheek.

He drags open his eyes and stares off with a glassy, blank look. "No."

"Are you sure?"

A slow nod.

I kiss his forehead. "Okay, but here's your phone." I set it on the nightstand." I'll check on you before we take off. Make sure to keep hydrated."

"Feel better, okay?" Tamsen tries to put herself in his line of vision, but it's as if he's looking right through her.

"Love you." I look back at him as we head toward the elevator.

Nothing.

★

BEFORE WE TAKE off I try calling Trick. He doesn't answer.

"I shouldn't have left him." I sigh while turning my phone to airplane mode.

Tamsen rests her hand on mine. "He'll be fine. He's probably in the bathroom, maybe taking a shower."

"It came on so sudden."

"Probably a virus."

I nod, not really convinced of it. "This trip is a waste of time."

"But you're curious?"

"Yes, but not just about what he might have there. As crazy as it sounds, I want to see her penthouse ... I've never been there. It's as if I want to confirm that she's the heartless bitch I've always thought her to be. I want to find pictures of some other guy, or men's shoes that wouldn't fit my father. As much as I despise her, a small part of me feels sorry for her that my father was always whoring around on her."

"So ... the whole fiasco over the open casket didn't prove it?"

I laugh. "You'd think, wouldn't you? But that's just Rachel. In her own twisted way she thought she was doing him a favor as much as herself. She always had a way of making my father look good in the public eye, politically and fashionably speaking."

AS SOON AS the plane lands I try Trick again.

No answer.

"Maybe I should see if Gemmie can check on him?"

"If you think it will ease your mind." Tamsen grabs our bags from the overhead compartment. "But if he chooses to ignore the door then it will only send you further into panic mode."

"I know." I frown as we exit the plane.

"Let's go back to my place. You can try him again, freshen up, and then we'll go to Rachel's so you can do what you came to do and get back home to Trick. Okay?"

"Okay."

I stare at my phone the entire way to Tamsen's, willing it to ring or at least chime with a text from him.

It doesn't.

Tamsen unlocks her door, dropping her bag just inside. "The bathroom is down the hall to the right if you need to use it and the guest bedroom is on the left." She sprinkles some food into her fish tank and presses the button on her answering machine.

"Fucking turn on your cell phone!"

My eyes go wide at the sound of Grady's angry voice.

Tamsen shakes her head and continues to focus on her fish. "Always the drama queen. He's been very high maintenance..." she looks back at me with the stink eye "...well, higher than usual since you and Trick moved to Mexico. I get all the calls and blown-out-of-proportion emergencies that Trick used to get." Another sour look over her shoulder. "Thanks for that. I think he's a little bipolar."

"Bet you're glad he's in LA At least you can ignore his calls. If he were here he'd be banging down your door."

"Amen, sister."

I call Trick again, and again it goes to voicemail. "I'm ninety percent worried and ten percent pissed that you're not answering your phone or any of the texts I've sent you. Please! Pick. Up!"

Tamsen giggles. "Now *you're* sounding like Grady."

I grimace. "Yeah, maybe you should call him back. What if it really is important?"

"Fine." She sighs while picking up her phone. "It's me. Sorry I missed your calls, but obviously I'm not the only one not answering their phone. I'm leaving to go to Rachel's with Darby. I'll have my cell phone *on*, so you can call me when you get this. Bye." She shoves her phone in the back pocket of her jeans. "Ready?"

I nod, eyes still glued to my phone.

★

WE ARRIVE AT the Manhattan high-rise and of course Rachel is not here.

"She's expecting me," I assure the fossil at the front desk.

She looks over the frames of her reading glasses. "Then you must know the code." She gestures to the elevators.

I grin. "Of course." Pivoting on the balls of my feet, I head toward the elevator with confidence.

"So you know the code?" Tamsen whispers.

"Nope, but I have a good guess."

When the doors open we step onto the elevator and I type in a four-digit code.

Tamsen grins as the doors close and the elevator beings its ascent. "Good guess."

"It's the year she started her company, the same four-digit code for the security at her other house. Rachel's dresses may be originals but that's where it ends."

"So where is she today?" Tamsen asks as we step out of the elevator onto a sea of black and white marble flooring.

"Beats me. I could call her but I'd rather she not be looking over my shoulder while I'm here."

"You mean while you're snooping around."

I check my phone again, unable to stop worrying about Trick. "Something like that." I frown when I see there are no notifications on my screen. We worm our way through the maze of expensive furniture and pedestals with nude sculptures until we reach the double doors to the master suite.

"Can you believe people really live like this?"

"People, no. Rachel, yes."

"Damn! Look at this bed." Tamsen runs her hand up one of the mammoth columns to the four-poster bed.

There are two walk-in closets with a bathroom in the middle.

"I'll go right, you go left." I flip on the light and this closet, that's larger than some studio apartments, should shock me, but it's

Rachel and I wouldn't expect anything less. My conscience reminds me that she could show up at any time and this is clearly not my father's closet, but my curiosity overrules all common sense. It's filled with miles of shoes and dresses and a wall safe at the far end—handbags, scarves, coats, hats. It looks like the entire women's section of a department store, not a closet. But what catches my eye is the box slid under the middle unit of drawers. I'm not even sure why. Maybe because everything looks so perfect—immaculate—but then there's this box that looks like it was haphazardly shoved there.

"I'm not seeing much, Darby. Are you?" Tamsen yells from the other closet.

I kneel down and slide the box out.

Kathleen Henderson.

I don't recognize the name or the Queens address. The box has been opened at one end so I tip it just enough for the contents to slide out. There's a receipt on top of … *the drawing.*

Holy fucking hell!

"I think you're looking in the wrong closet."

I startle and look back at a smug Rachel standing in the doorway.

"Darby—" Tamsen's voice cuts off as she comes around the corner and sees Rachel.

Rachel doesn't even acknowledge her.

"Where did you get this?" I look down at the drawing of the naked woman. "Who's Kathleen Henderson?"

"She's an old friend who works for an art gallery. She deals with online auctions and when she came across this very disturbing picture she bought it for me."

"I-I … I don't understand. Trick drew this."

"Yes, I know. But he shouldn't have, and he sure as hell should not have tried to sell it."

"You know her?"

"I *knew* her." She laughs and it's sadistic—vengeful. "Since Cal's gone, I guess it no longer matters, does it?"

"Darby—" Tamsen speaks with slow caution. I see the lines of nervousness along her forehead.

"Her name was Paula Bailey."

I close my eyes and shake my head. I haven't seen her, but the name is familiar.

"You were just starting college, but I'm sure you heard her name in the news. When the wife of the mayor of New York City dies of a drug overdose, it makes national news. I'd have loved to have seen the look on your face when he drew this. He doesn't even remember her, does he? There's no way he could; if he did he never would have sold it."

"Fuck you." I sneer.

She shakes her head, staring at me with condescending eyes. "I warned you to stay away from him, but not you, Darby. You've always been so headstrong, just like your father. Except he didn't hide behind some ridiculous gothic façade when he fucked everything that moved like you did your first two years of college.

"Let's go, Darby." Tamsen's voice cuts through the air with an urgent undertone.

"Darby's not going anywhere, not until she knows who she married."

"Darby, please…" Tamsen shakes her head "…don't listen to her. Let's just go."

I don't know if I could stand up, let alone walk away right now even if I wanted to.

Rachel licks her Botox lips like she's getting ready to eat her prey. "You may be stubborn, but you're smart … curious. Aren't you?"

My gaze falters. I should walk away. Trick's past isn't hers to tell, but I can't. I need to know.

"Shall I continue?"

My chin drops in shame as I nod.

"I saw Patrick, *Trick,* in Central Park early one morning on my jog. He was sketching some kids playing Frisbee with their dog. A small crowd had gathered to watch him. They were looking at his art; I was looking at him. He had a look to him, this raw sex appeal. So I gave him my business card and told him to call me. A week later he showed up at Hart Designs because he didn't have a phone to call me … he didn't have much of anything."

My eyes fill with unshed tears of pain and anger.

"I offered him a job, modeling my menswear." Her brow tenses for a moment, maybe in confusion. I can't tell for sure. "One thing led to another and we ended up having an affair."

The lump in my throat forces the tears out as my heart shatters into a million painful fragments.

She smirks. "Affair sounds too intimate. It was really just fucking."

I can't breathe as nausea and lightheadedness seize my body.

"Darby!" Tamsen brushes past Rachel and kneels beside me, pulling me into her arms. "Shut the hell up! You've said enough."

"Oh, I'm only getting started. I'll admit, he's the best fuck I've ever had. The kid sure did know his way around a woman's body."

A strangled sob escapes as Tamsen hugs me tighter.

"But we got a little reckless. I'd forgotten about my lunch date with Paula. The door to my office wasn't locked and she walked in on us." Rachel clears her throat. "But I have to hand it to Paula, she made the most of the situation. I thought we were friends, but then she threatened to expose us. That's when your knight in shining armor saved the day. He offered to let Paula in on our fun."

Oh my God!

I pull away from Tamsen and hug my stomach. It's too much.

"Don't act so disgusted. I'm sure during those two years you spent dressed in black, whoring around campus to piss off your father, you surely fell into the occasional threesome or orgy."

I shake my head. She doesn't know what she's talking about. I slept with more guys than I should have, and I *did* do it in a sort of rebellion, but that's it. They were just one-night stands, nothing sick and twisted.

"I'm sure you know he's a drug addict. Eventually that's all Paula craved ... drugs, sex, and Trick." Rachel picks up the drawing and laughs. "I bet he drew the last thing he remembered. Do you know what this is, Darby? Do you know what happened that night, the night he was hit by a car?"

I shake my head. "Stop ... no more."

"She's not sleeping in this picture ... she's dead."

"No! Stop it!"

Tamsen helps me to my feet.

"He drugged her, fucked her, and killed her."

"I hate you!" I lunge for her but Tamsen holds me back.

"Don't! She's not worth it."

Rachel smirks, stepping to the side as Tamsen pulls me toward the door. When we reach the elevator, I lean against the wall and collapse.

"I hate her ..." I sob. "I hate him ..." I clench and tug at my hair. "I hate this fucking life. Make it stop."

"Shh ..." Tamsen hunches down in front of me. "I'm so sorry, sweetie."

"D-did you kn-know?" I lift my head to look into her eyes.

"No, I didn't."

I trust Tamsen. I know she wouldn't lie to me. She's my friend ... my *only* friend.

CHAPTER FORTY-EIGHT

"**C**OCAINE?"

I shake my head.

"Alcohol?"

Another head shake.

"Have you fucked anyone but your wife in the past twenty-four hours?"

"No." Lifting my head from my hands, I watch Grady sit in the chair opposite of me. "How much did you know?"

Grady rubs the back of his neck and sighs. I've always known that Grady knew more than he was telling me, but in spite of the fact that he was driving the car that caused my memory loss, in a weird way I've felt like he saved me by not telling me everything and getting me the hell out of New York. I trust Grady; he's protected me. Until last night, I had no idea to the extent that he's had to go to protect me.

"I knew you were with Mayor Bailey's wife the night she died. There was a message on your phone from her earlier that evening."

I nod, rubbing my hands over my face. "She wanted to come over."

"Yes."

"Where did you get my phone? We couldn't find it after the accident."

"*You* couldn't find it. I took it from your belongings at the hospital. I was looking for family ... clues to what had happened. The morning after the accident all the headlines were about the tragic death of Paula Bailey. Mayor Bailey arrived home late and discovered that his wife had OD'd."

I stare at my hands. My whole fucking body feels numb.

"Someone moved the body, but I'm quite certain it wasn't you. However, when I had someone check into your phone records you made a call to a private number about fifteen minutes before you ran into the street. Do you remember who you called?"

I press my fingers to my temples. "The strongest memory I have is just how fucked up my memory was back then from the drugs." I look up. "Rachel Hart is the only person I would have called." I shake my head. "I think I called her … I don't know. I came out of the bathroom and Paula was …"

"Jesus, Trick … it *was* her, Rachel?"

I nod, eyes slipping to my hands as I clench my fists in front of me. "Why didn't you tell me when I sent you the picture of the drawing?"

Grady sighs. "For the same reason I didn't tell you years ago. Without your memory you wouldn't know what to do with the information. What was I supposed to say? 'Yep, that's Paula Bailey, the mayor's wife whom I imagine you snorted cocaine off her tits, then fucked her right before she died of an overdose.' What were you going to do with that little nugget of information? Tell Darby? Call the mayor and apologize?"

"And I know now?" I yell, not really meaning to lash out at Grady.

"At least now you can own it … make sense of why you did it." Grady shakes his head. "If you tell Darby, it will destroy her. It will destroy everything you have."

I grunt. "*If.* You can't be serious. There is no if. I have to tell her."

"She'll leave you and no one would blame her."

I feel so fucking dead inside, like she's already left me. "I'd rather lose her to the truth, than keep her because of a lie."

"I'm sorry." Grady scrubs his face with his hands. "Maybe I should have told you."

I shake my head. "No, you were right. It had to be all or nothing." I laugh, but it's devoid of humor. "I wish I didn't know."

Grady winces. "I knew it had to be quite the scandal, and that things were covered up. It's how I felt certain that no one would be looking for you, but … I never imagined Rachel Hart. How the hell did a homeless kid from Queens get involved with a married, millionaire fashion designer?"

I laugh through the sympathy I know he's feeling for me.

"And for the love of God, what are the odds that you end up marrying her stepdaughter?"

I let go of a heavy sigh and proceed to tell him *everything*, starting with the necklace that belonged to Darby's mom. The one that Rachel used to wear to remind me that her heart belonged to someone else. Impossible, considering the fucking bitch doesn't have a heart.

CHAPTER FORTY-NINE

Tamsen hands me another glass of wine and a new box of tissues then sits down on her couch beside me.

"You need to call him."

"I've tried all day." I sniffle. "He's not answering, not responding. And I don't know what I would say. 'Hope you're feeling better and oh, by the way, I know you fucked my stepmom and killed her friend?'" I release another sob and more tears.

"I know in my heart, Trick didn't kill her." Tamsen rests her hand on my leg.

"How? How can you know that? He was strung out on drugs and he owns a gun!" I sigh. "I'm sorry." I press a tissue to my swollen eyes. "I'm not trying to take it out on you. I'm just so ..."

"Angry?"

"Hurt. I'm dying inside, and I know he didn't mean to hurt me, but he did. Now what? He doesn't remember and I either have to tell him, forcing him to deal with actions he can't remember, or I have to pretend I don't know." I suck in a shaky breath. "He'll know. He'll see it ... feel it. He'll just ... *know*."

A sad smile pulls at her lips. "I love you, Darby. Because even now when you could be throwing things, screaming at him on the phone, or drawing up divorce papers ... your concern is for *him*. No matter what you decide, know that you are *my* friend and always will be ... with or without Trick in your life. Okay?"

Tamsen's words bring on a new round of sobs as we hug. In this moment I feel like she's physically holding my emotions together ...

holding all the broken pieces of *me* together. In *this moment* I don't know if Trick brought me to Tamsen or if she brought me to Trick when she and Grady saved him that night.

AFTER A LONG bath, Tamsen grins, sitting cross-legged on the guest room bed, holding up a hair brush. "How was your bath?"

"Nice." I force my lips to pull up fractionally.

"Sit. I'm going to brush your hair. It's soothing … at least I think so."

It's bittersweet that this girl friend moment is happening fifteen years later than it should be and under such heartbreaking circumstances.

"Me too. Thank you." I sit in front of her and let her treat me like the little sister she never had and vice versa. My phone rings on the dresser and we both freeze. I slowly get up and grab it from the dresser then sit back down. Tamsen rests a reassuring hand on my shoulder. "It's him."

She tightens her grip. "You can do this."

I swipe my finger across the screen and hold it to my ear. "Hey." I swallow back my entire heart that's beating in my throat.

"Hey."

One word from the voice that cuts me to my very soul is all it takes. Tears … they chase each other down my face, desperate to escape the monster of pain that resides inside me. I hold my breath and Tamsen hugs my back. I hear her sniffle and I know the pain she feels for two people she loves like family is ripping her apart as well, and her agony compounds my own.

"Sorry I didn't call you back earlier. I … wasn't doing so well."

I press my palm to my chest, lip quivering, eyes closed. "It's … okay."

"Darby, what's wrong?"

I can't do it. The pain is too great. My phone falls to the bed and my body slumps as the raw emotions annihilate my heart.

"Shh ... I've got you." Tamsen holds my shaking body. She grabs my phone. "You need to come, now." Tossing the phone aside, she lies next to me, soothing me ... helping me reach for my next breath. Tamsen is an angel from God, and tonight she's saving me.

MY EYES FEEL like they're about to explode; I can only open them partway. My head? It already has. Even the slightest movement brings on the percussion. I groan, sitting up. Tamsen's gone but there's a note.

> *At work. Ibuprofen on the bed stand. Call me if you* *need anything.* **He took the red eye, but I made him stay on the couch until you're ready. FYI – your mom's necklace—it triggered his memory, ALL of it. Love you, -T**

I suck in a breath, it feels like my last. He wasn't sick; he was in shock. The shards of my heart stir in my chest, making new cuts ... new pain. It's love, hate, fear, anger. I slide my legs to the edge of the bed and freeze.

Trick.

He's on the floor, curled up on his side, head resting against his arm—sleeping. The love I have for this man is enough to last a thousand lifetimes, but the pain is like a drop of blood on the whitest sheet. No matter how big the sheet, that little red dot will always stand out, and if it's your blood, it can never be ignored.

His eyes open with a slow blink. An eternity passes before he looks up at me and when he does, it's a wilted flower begging for water, a dying love, and pain ... so much pain.

I stiffen even more as he sits up on his knees. His hands move to my legs.

"Don't … please."

His eyes fall to the floor in defeat and he nods.

I bite my lips together and pray for strength to hold it together, one broken piece at a time. Yesterday's revelations haunt me, visions of my husband with Rachel. Life is so cruel.

"I forgive you," I whisper, and he looks up slowly while I blink away the pain. "But … it's not enough."

His eyes gloss over with tears.

"How did you recognize my mom's necklace?"

His brow furrows. "Does it matter? You don't need any more pain. I can't … I won't do this to you."

"Did Rachel wear it? Did my father give it to her?"

He nods.

I look up and shake my head. "What did she say the LC stood for?"

"Love Cal."

I laugh. *Unbelievable.*

"Lucy Carmichael. It stood for Lucy Carmichael!" I yell with more anger than I intend to.

Trick flinches. "I'm sorry … I didn't know." Each word is barely a whisper.

"Why was she wearing it?" I sob.

"To remind me that she belonged to another man."

My husband fucked my stepmom while she wore my dead mother's necklace. *This can't be happening.*

"She said you killed that woman."

His jaw twitches. "It was a drug overdose, period."

"But you gave her the drugs."

"No," he says through gritted teeth while standing. He paces the room, running his hands through his hair. "Rachel gave her the drugs. Rachel gave me the drugs. I wasn't a fucking drug addict until I met her!"

"You could have said no."

"She blackmailed me!"

I shake my head. "What are you talking about?"

He stops, resting his fists on his hips. "I didn't show up at her office to fuck her. I showed up to rob her. There, I've said it. She saw me in the park and told me when I was done doodling like a child that she had a real job waiting for me. It pissed me off so I went to even the score. When I got to her office I waited for the right opportunity. She stepped out for a few moments and that's when I took her wallet from her purse. I didn't want the money, I just wanted to piss her off in return. But when I sat back down with her wallet in my coat pocket that's when I noticed it."

He shakes his head. "It was stupid of me not to have looked in the first place. She had a security camera in her office—*proof* that I took her wallet. Before I could make another move she came back in with a security guard and confronted me about what I did. I tossed the wallet on her desk and she dismissed the guard. She said she wouldn't have me arrested if I agreed to work for her, so I did."

His gaze meets mine. "She took photos of me, but they were never used. She paid me in *gifts* that kept getting more elaborate. I went to fancy parties with her and that's when I started doing drugs—drugs she provided. Eventually the drugs and alcohol led to—" He closes his eyes.

I swallow hard, a few tears rolling down my cheeks. "Sex, they led to sex."

He nods. Somehow him actually admitting it cuts deeper than I imagined.

"Every time I tried to get out she threatened to turn me in and assured me when the cops showed up they'd find enough drugs at my place—the place she purchased in my name—to put me in prison for a long time."

"How long?"

"How long what?"

"How long did you fuck them?"

He flinches like a slap across the cheek.

"Two years."

"Did you love them?"

"I love you."

I close my eyes. "Did. You. Love. *THEM?*"

"I hated them … I hated myself—still do. Time will never erase my past; prison would have been better. Because I'm in hell right now, and I don't think I'll ever escape."

How fitting, I feel like I'm drowning and will never surface.

"I'm going back to Chicago—alone."

"Darby—" He moves toward the bed.

I scoot back, shaking my head. "Don't."

"I'm dying—" His voice cracks and a single tear bleeds down his cheek. "Why can't I touch you?" The pain in his face sucks a little more air out of my lungs … out of my life.

"Because right now all I see is you with them. *Threesomes!* I see your hands on them, your lips on them. I see you fucking them!" I shake my head and wipe my tears. "You could have fucked a million women that wouldn't have mattered, but instead you fucked the one that does … the one I can't forget. I-I just … can't … forget."

I know how much my words must hurt, and as much pain as I'm feeling, my intention isn't to hurt him.

"You'll never know how sorry I am." He turns, slamming the bedroom door behind him.

EXCEPT TO USE the bathroom, I don't leave the bedroom until Tamsen gets home.

"Hey." She opens the door, holding up a sack. "I brought you dinner. Trick messaged me earlier and said you hadn't eaten yet today."

I sit up, rubbing my eyes. "Thanks, but I'm not hungry."

She shuts the door and pulls the sandwich out of the bag, setting it on the nightstand. "But you still need to eat."

All I can do is stare at the ceiling.

"Trick said you're going home tomorrow."

"I am. You have work and I…" I shrug "…I need time."

Tamsen nods. "He loves you."

"I know."

"But it's not enough?"

I shake my head. "I wish it were. I know he didn't lie to me. I know he had reservations about us because of his past. I tried to think of every scenario and if it would be a deal breaker, but this … this I could never have imagined."

"*Is* this a deal breaker?"

I blink away the tears. "I don't know. I love him; I will always love him. It's not about forgiveness; I forgave him the moment the words fell from Rachel's lips. That was a choice, but forgetting is not a choice. So the question is can I accept it and … I. Just. Don't. Know."

"Whatever decision you make will be the right one." She kisses the top of my head. "Now, I've got to go shove some food down your husb—Trick." She gives me a sad smile. "He said he's not hungry either."

"Tamsen," I call as she opens the door. "It's completely inadequate, but thank you."

"You're welcome."

CHAPTER FIFTY

"YOU LOOK LIKE shit."

Sprawled out on the sofa, feeling a breath shy of dead, I stare at the ceiling. "Well then, at least I look better than I feel."

Tamsen lifts my feet, sitting down under them. "She needs time."

I nod. "And to think for years I wanted to remember. At least now when she leaves me, I'll understand why."

"You don't know that she's leaving you." She grabs my hand, giving it a squeeze.

"You didn't see her. She wouldn't even let me touch her. It fucking guts me. She's my wife, a room away and it feels like we're not even on the same continent. The ocean between us is so deep, but I want to cross it ... even if I die trying."

"You're a strong person ... one of the strongest I know. You will survive, no matter what."

"Tamsen..." I fight back the fucking emotions that feel like they're stabbing my soul "...I don't want to survive without her."

She stands then bends down, kissing my cheek. "I know, babe. But sometimes you do things you don't want to ... things you think you can't, and those are the defining moments in your life." She covers me with a blanket. "Night, sweetie."

"Night."

Today my friends stopped picking up after me. Grady offered to come to New York, but I told him I needed to do this alone. Tamsen listened, but she never tried to solve my problems or even offer false hope. I love the hell out of them for their ability to let me find my way, just as much as I've loved them for showing it to me.

Tomorrow morning Darby will leave me. I don't know if it's temporary or permanent—to my heart it doesn't matter. Every minute without her feels like a lifetime. I can't let her leave without the memory of my touch ... my hands on *her* ... my lips on *her* ... my heart next to *hers*. But I have no choice. I will *never* survive without this woman ... my friend ... my wife ... my life.

CHAPTER FIFTY-ONE

TAMSEN WAITS FOR me by the door as I sling my bags over my shoulder. The moment I look at Trick asleep on the couch, a river of tears breaches the bank. My friend has me in her arms in a heartbeat, her jacket absorbing my sobs. She hands me a wad of tissue and leads me out the door.

"Goodbye, beautiful," he whispers.

We both still. Tamsen grabs my hand, giving it a tight squeeze. The reassurance and strength I need to not look back.

We wait a few seconds. Nothing. And then we continue out the door, the sharp click of it shutting in the background.

When we get to Tamsen's car parked on the street, she grabs my bags and puts them in the trunk. As I open the passenger door, my heart stops, strangled by the grip on my arm.

Trick stands before me in a pair of jeans and nothing else, eyes red like they're bleeding with pain. Grabbing my head, he fists my hair and kisses me painfully hard—desperate, demanding, eternal. "I know you can't forget, so if you're going to remember something, remember this. You fucking own Every. Single. Piece. Of. Me." His voice breaks, our mouths a breath away. "I love you. I live for you. I fucking *breathe* for you. *That's* what you need to remember ... *only* that."

Ugly, harrowing sobs rip through my throat as my heart feels like it's rupturing in my chest. Turning, he walks to the door of the building without looking back.

⭐

IT TOOK EVERYTHING I had to walk away, and even then I left so much behind. Trick's not just my husband; somewhere along the way he became a part of me and I became part of him. I know he'll always have that part. I can never get it back. There's just two questions I need to figure out: Can I live without it? And do I want to?

There is no one to blame for any of this. It's like two cars crashing because they both merge to the center lane at the same time. It's coincidence, an unfortunate circumstance—bad timing. But even when there's no one to blame, there are still casualties.

"Hey, Nana. It's me."

She opens the door and without a single word or explanation of the past few days. She knows to hold out her arms to me. I fall apart in my safety net, and eventually, after many long emotional minutes, I tell her everything.

She hands me some water and a cool washcloth for my puffy eyes.

"What would you do?" I sniffle.

She sits in her chair, folding her hands in her lap. "It doesn't matter. I'm not Darby Roth and Trick is not my husband. This is your experience in life, my dear. Every woman has a place inside where she holds her truth. I think of it as our essence. It's where we recognize our greatest love, our greatest hope, and our greatest fear. It's where you'll find your answer. You're right. Forgiveness is not enough. But it's a package deal. You can't forget about Trick's past any more than he can erase it. When you look at him, can you love *all* of him? Can you look past his scars?" She leans forward. "It's not a test. This isn't a measure of your love for him. It's just a choice: left or right, chocolate or vanilla, ocean or mountain. But it has to be *your* choice."

★

AFTER LEAVING NANA'S to go back to the home that she refused to sell, I start counting—seconds to minutes, minutes to hours, hours to days. Eventually the days morph into weeks. I go back to working at the hospital on a temporary as-needed basis. Thanksgiving comes with little celebration, nothing more than dinner at a nice restaurant with Nana and a holiday greeting text from both Tamsen and Grady. Tamsen at least tells me she and Trick are in California with Grady for the holiday. Then I get the text I'm not expecting.

> **Trick:** BFF – I miss my wife. Could you tell her Happy Thanksgiving for me? And that I love her.

I cry, missing him so much ... but I'm still crumbling.

Every day I try to gauge my thoughts, putting them on a mental scale. On one side is Trick and on the other is his past. Nana's right. They are a package deal, because it's still so impossible to think about one and not the other. I keep hoping one day I'll wake up and just know, maybe the universe will give me a sign.

I welcome the days I get called into work. It's an emotional reprieve for a few hours. I even get invited out with Jade and a few other people from the ER. I laugh on cue, smile when someone looks at me, and occasionally contribute one or two words to the conversation. But mostly, I think about Trick.

> **Trick:** Wife – had toast, jelly, and eggs this morning. I miss my breakfast soul mate. Could you tell her I'm thinking about her?

I cry, missing him so much ... but I'm still crumbling.

By Christmas I'm numb, eight weeks without seeing him or hearing his voice. Two texts, that's all, and I couldn't even muster the emotional strength to reply to either one. I left him. He's being respectful of my wishes and giving me space. But sometimes I wonder if it's too much space. Is he still waiting on me? The last text was over three weeks ago. Will someone else fill the void I left? Before leaving for Nana's I call Tamsen.

"Merry Christmas! God, I miss you. We are getting together for New Year's and I'm not taking no for an answer."

I smile and it's genuine; I think the first one I've had since leaving New York. Tamsen has that effect. "Merry Christmas. I miss you too, and New Year's is definitely a huge yes."

"So I was late sending my gift, but you should get it by Monday."

"What? You shouldn't have done that. I didn't get you anything. Now I feel like a terrible friend."

"Whatever. It's nothing big. So did Santa come to Darby's?"

I laugh. "Not yet. I'm going to Nana's for brunch and we'll exchange gifts there. What are you doing?"

"Praying Grady doesn't burn down the joint. He and Trick are frying a turkey on the patio, which I don't think is allowed in my building."

Just his name has my breath held hostage in my throat, heart pounding, tears stinging the back of my eyes.

"Who are you talking to?" Grady calls in the background.

"Darby," Tamsen replies.

"Give me the phone. Hey, baby girl! Merry Christmas."

"Thanks, Grady. You too."

"Just because you're not talking to my boy doesn't mean you need to snub me. I haven't heard from you since Thanksgiving. Do I need to schedule us a spa day?"

I laugh, wiping my tears. "That sounds amazing."

"It's a date then. Before I head back out to LA we'll have a Grady Darby day. Deal?"

"Deal."

"Fabulous. I have to check on Turkey Tom. Love you."

"You too." The numbness I felt a few minutes ago has completely dissolved and the pain is pulsing from old wounds.

"Sorry about that." Tamsen laughs. "He's such an attention hog ... Trick, check the potatoes in the oven," she yells. "Ugh, it's crazy around here. I'd better go."

"Yeah, sure."

"Love you. Tell Nana Merry Christmas from us."

More tears fall. "Okay."

"New Year's ... call you soon. Bye."

"Bye," I whisper after we're already disconnected.

I cry, missing him so much ... but I'm still crumbling.

I TAKE A massive detour to Nana's. This morning's phone conversation put me into an unexpected tailspin, and now all I can do is think about Trick, but they're no longer just thoughts, they're a need. This sudden need takes me to Rogue Seduction. I frown when I see the *For Lease* sign in the window. I had no idea Grady gave up on finding a replacement for Trick. Part of me wondered if Trick went back to work, like I did—guess not.

As I pull around to the back of the building, I push the button to the garage door.

Empty.

I pull in, get out, and flip on the lights. Barren, there's absolutely nothing here. I take the elevator upstairs and step out into another completely bare room. Not a single piece of furniture or anything of Trick's or Grady's. I open a few kitchen cabinets and then the refrigerator.

Nothing.

I don't know why but right now, I'm feeling as hollow and *empty* as this place. As I turn to leave, something catches my eye. It's a package on the floor leaning against the glass wall to the bathroom. I move toward it with caution, a weird sense of fear. Bending down I take the envelope that's taped to it with my name on it. Pulling out a folded sheet of paper, I take a deep breath and let it out with tears ... so many tears. I have no idea what all these words mean yet, but just seeing his handwriting and my name at the top brings so many emotions to the surface.

Darby,

If you're reading this, it means you're here. I don't know why you came, but with no word from you I've come to believe it's to say goodbye. If it makes me a coward, so be it, but I cannot hear those words fall from your beautiful lips. So here's all I can give you right now. I hope somewhere in these words you'll find the closure you need.

Our story, although too short, was perfect because our life together was timeless. Still, losing you so quickly felt cruel, until I accepted my past. Now I know that you came into my life to give it back to me. As ugly and riddled with shame as it is, it's a part of who I am and without the memory of it, I would have always felt incomplete. Now the void in my heart—my soul—is you.

You are the most beautiful and extraordinary person I know. I pity the people who had the chance to be in your life and chose not to. For me, every second has been such a gift, one that I probably didn't deserve. I will never look at my ring finger without remembering that you said "yes." But the mark you left on my heart will live on long after my body is gone. It will transcend time to a perfect place where our past is forgotten and pain doesn't exist.

I will forever feel the lingering of your breath on my neck, your heart against my chest. I'll see your lips wrapped around my jelly spoon, brilliant blue eyes filled with love, and the blinding smile of my BFF—my breakfast soul mate—the woman who said "yes."

I know you love me—I really do. This is all on

me ... I did this to us. But I know I can't fix it, so I'm going to do the only thing I can. I'm going to give you your freedom and hope that someone deserving of your love can pick up the pieces and mend them with a love worthy of your heart.

Goodbye, Darby Carmichael
Trick

Carmichael—I can barely breathe.

Swollen eyes, blurred ink, and a bleeding heart.

With shaky hands, I lift the package and notice another envelope behind it. Setting the package back down, I open the envelope— divorce papers with his signature. If it's physically possible to die of a broken heart then this is where they'll find my body. The papers slip through my fingers and float to the floor in slow motion like a dream, because this just cannot be real. I buckle over resting my hands on my knees, my body wracked with sobs.

Tap. Tap. Tap.

My tears fall to the brown paper covering the package. I pick it up and rip off the paper with an uncontrolled anger, a death grip of pain.

"Oh ... my ... God ..." I sob even harder, holding the sketch— Just ... no words. A blown up black and white photo—every detail finished with such precision I can *feel* it, like I'm in the picture ... in the moment. It's Trick's lower abdomen with me pressing my lips to his black sanskrit tattoo and his hand fisted in my hair.

Don't look back in anger.

Leaning against the glass wall, I slide down it, completely drained. In this exact moment I realize something ... I'm no longer crumbling. I pull my phone out of my coat pocket and text my *husband.*

Me: *Come.*

CHAPTER FIFTY-TWO

T AMSEN RAISES HER glass. "A toast to my boys for not burning my house down and spending the holidays with your dateless, lifeless, will-die-an-old-cat-woman sister."

"Did you get a cat?" Grady asks as our glasses clink together.

"No, I'm referring to my vagina. In the straight world it's called a pussy. I'm going to die with an old and minimally used pussy."

We all laugh.

"I love that you think everything in the 'gay world' is different than the 'straight world.' Silly me, all these years I assumed it was just sexual orientation." Grady shakes his head.

"I have to go." I stand. "I'm ... sorry." I whisper, staring at my phone—lost for words.

"What's wrong?" They ask in unison.

I close my eyes and swallow hard. A week ago, after the last of my stuff was sold, I took the drawing, divorce papers, and letter to the place I knew she'd find it when she gathered the courage to face me ... to let *me* go. I gave thanks for the best days of my life, left the sketch, and then I did it so she wouldn't have to—I let her go.

Asking her to love me with the recent revelation of my past is too much to ask of anyone, especially the person that I'd die to protect. But just now she did what she does best ... She completely blew my mind, bringing me to my knees, reminding me that my heart still beats—many miles away.

"I'm going home." I look up from my phone—from that one word and hold it up to show my family.

Tamsen makes it only two seconds before she's a complete basket case, then Grady loses it too. I'd like to say that I hold my shit together—but I don't.

I throw most of my stuff in my bag and leave anything that's not in plain sight.

I give Tamsen and Grady quick hugs.

"So Chicago for New Year's?" Grady asks.

I turn before closing the door behind me. "I'm not going to Chicago."

CHAPTER FIFTY-THREE

I MANAGED A direct flight by just minutes. My plan was to leave tomorrow after spending Christmas with Nana, but when I showed her the drawing, the letter, and the divorce papers she was booking my flight and shoving me out the door to my "destiny" before I could slip in a single word of protest. I told her *if* Trick came, the chances of him getting here in the same day would be slim at best.

The sunset bid the day farewell, leaving me in a blanket of dark on our veranda, nestled in the old blue chaise lounge where we slept our first night here. I don't know that he'll come, but I'm not letting my heart in on that bit of doubt. He let me go and it could be too late. I can't stumble over the *what ifs*. I needed time and I never expected him to wait for me, but I couldn't hold him out of fear of losing him, that's not true love. Two months without a word from me—tears sting my eyes as I wonder if he felt abandoned, like the day his parents just … vanished.

I brush my finger over my tattoo. He may never know that my heart has the same mark as his, and if it's too late for us in this life, I will wait for him in my next. He's right … our love is timeless.

"Wife."

Oh God! Thank you.

I close my eyes, sucking in my lips—tears. With one word he breathes life back into me and I feel the crumbled pieces coming together again.

I turn and slowly stand. Looking at my whole world in the

doorway, I blink, releasing more tears.

With each step my heart swells more and more. His thumbs brush my wet cheeks. I close my eyes with a chill, taking in a shaky breath.

"Are you? Are you still my wife?" he whispers.

Looking up, I bite together my quivering lips and nod.

"I'm so sorry ..." His fingers thread in my hair, pulling my mouth to his.

I sob into our kiss, but he doesn't stop. This is the most beautiful pain. My hands clench his shirt, my lips bruising from his desperate touch. Lifting me to his body, he takes me upstairs, sucking and nipping at my neck. My heart clenches as he moans like he's starving, like his soul is bleeding into mine.

"Oh God ... I missed you." I fist his hair as he *possesses* me.

We fall to the bed in a tangle of frantic movements. He tears his lips from my skin just long enough to shrug off his shirt and mine. The clasp to my bra is broken with impatient hands.

"Ung!" I cry as his mouth covers my breast, the stinging bite of his teeth on my nipple.

Our hands spar, fumbling for leverage as we tug each other's pants off, lips refusing to let go. I shove down his briefs with my foot. He takes the quicker route and rips my panties off. Everything about this feels like the first time we made love. This is not just a physical need, it's an emotional reclaiming.

Interlacing our fingers above my head he sinks into me.

"Trick ..." I breath out his name, and for the first time in two months I feel *alive*.

He stills. I'm not sure if it's a moan of pleasure or pain that escapes from his chest with his face buried in the crook of my neck. Sex is usually the means to a release, not tonight. The urgency between us has been to get to this precise moment—this perfect all-consuming connection. I close my eyes and just hold him—this is love—we're making love.

Lifting his face to mine he looks at me. In his eyes are all those emotions that mean so much more than words ever could. Right now I feel like my whole body is connected to his. I may not want to lose my individuality, but right now I just want to be one with my husband.

"You came back to me," he whispers.

My lips tug into a sad smile as I see the unshed tears in his eyes. "I never really left."

EPILOGUE

I T'S BEEN FIVE years since I brought my wife and my Ducati back to Chicago. Darby works three days a week at the ER while I sketch. My drawings now sell for far more than either one of us ever expected. We travel the world attending art openings and living every day to the absolute fullest.

Tamsen moved to Chicago a year after we moved back from Todos Santos. She said she wanted to be closer to *family*. Fate stepped in for our favorite angel and gave her a husband a year after she arrived. Jordan works for the Chicago Fire Department, and according to Tamsen and Darby, he's a squirrel like me. Whatever the fuck that's supposed to mean.

Tamsen and Jordan are expecting their second child, another daughter, in two months. Darby is in love with Lyla, but I see the pain in her eyes that nobody else does. We've been trying to have a baby for over three years. Darby thinks it's karma for her promiscuity during college. I think it's just not our time and that patience bears the greatest gifts.

Grady refuses to jump on the relocation bandwagon. He loves LA too much. However, he hops on a plane to come visit every chance he gets, especially since Lyla is so crazy about him. She's been a good influence on him. He's given up his cavalier bachelor life for a committed relationship with Abel, a commercial property developer who is ten years his junior and *not* married.

Rachel Hart just finished a five-year jail sentence for possession of cocaine. How it ended up in the trunk of her car and who tipped off the police remains a mystery. We happened to be at a sports bar when the news of it played across the screen. Darby closed her eyes, took a deep breath, then asked the bartender to change the channel. What she did not do … ask me one single question.

Nana celebrated her eightieth birthday this year, but nobody told her it's okay to slow down. Her mind is razor sharp, except when she likes to pretend she's getting dementia just to mess with Darby. On a sad note, her friend, Mary, died three years ago and so Darby has filled in as Nana's shopping and lunch buddy, and I pick her up every Monday and take her to the shooting range. *Yeah, Darby loves that.*

"NANA WANTS ME to pick her up in twenty minutes." My tease of a wife hops up on the vanity in her Christmas red lace bra and panties. "Make me look beautiful."

"Done." I sink my teeth into the swell of her breast.

She grabs my face. "It's Christmas … I want the Trick special."

"I thought that's what you got in the shower." I fight back my grin … the one she calls her favorite subtle-but-cocky smirk.

"If you want your wife fix later then I suggest you get to work."

Of course I'm going to do her make up. There is absolutely nothing I wouldn't do for her.

With an air kiss and a quick tease to my cock, (she tortures it *all* the time) she's dressed and off to Nana's, leaving me to supervise Grady and Abel making Christmas dinner while Tamsen and Jordan keep Lyla out of the presents for a few more hours.

"What did you get Darby for Christmas?" Tamsen asks.

I stare at Lyla combing her baby doll's hair and wish my answer could be a baby … but I don't say it. Tamsen would see my disappointment. "I'm sending her and Nana to a spa for a week."

Tamsen jabs Jordan in the stomach. "Did you hear that?"

"You're popping out my kid in less than two months. I don't

think you'd get the full enjoyment."

"Whatever."

My phone buzzes just as I stand to go check on Grady.

Darby: BFF – Your gift is at the front door. Before you open it, I want you to know it's not just from me, it's from your whole family. We love you more than you could possibly ever know. You are the tie that binds us all together and this very special gift has been a long and grueling two years in the making. Love, your BFF, breakfast soul mate, and wife.

I roll my eyes at all *ten* holiday emojis. As if everyone else received the same text, Tamsen gathers everyone by the front door and then she starts crying.

Jordan shakes his head. "Don't mind her. It's just her hormones."

I nod and open the front door.

Darby and Nana stand off to the side videotaping me, but I'm … I'm so fucking speechless I can hardly breathe.

"Patrick."

I blink my eyes trying to register what I'm seeing as I hear my name from a familiar voice. *This can't be … there's just no way … they're … dead …*

"Son." Another familiar voice.

I shake my head and start to cry like a fucking baby … but I can't help it. "Mom? Dad?"

My dad hugs me and I fist the back of his coat like a young child. "We're so sorry, son." His voice breaks.

I release him and lean down to hug my mom—in a wheelchair. "Mom."

Her voice is helpless against her tears, so she just wraps one arm around me and kisses my cheek. My parents, they're alive. I just don't get it. I clench my fists to feel my nails dig into my palms—to confirm I'm alive and experiencing this surreal moment.

"Maybe you should invite them in," Darby suggests, chasing her own tears with a tissue.

I help my dad get her wheelchair inside. Then I grab my wife and hug her so hard I think I could break her. "My God, I love you. I don't know how they're even here or what you did but—"

She kisses me. "They're here for you … we're all here for you." She smiles past her tears. "From the very first time you told me about them, I just couldn't shake the unsettling feeling that maybe they didn't die."

This feels like an out-of-body experience. I haven't felt so disoriented and confused since I've been sober and clean. We make our way to the living room where everyone takes a seat—Darby on my lap.

"Alice, Ray, I'd like you to meet Tamsen, Jordan, and Lyla. And this is Grady and Abel." My wife introduces everyone to my parents when I should be introducing my parents to my wife.

My dad scoots to the edge of the sofa, resting his elbows on his knees. "Well, Darby's shared our story … with everyone but you, son. We wanted to be the ones to tell you."

Darby interlaces her fingers with mine.

"Your mom was sick. We didn't know what it was, but she kept having seizures and migraines." My dad, the strongest person I have ever known, chokes on his own words while my mom rubs his back. "You were fifteen and in school with friends, and we knew you'd be fine. By that point you had been taking care of us more than we were taking care of you. Somedays we felt like a burden. We knew eventually your talent would take you places, get you off the street. It was the hardest decision of my life. I knew if I told you, you'd insist on coming too, but I didn't think they'd accept you. I didn't think they'd accept me."

"Who?" I ask.

"Your mother's parents—your grandparents. I got enough money to get us on a bus to Minnesota. I was taking her home, praying to God that her parents would take her in and help her—save her life. I knew they hated me and so I was willing to leave her if they would agree to help her. They agreed to get her the medical help she needed and they even let me stay; although it wasn't easy for any of us.

She was diagnosed with a brain tumor. They removed it and by some miracle it was benign, but in the process of removing it there was nerve damage. She lost feeling in her left arm and leg. It's taken years of therapy to get her speech back and now she has some movement on her left side but not enough to get her out of the wheel chair yet. By the time we felt like we had the money to come back and find you, you were gone and nobody knew where you went." He clears his throat as everyone else in the room wipes their eyes. "Pastor Edwards told us about your accident and memory loss. He said one day you were asking questions about your past and the next day you were gone—no goodbye, no forwarding address, nothing."

"We thought we'd lost you forever," my mom whispers through her soft cries. "Until the private investigator showed up."

I look at Darby. She grins with a guilty shrug.

"My parents are both dead now and your dad and I are living in Des Moines. I just don't know how Darby did it, but I thank God she did." My mom looks at Darby with such love.

I squeeze her, kissing her neck.

"*We* did it." Darby looks around the room, and I can tell she's in awe of the people who are now our family.

All these years I let myself believe I was orphaned at the age of fifteen. It was too painful and unimaginable to believe my parents abandoned me. I'm not sure twelve years ago I would have understood. They never felt like a burden to me. But now I know what it means to love someone more than life itself, the way my father has loved my mother. I will forever feel honored to be Raymond Roth's son.

"I-I don't know what to say. I still can't believe you're here."

Everyone smiles at me, and as if on cue, Lyla yells, "Presents!"

We all laugh and agree to open presents before eating. I don't take notice of anything that's being opened, even when Darby bounces on my lap after opening the certificate for the spa getaway. I'm not sure how long it's going to take for the shock to wear off. I still swear this is a dream.

"Here, Patrick." My mom holds out a small box and Lyla brings it to me.

"You didn't need to get me anything. My God, you are the gift."

My mom smiles. "It's not from us, but it's for us too."

I squint, not understanding, but my brain is fried so I don't question it. For the second time this morning, all eyes are on me and the room falls silent. I tear off the wrapping paper. It's a long gold box. I think it's the box from Darby's bracelet that I gave her for our anniversary. I open the lid.

It takes me a few long moments to let *everything* about this day sink in. I look up at Darby, fighting back those fucking tears again. "Yeah?"

She nods, allowing her honest emotions to flow freely down her cheeks. "Merry Christmas, husband."

I fist her hair and kiss her senseless as our family laughs and cries together in celebration. Releasing her lips, I rub the tip of my nose against hers. "Mommy," I whisper.

I have the whole world on my lap, beaming at me with an enormous smile. Burying her face in my neck, she whispers back to me, "Daddy."

The End

Also by Jewel E. Ann

Holding You Series
HOLDING YOU
RELEASING ME

Stand-Alone Novels
IDLE BLOOM
UNDENIABLY YOU

Look for Jewel E. Ann's next release, *End of Day*, Book 1 in
The Jack and Jill Series coming summer 2015.

DEAR READER,

Thank you for reading *Only Trick*! I would love for you to share your thoughts. Please consider writing a review; I value your suggestions and feedback.

A special note: The word "sinceriously" is used in this book in support of Stephen Amell's campaign to raise awareness for Stand for the Silent and Paws and Stripes.

adverb

1. the ability to speak freely, openly, and honestly; about anything: *if you're going to say something, say it sinceriously.*
2. to initiate any action while spreading as much good karma as possible.

For information on upcoming books, exclusive excerpts, and giveaways please subscribe to my newsletter.

jeweleann.com

About the Author

Jewel is a free-spirited romance junkie with a quirky sense of humor.

With 10 years of flossing lectures under her belt, she took early retirement from her dental hygiene career to stay home with her three awesome boys and manage the family business.

After her best friend of nearly 30 years suggested a few books from the Contemporary Romance genre, Jewel was hooked. Devouring two and three books a week but still craving more, she decided to practice sustainable reading, AKA writing.

When she's not donning her cape and saving the planet one tree at a time, she enjoys yoga with friends, good food with family, rock climbing with her kids, watching How I Met Your Mother reruns, and of course…heart-wrenching, tear-jerking, panty-scorching novels.

CPSIA information can be obtained
at www.ICGtesting.com
Printed in the USA
BVHW03s1258190618
519440BV00001B/2/P